Praise for the novels of Jo Ann Brown

"A *Wish for Home* is a moving, fast-paced story about family, secrets, misunderstandings, and figuring out what matters most. This stirring romance is sure to capture readers' hearts."
—Suzanne Woods Fisher, bestselling author of *Mending Fences*

"Jo Ann Brown delivers a thrilling story filled with authentic Amish details, plot twists, wonderful characters and a satisfying romance."
—Patricia Davids

"Jo Ann Brown provides a lovely treat for readers with A *Wish for Home*, a delightful story of two opposites thrown together on a stormy night in Amish country. With a deft touch, Brown draws the contrast between Lauren, an ambitious advertising executive, and Adam, an Amish widower intent on raising his small daughter. Heartfelt and genuine, Brown takes readers along with her characters on the difficult and challenging road to home."
—Marta Perry, author of *A Springtime Heart*

"Jo Ann Brown's writing is both powerful and charming. She provides a respite from the cares of the day and gives the invitation to join her for a journey of peace that lingers in the heart."
—Kelly Long

"An Amish tale that is anything but plain and simple."
—*USA TODAY* bestselling author Vannetta Chapman

"A heartwarming, richly layered story of love and loss, betrayal and redemption with well-crafted characters. Readers of Amish fiction will love A *Wish for Home* by Jo Ann Brown."
—Mary Ellis, author of *Nothing Tastes So Sweet*

"In A *Wish for Home*, Jo Ann Brown weaves an intriguing story that readers of Amish fiction are sure to enjoy. A book about finding oneself, learning to forgive, and discovering the things that really matter in life—faith, hope, and love."
—Jennifer Spredemann

"A *Wish for Home* by Jo Ann Brown is a beautiful story of forgiveness and letting go of the past to return home. I really enjoyed this sweet, emotional story. I promise it will touch your heart!"
—Lenora Worth, author of *Seeking Refuge*

A
PROMISE OF
FORGIVENESS

Jo Ann Brown

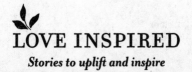

LOVE INSPIRED

Stories to uplift and inspire

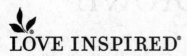

LOVE INSPIRED®

Stories to uplift and inspire

Recycling programs
for this product may
not exist in your area.

ISBN-13: 978-1-335-41875-3

A Promise of Forgiveness

Love Inspired
22 Adelaide St. West, 41st Floor
Toronto, Ontario M5H 4E3, Canada
www.LoveInspired.com

Printed in U.S.A.

For those special teachers in my life:
In third grade, Miss Barkley, who dared us to use our imaginations
In sixth grade, Mrs. Smith, who opened worlds to us
In high school, Mrs. Musser, who made even learning grammar fun
and challenged me to explore my love of writing
and Mr. Palumbo, who first read my work
and inspired me never to give up
And in college, Mr. Knott, who shared his respect
and love for popular fiction.
Your guidance, knowledge and support have meant so much to me.
Thank you.

And he said unto me, My grace is sufficient for thee:
for my strength is made perfect in weakness.
Most gladly therefore will I rather glory in my infirmities,
that the power of Christ may rest upon me.
—*2 Corinthians* 12:9

A
PROMISE OF
FORGIVENESS

Chapter One

Slippery little boys right out of the bathtub and wearing only a diaper weren't easy to catch.

Naomi Ropp knew that from experience, but she hadn't expected someone to knock on the front door as she was finishing her two-year-old twins' bath. She tried to grab them, but they eluded her. Tossing aside the towels she'd been gathering, she gave chase. They were out of the bathroom, along the upstairs hall and down the stairs, giggling the whole way, before she could stop them. As they skidded around the corner into the living room, she managed to catch their arms.

With a twist and more giggling, the towheaded boys escaped again. They raced toward the sofa and clambered onto it, making it rock against the wall.

"Jared, Jesse," she said as she stopped behind them. "You know you aren't supposed to run in the house."

"Fun!" chirped Jared, who was slightly taller than his twin.

"Fun!" Jesse echoed, his chipped front tooth visible in his grin. "Lots fun!"

Naomi started to answer, but halted when another knock came. This one sounded as if someone was pounding on the front door with a fist. She hoped not. The door, like many other things on the run-down farm, needed repairs. A solid hit might send it flying off its hinges.

"Coming!" she called, first in *Deitsch* and then in English, though not too many *Englischers* drove up the narrow lane unless they were lost. In the late summer, *Englischers* came looking for fresh vegetables. She'd put in her garden only last week, so the vegetables wouldn't be available for a couple of months.

She pushed her hair toward her *kapp* and grimaced when she realized how much had fallen out of her bun after a day of trying to keep up with a pair of two-year-olds. Smoothing her water-spotted black apron, she motioned for the boys to sit as she walked to the door.

They plopped down, but exchanged a look she could translate. They'd stay there until her attention was elsewhere, and then they'd return to their usual games.

Smiling, Naomi kept her back to the twins. She didn't want them to guess how often she found their mischievousness delightful. A *gut mamm* would be a bit sterner, but she couldn't keep from enjoying their antics.

Especially when there were so few opportunities for mirth in her life now.

Not for a long time. Six years, three months, two weeks and five days... The date was seared into her mind because it was the evening she'd discovered her husband had been cheating on her with a succession of other women.

Her late husband.

A tremor ran along her shoulders. She'd fought hard and futilely to save their marriage, but she didn't have to any longer. Marlin was dead because he'd been somewhere he shouldn't have been at the wrong time. That's what the police said when they came to let her know she needed to identify his body.

That had been only seven months, one week, two days, eleven hours ago.

Stop it! she told herself as she reached for the door. Her brain had a bizarre ability to remember every date and every detail of what happened each day from around the time of her second birthday. It'd served her well when she was a scholar, but there were things she wished she could forget.

But she couldn't.

Opening the door, Naomi was surprised to see an *Englisch* man and a woman with an astounding shade of bright red hair on her porch, which needed painting. That chore was far down her to-do list while she was trying to oversee the house and the yard and the vegetable garden by herself. Since Marlin's death, she'd sold the dairy herd and most of the equipment, but hadn't parted with the mules and the buggy horse. She wasn't sure how much longer she could afford to feed the animals and her family. Waldo, the buggy horse, had joined the household only a month before the twins were born, but the mules, Fred and Ginger, had been with them for almost the whole time she'd been married to Marlin.

Nine years, eleven months, three weeks, four days ago, her mind whispered. She didn't want to think about her upcoming wedding anniversary, the annual reminder of how stupid she'd been to believe Marlin's lies and accusations.

She realized the *Englischers* were staring at her. No wonder. She was so lost in thought they must think she'd forgotten her manners.

"Can I help you?" she asked, guessing they needed directions because they'd taken a wrong turn in the late-May twilight.

Neither the man nor the woman seemed to hear her. She realized they weren't looking at her. They stared beyond her at the living room, where her sons were scrambling over the furniture like a pair of chipmunks. Jared, the more daring, was trying to climb the couch.

When she asked the question again, the man's eyes snapped back to her. They were as cold as a snake's. He looked down a long nose at her. He and the woman were much taller than her scant five feet.

"Are you Naomi Ropp?" he asked in a raspy voice that suggested he must be a smoker. The odor coming off his light blue golf shirt and jeans confirmed it.

She wanted to put her hand over her mouth and nose. The remnants of cigarette smoke made her chest tighten and caused paroxysms of coughs if she breathed them too long. However, she was so shocked that the *Englischer* knew her name, she choked out, "*Ja*, I'm Naomi. Can I help you?"

"I'm Cole Yeatman. This here is my sister, Leslie."

"Are you lost?" Naomi glanced over her shoulder and discovered Jared had fallen into the couch's cushions, taking the quilt that covered it with him. Both little boys rolled about, convulsed with laughter, so she knew he hadn't been hurt.

"No. I own this dump."

Her head jerked toward the *Englischers*. "Own what?"

"This place." He hooked a thumb at the house and then pointed toward the barns. "It's mine."

"You're mistaken. This farm belongs to us." She gulped. "It belongs to me. I've owned it with my late husband for over ten years." She silenced her mind as it started its recital of the exact date she and Marlin had signed the papers before their wedding. "You've got the wrong house."

He shook his head. "What are you trying to pull, lady? Don't you think I know my own property?"

Though she wanted to fire the same question at him, she said, "As I told you, this farm had belonged to me and my late husband for a long time."

"Marlin Ropp, right?" asked the woman, drawing Naomi's attention.

Naomi hadn't forgotten the woman was there. She didn't forget anything, no matter how hard she tried. Most especially, she couldn't forget mistakes, hers or her husband's. She'd tried with Marlin's infidelities. He hadn't been her first mistake. Samuel King had been. He'd enticed her to kiss him more than eleven years ago and then spread nasty rumors about her. Horrified how people had looked askance at her, she'd accepted Marlin's proposal after he'd said he didn't put much stock in rumors. Only later did she realize that was because he didn't want her to believe the ones about him.

Growing uneasy that these strangers seemed to know too much about her—and she'd never met them—she said, "Like I said, you've got the wrong house."

She reached to close the door, but the man slapped his hand against it to hold it open. "No, we've got the right house. Playing stupid won't get you anywhere, Mrs. Ropp."

"I'm not—" She heard a crash and a wail behind her. She reached for the door again to shut it, but she couldn't as long as the man's hand was pressed to it.

Ignoring the *Englichers*, she ran across the room and scooped up one of the twins. Jesse, she knew as soon as she held him. He seemed fragile compared to his more robust brother. She checked he wasn't hurt, then discovered his tears were because his brother had gotten to the top of the couch and Jesse hadn't managed it.

"Mrs. Ropp." The woman's voice was impatient...and inside her home.

Naomi had miscalculated by taking her eyes off the Yeatmans. Not that it mattered. Cole hadn't intended to let her shut the door and keep him out.

Facing them, she said, "All right. I'm listening."

"That's right." Cole advanced on her, and she backed away, keeping the space between them the same. "It's time for you to listen, Naomi."

She frowned, knowing his use of her given name signaled change. Not for the better, she was sure.

"I'm listening." She put her hands on her twins' heads as they clamped their arms around her legs. The boys had sensed the tension in the room, though they couldn't understand. How could they when *she* had no idea what was going on?

She looked around the clean but worn room. The quilt had fallen onto the light brown couch cushions, revealing the burned spot on the upholstery left by one of Marlin's friends who hadn't listened when she'd asked him not to smoke in the house. A pair of mismatched chairs were draped by afghans to brighten the room. A table in the corner held the family's Bible and a small vase filled with the drooping dandelions her sons had picked that afternoon. Toys and books were scattered across the oak floors and the red-and-blue braided rug.

"Are those Marlin's kids?" Leslie squatted so her eyes were level with the twins. "You're cute. You look like your daddy."

The boys tightened their holds on her. Naomi guessed they weren't sure what to make of an *Englisch* woman who wore heavy eyeliner and bright red lipstick to match her outrageous hair. Her large earrings, bright gold with green stones inset in them, clanked when she moved her head. A half-dozen gold bracelets clattered on her arms when she held out her hands to the boys. They turned their faces to her apron.

Leslie's face hardened. "Not very friendly, are they?"

"They don't understand what you're saying," she replied, stroking their heads. "They speak only *Deitsch*."

"What's that?"

"It's what we Amish speak at home. The boys won't learn English until they go to school when they're six."

Standing, Leslie scowled at each of them in turn. "So you can brainwash them in your backward ways before they start asking questions? Poor kids. Probably never seen a cell phone." Pulling one out of her skintight jeans, she held it out to the twins. "Take a good, long look at what you're giving up, boys."

The phone made a buzzing sound, and Leslie transferred her frown to it. Jabbing a red nail at it, she said, "I hate this thing." She shoved it into her pocket.

Naomi bit her lower lip before she couldn't hide her nervous smile. The woman's words and actions didn't match. She guessed it wasn't the woman who intended to cause her trouble.

She refocused on Cole Yeatman as he said, "Leslie, give it a rest, will you? Or go out and sit in the car."

The woman spit a word that made Naomi want to cover her boys' ears. They wouldn't understand what it meant, but she did. She'd heard *Englischers* say it—and even Marlin once, on the night she discovered his cheating—but never had she heard it spoken in such a malicious tone.

Cole turned away from his sister. "You need to pack up your kids and any of this junk you want to keep and get out of here, Naomi."

"I'm not leaving my home, and it is *my* home." Her voice quavered, muting the anger in her words.

"No, it's not." He wagged a finger at her. "Let's get that one thing straight right now. This is my place. My family has owned it for years."

Yeatman. The name was clear in her memory. She'd seen it on the paperwork she and Marlin had signed when purchasing the farm. It was the name of the previous owners. That was what her husband had told her after he announced they were moving to Honey Brook in neighboring Chester County the day after their wedding.

She hadn't wanted to leave Bliss Valley and her parents, but it'd been her duty as a wife to heed her husband as head of their household. She hadn't been able to visit her parents more than twice a year. It was a long drive by buggy, more than two hours each way, and Marlin had been reluctant to hire an *Englisch* driver. Each trip home, especially after her *mamm*'s death when her *daed* had been despondent, had left her longing to return again soon.

"Your family," Naomi said with dignity, "sold the farm to Marlin and me."

"Prove it."

"Pardon me?"

He folded his arms over his full chest, which was already beginning the middle-aged slide down toward his belt. "You heard me. I said, 'Prove it.' You've got to have paperwork to prove you own this place."

"I do."

"Show me."

"Now?"

"I can wait while you get it."

Naomi hesitated, not wanting to leave two belligerent

strangers in her living room while she went to the kitchen cupboard where she kept household accounts.

"This way." She steered the boys into the kitchen and listened as heavier footfalls followed.

The kitchen was her favorite room because it'd been solely hers. Marlin had insisted they have their meals in the drafty dining room. Since his death, she and the boys had used the table in the kitchen. It'd been warmer because she never allowed the fire in the big black wood stove to go out. The room was scented with her day's baking. A loaf of bread sat on the cutting board next to a cooling peach pie. The stove she used for cooking was set between the refrigerator and sink. With its pale blue walls, the room was welcoming even on a cloudy day.

Putting the boys in their identical high chairs, she handed each of them a peanut butter cookie. They grinned in delight at the unexpected treat. They wouldn't stay diverted any longer than it took them to crumble the cookies and stuff the pieces into their mouths. Hurrying to the deep drawer where she kept important papers, she began to flip through them.

"We don't have all night," grumbled Cole from behind her.

She resisted reminding him that he'd said he could wait. Enraging the man wouldn't be smart.

Her shoulders stiffened as she heard Leslie say, "Hey, this pie is good!"

"Get your fingers out of that!" ordered Leslie's brother. "You don't know what they put into their pies."

Peaches, sugar, cinnamon, brown sugar, flour. Her brain rattled off the recipe she'd used as she looked through the drawer. Where was the folder with the papers from when they'd purchased the farm? In her mind's eye, she could see it, a bright green card-stock folder set between the bright blue one that held each year's dairy records and the yellow one with the receipts from her vegetable garden sales. The blue and yellow folders were there, but where was the green one?

She smiled as she pulled it out from near the bottom. Her smile vanished. The folder held only a few sheets. A quick scan revealed they had nothing to do with the farm's purchase. These pages had come from another folder, the one where she kept bills for propane and the barn's electricity. Where were the documents that should be in the folder? She closed it and the drawer.

God, I know I've asked for your help a lot lately, but I need it now. Reach into the Yeatmans' hearts and open them to my plight. Convince them to heed my words and let them know I'm being honest.

Naomi faced the strangers and made sure her demeanor was as calm as if God had already answered her prayer. He would. She believed that, but when and how were things that required faith. Her faith was shaky.

"I'm going to need time to find the papers," she said.

Cole crossed the kitchen in a few long strides and grabbed her arm. Tugging her away from the drawer, he said, "Okay, you've had your chance to prove it. You can't, but I can prove I'm telling you the truth." He pulled out a folded page, opened it and tossed it onto the table near where she stood. "Read it."

He had to repeat the order before she could make her fingers pick up the page. It shook as she raised it. The document was titled "Lease." She dropped into a nearby chair as she read the simple language that outlined how Marlin Ropp was granted full use of the farm and its buildings, including the house, for a period of ten years. Searching the page, she found the date on it.

Marlin had signed it five months before they were married... which meant there was just over a week left on the lease. *Ten days.* Ten days to move her and the *kinder* and the animals somewhere else?

If Marlin had leased the farm, why had she signed paperwork before their wedding? She'd handled the household accounts, and she'd been writing checks to pay the mortgage each month since they were married. In fact, she'd made the final payment to pay off the mortgage a month before Marlin died.

She raised her eyes to the two *Englischers*. "I gave Marlin a check for the mortgage each month. He took it to the bank, and the money came out of our account like clockwork each month. Where's that money gone?"

Cole shrugged. "You're asking the wrong man. You need to ask Marlin."

"You know she can't," choked Leslie and began to cry.

"Quit it, Leslie," Cole said in a disgusted voice. "Can't you see I'm trying to do business here?"

"I don't care!" his sister retorted. "The man I love is dead, and all you can think about is business."

"One of us has to." He paid his sister's sobs no attention as he narrowed his eyes at Naomi. "It's time to get to the point. You don't have paperwork to prove you own this farm, and I've got a signed lease agreement that proves I do. I told Marlin he could use the farm when he got serious with Leslie before you moved in. Now he's dead, and—"

"Don't say that word!" Leslie choked out a sob and hid her face in her hands. "It's not fair!"

Finally the redhead had said something Naomi could agree with. It wasn't fair Marlin had set up this house of cards. She must believe, as long as she trusted in God, things would work out somehow.

How would Leslie react if Naomi quoted the eighth and

ninth verses of 2 Corinthians chapter 4 that were flickering through her mind?

We are troubled on every side, yet not distressed; we are perplexed, but not in despair; Persecuted, but not forsaken; cast down, but not destroyed.

God had provided for her by giving her Jared and Jesse. If not for the twins, she wasn't sure she'd have been able to go on after taking care of Marlin's funeral and the farm in the weeks that followed.

"I told you to be quiet, Leslie." Again he jabbed a thumb out, this time in the direction of his weeping sister. "She's been like this since they got back together before he died…"

Naomi flinched, and she lowered her eyes to her hands folded on the table. This *Englischer* with the outrageous hair was another of her late husband's women? Leslie had been stupid to fall for Marlin not once, but twice. He must have cheated on the redhead, too. In shock, Naomi realized Marlin had cheated on Leslie with her. It was hard now to remember at one time, Naomi had loved him. Her heart had frozen in the middle of a single beat after he derided her for being so *dumm* as to have two *bopplin* at once.

That day, her love for him had dried up like an autumn leaf and blown away.

She had no idea how many women he'd been with. Some had been plain while others, like Leslie, were *Englisch*. He'd claimed for years it was because she wasn't a *gut* Amish wife who'd given him a house filled with kids to do the chores he hated. She'd offered to be a foster parent. She'd talked about adoption. He refused to listen about taking in *kinder* who needed a home, even after she'd been licensed. That she'd had more than a dozen miscarriages hadn't made any difference to him. Against the advice of her *doktor* and the local midwife, she'd continued to try to carry a *boppli* to term to show Marlin he was wrong.

She was the one who'd been wrong. Even when she gave birth to their twins, he hadn't stopped his running around with other women. Then he'd decided he didn't want to be stuck in the house with two crying *bopplin*. Too late, after risking her health and her *bopplin*'s health, she'd realized her miscarriages hadn't been anything but convenient excuses for him to break their marriage vows.

She'd been wrong about so many things from the minute she'd met Marlin Ropp and let his easy smile and well-polished words persuade her he was the man who could give her what she wanted. A marriage like the one her parents had, one not tainted by cheating and secrets and half truths. How many times had she heard *Daed* speak of how he and *Mamm* had never kept a secret from one another?

The day before he died in the crossfire of gunshots on a decrepit street in Lancaster, Marlin had told her he was jumping the fence to join the *Englisch*. He was doing it because he was in love with another woman—with Leslie Yeatman, she knew now—and planned to file for the divorce that wasn't allowed among the Amish. Other men and women had done the same thing to their spouses, so she knew what would have happened. Marlin would have gotten the divorce and gone on his way, free to marry whomever he chose. She would have held on to her vows of being his wife until death did them part.

Neither of them had guessed how soon death would change their plans.

Jesse let out a cry, and Naomi realized the boys had finished their cookies. Jared knuckled his eyes. The *kinder* were tired and ready for bed.

Standing, she said, "The twins need to be seen to."

"After we get one thing straight."

"What?"

"You and your kids need to be out of here by the first of June." He put his face close to hers. "Don't force me to make you sorry for staying here."

He whirled on his heel and headed toward the door. His exit was ruined when he tripped over a pile of plastic blocks. Kicking them aside with another curse that seared her ears, he stormed out with his sister following. The door slammed in their wake so hard the glass rattled in the window beside it.

Both twins let out cries, and Naomi wanted to join them. She couldn't. She had barely ten days to figure out where they'd go and what they'd do then.

The where was easy.

Her *daed*'s home in Bliss Valley. He'd asked her the day of Marlin's funeral to come home. She'd been too much in shock to make any decision, but now she wasn't. She had to think of her twins. As she lifted them out of their chairs and watched them toddle toward the stairs, she was certain of one thing. She was going to make sure they were loved and safe and never made the same mistakes she had.

Chapter Two

Naomi thanked God for how even-tempered her two mules were. Fred and Ginger plodded along behind the buggy as if they spent every day lashed to it. They pulled the farm wagon that held everything worth taking from the rickety farmhouse she'd believed was her home.

Most of the wagon was filled with the twins' toys and furniture and clothing. She had clothes, too, and the set of china *Mamm* had given her the day before her wedding. *Mamm* had received the same set of dishes from her *grossmammi*. Though there were fewer plates and cups. Naomi had broken one of each when she was a *kind*, and two more had cracked while she washed them in the old farmhouse in Honey Brook.

Then there was the night when Marlin had thrown a cup against the wall when she'd been upset he hadn't come home for three days.

At a squeal from the back seat, she looked over her shoulder.

Jared and Jesse bounced on the seat, waving to the mules and chattering to each other in their private language. She wasn't sure if they understood one another. She didn't comprehend a syllable, but guessed it was something twins shared. Neither she nor Marlin knew of twins in their families, so she didn't have experience with them.

Days of searching for the paperwork to prove she and Marlin had purchased the farm had been futile. She'd found none of the papers she'd signed. The stack of paperwork had been handed to her so quickly she hadn't taken time to read it. She'd been happy Marlin had found a farm they could afford to purchase and that they soon would be sharing their wedding day with friends and family.

If she'd read every page, she'd be able to recall each word. It was too late.

A visit to the bishop, Mervin Steiner, for his advice hadn't done her any *gut* once he'd looked at the pages the Yeatmans had given her. Mervin had said they seemed to be in order. Nothing could be done to stop the eviction. His offer to pray for her and send volunteers to help her pack had been kind.

So now Naomi and her *kinder* were traveling through central Lancaster County. Fields clung to the sides of the road. To her right, the bank was higher and formed an earthen hedge along the blacktop. She saw farmers, plain and *Englisch*, plowing their fields with mules and with tractors. Others were mowing and baling spring's first cutting of hay. Almost all the farmhouses, some small and others with additions going in every direction, were white. Barns backed them or stretched out along the rolling hills. Gray-topped buggies, identical to hers right down to the slow-moving-vehicle triangle on the back, waited in dooryards while laundry ran like rainbows from houses to the barns.

Going to her childhood home was her only choice other than living with her boys in the buggy. She'd never let her parents know about Marlin's cheating. Secrets seared her soul like poison. Yet she must endure it because she couldn't hurt her *daed* by revealing how she'd kept him in the dark for her whole marriage. She'd let him think it was as *gut* and honest as his own had been.

Naomi waved at a trio of kids going in the other direction on their scooters. They gawped at the odd procession she'd created after learning how much it would cost to ship her household goods by truck to Bliss Valley. Most of her savings had gone into buying seeds for the vegetable garden she'd never harvest.

She pointed at the scooters. "Doesn't that look like fun?"

"Fun!" the twins shouted and chortled.

Other *bopplin* said "*Mamm*" or "*Daed*" for their first word. Not her sons. "Fun" had been their first word and was their favorite.

Tears rose into Naomi's eyes at the sight of the farm where she'd lived the first two decades of her life. It didn't look like the others she'd passed. There wasn't any laundry hanging on a line, and there were three buggies in the yard. Her *daed* repaired buggies in his shop in the weathered outbuilding beside the white farmhouse with its *dawdi haus* tacked on the back. Nobody had lived there since her grandparents died when she wasn't much older than the twins, but her *mamm* had cleaned it every week.

Naomi hoped the living room, bedroom and tiny kitchen would offer the sanctuary she and her sons needed. More than once, she'd considered calling *Daed*'s shop and telling him she'd been evicted. She hadn't. Since *Mamm*'s death shortly before Naomi discovered she was having twins, *Daed* always was busy with work. Though she guessed he was losing himself in work so he didn't have to think about *Mamm*'s passing, it bothered her. The three of them had been close. Unlike most of her friends, who had lots of brothers and sisters, she'd been an only *kind*. Her best friend, Laurene Nolt, had been, too, which had been one of the first things that had drawn them together on their first day of school.

The farm had been home, and she was determined to make it so again. Only this time for her *and* her boys.

Turning Waldo into the farm lane, she called, "Boys, we're almost there!"

Excited cheers of "Fun!" met her words. The trip from Honey Brook had taken five hours because she'd had to make frequent stops to let the animals rest.

Maneuvering around the potholes in the farm lane, Naomi drove the quarter mile toward the farmhouse. She'd complained as a youngster about how far the house was set back from the road because one of her chores had been to collect the mail, no matter the weather. In the winter, when a cold wind sliced across the fallow fields, she'd hated the trek. Now she appreciated how the white farmhouse and the outbuildings were situated to give a spectacular view across the valley and the creek that snaked its way toward the Bliss Valley Covered Bridge. She and Laurene had spent plenty of warm afternoons splashing in the water under the bridge, trying to catch minnows.

Leave the past in the past, she warned herself as she had the past week. She wished she could leave Marlin in the past along with Samuel King and the other mistakes she'd made. Forgiving was impossible when her heart was so bruised.

Please, God, I know You gave me this gift of being able to remember everything, but could You take these memories out of my head?

A motion caught her eyes. Two men were emerging from *Daed*'s shop. They waited until she'd stopped the buggy after calling out to the mules to halt. Again she thanked God for how well trained Fred and Ginger were.

She climbed out, then lifted the twins from the buggy. They ran forward to greet their *grossdawdi* before heading for the tire swing hanging from the big maple in the front yard. It had hung there since her *daed* had been a boy.

As she came around the carriage, Naomi patted Waldo on the nose and thanked him for his work on the long journey from Honey Brook. She halted in midstep and stared at the man beside *Daed*. There was something familiar about him. He was much taller than *Daed*, whose head wasn't much more than three or four inches above hers now that he was bent after years of working on buggies. The man's hair shone like gold, but his eyes, the color of the weathered gray boards on the barn, were narrowed. The pale line of a ragged scar tore across his forehead above his left brow, and he leaned on a cane as he limped across the yard. He wore a half apron with large pockets tied around his waist, and she heard the clang of metal with each step he took. Was he carrying tools in it?

Who was the man? The last time she'd been home, almost two months ago, *Daed* had been talking about getting an assistant. Had he hired one?

"Naomi, what's this?" called *Daed*.

Instead of replying, she threw her arms around him. She didn't sob, though she wanted to. She wanted to be held as she hadn't been in too long, knowing she was loved. When he murmured how happy he was to see her, she closed her eyes and drew in the special scent of him. It was a mixture of wood shavings and the lubricating oils he used in his shop, and it was her favorite aroma.

Eager shrieks coming from where the boys were playing on the tire swing brought up Naomi's head. A quick check told her they were safe. When *Daed* asked again what was going on, she said she hoped he'd take her and his *kins-kinder* into his home.

"We can live in the *dawdi haus*, so we won't be in your way," she ended without telling him they'd been evicted. She didn't want to air her dirty laundry in front of the stranger.

"In the *dawdi haus*?" *Daed* shook his head. "No, you'll live in the main house. My assistant is living in the *dawdi haus* until the chicken barn is rebuilt." Motioning toward the other man, he said, "*Komm* and say hello to Samuel."

"Samuel?" Her voice sounded distant in her own ears as if the single word had been caught by a storm wind.

She took another look at the man who was limping toward them. No wonder he'd looked familiar. Samuel King had shared her first kiss and then told everyone about it, making her the laughingstock of Bliss Valley and ruining her reputation. How could she even attempt to forget the worst parts of her past when Samuel King stood right in front of her now?

Samuel King should have been prepared. When he'd accepted the job as Elvin Gingerich's assistant, he'd known there was a *gut* chance he'd bump into Naomi sooner or later. As the last three weeks had passed, he'd convinced himself he was in the clear because Naomi didn't seem to visit her *daed* often.

He'd guessed she hadn't recognized him when she first glanced his way. That wasn't any surprise. Even without the aftereffects of the car accident that had nearly killed him, he was taller than the last time she'd spoken to him. His growth spurt had come late, right after he'd left Bliss Valley to join the *Englisch* world with his friend Joel Beachy.

The past twelve years had been more merciful to Naomi than to him. She was as pretty as the day he'd noticed her when he'd walked into his new school after his family moved to Bliss Valley. Back then, her pale hair, the color of corn silk laced with sunlight, had been braided and twisted into a bun beneath a kerchief. Now it was confined beneath her white heart-shaped *kapp*. Her bright blue eyes were the same. That first day at school she'd looked at him with curiosity and welcome. Her offer of friendship had been retracted when he found friends who joined in his delight at teasing her and her friend Laurene heartlessly.

Had any of them, his friends Joel and Adam Hershberger or the girls, ever guessed he'd been frightened of her kindness? He'd never been made to feel welcome anywhere, especially not at home, where his *mamm* and his step*daed* never let him forget he was his *mamm*'s greatest mistake. A few times, he'd tried to protest to his parents that he hadn't asked to be conceived while his *mamm* was an unmarried *maedel*. His birth *daed* hadn't stuck around, and his *mamm* had been eager to get Samuel out of her life from before his first breath.

That was why, when he'd returned to Bliss Valley after the accident, barely able to stand alone, *Mamm* had slammed the door in his face. If he hadn't been able to rent a room with the Pfisters in Bird-in-Hand—Arlie Pfister was a third cousin's brother-in-law—he didn't want to think what would have happened. He'd picked up jobs wherever and whenever he could, looking for work that would complement the exercises he did with his physical therapy.

He'd healed and he'd survived and he'd jumped at the chance to work with Elvin Gingerich after a decade of odd jobs here and there to keep himself fed.

Now everything he'd struggled to get after he'd been taught

how to walk again was about to turn to sand beneath him. He'd learned enough from Elvin to work in another shop, but it would have to be beyond Bliss Valley, costing him any chance to convince his family to accept him.

"Naomi, this is Samuel King," Elvin said with a smile. "Samuel, this is my daughter. Those two imps over there are her twins, Jared and Jesse."

Samuel waited for Naomi to speak. She remained silent, looking at him as if he had stepped out of her greatest nightmare.

"Daed," she said, her voice unsteady with the emotion he could see in her clenched hands, "I need to get the twins something to eat before I start unpacking the wagon. If you'll excuse me…"

"Was iss letz?" Elvin couldn't understand what was bothering his daughter.

"How can you ask what's wrong? Why did you hire him?"

"Him? Samuel?"

"Ja."

"What's wrong with him?"

Naomi's eyes widened in disbelief. "How many days did I come home crying because I'd been teased? Two hundred fifty-seven days. Don't you remember?"

Elvin looked from her to Samuel, puzzled. "Of course, I remember. It broke my heart. There were three boys. Adam Hershberger, Joel King and—".

"Not Joel King! Samuel King!" She aimed a scowl at him that would have sent a bear fleeing into the woods. "Him!"

Elvin tugged at his beard, a motion Samuel had learned the old man made whenever he was confronting a problem he wished would go away. Not that Elvin would want his daughter and his *kins-kinder* to leave.

That left only one solution, the thing Samuel had known he must do from the moment he saw Naomi coming up the farm lane.

"I'll go," he said.

"What?" Elvin asked at the same time Naomi said, *"Gut!"*

"No," her *daed* argued. "It's not *gut*. I need an assistant, and Samuel has learned a lot. I don't want to start over. You two aren't *kinder* any longer. Let the past go. Naomi, what does the Bible teach about the past?"

"'Remember ye not the former things, neither consider the things of old,'" she replied. "Isaiah 43:18. All right, *Daed*. He can stay, and we'll—"

Elvin interrupted her. "If you're going to say you and the boys will leave, stop. The barn will be rebuilt soon. It would have been by now if there hadn't been so many fires in Bliss Valley this spring. Once that happens, you won't have to see Samuel. He'll be living next to my new shop."

She raised her chin, and Samuel realized anew how tiny she was. Even with her head held high, he could have rested his chin on her *kapp*. There was nothing diminutive about her emotions searing him. She turned her back on him. "Okay, we won't go."

"*Gut*. You're my *kind*, and I'm glad to have you home." Elvin touched Naomi's face with gentle fingers. The motion shouted the love between them more clearly than any words could have. "Let me see what those two little monkeys are up to." He strode past her with a grin.

Samuel hated the piercing pain as he wondered what it would be like to have a parent excited to see him. He tried not to be maudlin. He'd gotten this far. There wasn't any reason why, with God's grace, he couldn't someday have his family welcome him home.

As soon as Elvin was out of earshot, Naomi faced Samuel again. "You need to go. I don't want my boys' lives poisoned by you as mine was."

"You told your *daed*—"

"I didn't want to upset him. Find another job."

He frowned. In school, she and Laurene Nolt had been the best scholars. Now she was again acting as if she knew everything. He still didn't like it.

"I'm not leaving," he retorted, "and I'm not looking for another job. I've spent a long time trying to find a job like this. It's the first one I've had where my past hasn't been an issue."

"Your past?"

"I was in a car accident."

"Is that what happened to you?"

He didn't hear sympathy in her voice, but he hadn't expected to because she was furious. "*Ja*, I crashed the car Adam gave Joel and me." His brows lowered. "You must have heard about it. Everyone else in Lancaster County did."

Everybody had heard about the accident and then embroidered the tale to make the facts even more appalling. He knew the truth. He and Joel had been drinking and shouldn't have gotten into the car. He'd been driving and nearly died. Joel must have been hurt, too, but all Samuel knew for sure was his friend had fled. It was whispered he'd gone to jail. Samuel didn't know if that was true, because the same rumors had been spread about him. Though he'd been arrested, he'd never spent time in a cell. Warnings the judge wouldn't be lenient next time had kept him from ever having another beer.

"I've been living in Chester County." Something sad flashed through her eyes before she lifted her chin again.

Guilt gripped him. How could he have forgotten she'd recently lost her husband? She was a young widow with two rambunctious boys. He glanced toward the house and saw Elvin sitting on the porch steps. The boys were racing around the yard.

"Look," Naomi said, pulling his attention back to her. "I don't want to upset my *daed*, but I've got to think of the twins."

"Do I look like I'll be a bad influence on them?" He tapped his cane on the ground. "Most little kids don't want to come near."

As if to prove he didn't know what he was talking about, the twins ran toward them. They skirted him, not even looking in his direction as the bigger boy shouted, *"Mamm, komm!"*

"Just a moment." Looking at Samuel, she began, "It'd be for the best—"

"Mamm, komm!" The smaller boy grabbed her skirt and tugged. *"Komm, Mamm. Boppli!"*

Surprise turned her mouth and eyes into matching circles. *"Boppli?* What are you talking about, Jesse?"

"Fun, *Mamm*," the littler boy said.

"Fun?" Samuel repeated, confused.

"It's what they say when they're excited." Squatting, she said, "Tell me what you've seen, Jesse. What is it, Jared?"

"Boppli!" the twins said as one.

"The white barn cat is about to have a litter," Samuel said. "Maybe that's what they're—"

"Danki, but I'll handle this." She stood and took her *kinder* by the hands. Without another word to him, she went with her sons toward the house.

He shrugged and headed to the shop and the metal wheel that he'd been working on. It'd been bent when Ivan Keim, a neighboring farmer, had fallen asleep and driven his buggy into a ditch. Neither Ivan nor his horse had been hurt, but the same couldn't be said for the buggy. Two wheels looked like uneven ovals. Banging the rims into the proper shape was a loud, slow process. He had to take care he didn't crack the metal or break it.

Hearing an excited squeal, Samuel looked across the yard. Naomi's boys were leading her toward the small porch on the *dawdi haus*. That was his home. Why would the cat have had her litter there?

He hobbled toward the small porch, which wasn't big enough for a single chair. He had to sit on the steps when he removed his work boots. Unlike the broad porch on the front of the house, it wasn't inviting. Solitude hadn't been his first choice, but he'd accepted it in order to have a job that taught him a marketable skill.

Naomi paused at the bottom of the three steps, giving him a chance to catch up with her. When her mouth tightened into a frown, he looked at a brown paper grocery bag. Where had that come from? It hadn't been there earlier.

"*Boppli!*" crowed one twin while the other jumped up and down as he repeated, "Fun, fun, fun, fun!"

Had the cat used the bag to have her kittens? If so, why was the bag standing up? It should have tipped over when the cat crawled into it.

Samuel climbed the steps and looked into the bag. He gasped when he saw what was inside.

A slumbering *boppli* wrapped in a thick blanket.

Chapter Three

Samuel wasn't sure how long he would have stood there, staring into the bag, if one of the twins—he wasn't sure whether it was Jesse or Jared—hadn't run onto the porch and yelled, *"Boppli!"*

The noise woke the infant, and a thin cry floated up from the bag.

With a gasp, Naomi climbed onto the porch. She didn't elbow him away, but he stepped aside as she edged between him and the bag. His weak, right foot struck something, and a container tumbled, knocking over a *boppli*'s bottle. Catching the can before it could roll away, he saw it held powdered formula.

She gasped again and whispered a quick prayer before reaching into the bag and lifting out the tiny *boppli*. "It's a newborn," she said as much to herself as to him. "A newborn girl."

He peered over her shoulder to see the umbilical cord stump

was still attached. Whirling, he looked across the fields and along the road. Who had abandoned the *kind*? Why had they left her on his porch?

As Naomi cradled the tiny *boppli* next to her heart, the twins edged toward her, curious. He stepped back, overwhelmed by the explosion of emotions. Relief that the twins had led them to the *boppli* before something happened to her. Gratitude to God that Naomi was there to tend to the little girl. Elvin might know something about taking care of such a tiny *boppli*, but Samuel didn't.

Another *kind* as unwanted as he'd been. His *mamm* hadn't abandoned him on a doorstep, but she'd withdrawn from him so much he might as well have been alone. A recurring dream had plagued him his whole life. Sometimes the dream family was his *mamm* and his six half-siblings. Sometimes it was an imaginary one, but in each variation, he'd been the treasured member of a close-knit family. Every time he'd had that dream, he'd woken up and realized it wasn't true.

Now this tiny *kind*, through no fault of her own, would one day experience the pain of knowing she hadn't been wanted.

He shook the dreary thoughts from his head. The *boppli* needed to be taken care of, and she'd been left on *his* porch.

"See *boppli*," ordered one of the twins. "See."

"Please, Jared," Naomi replied without taking her gaze off the tiny face. She brushed her fingers over blond fuzz on the *boppli*'s head.

"Please see *boppli*."

"That's the nice way to ask, Jared." She leaned forward, holding the small bundle low enough so the twins could see over the thick blanket.

"*Boppli* no clothes," announced the other twin.

"That's true, Jesse. Would you share yours with her?"

He shook his head. "Me too big."

"We can make her clothes, ain't so?"

Samuel cleared his throat, and she looked at him. "You aren't thinking of keeping this *boppli*, are you? She's not a kitten someone's dropped off."

"I realize that." Her voice grew chilly again. "She belongs to someone."

"My *boppli*," the boy she'd called Jared announced.

As his brother began to protest, Naomi said, "The *boppli* isn't ours."

"Keep her?" Jesse grinned, and Samuel noticed he had a missing tooth. No, his little front tooth was there, but chipped. "Fun!"

"We'll have to wait and see." She smiled. "*Grossdawdi* usually has cookies in the kitchen. Let's go and see what we can find."

As they cheered and raced toward the front porch where Elvin sat, Naomi went down the steps. Over her shoulder, she said, "Samuel, you should bring the bag along. It may be an important clue to this *kind's mamm*."

He picked up the bag and folded it, so he could carry it under his right arm. He didn't trust the fingers of his right hand. Though he was doing better after years of physical and occupational therapy, the muscles could spasm without warning, and whatever he held fell.

The formula container and bottle were a bigger challenge. He couldn't carry them and use his cane at the same time. Managing such tasks was something he'd learned over the past seven years. He shifted the tools in his apron before placing the can in one pocket and the bottle in another.

Naomi walked faster than he could, so he had no hopes of

catching her. By the time he'd reached the front porch, she was already talking to her *daed* and showing off what she carried.

Elvin pushed himself to his feet as he choked out in surprise, "A *boppli*? You found a *boppli* on our porch?"

"On the porch of the *dawdi haus*," she said as the *boppli* began to cry. She rocked her arms, and that seemed to soothe the infant, but Samuel guessed the little one would be hungry soon.

Elvin's eyes cut to him as he asked in an exacting tone Samuel had never heard his boss use, "Is this your *kind*?"

"Not mine," Samuel said, holding up his right hand, "and before you ask, I don't have any idea where the *boppli* came from. Certainly nobody selected it off a shelf at Weis Market."

"Weis Market?" Naomi repeated.

He held up the bag with its grocery store logo. "There's a Weis Market on Willow Street and another in Gap. The bag could have come from either."

Another squawk from the blanket halted the conversation. Naomi led the way into the house, not stopping until she reached the kitchen. It was a large, cluttered room. Dirty dishes were piled in the sink, and Samuel doubted anyone had cleaned the stove since Naomi's last visit. Stacks of newspapers hid the table's top, and several more editions of *The Budget* had fallen on the floor.

If the mess bothered Naomi, she showed no sign of it. "*Daed*, do you have any goat *millich*? Cow's *millich* won't work for a newborn."

"There's this." Samuel pulled out the can and set it on the counter.

"Where did you get that?"

"It and a bottle were left with the *boppli*."

A faint smile tipped her lips. "At least whoever left May did one thing right."

"May?"

"She needs a name, and she was born in May. Why not call her that?"

Again the *boppli* began to cry, and Naomi moved with efficiency, directing the rest of them like a shepherd gathering sheep. She had Samuel open the can of formula. Getting two cookies for the twins and another for her *daed*, she instructed Elvin to pour *millich* for him and the little boys to drink on the porch. At the same time, she rummaged through a drawer until she found a soft dusting cloth. She improvised a diaper before using a dish towel to swaddle the little newborn.

When he brought her the bottle with a small portion of formula, she took it and sat at the table. "*Danki*. I didn't know you could do that."

"I've learned all sorts of things since the last time you saw me." He hadn't meant it to sound like sarcasm, but she lowered her eyes and focused on getting the *boppli* to suck on the bottle.

I don't want to go back to the way we used to be, God. Help me learn to treat her as if the past never happened.

He almost laughed at his own prayer. *As if the past never happened*? That hadn't worked for his *mamm*, though she'd made every effort to act as if she'd forgotten it and him.

Naomi looked at the *boppli*. "We need to call the authorities."

"Jonas should be informed first." When her brows rose in an unspoken question, he said, "Jonas Gundy is our bishop."

"Go ahead, but the longer we delay in getting social services here, the tougher they'll be on us." She raised her gaze to his. "That's something I learned when I was licensed as a foster parent before the boys were born."

He tried to hide his astonishment she'd stepped a toe into the *Englisch* world. Why had she obtained foster parent certification? Though he'd heard of other Amish families offering foster homes, it was unusual and he'd never met anyone who'd done it. As a flash of color climbed her cheeks, he wondered what she wasn't saying, what secrets she was trying to hide.

Secrets…

He hated that word. His earliest memories were his *mamm* cautioning his *aentis* and *onkels* not to speak of his illegitimacy. The overwhelming shame of his birth was a stain that must be a secret from everybody. Now he watched as Naomi nestled another unwanted *boppli* in her arms.

"I'll call Jonas from the shop," Samuel said. "I should be able to get him at this time of day at his shop."

"*Gut.*"

"Then I'll alert the police."

She nodded. "I'm glad you agree it's the best thing to do."

"If it is, why do you look like you're about to go to someone's funeral?"

He'd never imagined sorrow and fury could mix in anyone's eyes. With unmistakable dignity, she rose as their gazes locked. Her voice was soft, but the power behind it belied her petite stature.

"You've never thought about anyone besides yourself, Samuel King. I can see you haven't changed, though you've been given a second chance for a life. You're squandering what God has given you by not considering that doing the right thing is seldom the easy thing."

"You're wrong."

"Am I?"

"*Ja*, you are." He tightened his hold on his cane. "I'll make those calls after I unhitch your horse and mules." Sarcasm filled his voice. "You're welcome."

Her lips tightened before she again turned her attention

to the *boppli*. As she sat again, he limped out of the kitchen. He'd seldom gotten in the last word with pretty Naomi Gingerich. Everyone had been in awe of her odd memory, but he was grateful she had it instead of him. What *gut* would it be to resurrect every detail of your life when most of it had been miserable?

Later, Naomi wouldn't have been able to say who got to the house first: the police or the bishop. She hadn't seen either vehicle arrive because she'd been upstairs in the old farmhouse where she'd opened windows to air out two bedrooms. One for the twins and the other, smaller one for her.

And possibly the *boppli*.

She wanted to have Jared's and Jesse's bedding and favorite toys in their room before she tucked them in that evening. Though she'd never imagined she'd ever think the words, she was grateful for the help Samuel had given *Daed* bringing in the boxes and bags she'd packed in Honey Brook. The furniture would require more strong arms, because her *daed* must not risk himself carrying a mattress or headboard up either the simple front stairs or the tightly curved back stairs that led into the kitchen.

Now, a scant three hours after they'd discovered May in a paper bag on the *dawdi haus* porch, she stood in her *daed's* living room and listened to *Daed* confirm everything she'd said about finding the abandoned *boppli*. She looked at May, who was tasting the air as if it were the newest sensation. The *boppli* couldn't be more than a day or two old. It was *wunderbaar* to hold a brand-new infant. When the twins had been born, more than a month before her due date, they'd been whisked away and put in the neonatal intensive care unit. She hadn't held them for the first time until they were almost two weeks old.

"So you saw nobody, Elvin?" asked Officer Wigginton. Randy, as he'd urged them to call him, was short, stocky and had hair almost as bright red as Leslie Yeatman's. There was no mistaking the intelligence in his blue eyes.

She glanced around the familiar room with its worn furniture covered with the bright quilts her *mamm* had worked on throughout Naomi's life. Samuel loitered in the door between the living room and the kitchen. His face was as blank as a fresh piece of paper, but like the police officer, she guessed he was taking in every motion and word. Next to him was the bishop, Jonas Gundy. About the same age as Randy, he had a thick black beard that emphasized his thin face. He smiled when Jared, who considered everyone he met a *gut* friend, toddled over to show the bishop his favorite stuffed bear.

"Samuel and I didn't see or hear a soul other than each other until my daughter arrived." *Daed* sat in his favorite chair between the windows that gave him views of the road and his shop. "It's noisy in the shop, so we couldn't have heard anyone unless they'd made a powerful racket."

"What about you, Samuel?" Randy asked. "Did you hear anything?"

Daed chuckled. "Are you questioning my hearing ability?"

"If I was pounding on metal and around power tools all day like you are, I'd question my own hearing." The policeman smiled.

"Smart of you." Her *daed* looked past her to where Samuel stood. "Hear or see anything, Samuel?"

Shaking his head, Samuel replied, "I wish I had. Even a shadow might have told us if a man or a woman abandoned May."

"May?" Randy's smile turned to bafflement.

"May is," Naomi interjected, "what we've been calling

the *boppli*—the baby. Better than calling her 'baby' all the time, and it's the last day of May, so it seems kind of an obvious name."

"I get it." His smile returned. "Now what we'll need to do—"

A knock on the door interrupted him. As the twins whizzed past her, as eager to discover who was on the other side as they'd been at home, Naomi called them back. Her voice shook, and she repeated her request in a tenser tone.

When Samuel leaned forward to speak to the twins, distracting them, she went to the door and opened it. A dark-haired *Englischer* stood on the porch. He carried a battered briefcase and wore a suit that looked as if he'd taken it out of the washing machine and let it dry on him.

"Mrs. Ropp?" he asked.

"*Ja.*" Again her voice betrayed her disquiet. Cole Yeatman had asked her a similar question.

He pulled out a business card and handed it to her. "I'm Pierce Tedesco. I was contacted by the— Oh, hi, Randy!"

As the two men greeted each other, she read the card. Beside the emblem for the Commonwealth of Pennsylvania, Pierce Tedesco's name was listed as a social worker for the Lancaster County Children and Youth Social Service Agency. She handed the card to her *daed*, who glanced at it before holding it out to Jonas. The bishop passed it along to Samuel, who placed it on the table behind him before motioning for the twins to follow him toward the cookie jar.

Naomi almost called to halt him. Jared and Jesse had already had a cookie. Another might ruin their supper. She bit back the words. The twins' attention needed to be deflected. Nothing would do that better than a treat. Yet leaving Samuel to see to them made her even more uneasy.

She didn't have time to examine her feelings before May

began to cry. Feeling heat rush up her face as if she'd been caught doing something wrong, she hastened to say, "It's almost time for her next feeding."

"Go ahead, Mrs. Ropp," the social worker said.

"Call me Naomi."

He gave her a quick, professional smile. "Thank you. Go ahead, and we'll handle paperwork while you take care of that little girl."

Heading into the kitchen, Naomi stepped around her twins, who were jabbering like a pair of parrots at Samuel. She mixed up formula and put the bottle in a pan of water to heat. She made nonsense sounds to the *boppli*, knowing the only thing that would soothe May would be a bottle.

"*Boppli* crying," moaned Jesse as he inched over to her after finishing his cookie. "Owie?"

"No, she's not hurt." She bent and kissed her son's forehead, which was threaded with worry. "*Bopplin* can't talk the same way big boys like you and Jared do. Instead of asking for something to eat, they cry. That's how their *mamms* and *daeds* know they're hungry."

"Me big boy." He stuck out his thin chest.

"You're my big boy." She kissed the top of his head before straightening to check the bottle. The water was bubbling, so she removed the pan from the heat. Testing a few drops on the inside of her wrist, she smiled as she offered it to the *boppli*, who latched on to it as if she feared she'd never have another meal. "You're a greedy little darling, ain't so?"

Naomi stiffened as Samuel moved toward her with his uneven gait. She was about to dash into the living room when she froze at the sight of the social worker in the doorway.

"Thank you." Mr. Tedesco's smile had returned. "You saved a child's life today, and we appreciate you contacting the police right away. Doing so will allow us to get May into a foster placement today. As soon as you finish feeding her, I'll give you time to say your goodbyes, and then—"

"Why can't she stay here?" asked Samuel. "She was left here, and her parents may come back to look for her."

"They may, and you must call the police if they do. However, in the meantime, we need to place May in a licensed foster home."

This was the moment Naomi had been waiting for, but when she opened her mouth, Samuel spoke first. "You may not know this, Mr. Tedesco, but Naomi is a licensed foster parent."

The social worker's head snapped in her direction. "You're licensed?"

"Ja." She couldn't manage more than that single word, shocked at Samuel stepping in. Then she told herself she shouldn't be surprised. How many times had he and his friends stuck their noses into her business, especially after Laurene's family left Bliss Valley and they focused their nasty pranks on her?

He'd done the right thing this time.

"For infants?" Mr. Tedesco asked, opening his briefcase.

"From birth to age six." She paused as a soft burp emerged from the *boppli.* Offering May the bottle again, she prayed the social worker would agree to let her keep the infant until May's parents could be found. "I decided it'd be better to work with younger *kinder* until I was more accustomed to being a parent, because I was licensed before my twins were born."

"You were living here when you were licensed?"

Her hopeful heart fell as she shook her head. "I was living in Honey Brook. It was about four years ago, but I kept my paperwork up-to-date. If you want to check, I can give you the address."

"Why don't we have your current address?"

"Because we're in the midst of moving here to live after my husband died." She hurried to add, "I informed my contact at the foster care department in Chester County, and I was licensed again, this time as a single parent, three weeks ago." *Three weeks and three days and fifteen hours ago*, her mind whispered.

After Marlin's death, she'd hesitated about taking the time and energy to go through the process again, but she'd prayed for God's guidance and gone ahead. She drew the empty bottle out of May's mouth and put the infant up to her shoulder to burp her again. The little *boppli* might have been the reason she'd gotten a nudge to move ahead with being relicensed. At that time, she'd seen the process as a way to look toward the future instead of being sucked into thoughts of the past and her husband's serial infidelities.

A genuine smile creased the social worker's face for the first time. "That's good news. Let me make a couple of calls."

She nodded, understanding Mr. Tedesco needed to update his boss about what was happening and how she might be the possible solution for a temporary placement for May.

As the social worker went out of the house, she took a step toward the living room, where *Daed* and Randy were discussing the merits of fishing in the various streams crisscrossing Bliss Valley.

"Naomi?" Samuel called from behind her.

She wanted to pretend she hadn't heard him, but couldn't when Jared bounced toward her saying, "*Mamm*, Samuel. More cookies?"

"Not now," she replied. "How about some *millich*? Sit on the bench by the window, and I'll get you a glass."

Going to the cupboard where sippy cups were kept for the

boys, she took down two. She went to the refrigerator for the *millich*.

"Let me hold May," Samuel said, "while you pour the *millich*."

Naomi set the pitcher on the counter before she answered. "Can you?"

"Can I what?"

"Can you hold her?"

"I wouldn't offer if I didn't think I could do it."

She'd insulted him. She should apologize. The words stuck like peanut butter to the roof of her mouth. "Sit at the table."

When he complied, she slanted toward him to put the *boppli* in his waiting arms. He took the infant with a tenderness she wouldn't have thought existed inside Samuel King. Cradling her head within the crook of his elbow, he held her easily. May looked even smaller in his big, calloused hands as she closed her dark blue eyes and turned her face toward his heart.

Naomi raised her own eyes. He wasn't looking at her, only the *boppli*. She'd never seen such an unguarded expression on his face, and she was startled how it altered his features. No hint of the arrogant prankster who'd made her his target, accepting a dare from his friends to kiss her, then brag about it. Instead, he was gazing at May as if she were so precious he couldn't believe he was holding her.

Marlin had never looked at his own *bopplin* like that. Not once.

She edged away to get the twins their *millich*, but kept checking to make sure Samuel was being careful. From the way he was treating the newborn, she could believe he thought the *kind* was as delicate as a wisp of milkweed fluff, wafting on a summer breeze. Yet he held her with confidence.

Who would have guessed hard-hearted Samuel King, who'd acted out so badly his own family had disowned him before he jumped the fence, could be soft with May? She wouldn't have believed it if she hadn't seen it with her own eyes.

Handing the twins their plastic cups, she stopped before she could go to Samuel and take the *boppli* back. May had fallen asleep, and Naomi didn't want to disturb the little one who'd had such a tough day, being born and then abandoned.

She went into the front room to see if Mr. Tedesco had gotten approval for May to stay. She looked over her shoulder to make sure the *boppli* was safe. Samuel had been reckless as a kid, exploding into mischief or worse.

Rushing into the kitchen, she held out her hands in a silent order to him.

"She's sleeping," he whispered as if Naomi wouldn't have already noticed.

"Pass her to me carefully."

His mouth became a straight line as he growled, "You don't trust me with her, ain't so?"

"It's not…" She glanced toward the front door.

"Oh, I see. You don't want the social worker to know you left the *boppli* with me because I might endanger her."

"Please give her to me."

Without another word, he slid the infant into her arms. Their faces were close during the transfer, and Naomi straightened quickly. Too quickly because she jarred the newborn, who let out a soft cry at being woken.

"I hope you're happy," Samuel said as he pushed himself to his feet.

"It's not about either you or me being happy or unhappy."

"No?" He picked up his cane. "If anyone needs to talk to me, I'll be in the *dawdi haus*. I don't want to get in your way, princess."

She bristled. He'd snarled that name at her for their last years of school and after they were finished with schooling when they were fourteen. She'd hated the name in school, and she hated it more now.

Instead of replying, she retraced her steps into the living room. Her *daed* and Randy were still chatting, and the police officer pointed toward the door to let her know the social worker was outside.

Naomi took another look behind her. Samuel had left through the connecting door from the kitchen to the *dawdi haus*. On the bench, the twins were curled up together like puppies, their fingers linked together.

Somehow she had to make a life for herself and her *kinder* in Bliss Valley, in spite of Samuel King. If she'd known that, would she have returned? She almost laughed. What choice had she had? She didn't have any other place to go.

"You've been through worse," she murmured to herself as she went onto the porch. In the meadow, her horse and the mules were chomping on the grass along with her *daed*'s small herd of cows, already making themselves at home. She wished she could adjust as swiftly.

Mr. Tedesco was talking on his cell phone while standing near a light gray car beside the police cruiser. She didn't want the social worker to think she was trying to eavesdrop. She went to the glider that had been her favorite place to sit and shuck peas with *Mamm*. With a gentle toe-heel-toe motion, she rocked, watching as May's eyes closed again.

When a silver car drove up the farm lane moments later, Naomi was astonished. It parked next to the other two vehicles, and a woman got out. She wore a bright floral dress and the highest heels Naomi had ever seen. Large gold earrings hung from her ears and peeked through her blond hair, which had a stripe of bright green running through it. As she walked toward the house, not tottering on her heels, she took off large sunglasses to reveal a pair of bright blue eyes edged with dark eyeliner that led up to her garish green eye shadow.

"Is this the Gingerich farm?" the woman asked with bright red lips.

"*Ja*. Are you looking for Elvin Gingerich?" She couldn't figure out why the woman would want to speak to her *daed* until she remembered *Englischers* liked to buy old buggies to decorate their lawns. Perhaps the woman had bought one and needed to have it repaired.

That thought was shoved aside when the woman reached the bottom of the porch steps and said, "No, I'm looking for Mrs. Ropp. Naomi Gingerich-Ropp."

She flinched. She couldn't help herself. The last *Englischer* who'd said that had evicted her from her home.

"I'm Naomi. How can I help you?"

"I think you're my sister."

"Your sister?" Naomi shook her head gently, not wanting another sudden motion to wake the *boppli*. "That's impossible. I'm an only *kind*. Only child."

"In your adopted family maybe, but I believe that you, Naomi Gingerich-Ropp, are my mother's daughter, the child she gave up at birth."

Chapter Four

Naomi stared at the *Englisch* woman. Was this someone's idea of a joke?

She stiffened. If Samuel—

No, Samuel couldn't have been behind it. He wouldn't have had time to set up a prank in the short time since she'd come back home.

If all of this wasn't his work, then whose?

Horror clawed at her heart. Was this one of Marlin's mistresses? *Ach!* There had been plenty of women he'd cheated with, but why would one of them come to her *daed*'s house with a ridiculous story?

"Who are you?" she asked.

"My name is Skylar Lopez. My mother's name is Gina Marie Tinniswood. Has anyone ever mentioned her name to you?"

"No. I—"

A scream cut through the air. Not a frightened one, but an

angry one. Naomi knew that one could signal as much danger as the other. She whirled as she saw Jesse start to push Jared off the tire swing.

When had they come outside? She'd thought they were napping inside. They must have slipped out the back door. What sort of foster *mamm* would Mr. Tedesco consider her if she couldn't keep track of her own *kinder*?

"Just a minute please," she said to Ms. Lopez. "I've got to take care of this."

"But, Mrs. Ropp—"

"Just a minute," she repeated.

She pushed past Ms. Lopez and hurried down the steps, trying not to bounce the *boppli* and wake her. Aware of the police officer and the social worker witnessing the twins quarreling, she knew she needed to resolve their differences with the least possible amount of fuss.

"Fun!" Jesse announced, stamping his foot. "Me fun!"

"Me fun!" argued Jared. "Now me fun."

"Hush." She put one finger to her lips as she glanced at the *boppli*. "We don't want to wake the *boppli*, ain't so?"

"She cries. Loud!" Jared grimaced.

"No fun," added his brother.

Naomi tucked May into the crook of her left arm and held out her right hand. Jesse grabbed two of her fingers. When Jared hesitated, she didn't say anything, but caught his gaze and held it. He climbed off the swing and held on to her other two fingers.

Leaning down to them, she said, "*Komm* with me now. I've got to…" How could she explain to her sons what she didn't understand herself? Why would an *Englisch* woman come to the farm claiming Naomi was her sister?

She would have preferred to take the twins inside where

they wouldn't have been able to listen, but she didn't trust them not to slip out past her *daed* again. Leading the boys to the porch steps, she sat them on the bottom riser.

"Sit here," she said, "while *Mamm* talks to the *Englisch* lady."

As she'd hoped, the mention of the stranger got the twins' attention, and they began to jabber to each other again. Only this time their voices were filled with speculation and curiosity.

Gut! Distracted by the *Englischer*, they'd forgotten their squabble. At least, for the moment.

Naomi climbed the steps to where the woman stood with ill-concealed impatience. Forcing a smile, she said, "I'm sorry for the interruption. They aren't much more than *bopplin*, so I need to keep a close eye on them."

"I get that, but we need to talk."

"All right. Let's talk. Did one of Marlin's friends send you here?"

"Marlin? Isn't that a fish?"

Ms. Lopez's puzzlement seemed honest, but Naomi had been fooled too many times to trust her instincts. After all, she hadn't imagined her husband would have cheated on her within weeks of their wedding. She'd felt like such a fool for not seeing what was right in front of her eyes. It had been a bitter, disgusting feeling, and she didn't want to experience it again.

"I'm talking about Marlin Ropp, my late husband," Naomi said as she rocked the *boppli*. "Did you know him?"

"Never heard of him." She folded her arms in front of her. "Look. I'm here because, as I said before, I think you're my half sister."

"As I said before, that's not possible."

"How do you know?"

"Don't you think I'd know if my parents weren't my parents?"

"No!"

Startled by Ms. Lopez's vehemence, Naomi couldn't do anything but stare at the determined woman.

"Look," Ms. Lopez said again. "I know what I'm saying sounds like I've lost my mind, but what I'm saying is true." She held up her hands when Naomi began to speak. "We're not getting anywhere with you denying what I'm saying. Can I talk to your parents?"

"My *mamm* is dead."

Ms. Lopez murmured, "I'm sorry." Without a pause, she went on, "How about your father, then?"

"He's not available now." Guilt pinched her as she spoke the half truth. *Daed* was busy trading fishing tales with Randy Wigginton. She didn't want to bother them—most especially the police officer—with Ms. Lopez's claims.

"All right." Ms. Lopez seemed to deflate. "I can see I'm not going to get anywhere with you today. Will you talk to your father when he gets back?"

Instead of making a promise she didn't know if she could keep, Naomi asked, "Why is it so important after all these years to find your missing sister? I'm not far from thirty. That's a long time to wait for a family reunion."

For the first time, Ms. Lopez's facade cracked. She looked as young as the rebellious green streak in her hair suggested. Naomi guessed Ms. Lopez must be several years younger than she was.

Tears rose in her blue eyes. "I'm trying to save my mother's life. *Our* mother's life, if you're her missing kid as we suspect. Mom has cancer. Non-Hodgkin's lymphoma, and she needs a bone marrow transplant. I'm not a match, and neither are any of my siblings. My mother had twins before she was married, and they were adopted. We've been trying to find them."

"Have you contacted Joel Beachy's family?" she asked, sympathy clamping its grip around her. She knew what it was like to lose one's *mamm* from an illness. Her own had died from pneumonia, taken so suddenly they didn't have time to prepare. Now she wondered if any amount of time would have allowed her to face her *mamm*'s death. "Joel was adopted as a *boppli*. Have you thought that you should be looking for a brother rather than a sister?"

"I've contacted the Beachy family. They don't have any idea where he is. We're searching for him, but we've started looking at other people, too. Your birthday is a near match for my missing half-sibling."

"I wish I could help you." She glanced past Ms. Lopez to see Mr. Tedesco was still on the phone. "I know how important this is to you and your *mamm*. I'll be praying for you, for her health and for you to find the person you're seeking."

The other woman hesitated. "I can tell you don't want to talk to your family about this or consider they might have lied to you."

"My parents haven't lied to me. They've always been honest with each other and with me." Frustration edged into her voice. "You don't know them. I do!"

"All right. I get it." She held up her hands in a pose of surrender. "I didn't mean to insult you or your family. I want to get to the truth."

"I know." Naomi sighed. The conversation was going nowhere. How could it when they were at a stalemate? Naomi wasn't this woman's half sister, but the woman refused to believe it in her desperation to save her *mamm*'s life.

Ms. Lopez must have realized that, too. "Tell you what,

Mrs. Ropp. There's a simple way to figure this out. All I'm asking is for you to be tested. DNA and as a bone marrow donor."

"I don't—"

"It's not painful or anything. A couple of light scrapes on the inside of your cheek. It won't cost you anything. We'll pay for the testing."

"It's not about the cost. I'm not doing anything until I speak with my *daed*."

"You need his permission?" Her eyes widened.

"I'm Amish, and in our homes, the man is the head of the household."

Rolling her eyes, she said, "Okay. Talk to him. I'll stop back in a few days to get your answer. No, wait. I can't come then. I'll call you, and we'll arrange something. Do you have a phone?"

"There's one in the shop. The number's listed as Gingerich Buggy Repair."

"Okay." She turned to go down the steps, then paused. "You'll be here, won't you?"

"I live here."

"I know you think I'm being ridiculous, but I'm not. You're my half sister."

Though Naomi knew Ms. Lopez was mistaken, she couldn't help being shaken by the vehemence in the other woman's voice. If there had been any way to save her own *mamm*, Naomi would have scoured the whole world to find it.

She whispered a prayer for healing, then added another that Ms. Lopez would be successful in locating her half-sibling.

The prayer was interrupted when the twins, tired of sitting and poking at a bug with a stick, climbed up to her and gripped her skirt. She smiled and motioned for them to follow her inside.

Naomi wasn't surprised *Daed* and the policeman were still spinning fish tales while the bishop sat in the rocking chair, listening. She was amazed Samuel was seated on the sofa on the other side of the room. Why had he come back in from the *dawdi haus*? Maybe he didn't want to miss hearing what the social worker had to say about May's future.

She wished she had a way—any way at all—to convince him to leave. She didn't want him in her life or in her *kinder*'s lives.

He insisted he was staying because he needed the job.

Inspiration struck. All she had to do was find him another job, and then he'd leave. There were people looking for workers not afraid to get their hands dirty. All she needed to do was find him a job far from Bliss Valley.

Her eyes were caught by the pile of *The Budget* newspapers. Sometimes, people mentioned jobs that needed filling in their communities. Between scanning each issue and reading the local newspaper, she was sure to find something for him. How hard could it be?

Samuel watched Naomi as she walked across the living room with an ease he had to envy. Without interrupting the story Elvin was telling about landing a big bass out of a nearby pond, she gave the little boys each a picture book and sat them in a corner of the room.

When she turned, her face revealed her dismay. The only place to sit was on the sofa with him. Her steps faltered as his gaze met hers. Was that a challenge in her eyes? Did she think he was trying to intimidate her? If so, she was wrong. What would it take to persuade her he wasn't that hateful boy any longer?

He was still nettled after learning Elvin had hired him because the old man hadn't realized who Samuel was. Until Elvin said that by the shop, Samuel had dared to believe someone— Naomi's *daed*!—had forgiven him. It'd allowed him to believe it was possible *Mamm* would open her heart to him and stop blaming him for all the mistakes in her life.

Now that hope was nothing but cold ashes in the back of his throat.

He said softly so he didn't intrude on Elvin's story, which was becoming more outrageous by the second as, with every word, the bass got larger, "I heard a car come and go. Was the woman looking for the shop?"

"No, it wasn't anything important," she said as she sat on the sofa as far from him as she could.

She wasn't being honest. He'd seen how stiff she'd been while standing on the porch and talking with the *Englisch* woman.

Or maybe he was reading it wrong. Maybe the caller hadn't come about anything important. Naomi had been upset already with having to return home and waiting to hear if her offer to take care of another one would be okayed.

Not to mention arriving to find him working with Elvin. It was no *gut* trying to pretend their mutual past didn't exist. Even without her amazing memory, he couldn't forget any of the tricks he and Adam and Joel had devised, though he'd prayed so many times for God to sweep those memories out of his head forever. Especially during the night, when sleep eluded him as he cataloged his mistakes.

The social worker came into the house. He started to speak, then glanced at the corner. Samuel did, too, and saw the boys were sound asleep, leaning against each other and the wall.

The *boppli* stirred in Naomi's arms, but was soothed back to sleep when Naomi rocked her.

Samuel realized how different the situation would have been if Naomi hadn't been there. He didn't know much about *bopplin* as young as May. As a boy, he'd spent most of his time outdoors and had only occasionally assisted with his younger half-siblings. He thought he could still remember how to put a diaper on a *boppli*, but he had no idea how much formula he needed for May at each feeding. And, without Naomi's knowledge of the foster care system, they might have done everything wrong.

The social worker motioned with his head for the policeman to sit. Did anyone notice how Samuel stiffened at the thought of him taking the cushion between him and Naomi? Officer Wigginton said he'd rather stand. Samuel couldn't think of him as Randy. He couldn't feel comfortable around any cop. It'd been seven years since Samuel had been arrested for drunk driving following the accident. He couldn't forget a moment of the court hearing that could have ended up with him going to jail. The other petty crimes he and Joel had done were never brought up, because they hadn't been caught. If he'd had a rap sheet listing all he'd done... He was aware how close he'd come to ruining his life, and he was grateful to God every day the judge had decided to give him a second chance.

He shifted his eyes away as the cop gazed at the sofa. By now, the policeman most likely had checked Samuel's past record. Though Wigginton hadn't said anything, Samuel knew he'd jump in if he had any concerns about the safety of El-vin's family or May.

Jonas rose and motioned for the social worker to take the rocker.

Once he sat, Mr. Tedesco asked, "You all live here?" He looked at Samuel.

"*Ja,*" said Elvin, taking the lead. "Naomi is my daughter, and Samuel is my assistant in the shop."

"You live together?"

"Not exactly." Elvin smiled, but Samuel cringed.

Guessing the social worker had been delayed outside because a background check had revealed information about Samuel's drunk driving charge, Samuel said, "Elvin and his family live in the main house while I live in the *dawdi haus.*"

"Which is where?"

"It's attached to the back of the house. It's where we found May."

"I guess I'm confused." Mr. Tedesco looked from his notes to each of them in turn. "I thought a *dawdi haus* is where the elder generation lives."

Elvin explained about how a fire earlier in the spring had destroyed the barn where he'd planned to put his expanded shop as well as having separate space for his assistant to live.

"It was one of the arson cases, wasn't it?" asked Officer Wigginton.

"*Ja.*"

"Terrible thing, all those fires. That was more than thirty days ago. Don't you plain folk rebuild within a month after losing a barn?"

"There were so many fires we need to wait our turn." The old man sighed. "It's as it says in Isaiah, 'And they shall build the old wastes, they shall raise up the former desolations,' though it doesn't give us a timetable when that will be done."

"If I remember my Sunday school lessons, doesn't Ecclesiastes say something about a time to tear down, and a time to build up?"

"Isaiah 61:4 and Ecclesiastes 3:3," Naomi said under her breath, drawing Samuel's attention to her.

Was she trying to show off? Not likely. Naomi had been the well-behaved Amish girl, modest and unassuming.

Except for the night you kissed her and she kissed you back.

He thanked God nobody else in the room could hear his thoughts, most especially Naomi. Taking a dare from his friends had seemed like such a *gut* idea until he'd seen her shattered expression when the three of them had made sure she overheard them spreading rumors about how she was willing to kiss any boy, even Samuel, who'd teased her mercilessly for years.

A phone ringing echoed through the room. The *Englischers* looked at their phones. The call was for Mr. Tedesco. He answered it, said okay, then hung up.

In the corner, neither of the twins stirred. They must be exhausted not to jump up to see what was going on.

"That was my supervisor. She's finished a quick check on—" Again he glanced at Samuel. "Because you're licensed, Naomi, she's given the go-ahead for a temporary placement here, subject to a more in-depth review of the household."

Naomi grinned with unabashed happiness. It was an expression that added a bright glow to her eyes. "*Danki.* That's *wunderbaar* news, and I'm so grateful to you for speaking on our behalf."

"My pleasure." The social worker smiled at her, and Samuel felt something uncomfortable in his gut.

The *Englischer* had reacted to Naomi's joy. Nothing more. Nothing less. So why had Samuel's center clenched like he'd tightened it into one of the big clamps out in the shop? She would have laughed in his face if Samuel admitted that the social worker's easy smile bothered him. She would have asked

him why he thought he had any claim on deciding who should
or shouldn't smile at her.

"When will you do the home study?" Naomi asked.

"I can come back next week. Monday or Tuesday."

Her *daed* interrupted. "Monday isn't any *gut*. Samuel and
I will be busy finishing up the Keim buggy. They need it
on Tuesday to visit family in Quarryville, and I told them it
would be ready."

"Then Tuesday it'll be." Mr. Tedesco pulled a small notebook out of his pocket and paged through it. "How is eleven,
Naomi?"

She glanced at her *daed*, who nodded before saying, "That
will be fine. I assume you want to speak to all of us."

"The standard practice is to speak to everyone who lives in
the house." His glance at Samuel was swift. "Just under *this*
roof is all that's necessary."

"We'll be ready to answer any questions and give you a tour
upstairs and down," she replied.

"Good."

The social worker jotted in his notebook, returned it to his
pocket and stood. Bending to pick up his briefcase, he said,
"I'm done here. Anything else?"

Samuel knew the question wasn't aimed at him because Mr.
Tedesco looked at the bishop and the policeman. Both assured
the social worker they had no questions.

As the three men left together, Elvin set himself on his feet,
saying, "I'd better get back to working on the Keim buggy.
Coming, Samuel?"

"I'll be right there," he replied, but he didn't know if the
older man had heard him because Elvin was already out the
door.

When Naomi stood, heading toward the kitchen, he called

her name. She turned, not hiding her reluctance to spend a second longer in his company.

"I need to get a bottle ready for her," she said as he limped to where she stood in the doorway between the two rooms.

"This will take only a moment."

"All right. What is it?"

He almost asked her to give him a second chance, but that would be a waste of time. After all, she'd given him far more chances than that when they were teens, and he'd thrown them away. Why should she take his word he wasn't that person any longer?

Even so, he might have asked her to reconsider when they'd be living almost under the same roof if he hadn't seen the shadows in her eyes. What had the *Englisch* woman said to her outside? If he asked, he doubted Naomi would say anything other than it wasn't his concern.

Maybe he should acquiesce and accept she was being smart. Picking at old wounds and scars would get them nothing but more pain.

He said, as if it were the only thing on his mind, "You've been through a home study before. Is there anything I need to do to prepare?"

"I hope you won't need to be involved at all."

"Mr. Tedesco said—"

"He said the home study would focus on the house where the *kind* will be living and the residents of that home. You don't live here. You live in the *dawdi haus*, which has its own kitchen and bath. That makes it, from the *Englisch* point of view, an apartment. As such, it isn't part of our home. You don't need to be here when he comes on Tuesday." She turned toward the refrigerator. "On the off chance he wants to speak with you, he can go to the shop."

She didn't say anything else, and he knew he'd been dismissed as if she were queen and he a peasant.

He opened the back door and went out into the afternoon air, which was far warmer than her icy conclusion to their conversation. They'd talked long enough to make one thing clear. In spite of everything that had happened during the past decade, she wanted him to know one thing hadn't changed. She didn't want him in her life.

Chapter Five

The next morning, Samuel was stifling a yawn as he stepped out of the *dawdi haus* and headed for Elvin's shop. The older man had been using the small space for years, but had planned on renovating the larger chicken barn to increase the size of his shop and also to give his assistant privacy. Elvin had hired Samuel, having him start work before the embers of the barn had cooled.

He paused for a moment as the yawn escaped. Though he was much steadier on his right leg than he'd been a couple of months ago, something as simple as a yawn or a cough or sneeze could threaten his balance and send him crashing to the ground. His physical therapist, Hazel, had taught him to roll with a fall, because his right arm was too weak to catch him.

A chuckle escaped into the morning humidity. Hazel Burroughs might have looked like a sweet *grossmammi* with soft white hair and chubby cheeks, but she'd worked like a Marine Corps drill sergeant. She expected nothing less than one hundred and twenty percent every session.

"*Danki*, Lord, for having her stick by me." He said the prayer he'd repeated almost every day since he'd met the tiny taskmistress who'd not only gotten him on his feet but also helped him relearn how to walk and overcome the weaknesses left in the wake of the accident.

More important, she'd guided him in accepting his new reality. She'd allowed him no self-pity. Complaining earned him a few extra of the exercises he hated most. While he'd suffered under her eagle eyes, he'd known she wanted what was best for him. She felt he deserved a normal life again. It was a stark reminder of how seldom he'd experienced compassion.

He sighed as he looked at the cane he depended on. The day he'd finished his therapy, he'd had to fight back tears as he thanked Hazel for all she'd done. She'd acted as if it was nothing, but it'd been far more than helping him rediscover what he could do with his new and battered body.

Raising his head, Samuel gazed across the gently rolling hills beyond the farm. They were green with the burgeoning crops, and as the breeze passed through them, shifting the remnants of the early-morning mists so they danced across the tops of corn and barley, the tree leaves rippled in the same tempo. Near the road, a creek whispered its secrets as the water slid past the rocks.

He'd missed Bliss Valley. After he'd first run away, he couldn't have imagined returning to the place where he'd grown up. Then he'd come home.

Mamm had slammed the door in his face and refused to re-open it then or when he'd returned five more times over the next two weeks. Hoping she'd come to see reason and forgive her oldest son, he'd waited another week before making a final attempt to speak to her. That time, his step*daed* had come to the door and told Samuel never to return. Neither had offered any explanation, acting as if it shouldn't be necessary because he already knew.

He hadn't. For the past six years, he'd asked himself the same questions over and over. Had they been angry because he'd been *dumm* and wrecked a car and himself by driving drunk? If so, why hadn't they offered him the chance to atone and ask for forgiveness? Wasn't that the way of the Amish? Or had the rage been because his return meant he once again was a living, breathing reminder of his *mamm*'s sin? That he couldn't atone for, though his family had made it clear from his earliest memories the fault was his for being born.

If Arlie Pfister hadn't let him live in their unused cabin up in Bird-in-Hand, he doubted he would have survived long enough to find this job with Elvin.

When his *mamm* had shut him out of her house and her life and refused to let him see his six younger half-siblings, he'd thought he was homesick only for family. He'd realized how wrong he was when he'd started working for Elvin last month. He'd missed Bliss Valley itself. There was something timeless in the changing seasons and the sowing and reaping.

Not that he wanted to be a farmer. He'd watched his step-*daed* and other men alternately worrying about the vagaries of the weather and the ever-changing prices for their *millich* and their crops. Early on, he'd learned a man could toil long hours, day after day, for months, and all it took was a single bad storm of hail or flooding rains to wipe everything out.

Better, he decided, to learn a skill and work with his hands. *Or hand,* he amended as he shook his right hand, which had the unfortunate habit of going dead at the worst possible moment.

Making sure his cane didn't catch on the grass, Samuel crossed the yard to the rickety buggy shop. It was about the

size of a one-car garage, and it had a big door on the front
that required his and the older man's heft to raise or lower it.
Maybe if he had two usable hands…

No, he wasn't going to start the day with depressing
thoughts. He was alive and had found work that challenged
him and was enjoyable. No longer was he living hand to
mouth as he'd been during those years on the other side of
the fence with Joel. He wasn't dependent on others as he'd
been when he lived in Bird-in-Hand. God had listened to his
prayers and brought him here.

Then God had deposited Naomi back into his life.

Why?

He sighed again. He knew the answer. God wanted him to
seek Naomi's forgiveness, not for Samuel's sake, but for hers.

Where to begin when she'd made it clear the less she saw
of him the better?

Walking into the shop, he wasn't surprised to see Elvin had
arrived before he did. The man might be closing in on sixty,
but he worked every day except Sundays as hard as a teenager
eager to prove himself on his first job.

Samuel had learned his first day that his most important task
was to put away the tools the old man used each day. While
Elvin seemed able to put his hand on any tool he wanted at any
given moment, Samuel had found himself wasting too much
time looking for the specific screwdriver or wrench he needed.

Checking that most of the tools were still in place, Samuel
went to the buggy they were currently working on. He skirted
two others with the ease of practice. One of the buggies was
leaning against a wall because its back axle was broken. The
other had lost a rear wheel. They'd come in for repair after
the same accident. Though no one, not even Elvin, had men-

tioned the cause, Samuel guessed from a single glance that the buggies had been damaged in a drag race.

Though Samuel, after tough lessons, now knew better, young men couldn't resist the opportunity on a moonlit night to discover which buggy was faster. They'd been forewarned, as he'd been, but they'd learned, as he had, it was simpler to heed *gut* advice than to discover the truth the hard way.

As if answer to his thoughts, his right knee twinged, sending pain to his toes. His fingers curled around the edge of the buggy as he fought it back.

"Check the connections on that front wheel, will you?" asked Elvin.

The old man never offered outright sympathy, which Samuel appreciated. Elvin had hired him to do a job and expected him to do it.

"All right," he replied, leaning his cane against the wall and awkwardly getting down on his hands and knees to slip under the buggy.

His boss didn't look in his direction. Elvin continued to focus on adjusting the door so it would close properly. Tipping the buggy into a ditch had skewed its whole body, but they were getting it realigned.

Samuel flipped onto his back and pushed himself under the buggy. If he mentioned how impressed he was with the old man's skills, Elvin would lecture him about how Samuel must have forgotten compliments and plain folks didn't mix. Samuel remembered the tenets of a plain life, but he'd picked up *Englisch* habits that clung after almost seven years back in Lancaster County.

"Don't you think it's too much for her?" Elvin asked.

Accustomed now to the other man starting a conversation somewhere in its middle, Samuel checked one bolt on the front driver's side wheel before answering. When Elvin said "her," he meant Naomi. Samuel wanted to say that he preferred work to be a Naomi-free zone, but he didn't.

Instead, he asked, "What's too much for her?"

"That *boppli*. She's already got two of her own who run her ragged. Why should she be responsible for someone else's *kind*?"

Samuel clenched his jaw. He didn't want to react each time someone suggested a *kind* was unwanted, but he couldn't help it. After spending nearly thirty years listening to his *mamm* complain about how he'd ruined her life, he'd gladly help any other kid from suffering the same.

"Has she complained?" he asked, picking his words with care and glad Elvin couldn't see his face, which must broadcast his distaste with the question.

"Naomi doesn't complain."

"No?" He'd heard her grouse about the paperwork ahead of her if May stayed on as her foster *kind*.

"Not about important things. Not even when you and the others were harassing her."

This time, Elvin's words made him flinch. He scraped his knuckle on a wheel spoke. Yanking it back before blood splattered the wheel he'd spent hours cleaning, he forced his voice to remain calm. "If she didn't want May to remain here, she wouldn't have pushed the idea with the social worker."

A sound like a rusty hinge closing came from Elvin. It was his idea of a laugh. "Boy, you don't know anything about her. She jumps in to help before her brain has time to tell her it isn't a *gut* idea."

"Do you want me to talk to her?" He couldn't figure out why else Elvin would have mentioned this. Before now, they hadn't spoken of anything but work.

"Don't waste your breath. She won't listen to me." Again his raspy laugh filled the shop. "She most certainly won't listen to *you*." Without a pause, Elvin went on, "The barn raising will be early next week. Once the barn's up, we'll be able to move the shop out there and have more room to work."

Glad his boss had changed the subject, Samuel picked up a rag. He wrapped it around his bloody knuckle as he pushed himself out from under the buggy. "I can move there and get out of your way, too."

"You?" Looking around the front of the buggy, Elvin frowned. "I figured you'd want to stay in the *dawdi haus*. It's more comfortable than the barn will be."

"Don't want your own place again? The kids have taken over the house." He wondered if his boss had brought up the *kinder* to get to this point.

He realized how wrong he'd been when Elvin shook his head. "*Ja*, but Naomi needs an extra set of hands to help with them. The boys are great at thinking up mischief, and they keep her hopping all day long."

Samuel couldn't argue with that.

"She's taking on too much," Elvin went on, his voice dropping to a grumble, "when her husband's barely cold in the ground."

Not sure how to respond because he couldn't miss the grief in the old man's voice, Samuel decided the best thing to say was nothing. Elvin must have agreed, too, because he talked only about their current project as they worked side by side. When Elvin went into the house for his midmorning cup of *kaffi*, Samuel picked up the tools the old man had tossed aside and wouldn't need the rest of the day.

He was hanging the tools on the pegboard behind the workbench when footsteps sounded by the doorway. Grabbing his cane so he could maneuver through the crowded space, he hobbled toward the tall silhouette in the doorway.

"Samuel?" Neither the question nor the voice were unexpected.

Feeling the familiar flush of embarrassment washing over him, Samuel heard the shock in his one-time friend's voice. The last time Adam Hershberger had seen him, Samuel hadn't needed a cane.

"Ja," he answered. "I would have recognized you anywhere, Adam."

That was the truth. His friend's hair was the same floppy brown, and his dark eyes as fearless. Time had broadened his shoulders, but his clothing was identical to what he'd worn during their years in school together right down to a spot of grease on the left sleeve of his light blue shirt.

"You, too."

He wanted to call his friend out on that. Samuel knew he'd changed. The limp, the weak right hand, the scar over his eyebrow...the years of scrounging jobs where he could find them and feeling like an outsider. He'd left Bliss Valley as a cocky kid and returned a battered man.

"I'd heard Elvin had hired an assistant." Adam looked uncomfortable.

Samuel wanted to tell him it was all right. Nobody except Elvin seemed at ease around him. The twins might have if Naomi didn't do all she could to keep them from getting near him. He'd almost told her—more than once—his teenage rebellion wasn't contagious. Even if it had been, it'd been ground out of him.

"I'm not exaggerating when I say it's a blessing Elvin hired me."

Adam laughed.

What was so funny?

As if Samuel had asked that aloud, Adam said, "Now *that's* one thing that hasn't changed. Do you know how many times you used to say, 'I'm not exaggerating when I say...'? Then the next thing you'd say was exaggerated."

"I don't remember that."

Adam laughed. "I do. It's a habit I picked up without realizing it. My great-*grossdawdi* told me to kick it. Let me tell you, I learned it wasn't as easy to quit a bad habit as it was to take it on." He chuckled. "*That* is no exaggeration."

Samuel felt something heavy fall off his shoulders as he grinned. Back when the three of them had been close friends, he, Adam and Joel had cracked jokes whenever they were together. There was something so comforting, so ordinary, so right about laughing with Adam again.

"What can I do for you today?" He glanced at Adam's gray-topped buggy, but couldn't see anything wrong. He'd learned not all problems were visible.

"Actually I came over to speak with Naomi. I've heard she's back."

"*Ja.* She and her boys got here yesterday."

"To stay?"

"From what she's said, *ja.*"

"I'm glad it's not a rumor. Laurene will be glad to hear she's here to stay. I'll let her know tonight."

"Tonight? You're seeing her tonight?"

"Guess you didn't hear. Laurene and I are walking out together."

Shock almost knocked him off his feet. "You and Laurene? Laurene Nolt?"

"*Ja.*" A flush rose up his friend's cheeks. "If you'd told me last winter she'd forgive me, I would have said you were *ab in kopp*. What could be more unexpected than that?"

"Not much," he replied, knowing that was what Adam wanted to hear. He thought it was far more unexpected that he lived on the same farm as Naomi and her *kinder*.

"Laurene's going to want to come and see Naomi," Adam said, "as soon as she can get away from helping her great-*aenti* at the inn."

"There was a fire there, too, ain't so?"

Adam nodded, his eyes abruptly snapping with anger. "The last of the fires we had this spring. Since we put a stop to them, we haven't had many calls for the fire department." His *gut* humor reappeared. "Hey, would you like to join us?"

"Who?"

"The fire department. We're always looking for hardworking volunteers, and if you're working for Elvin Gingerich, you're used to hard work."

Looking at his impaired right side, he shook his head. "I doubt any fire department would want me when I can't walk some days without this cane."

"You'd be surprised. We've got lots of jobs to fill, and there are several you could do." He held up his hands to forestall an answer. "Think about it, Samuel. We could use you, and it'd give you something to do other than fix buggies."

"I've got other things to do than fix buggies."

His friend nodded, serious again. "Jonas told me about the *boppli* left here."

"A little girl wrapped up in a blanket and put into a grocery bag."

Adam sighed. "There's no need for a *kind* to be abandoned. The safe-haven law allows for an unwanted *boppli* to be dropped at a hospital or a police station without any consequences. If the parents are plain, they could have come to any of us for assistance."

If the safe-haven law had been around when he was born, would Samuel have been dumped on strangers? It would have been a simple way for his *mamm* to get him out of her life, once and for all.

"Naomi is a licensed foster parent, so she's arranged for May to stay here."

With a whistle, Adam shook his head. "With two-year-old twins? I guess she knows what she's getting herself into."

"I'm not sure she does," he said, glad to be able to be honest. "That *boppli* could be taken away at any point, and I don't think she's prepared for that."

"If you—or she—need someone to talk to…"

"I'll let her know."

"*Danki*. Guess I should get going, but think about the fire department."

"You don't need me tripping over hoses and falling flat on my face in a puddle of water."

"Could give the others a chance to practice their resuscitation skills."

Laughing in spite of himself, Samuel said, "*Danki*. I think."

Adam chuckled, too. "Give the idea some thought. Like I said…"

Another set of footfalls, far lighter than Elvin's, came toward the shop. Samuel recognized them with an ease that was troublesome. How quickly Naomi had become a part of his life again.

Too quickly…for his own *gut*.

"Samuel, could I have a moment?" Naomi asked as she blinked to make her eyes adjust from the bright sunshine to the dim interior of the buggy shop. She'd gone through most of the issues of *The Budget* and found a single job she thought might be a match for him. Best of all, it was far away in Indiana. As her vision cleared, she saw two people there. "Oh, you're not alone. I can…"

Her voice trailed away as she realized who was standing beside Samuel. Adam Hershberger! What was he doing here?

Every instinct told her to flee. These two together could mean only one thing: they were plotting a new atrocity to inflict on innocent people. Her legs tensed, preparing to run as fast as she could in any direction.

Stop it! This is my *home. I don't have to put up with their nasty pranks here.*

Raising her chin, she glared at both men. She wouldn't give them the satisfaction of making her scurry away like a frightened rabbit. She wasn't going to let any man have that hold over her.

Not Samuel.

Not Adam.

Not Marlin.

Her shoulders ached as she fought the wince at the last thought. She'd never linked her late husband with these two men who'd treated her badly. She didn't want to now, but it was impossible not to. Not after he'd lied to her about purchasing their farm and the many women he'd seduced after he'd vowed before God he'd be faithful to her.

Tears burned in her eyes, but she refused to let them dribble down her cheeks. Her grief was hers alone, to be hidden in the darkest hours of the night when nobody else could hear her weep. To break down when so many depended on her would be useless and, most especially, she didn't want to show any weakness in front of Samuel King and Adam Hershberger.

"*Gute mariye*, Naomi," Adam said quietly.

She waited. Had time changed him as Samuel claimed he'd

been changed? Or would Adam fling an insult at her as he had the last time she'd seen him?

When she didn't answer, Samuel said, "Adam came over to see if it's true that you'd moved in with your *daed*."

"As you can see, Adam, it's true."

The men exchanged a glance. What did they expect? For her to welcome another of her tormentors with open arms and a broad smile?

"Is there anything we can do to help?" Adam asked. "I'd be glad to speak with Jonas." When she didn't answer right away, he added, "Jonas is our bishop."

"I know that. What I don't know is why you'd speak on my behalf to him."

"As your deacon, I—"

"You? You're our deacon?" Had the whole world gone topsy-turvy? Adam Hershberger, who'd taken any excuse to cause trouble, was a deacon? What had the *Leit* been thinking? At least three of them would have had to put forward his name for the lot.

"Kind of ironic, ain't so?" His self-deprecating grin was something she'd never seen. "I used to be one of those who caught the deacon's attention too often. Now I'm the one who's in charge of reminding others of their misdeeds."

"Is that why you're here?"

"No, no." Again he looked at Samuel as if his buddy would step up to confirm the truth.

She wasn't impressed by Adam's protestations. She'd seen the three of them—these two and Joel Beachy—lie to get themselves out of trouble. After years of enduring their mischief, she was pretty wise to their tricks.

"Naomi," Adam said into the strained silence, "I know you've got every reason to distrust me and none to believe me, but I'm asking you to believe me anyhow. I'm here to make sure you and the *kinder* have everything you need."

"We're fine."

When she didn't say anything else, he said, "I'm glad to hear that. I also wanted to tell you—"

"Look. I'll tell you what I've told Samuel. I don't need or want any apologies. I don't have time to rehash the past. I've got three little ones dependent on me." She spun on her heel and began back toward the house.

"Naomi?" called Samuel.

She paused, but didn't turn. *"Ja?"*

"What did you come out here for?"

"Nothing important," she replied. She didn't want to admit she'd forgotten why she'd come out to the shop as soon as she'd seen the two men standing there together and laughing. Just as they'd done the day after she'd let Samuel kiss her.

Chapter Six

It took until the following week before Naomi found time to empty the last box from her old home. She might not have had the opportunity if Mr. Tedesco hadn't postponed their appointment.

"Something's come up I can't postpone," had been the message in the social worker's precise tone on the machine in the shop. "I'll let you know as soon as I can reschedule. I should be able to give you at least seventy-two hours' notice so you can let me know if the time and day are convenient. In the meantime, if you've got any questions or need anything, don't hesitate to call the office."

She hadn't had any reason to call. May had settled into their home and their daily routine as if she'd been part of their family for months instead of days. The twins didn't seem to mind sharing her time with the *boppli*, because they enjoyed their *grossdawdi* at the end of every workday.

She'd tried several times to bring up the job in Indiana to

Samuel, but each time, either he changed the subject or some-one else did. The last time she'd started to mention it, *Daed* had given her a scowl that warned he'd guessed her intention and he wanted her to stop.

She did, and she began to try to figure out how to live with Samuel right next door in the *dawdi haus*. In spite of that, she was happy to be home. She smiled as she took the last small pile of the twins' clothing and carried it to the dresser that once had been hers. *Daed* couldn't hide his delight that she and Jared and Jesse were now living with him.

Closing the drawer, she wiped sweat from her forehead. The early-June morning was heavy with humidity, as uncomfort-able as a day in July. Last summer had been a long one, and it appeared as if this one would be as hot.

She set the empty box out in the upper hallway before she looked around the room. It was larger than the room the twins had shared in Honey Brook, but didn't feel that way. The dou-ble bed that had been in the room for as long as she could re-member had been dismantled and the headboard leaned against the wall. The mattress had been shoved in front of one win-dow to allow enough room for the cribs the boys used. It cut off any air coming through that window.

There wasn't any other choice if she wanted to put two cribs in the same room. She'd considered leaving them behind on the farm and putting the boys into beds, but was glad she'd brought them. Having their familiar cribs gave Jared and Jesse a sense of home.

She hoped.

It wasn't easy to tell what the two-year-olds were think-ing. They seemed content to be living with their *grossdawdi*. They'd dubbed the *boppli* "fun." It was, she believed, the high-est compliment they could give anyone or anything.

She paused to check on the *boppli,* who was across the hall in Naomi's room. May seemed so tiny in the cradle beside her bed. Asleep, the *kind* looked as sweet as a ripe strawberry, but already her personality was making itself known. Everyone knew when May was hungry or uncomfortable or wanted to be held. *Daed* remarked on how *gut* her lungs were, and the twins put their hands over their ears when she started crying. The first couple of days, Samuel had asked if May was all right, but now he seemed to have learned which cries demanded instantaneous attention and which could wait a moment.

In spite of herself, Naomi was impressed at how he'd adjusted to having a *boppli* in the house. He handled May with ease. She'd wondered if he could after being injured in the accident years ago.

She had no idea how long ago the accident had been or what had happened. Samuel changed the subject or acted as if he hadn't heard her when she mentioned it.

Why?

Sternly she told herself to stop thinking about him. It was bad enough he lived in the *dawdi haus* and took most of his meals with the family. She didn't need him taking up space in her head as well.

Going into the twins' room, she found Jared had climbed into an empty box. Jesse was standing behind him as they pretended to be rowing a boat. She smiled as she remembered the day she'd taken them to a nearby park to watch canoe races. That had been several months ago—three months and five days ago—so she was amazed they recalled it, too. Had they inherited her memory skills?

"See? *Grossdawdi* show us. Fun!" Jesse announced.

"Book!" Jared added, his eyes sparkling.

Naomi translated that to mean that *Daed* had read the boys

a story about a boat. She was grateful how every evening, while she was getting their meal on the table, *Daed* read to the twins. It gave them time together, as she once had with him. In addition, sitting on their *grossdawdi*'s lap while they turned the pages of a picture book calmed two little raucous boys at the end of a long day of exciting play. Since she'd brought the boys to Bliss Valley, she hadn't had to chase them a single time while giving them their daily bath.

She smiled when she thought of her *daed* sitting in his favorite chair and giving May a bottle while Naomi oversaw the twins' bath. Marlin never had offered to help. Even when she'd insisted once or twice when she felt particularly overwhelmed, his help had been so reluctant she'd wished she'd never asked. She hadn't let Marlin off the hook—though it'd taken more than twice as long for him to complete the few tasks she'd asked him to do—because she didn't want to curtail a second of the time the boys had with him.

Now she was grateful she'd been firm about Marlin helping. Those times, if the boys could recall them later, would be the only memories they had of him.

The past was in the past. She didn't want to let her memories, clear and precise, creep out and torment her. She'd spent many nights alone wondering what mistake she'd made, what she'd said or not said, done or not done so Marlin sought another woman's arms. How had she failed to be the wife he'd needed?

"*Mamm*, look!"

"Fun!"

Her darling twins' excited voices spared her from more self-accusations. Refocusing her eyes on where they played, oblivious to her taunting thoughts, she thanked God for their *wunderbaar* innocence.

"Jared and Jesse got boat. Fun." The little boys giggled with excitement, not bothered by the heat that plastered their fine hair to their scalps.

Smiling, she asked, "Is there room for me?"

They looked around themselves, so somber she had to bite her lip not to burst out laughing.

Jared gave her a pitying look. "No, *Mamm*."

"Other boat!" Jesse pointed at another box, then deflated. "*Mamm* too big."

"I'll wave as you paddle by. How's that?"

Both boys brightened and began their imaginary journey with the gusto of their ancestors setting off across the Atlantic to escape persecution in Europe almost three hundred years before.

Naomi left them to their adventure as she gathered up the other boxes and knocked them flat. Looking at the pile, she wondered if she should get rid of them. No, the boxes could be used again. The room at the end of the hall was one her parents used for storage. She'd put the boxes there.

When she turned the knob, the door didn't open. She pushed against it, wondering if hot weather had caused the wood to swell. The door refused to move. Putting her shoulder on a raised panel, she shoved harder. It shifted, but only a couple of inches. She heard something inside bump into another box.

Memories burst through her mind like sparks from fireworks. *Mamm* coming up the back stairs, toting boxes or stacks of clothing or toys and books Naomi no longer used. Naomi couldn't remember her *mamm* taking anything out of the room, just putting things inside. Had the room ever been cleaned out?

There was only one way to find out. She leaned into the

door again and shoved. "Open!" she ordered through gritted teeth. "Why won't you open?"

No *gut*.

The door refused to budge more than the scant two inches it'd opened.

She peered around the edge of the door and gasped. Boxes were set on top of other boxes, the stacks leaning precariously against one another and looking as if a single breath would send them tumbling.

"Go in?" asked Jared as he slipped under her arm and tried to peek past her.

"Fun!" his brother crowed.

She shook her head and stepped back. Taking their hands, she drew them away before they put the mischief in their eyes into action. "I don't think you two could squeeze in there." When the twins looked at her in confusion, she said with a smile, "You're too big."

They grinned, but her own smile wavered. For the past week, as she'd done what she could to make them feel at home in their *grossdawdi*'s house while her attention had been taken up so often with the *boppli*, they'd been told time after time they couldn't do something because they were too little.

The boys, however, were beginning to feel cramped staying in the house with her and the *boppli*. She completely agreed with *Daed* that the boys shouldn't spend time in the shop without her there to supervise them. There were too many tools that could be dangerous in a *kind*'s untutored hands. Staying away from the remnants of the large chicken barn was also a *gut* idea.

Perhaps she should take the boys out to the shop when she could keep a close eye on them. She'd enjoyed visiting it when she was little. She guessed they would, too.

She almost spoke her thoughts, then paused. If she went out to the shop, she'd see Samuel. He was intruding on their lives already too much. Maybe if *Daed* hadn't insisted Samuel take his meals with them...

"It was what I offered him as part of the job, Naomi," *Daed* had told her in the tone that warned she shouldn't waste her breath trying to change his mind.

So she hadn't, and she realized she'd made herself as much a prisoner in the house as the boys were. She'd given up without standing up for herself.

She sighed. It was a bad habit she'd gotten into. Most days, she'd found it easier to ignore what was right in her face than confront it. When she'd spoken her mind, sometimes raising her voice to Marlin, she'd ended up feeling as if she was wrong. She hated the heavy pressure of guilt, especially when her logical mind argued she wasn't the one who'd made the mistake. It didn't matter. The burden was hers, and Marlin was content to let her carry it alone.

Marlin was gone. So was her home. She needed to find a new life in Bliss Valley. That must include Samuel King, but she wasn't the same pushover she'd been as a teenager. This had been *her* home long before it was his.

Leaning the boxes against the wall, she closed the door and smiled at her sons. "Let's go for a walk after the *boppli* wakes up."

As if on cue, May began to whimper from the bedroom. The boys exchanged an eager look and nodded. She wasn't surprised when they followed her in. They watched while she bent to lift the infant out of the cradle, one on each side, holding it still. Thanking them and touched by their kindness, she changed the *boppli* and led the twins down to the kitchen. She walked sideways so she could keep an eye on them. The steps were taller than they'd been accustomed to in Honey Brook, and she didn't want them to fall.

She prepared a bottle for May and took it out on the porch. The boys followed. They let out cheers and ran to the tire swing as she sat to feed the *boppli*.

By the time she was burping May, the boys had gotten bored and were clambering back up the steps, looking for something to do. She saw them glance toward the concrete foundation that was all that remained of the chicken barn. Knowing she needed to make sure they stayed away until the building was whole again, she didn't say anything. She'd learned that telling them not to do something was, too often, something they perceived as an invitation to get into trouble.

"Let's go see *Grossdawdi* Gingerich," she said, coming to her feet.

Renewed cheers met her words, and the boys bounced like maddened rabbits ahead of her across the grass. She looked at the ruined building again. When she'd lived on the farm, the chickens had been her responsibility. Her nose wrinkled as she recalled the acrid smell of the hot chicken barn on a summer afternoon. She'd kept chickens for a while in Honey Brook, but when a fox had taken off with the last ones, she hadn't replaced them.

Marlin hadn't noticed.

Naomi pushed that memory away as she had so many connected with her late husband. When she saw *Daed* coming toward her, she was glad only May could hear her soft sigh. The *boppli* wouldn't ask why she sounded relieved.

"You're *gut* at keeping secrets, ain't so?" she whispered to the infant.

Sorrow surged through her as she realized how true her words were. Little May couldn't tell them about her true *mamm.* Would the woman be found? In spite of herself, Naomi couldn't keep from thinking about Skylar Lopez and her need to find her sister. Years from now, would May's *mamm* be seeking her, too?

By the time she reached *Daed,* who had the twins draped over him, she had her emotions under control. She smiled when *Daed* asked what she'd been up to.

"Your *mamm* was a frugal woman," he said after she'd explained how she couldn't open the storage room door. "She didn't like throwing out things."

She almost said there was a fine line between frugal and hoarder, but she didn't. Unspoken between her and *Daed* was the rule that, since *Mamm*'s funeral, neither of them questioned how *Mamm* had handled the household.

"I'll give the boys their midday meal," *Daed* said, startling her.

"I can—"

"You go with Samuel."

Her eyes widened, and she stiffened so hard with shock that the *boppli* let out a mew of protest. "Go with Samuel? Why would I go anywhere with Samuel?"

"Because I asked you to."

Though Naomi wanted to retort she wasn't a *kind* any longer and *Daed* shouldn't treat her that way, she reminded herself how she owed him for taking them in when they had nowhere else to go. She couldn't insist she needed his permission for the testing Ms. Lopez wanted her to have and then turn around and resist her *daed*'s request.

Something on her face must have shown her reaction because her *daed* sighed deeply. "He's picking up a buggy that needs work. If you take him in your buggy, you can drop him off and then come home."

"I understand." She understood she needed to stop reacting each time Samuel's name was mentioned. Had either he or *Daed* noticed last night when she almost dropped a whole bowl of chicken and noodles because Samuel had brushed past her, his elbow grazing hers, as he walked into the kitchen?

"*Gut.*" He smiled. "You can help me out, and I'll get to spend more time with my *kins-kinder.*" He held out his hands for the *boppli.* "Go ahead, Naomi. I'll take *gut* care of the three of them. We've got leftover potato-and-ham casserole Ephraim Weaver sent over. I'll warm it up for all of us, except little May. She'll want her next meal in a bottle."

"I have several already made up in the refrigerator. If there's not enough of the casserole, there's taco meat in the freezer."

"From the Millers?"

She nodded, then laughed as he smacked his lips.

"*Ja.* One of the nice results of you coming home, Naomi, has been our neighbors bringing over their best dishes to share." He waved her away. "Don't keep Samuel waiting. He needs to get that buggy here so we can start figuring out what the problem is with its wheels. Run along, and don't worry about the *kinder.* I can take care of them as I did with you."

Settling May into the crook of his arm, she said, "I'm sure of that."

"*Ach,* Naomi!" he called to her back. "I forgot. The social worker called. She's coming tomorrow."

"Tomorrow?"

"*Ja.* That's what the message said. Tomorrow at ten."

Swallowing her groan of dismay, Naomi nodded. "*Danki, Daed.*"

She hurried toward the shop. She'd drop Samuel off wherever he needed to go and hightail it back. With *Daed* preparing a meal for the *kinder,* the kitchen would be a mess. She'd clean it and check the rest of the house so it would meet Mr. Tedesco's standards.

Her steps faltered. She? *Daed* had said *she* was coming tomorrow. That meant the home study would be done by a different social worker. Naomi hoped the woman would be as open to leaving May on the Gingerich farm as Mr. Tedesco had been.

Seeing Samuel hitching Waldo to her buggy, she sighed as she prayed the day wouldn't hold any other surprises.

Would someone walking to the gallows look more reluctant than Naomi did as she approached the buggy? Not likely, Samuel decided.

He could see vestiges of the young girl she'd been in her easy, barefoot stride, but an invisible weight burdened her shoulders and made her shrink into herself. Grief at her husband's death? She seldom spoke of Marlin Ropp. Was that a sign of how deeply she mourned the man? Others might see it as odd.

He didn't.

He knew how necessary it was to shroud one's most poignant hurts in shadows. His reticence had to do with wounded pride. His own *mamm* didn't want him in her life. What was Naomi's reason?

"*Daed* told me you needed me to go with you to pick up a buggy," she said without a greeting.

"I'd appreciate it."

"Where are you headed?"

"If you can come as far as the Acorn Farm Inn, I can walk from there."

She frowned. "Why would I take you only partway?"

"I thought you might want to stop at the inn. Your friend

Laurene has been helping her great-*aenti* rebuild after the fire there."

"There was a fire at the inn, too?"

"*Ja.* A few weeks ago. The smoke and water damage has already been repaired, but the whole back of the house is gone. That will need to be rebuilt before they can reopen."

"So Laurene is still in Bliss Valley?"

"She is. I thought you'd like a chance to catch up."

She nodded, but she remained silent. Even after he'd opened the door on the driver's side of the buggy and stepped in, she didn't say anything. He wondered if she'd say anything during the ten-minute ride to the Acorn Farm Inn.

When she sat on the other side of the seat as close to the door as possible, he readjusted his cane between them, so it wouldn't fall against her when they went around a corner. He picked up the reins and turned the horse toward the farm lane.

"*Danki* for coming along," he said, "so I didn't have to figure out how to get two buggies back here."

"You could hook up Fred or Ginger as I did."

He almost laughed at the idea of having one of the mules pulling the other buggy, then realized there hadn't been any humor in her voice. Annoyance sharpened his voice as he said, "We need to talk."

"About what?" Her tone remained prim and ever so polite.

"About Elvin and problems he's having."

Her head jerked as if he'd tugged on it with a string. "Problems? What sort of problems?" Her cool voice broke. "I left him alone with the *kinder*. If—"

"They'll be fine. It's nothing like that." He glanced at her ashen face. "Naomi, it has to do with work."

"Why didn't you say so instead of scaring me?" Her mouth grew into a straight line. "Just like you used to do."

He held up his right hand, exerting all his strength to make the fingers straight. Focusing on that helped him ignore how painful—and how accurate—her accusation was. "This is nothing like that, and you know it. You jumped to conclusions before you gave me a chance to explain."

"I know," she said so softly he barely heard the words over the sound of the horse's hooves and the clatter of metal wheels on asphalt as he turned onto Walnut Run Road. "Tell me what's wrong with *Daed*."

"He won't admit it, but he's having trouble with his eyes. I've noticed in the past week or so he's taking parts he's working on closer to the door or the window. A couple of times, he's stumbled when moving around in the shop. I think he should have his eyes examined."

"He doesn't like *doktors*."

"So he said to me when I suggested he go to the eye *doktor*." A smile tugged at one corner of her lips. "You see how stubborn he is."

"That's something I knew before I started working for him. I was told it would be easier to move the Susquehanna than Elvin Gingerich when he's made up his mind." He looked at her again. "I thought you should know."

"*Danki*. I'll try to find a way to bring it up after the home study tomorrow."

He nodded. "Elvin told me the social worker had called. What do you think the chances are that he'll leave May with you?"

"*She*. It's a different social worker. I pray God will help the social worker see fit to let May stay, but it's in His hands."

Samuel guessed Naomi wasn't as calm as she tried to sound. He wondered if she'd revealed any honest emotions since she'd returned home. Other than the contempt she showed him and the love she had for her family. Every other reaction seemed calculated to keep the world at bay.

"I can't imagine anyone who'd take better care of that *boppli* than you."

"*Danki.*" A faint hint of rose brightened her cheeks.

Warmth glimmered inside him. It was a small connection, but her appreciation stripped away a paper-thin layer of the anger he'd forced her to raise against him. He couldn't imagine how many more layers needed to be torn away so she could reach the point where she could offer him forgiveness.

Why should she forgive you?

The question taunted him as it had so many times when he'd tried to devise a way to convince his *mamm* to open her heart to him.

God, I understand how I must seek forgiveness for my own sins and I'm trying to do that, but how can I atone for something I had nothing to do with other than being born?

"You're left-handed?" Naomi asked, breaking into his thoughts. "I don't remember that."

"If you don't remember me being left-handed, then I couldn't have been." He regretted the abrupt venom in his voice. "I'm sorry, Naomi."

She glanced at him and away. Was she checking to make sure he wasn't trying to confuse her by sounding nice while wearing an arrogant smile? One *gut* thing about her memory was she could recall every prank he'd pulled on her.

Another bad thing about her memory was she could recall every prank he'd pulled on her.

Realizing she was staring at her fingers on her lap, he sighed. She was clenching her hands so tightly her knuckles were almost as pale as her *kapp*.

"You're right," he said. "I used to be right-handed. The

injuries I got in the accident forced me to learn to use my left hand because I can't depend on my right one any longer."

"I'm sorry."

"You don't need to be. I don't have anyone to blame other than myself for the accident."

"I shouldn't have said anything."

He steered the horse around a corner. "Why not? You've always asked questions to satisfy your curiosity."

"Sometimes it's better to remain curious than to find out the truth." Before he could ask what she meant by that, she hurried to say, "I'm not that silly girl I used to be."

"I never meant to suggest you were."

"Maybe not, but I wanted to make sure you understand I'm not as *dumm* as the girl you kissed and then told everyone about."

He hoped his wince wasn't visible. He'd known it was inevitable she'd mention the night he'd tried to forget. For a moment, he considered telling her the truth. That he was sorry he'd given in and accepted his friends' dare before rushing back to them like a pilgrim thrilled to have reached his journey's end. Would she believe him?

Probably not, because it wasn't the complete truth. He might be sorry he'd accepted the dare, but he'd never—not for a single second—been sorry he'd had a chance to taste her soft lips. He'd known, even then, it was the only opportunity he'd ever have to kiss a girl as amazing as Naomi Gingerich.

Chapter Seven

The recent fire had left its scars on the old stone house. Windows were opened wide to let in fresh air to wash away any odors of clinging smoke, and as Naomi walked across the lawn toward the scorched front porch, she saw some panes were broken or cracked. Blackened timbers were piled not far from the barn behind the house, and she guessed they once had held up the section of the inn that was now only the gaping maw of a foundation.

Her eye was caught by the uneven motion of Samuel's steps as he walked toward a neighboring farm. She had to admire his determination to do what he could have easily done before the accident. One of the elderly ladies who worshiped in her former district in Honey Brook had needed months and months of physical therapy after breaking her wrist. Samuel had suffered far more injuries, so he must have gone through longer sessions of physical therapy. For a man who'd wanted nothing to do with anyone but his two friends, being dependent on others must have been excruciating.

"Naomi? Naomi Gingerich, is that you?"

The call of her name brought a smile as a familiar face with warm purple eyes emerged from around the other side of a large tree in the yard. Laurene Nolt was wearing plain clothing, but her time among *Englischers* was still evident in how she pushed strands of light brown hair back toward her *kapp*. It wasn't long enough to stay in place, and Naomi guessed her friend had cut her hair soon after her family left their plain lives behind fifteen years ago. Laurene had hated having to brush snarls from her long hair, even when the two girls had taken turns smoothing each other's hair as youngsters.

Happiness gushed through Naomi. Since the Nolts had disappeared from Bliss Valley in the middle of the night, she'd longed for another chance to spend time with Laurene, sharing a cup of tea and cookies and talking.

Why hadn't Laurene warned her best friend she was leaving? Or had Laurene not known what her parents planned?

That was in the past, and Naomi wanted to put it behind her. She wanted to find the girl she'd been before cruelty and betrayal had shattered her belief that love could cure everything.

Hurrying forward, Naomi grasped her friend's hands. "Laurene, I'm so happy to see you again."

"Did I hear right?" She hugged Naomi close before stepping back and smiling. "Are you in Bliss Valley to stay?"

"*Ja.* We've moved in with *Daed.*"

"He must be so happy. *Aenti* Sylvia told me he's been so lonely since your *mamm* died."

Naomi was startled. "He never said anything to me."

"He wouldn't. You know he's tight-lipped about things like that."

"Maybe that explains why he hired an assistant after all these years. He wanted someone to talk to."

"Now he has you." She motioned for Naomi to follow her to a bench under the tree. A table had been set in front of it and was covered with long sheets of paper. Building plans, Naomi realized as she glanced at them. They must have been drawn to aid in the reconstruction of the inn.

"How's this going?"

Laurene smiled. "Slower than my great-*aenti* Sylvia would like, but there are a flurry of decisions to be made every day." She sat and waited for Naomi to do the same. Taking Naomi's hand again, she said, "I've been praying for you."

"I never doubted that." She smiled. "Tell your great-*aenti* how much the twins loved the chocolate-and-peanut-butter whoopie pies she sent over a couple of days ago. They got as much on their faces and their clothes as in their mouths."

"Peanut butter facials, ain't so?" She sighed. "A facial is one thing I miss from the other side of the fence."

"*Englischers* use peanut butter on their faces?"

Laurene chuckled. "Not only peanut butter, but one of the gals who worked in the building where I did once bragged about what wonders dark chocolate did for her face."

"What a waste of perfectly *gut* chocolate!"

"My thoughts exactly."

They laughed but as the sound faded, Naomi couldn't think of anything to say. How was that possible? After waiting fifteen years, two months, one week and a day, how could she already have run out of things to say?

When Laurene sighed, Naomi wondered if her friend's

thoughts matched her own. She decided to be as frank as she'd been when they were scholars.

"This isn't," Naomi said, "how I imagined it would be when we got back together again."

"Me, either." Relief shone on Laurene's face. "I remember us talking about everything and about nothing." A wry grin tipped her lips. "Of course, *you* remember that, too. Do you still remember every day and how long ago it was?"

"*Ja*."

"I'll tell you something I never told you when we were kids. I was envious of your ability."

"Don't be. There are things I wish I could forget. Lots of things."

Laurene's hold tightened on hers. "I know." She glanced in the direction Samuel had walked. "I'm glad you've made peace with—"

"The Fearsome Threesome?"

"I'd forgotten we used to call them that." She laughed sadly. "You're right. There are things better forgotten."

Again, Naomi wondered what to say next. She didn't want the conversation she'd looked forward to since she'd heard Laurene and her family had jumped the fence to turn into a litany of the appalling pranks played upon them. She needed to shove aside her discomfort and reestablish the connection that had been so strong between her and Laurene.

"How are you adjusting to plain life?" she asked, praying her friend would see the question as the hope their conversation would go on.

"Better than I expected. I do miss my computer, but I don't miss my cell phone." She laughed as a faint ring came from her apron pocket. "Because I haven't had a chance to miss it yet." Fishing it out of her pocket, she glanced at the screen.

"That can wait." She put it back. "I'm keeping it to help with work on the inn, though I'll get rid of it before I'm baptized."

"I'm glad to hear you're going to be baptized." Naomi hugged her friend again. "When I saw you last month at your cousin's wedding, I thought I was dreaming. I thought I'd never see you again."

"I hadn't planned on coming back, but God had different plans. I hear God has brought you another blessing in addition to the twins."

Naomi explained about May and how she was taking care of her.

"On the *dawdi haus* porch?" Laurene tapped her finger against her chin. "Do you think whoever left May knew Samuel lived there?"

"I don't know, but I do know the porch isn't visible from the road."

Laurene nodded. "So expediency may have had more to do with the decision than an expectation Samuel would take care of her."

"*Ja.*" She didn't add more because it was unsettling to think May's *mamm* abandoned her to Samuel's care. Trusting her own boys to him was inconceivable.

Her friend must have sensed Naomi's discomfort, because she returned to a safer subject. "How is your *daed* adjusting to having you home?"

"We're all getting adjusted to it." She smiled. "Slowly, as you are to the changes in your life, I'd guess. Like I said, I'm so glad to hear you're going to be baptized and are making a commitment to a plain life."

"Baptism is a requirement before I can get married."

"Married?" Naomi paid no attention to her stomach tightening at the thought of her friend taking that step. Was the cramp from dismay at Laurene facing the same betrayals she had or from envy her friend might have the life Naomi had believed would be hers? Hastily, before her friend could guess her thoughts, she added her congratulations.

"*Danki.*" Laurene's smile grew shy. "Would you be one of my *newehockers*? I know wedding attendants aren't supposed to be married, but—"

"I'm not. Not any longer."

Laurene's smile fell. "Naomi, that's not what I was going to say. I didn't mean to suggest you being widowed..."

Giving her usually glib friend a hug, she said, "I know you didn't, Laurene. I know you were trying to explain why you were asking me."

"I'm asking you because you're the best friend I've ever had."

"You are mine." It was startling to realize she couldn't name a single female friend she'd had since she'd gotten married. Early on, any time she'd made plans to get together with one or more of the women in Honey Brook, something had come up on the farm or with Marlin's schedule that required her to cancel. Eventually the women, though they were friendly on church Sundays or at mud sales, had stopped asking her to join them at work frolics and other gatherings.

She'd been so focused on making a home and providing a family for Marlin she hadn't noticed how her chance to make those connections had slipped away.

Until it was too late.

"Then will you be one of our *newehockers*?" Laurene asked.

"*Ja.*" She gave her friend another hug. "I'd be honored."

Laurene clapped her hands as if no older than the twins. "That's *wunderbaar.* I can't wait to tell Adam you've agreed."

"Adam?" A dribble of ice slipped along her spine as she told herself it wasn't an uncommon name among the Amish.

Her shock must have been visible, because Laurene took her hand again. "I thought you knew I'm marrying Adam Hershberger."

"You and Adam? After all he did to make our lives miserable?"

"He's not the same person he was. He's grown up." She took a deep breath and released it. "So have I. We know what's important in life."

Naomi stood, unable to listen to her friend spout nonsense that could ruin her life. As Naomi had, but she hadn't known how Marlin would ignore their vows of faithfulness. She'd gone into their marriage with a grateful heart and hope for a blessed life together.

"How can you be certain," she asked, "he's not setting you up to be hurt again? Laurene, think how we were *dumm* enough to believe they'd changed. Every time—*every time*— we found out the worst possible way we were wrong."

Coming to her feet, Laurene blinked back tears. "Samuel brought you here. Is that any different?"

"It's very different. I'm not marrying him!" She realized how her voice had risen, so she paused to compose herself by delving into her memories. Not the appalling ones of the Fearsome Threesome, but the ones of friendship with Laurene, memories she should enjoy more.

One memory pushed to the forefront. It was a conversation she'd overheard her parents having. She didn't bother to recall the specifics of why she'd gone to them with a request about something she and Laurene had wanted to do. That wasn't important. What was important were the words her *mamm* had spoken.

"Elvin," she'd said, "you know Laurene Nolt is the most sensible girl in the district. She makes *gut* decisions, and she's teaching Naomi to be less impulsive. Let's be grateful to God for every moment the girls spend together."

Most sensible girl in the district. With ease, Naomi could recall other people saying the same thing about her dearest friend.

"I'm sorry, Laurene," she said, ashamed of her outburst. When would she learn to curb being impulsive as *Mamm* had mentioned all those years ago? *Seventeen years, three— Not now,* she told her bizarre brain. "I shouldn't have spoken to you like that."

"I'll never be angry at you when you've got my best interests at heart, but I need you to trust me, Naomi. I love Adam, and he loves me."

"You're my best friend. If you think marrying Adam Hershberger is what God wants you to do, I'll stand beside you."

"Literally and figuratively?"

She chuckled. "You sound *Englisch* now."

"It comes from my public relations work. Dotting the i's and crossing the t's. Will you be an attendant at my wedding?"

"Ja." Joy swelled through her as she envisioned how beautiful her friend would look that day. "I'll be the first to wish you blessings on your life together."

Flinging her arms around Naomi, Laurene burst into tears. Happy tears, her friend assured her.

Naomi closed her eyes and prayed her friend's tears didn't change to sad ones as hers had the day the twins were born and Marlin walked away.

Early the next morning, before she prepared breakfast, Naomi went to the shop. She carried a flashlight because she didn't want to switch on the electric lights in the shop. No lamps were on in the *dawdi haus*, and she didn't want to alert Samuel that she was out there. Dealing with him when she had the home study coming that afternoon was something she wanted to avoid.

She skirted the buggy parts on the floor and edged between the buggy that Samuel had driven home yesterday and had stored in the shop before she returned from the Acorn Farm Inn. Running the light along it, she immediately saw the problem. A front wheel was worn unevenly. It could have been because of damage by hitting a rock or other debris in the road, or the brakes could be failing. *Daed* would be able to figure it out faster than she could ask him.

She was trying to distract herself from the reason she'd come into the shop. After a long night of being unable to sleep between May's feedings, she hoped by listening to the answering machine herself, she could get an idea how the social worker felt about the *boppli* staying on the farm.

After turning the volume down, she pushed a button on the dusty machine. She leaned forward to put her ear close to the speaker. There were two messages before the one from the social worker, both about work in the buggy shop. She held her breath when she heard a woman who identified herself as Pam Andrews. The woman's voice was calm and friendly and offered no clue to how she felt about May remaining with Naomi.

Straightening, Naomi reached to turn off the machine. Her fingers halted when she heard another woman's voice. "This is Skylar Lopez. I'm calling for Naomi Gingerich-Ropp."

She clasped her hands behind her before she could reach out and stop the message. No! She didn't need Ms. Lopez intruding right now.

"I'll be out your way tomorrow afternoon," the message continued. "I should be by your house around three o'clock."

Naomi breathed a quick prayer of gratitude. At least, Ms. Lopez's path and the social worker's wouldn't cross.

"I'd like to talk to you and your father about Gina Marie Tinniswood," continued the message. "That's my mother, and maybe… No, I'm not going to say it again so you can disagree. All I'm asking is you give me a chance to speak to you and your father. Please. My mother's life may depend on you. Please, Naomi. Agree to do the test, and if you don't want anything else to do with us, that's fine. Call me to confirm. Please!"

Though she wanted to dismiss the plea as a mistake, Naomi's heart broke as she heard the desperation in the other woman's voice. Even so, she didn't hesitate to push the button that deleted the message.

Then she heard another voice, this one much deeper and more familiar. "Who was that?"

When Naomi whirled to stare at him, Samuel doubted he'd ever seen such a guilty face. Maybe his own had looked more shamed when he'd stood before the judge, but not much. What could she have been doing in the shop that compelled her to wear that expression?

"*Ach*," she said, "you scared me."

"I didn't mean to." Deciding not to let her take the offensive again as he had too often since she'd returned to the farm, he asked, "What are you doing out here so early?"

"I came to listen to the message from the social worker." She glanced at the answering machine, which was blinking the same number it had for the past day.

"Who's Skylar?"

"You heard that?" She flinched, and he couldn't help wondering why.

Naomi had made it clear she didn't want him taking any part in the home study. She'd used the excuse that he didn't live under the same roof as May, but he knew she feared the social worker would find out about his past and snatch the *boppli* out of the house.

"I heard her asking you to call. She seemed anxious to talk to you. Skylar is the social worker?"

"No, the social worker's name is Pam."

"Then who's Skylar?"

"The message was for me, not for you." She walked past him.

His eyes narrowed. "Does this have something to do with your late husband and how he died?"

"Why would you ask me such a thing?"

She was stalling. Unlike him, Naomi had never delighted in telling half-true stories. He didn't lie any longer, but there were a lot of people who wouldn't believe that.

Going to where she stood, he stopped a couple of feet from her. If he moved closer, he might spook her and send her fleeing back to the house. Folding his arms in front of him to mirror her pose, he said, "Elvin told me Marlin died in Lancaster. Something about a fight, and he was injured so badly he died. He said the police are still investigating what happened, so we might get calls from them. He couldn't explain why. Can you?"

"*Ja.* It's because Marlin was shot."

His face grew cold. "Elvin didn't mention that."

"I don't know if *Daed* knows, and I don't want him to know."

"So why are you telling me? To distract me from Skylar's call?"

She scowled. "You work for my *daed*. You're not part of our family. You don't have the right to question me about my private life."

"So you'll tell me about your husband's death, but you won't explain what a call to the shop is about?"

That was, he discovered, one question too many. She stomped away across the wet grass.

He watched until she'd disappeared through the back door to the main house. Walking to the buggy he'd brought to the shop yesterday, he leaned his elbow through the door and onto the seat. He stared at the house where a light glowed in the kitchen.

Since Naomi had come to the farm, Samuel had been certain she was hiding a terrible secret. She'd made every effort to act as if the secret didn't exist and everything was as *gut* as it could possibly be for a widow with two young *kinder*.

She hadn't told her *daed* her late husband had been shot, apparently during a fight, in Lancaster. Too many other questions battered his brain. Why had Marlin been in a fight in the city? Why were the police still investigating? Didn't they have a suspect in custody? It sounded like an open-and-shut case with plenty of witnesses. When he'd worked construction, some men had a weekly tradition of spending most of their paycheck at a bar where fights broke out. Each week, a few had to be excused from work to throw themselves on the mercy of the court, promising never to use their fists like that again. They'd usually kept that promise for a week or two before it started all over again. They complained about the snitches who told the police the names of everyone involved in the fight.

So why hadn't the police arrested someone for Marlin Ropp's death? Surely a plain man would have caught enough eyes.

"It doesn't make sense," he mumbled to himself as he picked up a screwdriver that had gotten missed when he'd cleaned up last night. Holding tight to the buggy, he made sure he didn't tumble on his face when he bent. He kept trying to puzzle out what was bothering him about the conversation with Naomi.

Instantly he knew the answer.

She'd told him about her husband's death too readily. She usually guarded every word she spoke as if she feared the next one would reveal what she hid.

That meant she didn't care if he knew about Marlin's death.

If she wasn't trying to hide her husband's death, then what was she struggling to keep anyone from knowing about?

He couldn't begin to guess, but he shivered. What she hid must be worse than her husband being shot in cold blood in the middle of a Lancaster street.

Chapter Eight

The home study proved to be simple and painless. Naomi was grateful for how kind Pam Andrews was from the moment she arrived at ten a.m. After the conversation with Samuel, she wasn't sure if she could face another interrogation. He'd regarded her with open curiosity when she'd delivered breakfast to him and *Daed* in the shop, apologizing for the simple egg sandwiches that had allowed her to keep the kitchen neat in preparation for Ms. Andrews's arrival. She wasn't sure if it'd been her own refusal to do more than glance in his direction or *Daed*'s presence that kept Samuel from asking more questions.

She wasn't going to satisfy his curiosity. If she did by telling the truth about Marlin, her words might one day come back to injure her sons. That must never be allowed to happen. They were innocent and kind and *gut*. She prayed they'd stay that way. She'd begged God to let her believe Marlin's sins had died with him.

Concentrating on the meeting with Ms. Andrews allowed

her to untangle herself from the briars of thoughts that tormented her.

Ms. Andrews had first apologized for Mr. Tedesco not being able to meet with them. She'd listened, with Naomi translating, as the twins told her about everything they'd had for breakfast. To *Daed,* she'd offered deference and often turned to him with her questions, though he looked to Naomi to give the answers.

One thing became obvious. Either Pam Andrews hadn't been told about Samuel, or he truly wasn't pertinent because he didn't live in the house. Ms. Andrews didn't ask a single question about anyone but the five of them. She focused on where the little girl slept and how Naomi planned to balance her time between the demands of two toddlers and an infant.

Naomi had self-assured answers. May was using the family's cradle set next to Naomi's bed. The social worker, who'd told them to call her Pam—"because we're equal team members in helping this little girl"—was delighted when *Daed* mentioned, during their tour upstairs, that it was the same cradle where Naomi had slept after she was born. Pam hadn't been as pleased when he said they'd be getting an old crib out of the storage room and setting it up for the *boppli.*

"How old is it?" the social worker asked.

"My *daed* built it when my oldest sister was born," her *daed* replied, "so sometime in the 1950s. It's served us well. Did I tell you my dear wife gave birth to Naomi all alone? I was out in the fields working, and when I came home, there was my wife and a sweet gift from God. Naomi means 'pleasant,' because my wife said everything about our little girl was pleasant, even her birth."

Daed continued to prattle while the twins opened an empty box and decided it was an airplane. Naomi shot a look of apology to the social worker. Pam surreptitiously waved away her concerns and let *Daed* continue on about the crib and all who'd slept in it.

Pam said, as soon as he paused to take a breath, "You'll need to get another crib for May." She reached into her attaché case and pulled out a piece of paper. "Here's information on acceptable cribs. You'll see that the rails on them are much closer together than one you might have used yourself, Naomi. We don't want the baby getting her head stuck between the rails." Handing the sheet to Naomi, she said, "If you need assistance in finding or paying for a crib—"

"We'll be fine," she said hastily, knowing *Daed* would be upset if the social worker suggested he couldn't provide for his family. "As you saw in their room, the twins' cribs are correct. It's time for them to be moved to real beds, so May can use one of their cribs."

"Excellent." Pam closed her briefcase. "Do you have any questions for me?"

"How long will it take to know if May is staying with us?" Naomi shook her head. "I know if her *mamm* or her *mamm*'s family is found, the plan will be to reunite them. That's not what I'm asking. I'm asking how long will it take to know if I'm approved for her continued care."

"You should hear within seven business days." She smiled. "You're going to have my recommendation, and Pierce feels this is a good placement for her. However, ours aren't the final approvals. You know the wheels of the commonwealth's bureaucracy turn far more slowly than any of us would like."

"Has anything been discovered about May's parents?"

"Not yet. Whoever left her here took great pains to make sure there was nothing to trace the child back to him or her."

With another sigh, she asked, "The phone number you gave Pierce is still good?"

"*Ja*. It's in the shop, so leave a message. I'll get back to you."

Pam nodded, then turned toward the front door. "Thank you for your time. I've got everything I need. Thank you for offering this sweet little one a home."

"Our pleasure," Naomi said at the same time *Daed* did. They looked at each other and laughed.

"Well," Pam said with a grin, "I can see you two are in agreement about May." She reached for the doorknob. "I'll get you an answer as soon as I can. Enjoy the rest of your day with your lovely family."

Thanking her, Naomi closed the door after the social worker. She watched Pam get into her car. As soon as the vehicle was moving along the farm lane, Naomi let her shoulders sag, hoping the tension would roll off them. The meeting had gone as well as she'd prayed it would, but she was glad it was over.

If only tomorrow's visit from Ms. Lopez could be over and done with, too. She needed to talk to *Daed* about that. How to begin such a conversation? It wasn't like she could say, "You know, I've heard you aren't my *daed*."

"That's it? It's that simple?" *Daed* asked, startling her because for a half second she wondered if she'd spoken her thoughts out loud.

He was talking about the home study. He had no idea what was about to explode into their lives. She wished Ms. Lopez's visit could be as straightforward as the home study, but she suspected it wouldn't be. If she had any inkling Skylar Lopez would listen to her without disrupting the whole family, she wouldn't have kept the truth about the message from Samuel.

Or from *Daed*.

Now would be the perfect time to broach the subject. She opened her mouth to tell him, but instead she fell back on discussing the home study. She couldn't bear the thought *Daed* would be hurt by her giving the question of her parentage enough credence that she brought it up to him.

"There'll be additional paperwork to fill out if May stays here," she replied.

"She doesn't want to talk with Samuel?"

Seeing her *daed*'s high color, she decided she'd been right not to listen to her instincts and tell him about Ms. Lopez. "He doesn't live in the house."

Daed sniffed. "That's silly. The *boppli* was found on his porch, not ours."

She wasn't going to change his mind. Nor was she going to allow anything to change hers. Samuel and his cohorts had tried to ruin her life. She wasn't going to let him do the same to her sons and May.

"Will you watch the *kinder* while I get us dinner?" she asked.

"*Ja.*" He reached out a trembling hand toward his chair and sat heavily in it.

"Are you okay? You look like you're not feeling well."

He waved her away. "Just a headache. Probably allergies. Everyone around here is cutting hay, and I'm stuffy at this time of year." He shooed her toward the kitchen. "A *gut* meal is the best prescription for a headache."

Giving the twins crayons and coloring books, she took them into the kitchen. She left them coloring under the table, where they were out of her way. Returning to the living room, she picked up the *boppli*'s carrier and brought May into the kitchen, too. She glanced at her *daed* and saw his eyes were closed though he'd picked up a copy of *The Budget* from the stack by his chair.

The date on the issue was more than two months earlier. Samuel had noticed how *Daed* needed more light to work. Was he having trouble reading, too? Was that why the newspapers had been piling up in the kitchen?

A tendril of worry wove around her heart. *Daed* had been overdoing it, trying to work as if he were as young as Samuel and spending time with his *kins-kinder*. He enjoyed it, but she needed to make sure he got to bed early, as she did with the boys. A smile teased her as she wondered if he'd be as resistant to a bedtime as Jared and Jesse were.

Preparing a hearty meal of roast beef sandwiches with cold potato salad and chow-chow and applesauce, as well as fresh asparagus spears she'd picked in the garden that morning, Naomi focused on keeping the *kinder* quiet so *Daed* could relax. She had to pause to give May a bottle, and the little girl drained it so quickly Naomi spent more time burping her than feeding her. The little boys giggled each time May released a loud burp.

When Samuel didn't appear as Naomi was putting the food on the table, she wondered why. The answer came as quickly as the question. He didn't want to intrude on them and the home study, though the social worker had left. She realized he didn't know anything about what a home study entailed—because she hadn't answered his questions as she had her *daed*'s—so he might believe it was ongoing.

First she'd wake *Daed*, then she'd get Samuel. That would give *Daed* time to oversee the boys picking up their crayons and putting them away.

Wiping her hands on a towel, she called, *"Daed?"*

She didn't get an answer, so she went to the living room

door. Looking in, she discovered he was sitting in the chair, staring across the room instead of looking at *The Budget* on his lap.

He moaned. "Na-Na-Na..."

She wanted to groan herself when she saw how gray his face was. Fear riveted her at the sight of his mouth pulling down on the left side as he struggled to speak. She ran to his chair. The twins started to follow, but she ordered them back so sharply that, for once, they obeyed without protest.

Putting her hand under his elbow, she said, "Let me help you."

"Make sure the *kinder* eat. They must be hungry." His mouth was balanced as it should be. Maybe she'd been fooled by a trick of light and shadows. "I'm hungry, too."

"If you'll be okay—"

"I'm fine, girl. Go and take care of your *kinder*." He frowned. "Get Samuel in here. He must be starving by now."

"I'll call him."

"He won't hear you. He's working on that wheel."

She nodded. "I'll get him. Do you want me to help—?"

"I'm fine. Go!"

A *gut* daughter heeded her *daed* while she lived beneath his roof. Wasn't that what she'd told Skylar Lopez?

No! The last thing she wanted to think about now was the woman and her outlandish theories.

Hurrying into the kitchen, she called to the boys as she lifted May out of her *boppli* seat. She'd have to take all the *kinder* with her to the shop, knowing she would need to keep a close eye on the twins. Their inquisitive little noses and fingers would be poking at everything in the shop. She didn't want *Daed,* who was clearly exhausted, to have to watch them. She'd—

A dull, hollow sound struck Naomi like a blow between her shoulder blades. Whirling, she stared at her *daed* lying on the floor. His head lolled from one side to the other, and she realized the thump had been it hitting the floor.

"*Daed!*" She ran into the living room.

Putting the *boppli* on the sofa, she knelt by her prone *daed*. He kept moving his head side to side as if he was trying to shake something off of it. She clasped his face between her hands and halted the eerie motion, though he fought her.

"*Daed?*" she whispered. Loudly and in a tone she'd heard *Mamm* use whenever she needed him to heed her, she snapped, "Elvin Ropp, look at me!"

"Don't yell, Flossie!"

Ignoring how he'd used her *mamm*'s name, she asked, "Are you all right?"

"My head hurts. It hurts bad."

She guided him to sit, then grabbed a pillow off a chair. Putting it beneath him, she eased him back onto it. "Does that help?"

"*Ja*, Flossie. I think I need to sleep now."

"No, don't sleep." She wasn't sure how hard he'd hit his head. If he had a concussion…

Then she noticed how his mouth was drooping, and she guessed the situation was far more dire than a concussion. The twins crept around the edge of the doorway between the living room and kitchen. She motioned them away. She didn't want them to see their *grossdawdi* like this.

"*Daed*, raise your arms," she said as she knelt beside him. When he ignored her, she swallowed another groan, then ordered, "Elvin, raise your arms! I need to measure you for a new shirt."

"My old shirt…" His words faded into a mumble.

"Raise your arms!"

His right arm rose, but his left stayed at his side, unmoving. *God, help me! He's having a stroke!*

She looked around. Why was this the one time that Samuel wasn't skulking around, invading her life? She was ashamed of the thought the moment it formed, but now she didn't have any choice but to leave her *daed* while she went for help.

"*Daed*, I'll be right back. I'll—"

"My head...my head..." he groaned, putting his right hand to his temple.

"I'll be right back." She kissed his cheek, then pushed herself to her feet.

Hating to leave him a second, she scooped up the *boppli* and called to the twins to come with her. She held the door open for her *kinder*, looking back at her *daed* lying on the floor. She tossed a prayer in heaven's direction and ran out with the little boys trying to keep up.

Samuel aimed his hammer at the metal wheel he'd removed a few hours before. It was almost round again. The young driver must have hit the obstruction in the road at a near gallop to do so much damage. He started to swing the hammer, but halted when a motion in the direction of the house caught his eye. He straightened and looked out.

Naomi, carrying May, and with her twins trying to keep up, was racing toward him as if a rabid dog nipped at everyone's heels. He put down the hammer and hobbled toward the door, not bothering to get his cane. He rubbed his right thigh when the muscles tightened into a cramp. Pausing in midstep, he bent to catch the little boys before they could rush past him and into the shop. He had tools set out on the table.

"Get out of the way! I need the phone!" Naomi yelled.

"Naomi—" He started to ask what was wrong, but she elbowed past him.

"I need to call 911!"

"What's happened?" He hated his leg that slowed him as he tried to follow.

"It's *Daed*! I think he's had a stroke." She pushed the *boppli* into his arms, shocking him because she'd kept him from holding May since the day they'd found the infant.

As he shifted the little girl so he wouldn't drop her, he put out his right hand to halt the boys again. "Wait," he ordered.

"*Mamm*—" Jared began.

"Not now!" Naomi called as she grabbed the phone off the work table.

"*Grossdawdi.*" Tears welled into Jesse's eyes. "No fun."

"I know, buddy," Samuel said, motioning the *kind* to come closer.

Jesse leaned his face against Samuel's pants and began to cry. As if it were a signal, Jared and May began to wail, too. Naomi glared in his direction as she punched the number into the phone. What did she expect him to do?

Take care of the kinder *while she gets help for Elvin*, came the answer from inside him.

He almost laughed at his thoughts. Naomi didn't think him capable of watching the *kinder*. He was the last person she trusted to—

Again he halted his thoughts. He *was* the last person she could depend on if Elvin had had a stroke. A stroke! *Please, God, not that!* He glanced at the house and started to take a step in that direction.

"Don't!" she yelled.

"Don't?"

She looked from him to the twins, and he guessed she didn't

want the youngsters seeing their *grossdawdi* suffering. Yet Elvin was in the house alone.

He glanced from the house to where she was waiting for the 911 dispatcher. Elvin needed someone with him. The kids couldn't be left alone. Too many tools were scattered through the shop, and he had no doubts that the twins would find the most dangerous ones the moment he took a step toward the house.

Take care of Elvin, he prayed as he realized the dilemma that Naomi must have faced before she burst out into the yard. The only way to help her *daed* was to leave him alone.

Squatting wasn't possible, so Samuel dropped to sit on the edge of the shop's concrete floor. The twins scrambled to find a place on his lap, and he lifted May out of their way. How could two little kids seem to have a dozen limbs? They curled up against him, their only bulwark against their fears.

"Let's ask God to help your *grossdawdi,*" he whispered.

Behind him, he heard Naomi's voice, shockingly calm as she gave the 911 dispatcher the pertinent information. He began a simple prayer the twins would understand, but halted when she shoved the phone into his right hand. He almost dropped it but managed to get his fingers to close around it in time.

"They want someone to stay on the phone," she said. "I've got to get back to *Daed.* I don't want him to be alone if..." Without saying more, she plucked May from the crook of his arm and ran to the house.

"I'll wait here for the ambulance," he called to her back. He looked at the twins. "*We* will wait for the ambulance, ain't so, boys?"

She didn't answer as she sped onto the porch.

"If what?" asked Jesse, jumping to his feet.

Samuel looked at the younger twin as the other boy scrambled to stand, too. "I don't know what you're asking."

"*Grossdawdi* no alone." He raised his fearful eyes from his clasped fingers. "If what?"

How was he supposed to answer such a question? With the truth? He didn't want to lie to the *kinder*, but to say Naomi was worried their *grossdawdi* would die... He couldn't tell them that. He hadn't heard them speak about their *daed*. Did they understand he wasn't coming back? Did they remember him?

He listened as the twins began to chatter like a pair of manic squirrels. He'd noticed they had a language of their own they used whenever something unsettled them. Although they could have no idea of what had happened to their *grossdawdi*, they'd sensed how upset Naomi was. Why had he never noticed before now the *kinder* were an emotional barometer for their *mamm*?

Both boys looked at him, and he knew he had to answer Jesse's question. He resorted to asking a question of his own, "What happens when you're alone?"

The twins exchanged a look, then threw their arms around each other.

"*Ja*," Samuel said, relieved their response had given him enough insight to know how to answer Jesse's question. Hauling himself to his feet, he nodded. "You're right. When we're alone, we want to be with someone else. Though God is with us always, we sometimes want someone we can hug."

"*Mamm* hug *Grossdawdi*," Jared said with the certainty of a two-year-old. "Me hug *Grossdawdi*."

Putting his hand on the boy's shoulder before Jared could run into the house, Samuel said, "Don't forget. We've got a job to do."

"Wait," Jesse interjected with a grin.

"*Ja.* Wait for the ambulance. Watch the road. It'll be here soon."

"See it!" Jared bounced from one foot to the other.

"Soon," Samuel assured him. "Look for its lights and listen for its siren."

The twins looked at each other, and he realized they had no idea what he was talking about. Maybe they'd never seen an ambulance before. They wouldn't have when their *daed* had died because he'd been far from them. What had Naomi told her sons about Marlin Ropp's death?

Astonished, he realized how seldom Naomi spoke of her husband. Because grief ate at her with every breath? However, Elvin hadn't spoken of the man, either. Had his boss and his son-in-law been close? Not likely, when Elvin had mentioned several times how he wished his daughter and *kins-kinder* would visit more often. He hadn't ever said anything about Marlin Ropp, *gut* or bad.

Why did Naomi and Elvin act as if the man hadn't existed?

Keep your nose out of it, warned his conscience as he huddled with the *kinder.* It was *gut* advice, and he needed to follow it. If he didn't, too much could change. Every bit of hope he'd gathered since he started working for the old man might be ending...

He wasn't sure how he'd find a way to begin again.

Chapter Nine

With a sigh, Samuel leaned forward on the chair in the hospital waiting room and clasped his hands between his knees. He longed to pray, but after two hours of sitting there alone, he'd run out of ways to ask God to spare Elvin's life.

The ambulance had taken Elvin to Lancaster General Hospital. A quick call had gotten Morris Transport to bring Naomi, the *kinder* and him there, as well.

Samuel was grateful Keith Morris, the driver, hadn't said anything to him when the van arrived. Years ago, Samuel and his friends had soaped the windows of their vans every night for two weeks in a row. Naomi's wasn't the only long memory in Bliss Valley. He'd known that was true when Keith glared at him while Naomi's back was turned. He'd wanted to apologize, but Naomi had urged him to hurry when they'd reached the hospital. Something more to add to his to-do list.

He looked up as a shadow announced someone was walking past. Banished there by the staff, he'd wished Naomi would come and tell him how Elvin was doing. His hopes had been dashed dozens of times, but not this time.

Pushing himself to his feet, he tightened his fingers on his cane. He forced them to loosen before he snapped it in half. In silence, he waited while Naomi walked toward him. Each step was as labored as if she carried a pair of elephants on her shoulders. His eyes narrowed as he looked past her.

"Where are the *kinder*?" he asked.

"Laurene came to take them back home. She's going to stay with them until I get there." Her voice was dulled by fatigue and worry. "Her car hasn't sold yet, so she used it to pick them up. I think under the circumstances, God will understand."

"I'm sure He will. Laurene is a *gut* friend."

"When she and her family left, nothing was the same." Her gaze shifted, warning she was thinking of the uncomfortable past they'd shared.

"If I could change—"

"Don't, Samuel," she whispered. "Not now."

He nodded. She was right. Her burdens were too enormous for her to listen to his apology, which would be a decade too late.

So he asked the question haunting him, "How's Elvin?"

"Stable. That's the word the nurse used. I guess it means he's not worse." Tears welled into her eyes, making them glisten like a blue sky after a shower. "I think it also means he isn't any better."

He took her arm and steered her toward the hard plastic chairs where he'd been waiting. Seating her, he sat beside her. "I'm glad to hear he's no worse."

"What if he never gets better?" She worried her fingers together. "I wish they'd let me see him."

"They will once he's in a room."

Her head jerked up, and she looked at him as if she'd just noticed he was there. "That's what the nurse said. How did you know that?"

"I've spent more than my fair share of time in hospitals." He tapped his right knee. "I learned about how they do things."

When footsteps sounded outside the waiting area, her eyes cut toward the doorway. He wanted to tell her not to get her hopes up with every noise, because the hospital was filled with them, but he couldn't. Not when his own hopes rose, too, to fall when a stranger walked past without looking in their direction.

Naomi stood, rubbing her hands together as if trying to get sticky pine pitch off her fingers. He wasn't surprised when she began to pace the breadth of the room. It was only four or five steps each way. He knew. He'd counted those steps for almost an hour before his weak leg demanded he sit.

"This is all my fault," she moaned.

"None of this is your fault," he answered, hiding his shock at her words.

"You don't know what you're talking about!"

He was shocked by her caustic tone, then realized he shouldn't judge anything she did or said when she was distraught.

"Maybe not," he said as he pushed himself to stand. He flinched as pain rushed down his leg. "I do know that, if indeed your *daed* has had a stroke, it had nothing to do with you."

She didn't pause in her frantic pacing from one side of the wide doorway to the other. "I'm not talking about the stroke. Afterwards! I pray to God I didn't cause him more harm."

"More harm? How?"

"I moved his head to put a pillow beneath it. I didn't want

him lying on the hard floor when he was complaining of a horrific headache." She continued to knead her hands together until he worried she'd scrape her skin right off. "I realized— too late—nobody's supposed to move someone who's taken a fall. Only a *doktor* or nurse who knows the right thing to do."

He walked in front of her. She started past him, and he put out his arm.

"Get out of my way!" she said, but halted.

"Not until you listen to me."

"You don't have anything to say that I want to hear." She folded her arms in front of her. "You don't need to be here. Why don't you go back—"

He seized her arms. Fighting his instinct to shake her, but needing to make her see sense, he tightened his grip when she twisted to escape him.

"I'll let you go," he said, "when you calm down. Nobody's to blame for this. Everything that happened today is God's will, as surely as it is His will you were in the best place to help Elvin when he collapsed. Your *daed* could have lain there for quite a while if you hadn't been there, too. When he wakes up in his hospital bed, his last previous memory will be of the two of you getting ready for the dinner with the *kinder*. A *gut* memory because you're a *gut* daughter."

"I don't know…"

He released her, but before she could turn and walk away, he caught her chin between his thumb and forefinger. Instead of tilting her head up so he could hold her gaze, he bent down. It wasn't easy to keep his balance, yet he knew he must. What he had to say was important. Not for him to speak, but for her to hear.

"Naomi, I do know. I know you're a *gut* daughter, and I know your homecoming has brought joy into his life. All he talks about, most days in the shop, is what he did with you and the twins and the *boppli* the previous evening."

"Maybe it's been too much."

"Only if too much has put a sparkle in his eyes and taken aches and pains out of his body. Since you got back, he's acted as if he's two decades younger. That's why I know nothing you did could have harmed Elvin."

He held his breath, hoping she was listening to him instead of hiding behind her fear and ridiculous guilt.

Her mouth became a taut line. "You don't know that. You're not a *doktor.*"

"That's true, but a stroke—if that's what made Elvin fall—isn't something caused by happiness or you urging him to get up off the floor."

Her eyes grew so wide, he could see white all around her blue irises. "How do you know...?" Her shoulders stiffened. "Were you eavesdropping?"

"You know I wasn't. How could I have gotten from the house to the shop before you did?"

She closed her eyes and sighed. "I know you couldn't have, but if anything I said or did upset him so much that something happened to cause—"

"Even if it were physically possible to cause a stroke, which I'm pretty sure it's not, *you* couldn't have said anything to him to bring it on."

"How do you know?"

He heard an uncertainty in her voice he'd never heard before. In school, Naomi had been the one who could pinpoint any fact.

"Because I know you. You may not believe it, but I'm a pretty *gut* judge of people." His mouth pulled into a grimace. "Something I learned after a lot of hard lessons. One thing

I've discovered since you returned to the farm is you try to do your best for those around you."

"But…" She drew away and hurried to the door, looking along the hall.

A group of nurses rushed past, and she jumped back as if she feared they were going to bowl her over. Running her hands up and down her arms, she edged closer to the side of the door again.

"You should sit," he said. "It may take a while before anyone comes."

"I want to know what's going on."

"You won't find out by loitering in the doorway. All you're doing is risking getting in someone's way."

"Leave me alone! You aren't my husband. You can't tell me what to do!"

He stared, shocked at her outburst. He'd never seen Naomi lose her cool before, not even when he and his friends had played an annoying prank on her. Horror rushed through him as he tried not to imagine what her late husband had done. It must have been more appalling than their stupid teenage tricks. What had Naomi's marriage been like?

Knowing she'd said too much, Naomi wrapped her arms around herself. They were a poor substitute for Samuel's strong ones.

Have you lost your mind? The accusation echoed through her head, wiping away any vestiges of silly thoughts. She usually didn't need to be taught the same lesson twice. Hadn't she learned not to trust him after Samuel pretended he wanted to walk out with her and then kissed her?

Looking at his shocked face now, she wasn't going to explain why she'd said what she had. She hadn't mentioned a word to her parents about the sad state of her marriage. Even if she had, the last person on the planet she'd confide in was Samuel King. He'd shown already he couldn't keep his big mouth shut. If he spread the truth through Bliss Valley about how Marlin had cheated on her, it could have a terrible impact on her sons' lives.

She turned and stiffly walked back to the chairs. She was about to sit when a shadow crossed the door. It became an Amish man carrying his straw hat.

Samuel said, "*Danki* for coming, Jonas."

She straightened as Jonas Gundy entered the room. As she'd noted the day he came in the wake of their discovery of May on the porch, he was a powerful presence, though he wasn't tall. His dark beard added strength to his narrow face. As he held out his hands to take hers, she recalled he'd been chosen by lot shortly after she was married. There had been concern because he hadn't been at least forty years old, but he'd gained the *Leit*'s respect with his kindness, his knowledge of the Bible and his ability to find solutions.

She didn't recognize the two men with him, though it was clear they were related. When Jonas introduced them as the district's ministers, Gerald Hooley and Orus Hooley, she understood why. She remembered the first cousins from school, where they'd been several years ahead of her, and she knew they were related to a large portion of the plain folks in Bliss Valley.

"*Danki* for coming," she said.

"Adam would have been here if he could have," Jonas replied.

"I'm sure he would have." She suppressed the dismay at the idea of facing her *daed*'s possible death with two of her three tormentors in the room. Though, she had to admit, Samuel had been a great help in getting *Daed* to the hospital.

"How's Elvin?" the bishop asked.

"We're waiting to hear." She gestured for the men to sit, but nobody moved.

She understood why when a woman in a white lab coat came into the waiting room. Her sleek black hair was pulled back in a bun not so different from Naomi's. She carried a clipboard, but didn't look at it as she asked, "Gingerich?"

"I'm Naomi, Elvin Gingerich's daughter." Her teeth chattered as if she'd stepped into a walk-in freezer set at its lowest temperature. "How's my *daed*?"

"I'm Dr. Dayal," the woman said instead of answering Naomi's question. "I'm a neurologist. Do you know what that is?"

"*Ja,*" Naomi answered. "You're a *doktorfraa* who deals with the nervous system." She used the term for a female *doktor*, then wondered if she should have. *Englischers* seemed to prefer terms that didn't define jobs by gender.

"That's right," Dr. Dayal said with a faint smile, and Naomi relaxed, glad the woman wasn't offended. The *doktorfraa* glanced at the men. "I'd like to speak to you about your father's present condition. Are these family members?"

"No." Naomi introduced the bishop, the two ministers and Samuel before they left when the *doktorfraa* asked for privacy.

A single, fragile bubble of hope floated in her heart. Wouldn't the *doktorfraa* have insisted Jonas and the Hooley cousins remain if her *daed* was dead? The bubble threatened to pop when she realized how little she understood about a hospital. She'd been in one only twice before. Once when the twins were born, and shortly after, she'd returned because of postnatal complications. She hadn't gone to a hospital when Marlin was shot. He'd been sent to one—most likely the same one she stood in now—when he'd been found on that Lancaster street, but by the time she was able to get there, he'd been moved to the morgue.

"Ms. Gingerich," the *doktorfraa* began.

"I'm Mrs. Ropp, but please call me Naomi."

"Of course, Naomi. First of all, I must tell you that you did everything right for your father. He's alive because you knew what to do."

Tears, mixed with relief and gratitude, filled her eyes. She thanked God for putting the words into the woman's mouth. Naomi needed to hear them. *And* danki, *Lord, for letting* Daed *stay here with us a while longer.*

"As I'm sure you guessed, he has suffered a stroke," Dr. Dayal continued. "The damage has affected the left side of his body, but we won't know the extent of the impairment he's suffered until he's fully conscious. We have him sedated now to give his brain a chance to try to heal. Once we've completed our tests and can give you a prognosis, we'll have him moved to a rehabilitation center."

"He can't come home?"

"He's going to need round-the-clock care in addition to physical and occupational therapy. Perhaps speech therapy, as well. That will put a heavy burden on you and your family, Naomi."

"In a plain community, everyone pitches in when someone has a need."

The *doktorfraa* regarded her steadily for a long minute. "My mother said it was the same in her village in India. I'm sorry we've lost that part of our lives in the modern world." Her phone buzzed, and she glanced at it. Raising her eyes, she said, "Let's not make any decisions about where your father will do his rehab until we know what challenges he'll have. Okay?"

"*Ja.*"

"Good. Someone will come in to get you once your father has been moved to a room. I'll check in with you later."

"*Danki*. Thank you, I mean."

Dr. Dayal smiled. "I got what you meant. Your father isn't my first plain patient. I've picked up a little of your language along the way." She didn't add anything else as she strode out.

Naomi sank onto a chair and covered her face with her hands. She was too numb to pray other than thanking God over and over that her *daed* was still alive.

When someone sat beside her, she didn't lower her hands. She didn't need to. She knew, with some sense she couldn't name, it was Samuel. He didn't speak, and neither did she. She owed him an apology for lashing out, but didn't want to leave the fragile haven behind her palms. There, she could feel God's grace. It was her only sanctuary, as it'd been the night Marlin was shot.

Like that night, Naomi wasn't granted much time to savor God's love in quiet. The passing hours became a blur with paperwork she needed to review and sign. At long last, nearly six hours later, a young woman came to let her know she could visit her *daed* briefly in the cardiac intensive care unit.

She hurried to the elevator. Samuel and Jonas went with her. The ministers excused themselves to head home because visitors would be limited. She thanked them for coming, her voice rough because unshed tears clogged her throat.

The CICU was eerily quiet except for the pinging from machines monitoring patients and keeping them alive. When a nurse told them only two visitors at a time, Samuel hung back and motioned for Jonas to go with Naomi.

Something else she would need to thank him for.

Later.

Now, all she wanted was to get to *Daed*.

Pausing by the door where a curtain had been pulled back to give the nursing staff easy access and visibility, Naomi breathed a prayer for God to hold her up. She walked in with the bishop by her side.

Daed looked barely alive. His chest rose and fell slowly. He was attached to tubes and machines that made annoying beeps. No, not annoying. She should be grateful the sounds were regular, offering proof her *daed* was alive.

"Are you all right?" Jonas asked her.

"No, but I'll manage."

He gave her a swift smile. "I'm glad you've inherited Elvin's and Flossie's strength."

Naomi took her *daed*'s hand as Jonas offered up heartfelt prayers. He prayed for God to heal *Daed*, asked for a surcease of any pain and then implored all of them to accept God's will. He finished with a verse from 2 Peter: "'The Lord is not slack concerning his promise, as some men count slackness; but is longsuffering to us-ward, not willing that any should perish, but that all should come to repentance.'" He put his hand on *Daed*'s shoulder before facing Naomi.

"Danki," she whispered.

"Don't hesitate to send for us any time of the day or night," the bishop said.

She nodded, knowing he was speaking of what she should do if her *daed* lost his fight to live.

"Do you want me to send Samuel back?" he asked.

She opened her mouth to say no, but heard herself say, *"Ja."*

Gripping her shoulder as he had *Daed*'s, he said, "I'll be back when I can."

Naomi nodded again. She knew the bishop was busy with many matters for his districts, as well as running his business and taking care of his own family.

When Jonas had left, a nurse came in. She gave Naomi a bolstering smile when Naomi moved away from the bed to let the nurse do her job. The nurse talked to *Daed* while she took his vitals and wrote information on a clipboard.

"You should talk to him." The nurse rehung the clipboard on the bed.

"Can he hear me?"

"We can't be sure, but if he can hear you, don't you want him to know you're here?" She didn't wait for an answer before she moved to the next room.

Naomi edged toward the bed, taking care not to jostle any of the wires or tubes. She folded the fingers of his right hand between her hands. "*Daed*, it's Naomi. I'm here. Don't worry about me or the kids or anyone or anything else. Focus on getting better."

His face, the left corner of his mouth still drooping, was as immobile as a statue's. She bent and kissed his cheek and whispered she loved him.

The flutter of a motion against her palms brought a gasp. "*Daed!*"

"Is something wrong?" asked Samuel from the doorway.

Looking at him, she said, "His fingers moved when I told him I love him." Wonder rose like a wave through her heart. "He's here with us. He really is."

Samuel walked to stand beside her. "That's *wunderbaar.*" A mischievous smile brightened his eyes as he leaned toward *Daed*. "I've been trying to tell her you're stubborn enough to persuade God to give you more time with your daughter and *kins-kinder.*"

Genuine affection was laced through Samuel's teasing words, and she realized he'd been honest when he said how much he appreciated *Daed* giving him a job and a chance to start over in Bliss Valley. As she related to *Daed* all that had happened following his collapse in the house, Samuel added silly stories about the questions the twins had asked him on the way to the hospital. She was surprised when he added a story about how he and Adam and Joel Beachy had vandalized the Morris Transport vehicles.

"Thought when Keith Morris recognized me, I'd have to walk here," he finished with a laugh.

Daed didn't react, but she was comforted to know he was hearing them. They talked to him for a little longer, then grew silent as snores came from him.

Naomi led the way out of the room and past the nurse's station. Beyond it was another small waiting room. Neither of them spoke as they each chose one of the uncomfortable chairs on either side of a table topped with a lamp and multiple copies of the same health magazine.

"I'm not planning to go home tonight," she said.

"I assumed that."

"Laurene knows where the formula for the *boppli* is, and the boys can show her where their clothes are stored."

"After they show her all their toys."

She nodded, too worn out to smile. "She mentioned that, too, so I told her not to let them try to show her everything downstairs."

"Did you mention to Jonas you're going to need help in the house?"

"No." She kneaded her forehead. "To be honest, I didn't think about it. Right now, I'm focused on getting *Daed* through each hour of tonight and then each hour of tomorrow and each hour afterward."

"I know that, but you've got to think about what awaits you when you get home. Elvin can't manage stairs now."

"There's the extra room off the kitchen. If a bed is moved in there, *Daed* can use it until he's able to handle stairs again."

He didn't say anything, but she saw the truth on his strained face. He wasn't sure if her *daed* would ever manage to walk on his own again. She couldn't let his pessimism overwhelm her hopes.

When he finally spoke, he said, "I want to help."

"I appreciate that." When he started to reply, she cut him off by hurrying to say, "I do because I can't handle the house, the *kinder* and *Daed*'s needs in addition to the shop. If you can take over the shop, then I—"

"Don't worry about details tonight, Naomi."

"I have to. It keeps me from thinking about—"

He put his finger to her lips to hush her. Or so she thought until his fingertip grazed the curve, and his gaze held hers, daring her to react. She jerked away, but not quick enough. A spark, as bright and hot as an ember at the heart of a fire, jumped from his skin to hers. In his eyes, she saw a matching warmth. She looked away. Was this another prank? How could Samuel, who'd been a master trickster when they were kids, make her feel a flash of attraction to him?

That was all it'd been. Something she'd felt only because she was exhausted and on edge. Every nerve was ready to jump to attention. Something that wasn't lasting, wasn't heartfelt, wasn't real.

It hadn't been longing for his touch. It couldn't be.

Not with Samuel King!

Chapter Ten

For Naomi, going to church in Bliss Valley for the first time without her *daed* three days later seemed strange, but, according to his *doktors*, he wouldn't be released from the hospital until Monday or Tuesday at the earliest. His progress was slow, and the staff wanted to have support in place for him before he was allowed to go home. He could say a few words, often not the ones he wanted, though he was able to scribble notes, including the one that told her to attend services instead of coming to the hospital. She was grateful his right side seemed unaffected, but he could not make anything on his left side function.

The physical therapist was going to start working with him today on strengthening exercises which could lead toward him standing alone, and *Daed* didn't want an audience. Most especially her. He'd refused to let Naomi witness any of his PT sessions, but he hadn't realized one of the therapists was capturing his efforts on a cell phone camera. Those were shared with Naomi along with reports of his frustration and stubborn refusal to do what he must sometimes. Another reason, she knew, why *Daed* needed to come home to continue his therapy. He would be determined not to look weak in front of her and the *kinder*, so he'd master each exercise as fast as he could.

She couldn't wait for him to come home. It was going to be hard, she was told, especially with the responsibility of two toddlers and a *boppli*. In addition, there was the buggy repair business to oversee. Samuel wanted to help, but he'd admitted he didn't know anything about prices or scheduling work. *Daed* had done that himself, so either Naomi would have to take the time to teach Samuel what her *daed* had taught her years ago or handle it.

It was going to be a challenge, but *Daed* had conveyed to her he wanted to come home as soon as possible. Bringing him home was what she intended to do.

The Sunday morning was hot and without a whisper of a breeze, though it was barely eight o'clock. She'd set up battery-operated fans in both bedrooms last night, but they'd been too feeble. She'd brought the cradle downstairs along with the crib mattresses. She and the *kinder* had spent the night in the living room.

Jared and Jesse had decided being downstairs must mean it was playtime, and May had been awakened and more than a bit annoyed by their eager whispers and tiptoeing around the room. Though it was cooler downstairs, nobody slept.

Naomi stifled another yawn. She was comforted by the welcome of the *Leit* when she joined the other women and young *kinder* by one side of the door leading into the former Nolt house not far from the Bliss Valley Covered Bridge. Another family had moved in after Laurene and her parents had slipped away in the middle of the night, leaving Naomi alone to face the bullying of the Fearsome Threesome. Her hope she'd see Laurene disappeared when someone mentioned that Laurene's great-*aenti* wasn't feeling well, so she'd stayed home with her.

How long would be it before Naomi could attend another of the every-other-week Sunday services? Getting *Daed* there would be difficult, and she guessed it would take time before he was strong enough to sit, even in a chair with a back, for the three hours of a worship service. He grew exhausted in less than fifteen minutes of having the head of his bed raised.

As each woman came to welcome her, coo over the *kinder* and tell her how *Daed* was in her prayers, Naomi kept her familiar fake serenity in place. She'd worn it through her marriage and had perfected it while thanking those who came to Marlin's funeral. Now it was so easy to bring it out and drape it over her like an invisible cloak. Though it weighed more heavily on her each time she pulled the protective guise out, she found a haven within it.

She looked at the other side of the barn door. There, Samuel was answering questions from the men who'd gathered. She saw several glance in her direction.

Were they asking about the future of the buggy repair shop, or were they asking how they could help? Her shoulders grew taut. Adam Hershberger, as their deacon, would soon come to the house to discuss how the community would assume the debts from hospital bills Naomi couldn't pay. She dreaded the moment when she'd have to admit she didn't have any assets other than the clothes on her back, a couple of vehicles and her animals. Saying that might bring questions of what had happened to the farm she and Marlin supposedly had purchased.

Ach, why had she listened when Marlin had insisted she didn't need to read the paperwork before signing it? So many questions could have been answered if she was able to pull images of those pages from her memory.

Those thoughts plagued her through the service, so she had to struggle to keep her attention on the sermons. Twice, she had to excuse herself and go into the small storage room that had been set aside for *mamms* of small *kinder*. She went once, bringing the twins with her, when May needed to be fed. The second time, she ended up changing the diapers for all three *kinder*. Her plans to potty train the twins had been interrupted by the move from Honey Brook.

Though she missed more of the service than she attended, Naomi was glad she'd come. She enjoyed watching Jared and Jesse play with other little ones while the women prepared and served the meal following the service. When she had a chance to sit and watch the boys eat their sandwiches with church spread—marshmallow cream and peanut butter—she listened to the women talk about events during the past two weeks. She appreciated the reassurances that when *Daed* came home, she'd have the help she needed. In the meantime, prayers offered eased the weight on her heart. These people were *gut*. She couldn't let herself forget that as she had when her memories had become mired in the cruel capers perpetrated by Samuel and his friends.

When the last of the dishes were washed, they were stored in the bench wagon so it could be moved to where services would be held in two weeks. Both twins were yawning. Leading them toward where the buggies were parked in front of the barn, she heard her name called.

"Laurene," she said as she looked over her shoulder, "I didn't think you were coming today. How is your great-*aenti*?"

Her friend, who carried a large plastic container, smiled. "She's feeling better. I think she overdid it in the heat yesterday. She was at the inn supervising the contractor she hired to rebuild it. She says he's the best in the area, but still she feels she needs to keep a close eye on him."

"I'm glad to hear she's okay."

"How's your *daed*?"

Naomi gave her friend a quick update, ending with, "I hope he'll be home by the middle of the week."

"If you need anything, don't hesitate to ask. I saw how much help *Aenti* Sylvia needed when she was in her wheelchair, and your *daed* will need more."

"I'll let you know."

"Don't try to do it all on your own." Laurene's voice became stern. "I know you'll run yourself ragged because you don't like to ask for help."

"I'm going to have to now." As soon as she spoke the trite words, she knew they were true. What lay ahead for *Daed* and the whole family was going to be like nothing else they'd ever faced.

"*Gut*. I'm glad you're going to be sensible." Her friend's smile returned as she looked at the twins. "*Aenti* Sylvia sent me over with cookies for the singing tonight. Adam is going to be one of the adults there, so she made his favorite coconut cookies. I'm supposed to make sure he gets at least one. Do you know anyone else who might want a cookie? I seem to remember two boys who liked *Aenti* Sylvia's cookies when they were with me a few days ago."

"Cookies?" asked Jesse, hope in his voice.

"Fun!" asserted his brother.

Squatting, Laurene opened the top of the container, which was large enough to hold a multilayer cake.

"One each," Naomi said.

Laurene laughed. "You've never gotten by with just one of my *mamm*'s or my great-*aenti*'s cookies."

"True." Smiling, she said, "All right, boys. You can each have two. One for each hand." As they shoved each other to be the first to select cookies, she frowned. "Remember your manners."

The twins looked at each other, which was *gut* because Laurene was trying not to smile at their antics and failing. As one, they turned to Naomi.

"*Mamm*, cookie?" asked Jared, again the leader.

Jesse pointed at Laurene. "Cookie lady!" He put on an endearing smile Naomi didn't believe for a moment. "Cookie lady, cookie? Please?"

"*Ja,*" Laurene replied, her lips still twitching. "You heard your *mamm*. You may each have two."

The boys looked at the cookies, then frowned.

Laurene sat across from them. "They're coconut. Do you like coconut?"

Jared reached for a cookie, then drew his hand back. He looked to his twin.

Jesse stretched out a finger toward different cookies in turn. "Jesse's cookies. Jared's cookies. No *Mamm* cookie?"

"Where *Mamm* cookie?" Jared asked.

Touched by their concern, Naomi took a cookie. "How's that?"

"Jesse's cookies. Jared's cookies." He gave her a big grin, the sight of his chipped tooth touching her heart. "*Mamm*'s cookie. May?"

"May no cookie," Jared said.

"No fun. May cookie." Jesse shot his brother a glance to show he'd gotten the last word.

Before they could go on and on in an effort to outdo each

other, Naomi said, "May is too young to eat cookies. Tell Laurene *danki* for the cookies."

Laurene couldn't hide her grin as the twins thanked her and Jesse added, "Jared cookies. Jesse cookies. *Mamm* cookie. *Boppli* no cookie. *Gut.*"

"Fun," his twin said before a big bite filled his mouth with coconut.

Naomi thanked her friend, who went to find Adam. She was glad Laurene hadn't asked her to go, because she didn't want to insult her friend. Naomi wanted to avoid any interaction with Adam Hershberger, who'd been instrumental in spreading the tale of how Samuel had kissed her all those years ago.

Get over it! she told herself, but she couldn't forgive herself for being lured into their stupid games again.

Suddenly, all she wanted to do was go home and find something to keep her too busy to think. Putting the *boppli* into the special carrier set on the buggy's front seat, she realized the twins, now covered with crumbs, were eagerly pointing at ducks floating on a nearby pond. She caught their eyes and shook her head.

For a moment they deflated, but then they ran toward a cat sunning itself near the barn.

"Fun!" shouted Jared.

"Fun!" echoed his brother.

"Not for that poor cat," Naomi muttered as she chased them, scooping one boy up in each arm. "Not fun for you," she added, setting the boys on the ground, "if that kitty scratches you."

The twins looked at her with furrowed brows as they tried to figure out what she meant.

"Remember the cat that snarled at you and scratched your hand, Jesse?"

"Owie!" The little boy moaned and clutched his hand.

"Cats can be tough to deal with," said Samuel from behind her.

How had she missed the sound of his uneven steps and the soft thud of his cane against the ground? She wanted to sigh at the thought of how close she'd come to leaving without speaking with him.

Instead she said, "Boys, *komm mol.* It's time to go home."

"Can't you stay a bit longer?" Samuel asked as she herded the twins toward the buggy. "I thought the boys might want to go fishing."

"We don't have any poles."

"Easily remedied." He pulled out a pocketknife. "A couple of short saplings and the string and hooks I've got in my other pocket, and ta-da! We'll have fishing poles." He grinned, and she wondered if it was the first time she'd seen a genuine smile on his face since she returned to her *daed*'s house. It was certainly the first time he'd offered a sincere smile in her direction.

She was amazed when a dimple appeared in his left cheek. It softened his face, but she wouldn't be fooled. No doubt, it'd been there when they were scholars. Then, she'd learned not to look at him because he'd seemed to take it as an invitation to cause more trouble for her. After he'd kissed her and spread rumors about how she'd initiated the kiss, she hadn't wanted to see him again.

Opening her mouth to say she hadn't changed her mind about taking the *kinder* home, she didn't have a chance before Jared announced, "Fishing? Fun!"

"*Ja,* fun!" his twin echoed, not to be outdone. "Fish, *Mamm*?"

"Do you know what fishing is?" she asked, then regretted her sharp tone.

Marlin had never done anything with his sons. When she'd suggested he might want to read the Bible to them as she did each evening, he hadn't given her the courtesy of an answer. Instead, he'd found his hat and left. He'd come home two days later smelling of alcohol and perfume.

Looking at their eager faces, she thought of how little time she'd had with them since *Daed*'s stroke. They'd spent one day with Laurene, and generous neighbors had watched them the other days. The only time she'd seen them had been first thing in the morning before she took the Morris Transport van to the hospital or when she came home to find them up later than their usual bedtime. She'd been wiped out by anxiety and flagging hope, barely able to keep up with their chatter while she gave May a bottle before falling into bed to try to sleep.

"Fun?" asked the boys at the same time.

She raised her eyes to Samuel. If she could trust him, she would have asked him to take them fishing while she went home with May... She didn't trust him with her most precious gifts from God.

His eyes narrowed, and she guessed he could discern her thoughts. She abruptly felt bad for accusing him of something he hadn't done. He'd never endangered any of the *kinder*, but she couldn't be like Laurene. She'd couldn't put the past behind her as her friend had.

She couldn't, could she?

A shiver sliced through her. Whether she could or not, she didn't want to. At the same time, she didn't want to disappoint her boys, who'd been so *gut* through the traumas of the past week.

"All right," she said, hoping she wasn't making the same mistake she'd made the night she'd let Samuel kiss her, "let's go fishing."

★ ★ ★

Samuel was surprised when Naomi agreed to his spur-of-the-moment offer. However, he wasn't surprised that, after she got the *boppli* from the buggy and took one twin by the hand and had the other twin hold his brother's hand, they were stopped time after time by the *Leit*. Offers of help and meals inundated her until she began to say *"Danki"* almost before the person finished speaking. Most of the questions about Elvin were asked by the men, so he assumed the women had satisfied their curiosity while sharing their meal.

If anyone was amazed to see him walking with Naomi's little family toward the creek, he saw no signs. Were they hiding their astonishment? *He* still couldn't believe she'd consented to bring the *kinder* fishing with him. He'd seen her struggle with the idea, but her love for the twins had convinced her, not Samuel.

He waited until they'd reached the line of trees edging the creek before he asked, "Are you okay?"

"Okay?" Confusion glittered in her eyes. "With what?"

"All that well-meaning kindness can be a bit overwhelming, ain't so?"

"I'd be ungrateful if I didn't appreciate it."

"You'd be honest you're running out of ways to express your thanks."

She smiled, and it was the first real smile he'd seen on her face that day. Her voice lightened as she said, "You're a scoundrel to think such things, let alone say them, Samuel King."

"I guess that makes you a scoundrel, too."

"So you're a mind reader now?"

"Far from it. I know what I'd be thinking if I were in your place."

When she didn't answer, he wondered if he'd said too much.

How could he presume to know what was on her mind when all her thoughts were focused on her family...and he didn't have one to call his own? To speak the truth—that he knew what she was thinking because he would have had similar thoughts if he had a family member to worry about—would sound pitiful, and he didn't want her pity.

In fact, he was glad she hadn't shown him any. Though he knew it was because she harbored anger toward him, that was, he'd decided, better than having her look at him as if he were nothing more than the wretched results of an accident. He forced the fingers on his right hand to spread. What once had been as simple as blinking now took effort. Not that he minded. He was grateful he still could draw a breath. Nobody had to tell him how close he'd come to dying the night the car had plowed into a telephone pole. Months later, when he could finally move well enough on his own, he'd gone back to the site of the accident. The damage to the telephone pole had been obvious from the road, but when he'd gone closer, he could see pieces of car driven into the wood.

Turning his attention to making the short fishing poles he'd envisioned for the twins, Samuel's appreciation for all Naomi did grew. The boys offered to help, and with that, it took him about three times as long as it would have if he'd cut the saplings and tied the strings on himself. He refused to let them use the knife or handle the hooks, but he showed them how to dig up worms from the grass in the cooler shadows. He chuckled at their squeals as he put the worms on their hooks and taught them how to drop the lines into the water at the edge of the creek.

Going to where Naomi was in the shade with little May, he sat beside her, resting his cane across his knees. He listened to bugs in the grass on the other side of the creek. He swatted a fly away. Leaning back against a stump, he watched as the twins slapped the water with their poles.

He chuckled. "I don't think they're going to catch many fish that way."

"They like to play in water." She looked up as she drew the empty bottle away from the *boppli* and set May against her shoulder.

When the infant burped loudly before Naomi patted her back, he laughed again. "That's a healthy sound."

"She's a little piglet, sucking in the *millich* as fast as she can. Of course, she draws in plenty of air, too."

"Can I burp her?"

Again he could see incredulity in her gaze. "She spits up sometimes."

He slipped off his *mutze* coat and held out his hands. "She can't hurt this shirt. It got stained one day when I was helping push a buggy out of the mud." He pointed to a brownish blotch that had been hidden beneath his black coat. "One more stain isn't going to make any difference."

"Have you burped a *boppli* before?"

"I've got six younger half-siblings," he replied, not wanting her to know how his mamm and stepdaed had done their best to keep him away from them. It'd been as if he'd been put under the *bann* from the moment he'd taken his first breath.

"All right," she said, shifting the *boppli* far enough away from her so he could grab the clean diaper she'd flung over her shoulder to protect her dress.

He draped the diaper over his right shoulder and carefully took little May from her. Knowing she was watching him as closely as a hawk did her nest, he settled the *boppli* against his shoulder. He drew in a deep breath of her sweet scent as he gently patted her back.

"Keep one hand at the base of her head so it won't wobble," Naomi urged.

Could he? He raised his right hand along the infant's back and let his palm cup her head. "Like that?"

"*Ja.* You—" She jumped to her feet and ran to the twins before they pushed each other into the water. Taking their hands, she brought them to sit in the shadows. "Enough fishing for now."

"Fun!" Jesse said, but yawned.

That set his twin to doing the same, and Jared barely managed to say "Fun" before his eyes closed.

By the time Samuel had finished burping May, she was asleep, too. He placed her on the diaper on the grass, and she stuck two fingers in her mouth.

"When did she start doing that?" he asked.

"Yesterday."

"My two youngest sisters used to do that. It's so cute."

"*Ja.*" She didn't add anything else, and the sounds of the insects seemed to rise in volume as all three *kinder* slept.

Tempted by the sultry afternoon to do the same, he forced his eyes to stay open. He'd been waiting for days to have the discussion he and Naomi needed to have. Now might be his only chance.

He rolled up one sleeve as he said, "Elvin will be coming home soon."

"In the next couple of days, I hope."

"I told you at the hospital I wanted to help."

"I know, and I appreciate you'll be in the shop."

He shook his head.

Her voice was puzzled. "You *won't* be in the shop? Are you quitting?"

"That's not what I meant." Sitting straighter, he looked

at her steadily. He saw fatigue and worry on her pretty face. Knowing he could ease both—even a little bit—he added, "I'll be working in the shop as I normally would, but I can help much more than that."

"Knowing I don't have to deal with customers will be a huge help. That's been a part I didn't—"

"Listen to me!" His voice was whetted, but he didn't raise it, not wanting to wake the *kinder*. His left hand grasped her shoulder, halting her. He shifted so he faced her and slowly brought up his right hand to her other shoulder. "Listen to me, Naomi. You need my help with Elvin once he's home."

"I've had lots of offers today. More than I know what to do with."

"I heard many of them. How many were offers to help during the night?" When she didn't give him a quick reply, he nodded. "I thought so. Lots of folks are willing to clean the house or bring a casserole, but you're going to need someone there to help Elvin at night with his most basic needs. Things he won't want his daughter to help him with. In addition, you're going to need my help to make sure he does his PT exercises."

"I can help him with that."

"Not as I can." His hands softened on her shoulders. He didn't want her to feel like a prisoner. He wanted her to listen. Really listen as if he wasn't the adult version of the kid who'd made her teen years a misery.

Seeing the uncertainty in her eyes, he sighed. What right did he have to ask her to trust him when he'd done everything possible to show her how untrustworthy he could be?

"'Withhold not good from them to whom it is due, when it is in the power of thine hand to do it,'" he murmured as he tried to find words of his own to help persuade her.

"Proverbs 3:27."

"Ja." He'd known she'd be able to cite the book and verse of the quote, and, for the first time, it didn't bother him as it had before. For the first time, he realized it was her way of confirming what he'd said. "I can help, Naomi. What Elvin is going to go through, I've been through. I know what it's like to have your body refuse to do the simplest tasks, to feel as if you've been betrayed by your own limbs. He'll be angry, as I was, at everyone, as well as furious with himself and God. He'll wonder, too, why he has to endure more pain and indignity than he already has. At night, when he can't sleep and a thousand thoughts fly through his head, I'll know what each one will be because I've had those same thoughts myself. Thoughts of not wanting to be a burden on anyone—"

"Daed will never be a burden. Not to me."

"You know that, Naomi. I know that. Even Elvin knows that, but there will be times when he doesn't believe it. When he won't let himself believe it because he sees how tired everyone is. He'll feel as if he's let everyone down because he can't master the next challenge in front of him."

"He eventually will. I know my *daed.* He'll keep going until he does what he's set out to do."

"Then the process will start all over again. The hopes, the disappointments, the self-doubts slithering like serpents through your brain. It's not a one-time set of circumstances. There are no quick fixes for the recovery ahead of your *daed.* Those snakes keep slithering back over and over and over." He sighed and released her, leaning back against the tree. "It never ends."

"It hasn't ended for you?"

"No." He raised his right hand and tried to bend his fingers into a fist. Only two did as he'd hoped. "See? I'm still working toward being able to do what I used to do." Lowering his hand, he said, "Let me help, Naomi. I owe Elvin more than I can ever repay for taking a chance on me."

For a long moment, she didn't answer. He could come up with the many reasons she'd say no, but he could as easily think of ones why she should, especially because he was right. The best way to help her beloved *daed* was to accept his offer. It wouldn't change anything between Naomi and himself, but their damaged relationship wasn't the crux of the matter. Elvin's future was.

She must have realized that, too, because she said, "All right, but if there's a hint of funny business or I hear about you gossiping about my family, you're done. Not only with helping *Daed* but with working for him."

He knew she thought that was a harsh standard he never could achieve, but she hadn't let him show her the man he'd become. At last, he'd have the way to prove he wasn't the horrible boy he'd been and maybe—just maybe—she'd acknowledge the truth, too.

Chapter Eleven

"*Mamm*, fun!" Jesse gave Naomi a big grin on Tuesday morning as he splashed both hands in the water on the table at once.

"Fun, fun, fun," his brother repeated in rhythm with his splattering water in every direction.

"I see that." She ran a dishcloth between them, soaking up the water Jared had spilled when he decided not to wait for Naomi to come and refill his cup. Fortunately he hadn't tried to add *millich* to his cereal.

Giving the clock over the stove a quick glance, she realized she had time for a cup of *kaffi* and a piece of toast before the Morris Transport van arrived to take her to the hospital. Her hopes *Daed* would come home yesterday had been for naught, and the nurses said it would be more likely he'd be staying a few more nights until they got his vital signs more stable.

She didn't bother with cream or sugar as she took a deep drink of the black *kaffi*. How long would it take for the caffeine to make her feel like she wasn't sleepwalking? She had to look rested and upbeat when she stepped into the room *Daed* had been moved to after leaving the ICU.

"Where do you two get all your energy?" she asked as she peeled a banana and gave half to each boy.

"Fun, *Mamm!*" was their answer in unison, which made them giggle before they began to eat their halves of the banana. They squished the fruit between their fingers and laughed as they licked it off.

Naomi checked on May, who was fascinated with her right foot. Like her fingers, she was zealous in tasting it. Rubbing the little girl's belly, which seemed to please the *kind* as it had the boys, Naomi said, "You'll be joining them in causing me all sorts of trouble in no time, ain't so?"

May wiggled in her carrier, but a motion through the window caught Naomi's attention.

Samuel walked toward the shop with his uneven rhythm, his cane matching his motions with the ease of years of practice. What must it be like to be unable to trust your body? She shivered as she imagined the struggle ahead for *Daed*, who couldn't stand without someone assisting him. Would *Daed* be able to walk again or feed himself or get in and out of bed on his own? She tried to imagine caring for three *kinder* and her *daed*, as well as keeping his buggy business running.

God, show me how You are here to guide me. I can't let my faith flag. Not now. Not when I'm so alone and so responsible for everything.

As she opened her eyes at the end of her prayer, which never stopped as it replayed in her mind, she noticed Samuel hadn't spared a glance at the main section of the house. Even so, she backed away from the window. Had she made a mistake when she agreed he could help *Daed*? If it had been anyone else, such an offer would have been a *wunderbaar* example of God's grace. The offer hadn't come someone else. It'd come from Samuel King.

God, if I'm making a horrible error, don't let Daed *suffer for it.* Honesty compelled her to add, *If Samuel's help is Your will, forgive me for not seeing that.*

Hearing automobile wheels slowing in front of the house, Naomi whirled. The clock said she still had more than twenty minutes before the van was supposed to arrive. Celesta Umble, the teen who lived on the neighboring farm and was taking care of the twins and May while Naomi went to the hospital today, hadn't shown up yet. Delaying the transport van could have repercussions all day long because each pickup would be late.

Ask Samuel to come in and watch the kinder *until Celesta arrives.*

She turned to the back door, hoping he'd hear her call across the yard before he began work. A knock on the front door halted her.

A knock? Keith Morris beeped his horn when someone was slow coming out. She'd witnessed that a couple of the days he'd taken her to Lancaster.

Rushing to the front door, she threw it open and stared at Skylar Lopez, who regarded her with anger. The woman wore a bright red tank top over denim shorts. The streak in her hair matched her shirt and her vibrant lipstick. She wore red-rimmed eyeglasses shaped like cat eyes.

"Caught you!" Ms. Lopez fisted her hands on her hips. "I'm tired of you avoiding me."

"I haven't been avoiding you. My *daed* has been ill."

Ms. Lopez regarded her. "Is he as ill as our mother who's going to die if she doesn't get that bone marrow transplant?"

"He's had a stroke."

She opened her mouth, then closed it so hard and fast Naomi heard her teeth click. "I'm sorry. I didn't know."

"I know you didn't. I should have called you. I'm sorry. I haven't—"

"I understand."

Naomi heard the truth in those words. Ms. Lopez understood what it was like to deal with a gravely ill parent.

She moved aside. "Do you want to *komm* in? I can't talk long. The van is coming to take me to the hospital in Lancaster."

Taking a single step inside, Ms. Lopez glanced around the room, clearly curious about the interior of a plain house. She faced Naomi. "I'm sorry to push this, but I have to. Have you spoken to your father about taking the DNA test?"

"No. I didn't have a chance." The ice cutting through her was because she wasn't being honest. She'd had plenty of time to speak with him, but hadn't found the right time.

"Mrs. Ropp—"

"Naomi, please. We don't like to use titles."

"Okay, whatever. Call me Skylar. Using Lopez reminds me of that cheating creep I dumped. Happiest day of my life was when I signed those divorce papers."

Naomi knew she'd have more sympathy for the young woman. She could commiserate about a faithless spouse, though she wasn't about to air her own dirty laundry. If *Daed* learned the truth, it could upset him, and the hospital staff had been adamant about one thing. He had to avoid stress during his recovery.

"How soon can you talk with your father about this?" Skylar asked, pushing her glasses up her nose.

"It's not a matter of how soon. It's a matter of why I should upset him over something that doesn't make any sense." Her words came out sharper than she'd intended. "I can't be your missing half sister. Don't you think my own *daed* would know the truth about his daughter?"

"Maybe he's lying."

"My parents have always been honest with me, as they were with each other. It's probably the thing I've admired most about them. Their honesty."

"Something doesn't add up." Now Skylar seemed to be talking more to herself than to Naomi. "Your birthday is right around the baby's birthday. You live in this community. It all holds together."

From the kitchen came excited shouts from the twins and a cheerful *"Gute mariye!"* in Celesta's chirpy voice. At the same instant, Naomi saw the white van pulling in next to Skylar's car.

"Look," she said, "that's my ride. I've got to go."

"I can drive you to the hospital," Skylar argued. "Then we'll talk to your father."

"No." She shook her head. "His *doktors* have emphasized nothing must upset him while he's fragile." She sighed. "I'm praying for your *mamm*, Skylar, and for you. I hope you find the person you're looking for."

"I *have* found the person I'm looking for, and it's you. I don't know why you won't agree to be tested."

"My *daed* didn't give me permission."

"You said he had a stroke. Can he talk?"

"Not much yet, but he's getting better every day."

Skylar stamped out the door, before turning. "My mother doesn't have time to wait for your father to get well enough to tell you it's okay to do what anyone with a heart would do. You're a grown woman! You're older than I am, and I don't have to get Daddy's permission to do something."

"My *daed* is the head of our household, and—"

"My mother may die, " Skylar snarled, "because you cling to your old-fashioned ways of believing a woman doesn't have the ability to make up her own mind."

"I can make up my own mind, but this is too important to do without speaking with my *daed*."

"So speak with him."

"I will. As soon as I can without endangering him. I promise."

Skylar eyed her up and down, then sighed. "I guess that's the best I can hope for now. I know you're going to keep that promise because I'm sure you people would think it's a sin if you don't. I can give you a few more days because we're still waiting to hear from the private detective we hired. If he can't come up with any other info, you've got to ask your father. You've got to!" Tears spilled from her eyes, dragging her eyeliner with them. Rather than looking garish, the thinning makeup made her more vulnerable.

Naomi's heart went out to the younger woman. She wanted to see her *mamm* well as Naomi longed to have *Daed* on his feet, but Skylar was asking for the impossible. Naomi couldn't be the person Skylar sought, and bothering *Daed* could jeopardize his recovery. Yet, somehow, she felt like there was something she must do to help. She'd ask *Daed* about Skylar's search. Not about Naomi being the missing *kind*, but that a *kind* adopted around the time Naomi was born needed to be found. Who knew? Maybe mentioning the search to her *daed* would jog his memory, and he'd be able to point Skylar in the right direction.

It wasn't much to hope for, but it was all she had.

"*Du rei do*, Samuel?" came a call from the doorway of the shop.

"*Ja*, I'm in here." Samuel looked up from the seat he was

patching and motioned for Adam Hershberger to come into the shop.

"How's Elvin doing?"

"As well as can be expected." He glanced at the house. "Naomi has been visiting him at the hospital each day and hopes she can bring him home. That hasn't happened yet. He's had a couple of small setbacks with test results that didn't match what the *doktors* hoped for with him. They're talking about him coming home by week's end."

"Having him here will be a challenge."

"*Ja.*" He set the awl he'd been using to pierce the leather on the seat and wiped his hands on his trousers. Palming sweat off his forehead because the humidity was rising by the hour, he said, "She's agreed to let me help with his physical therapy, using what I learned during mine."

"I'm glad to hear that." He sighed. "It's going to take the efforts of the whole community and others beyond our district to pay for his hospital bills and care now. With all the fires we had this spring, any money put aside for emergencies has already been tapped."

"Are you still planning on rebuilding the old chicken barn here?"

"We will, but we pushed that project back to put in a few days' labor to help Sylvia Nolt at her inn. She's provided the materials, so we only need to lend her a hand in getting the new kitchen and rooms above it framed. We're having the workday a week from this Saturday."

"Count me in. I can swing a hammer with my left hand." He held it up and flexed his fingers. "I'll let Naomi know about the delay. She's sure to understand Elvin would want to be here to oversee the project."

"That's what I thought." Adam hesitated, then said, "None

of that is why I came over this morning. I came to tell you your youngest sister has run away."

"Kara?"

"*Ja*. She seems to have jumped the fence."

Samuel swallowed hard. His youngest sister couldn't be more than fifteen. No, she'd be sixteen because she'd been born in early June. Unlike when he'd left, *Mamm* and his step-*daed* must be devastated and fearful of what a young, naive girl like Kara would face in the *Englisch* world. Bitterness rose like bile in his throat. No doubt, they'd blame him for setting the example of abandoning his family, though, in truth, his family had abandoned him long before.

Not his two youngest sisters. They'd trailed him like adorable puppies. Now Kara had followed him in leaving the plain life.

"Have you spoken to her?" he asked.

"I tried, but she said she didn't want to talk to me. However, something she said makes me think she'll talk to you."

"What?"

"She said you'd understand why better than anyone else." Adam's brows lowered. "Has she contacted you?"

He shook his head. "No, and I can't imagine why she would. *Mamm* refused to let me back in our house after I returned. Kara was young when I left with Joel. I may have seen her once or twice at a mud sale or some other event since I got back, but if she said more than hello to me, I don't remember it."

"Too bad you don't have Naomi's memory. You'd be able to call up the facts like that." He snapped his fingers.

"*Ja*, but you're not dealing with Naomi. You're stuck with me."

"You're the person we need. You've left Bliss Valley and

you've come back. Maybe you can persuade her to do the same."

"I'd try if I knew where she was."

"She's working at the ice cream shop in Strasburg. I've tried going back to talk with her, but she avoids me. She must have the other employees keeping an eye out for me because she's in the back room or on break or 'not available.'" He made air quotes with his fingers. "I was able to talk to one of the other kids, who said she usually works the closing shift."

"You remember how it was, Adam. We dreaded running into the deacon and getting a lecture about how every member of the *Leit* is vital to the community."

He chuckled without any humor. "*Ja*, I remember those conversations well. I don't know about you, but I was terrified of the idea of the deacon finding me and marching me home to *Grossdawdi* Ephraim."

Samuel arched his brows.

"Okay, I get it," Adam said with another laugh. "Your sister sees me the same way we did the old deacon. Do you think she'll talk to you?"

"Maybe she'll talk to me. Maybe she won't."

"Would she talk to Naomi?"

The question astounded Samuel. "I don't know."

"You don't know whether Kara would talk to Naomi or whether Naomi would help?"

"No, Naomi would help." He laughed without mirth. "Not on my behalf, but because she won't want to see my sister making what could be a huge mistake."

"Laurene said much the same thing." He leaned his elbow on the door's molding. "If you'd rather, I can ask Naomi."

"Do you think she's more likely to listen to you than to me?"

With a sigh, Adam said, "I was hoping she'd forget I was that awful kid long enough to let me talk to her as the deacon."

"Naomi doesn't forget anything. Not a word, not an action, not anything."

"*Forget* was the wrong word. I'm asking if you think she can put aside her anger long enough to listen and help."

"She will. Not for you or me, but for Kara."

He sighed again. "I'd prefer for us to talk about atonement and forgiveness, but I can work with this."

"Give her time, Adam."

"I will, but I know this bothers Laurene. She wants her best friend to put the past behind her as Laurene has."

"You want to keep your soon-to-be wife happy."

"Happy wife, happy life. At least that's what I've heard people say."

"Probably some truth in that." Was that why everyone in his family had followed *Mamm*'s lead and turned their backs on him as soon as they were old enough to listen to her comments about how he'd ruined her life? Early in the days when his step*daed* had been walking out with *Mamm*, Ernest Slabaugh had been kind to Samuel. That all changed after they were married.

The rest of the afternoon, Samuel debated how best to approach Naomi with his request. It had taken him several days to find the optimal way to convince her she needed his help with Elvin.

Shadows were stretching deeply into the shop when the white van drove up the farm lane. Putting away his tools, Samuel walked out into the yard. The day's heat wasn't leaving as the sun dropped toward the western horizon, and the windows in the house were open to let in any whisper of moving air. Hearing a thin cry from the house, he saw the Umble girl picking up May to comfort her.

He wasn't sure why Naomi hadn't arranged for the girl to stay overnight. She must be wiped out after a day at the hospital. Samuel had gone two days with her, and he'd been relieved to return to work instead of sitting in the hospital room and trying to pretend as if everything was going to be fine as soon as Elvin came home. He knew it wouldn't be, and Naomi knew that, too, though he wouldn't have guessed that by her optimism and easy smiles with her *daed*.

For a moment, he let his gaze linger on the house. To have a home of his own with a family was a dream he'd forfeited the night he'd gotten behind the wheel drunk. How could he trust himself not to make a stupid decision again? If he'd known then the emptiness that filled his soul, would he have blithely been so *dumm*? That night, neither he nor Joel could have imagined how their lives would be altered in seconds. He wondered if, through God's providence, he could go back in time to confront himself, how much he would have listened to his own advice. Back then, the two of them had thought they were invincible and knew more than anyone in the world. Too bad, it'd been the opposite.

They hadn't known anything.

"Just finishing up?" Naomi asked as she walked past him toward the house.

"*Ja.*" He fell into step with her, glad she slowed her pace so he could keep up. "How's Elvin doing today?"

"The same. Annoyed at his inability to do what he believes he should be able to do and giving the nurses and *doktorfraas* sassy smiles to make them grin."

"He can be a charmer when he wants to be."

"I'm glad something about him hasn't changed."

He nodded, then realized she wasn't looking at him but at the house. What did she see when she gazed at it? A past when her *daed* and *mamm* were alive and she was a young *kind*, not yet being subjected to the heartless pranks he and his friends had dispensed upon her?

"Naomi?" he asked as they neared the kitchen door. After hours of pondering how he should ask her, he said, "I need a big favor."

"What is it?"

As he explained what Adam had told him, he watched dismay wipe despair from her face. Samuel had been right when he told his friend Naomi would put aside her feelings about him to help his sister.

"She's working at the ice cream shop in Strasburg?" she asked when he finished. "That's right in the center of town by the stoplight."

"I know."

"When do you plan to talk to her?"

"That's the favor I wanted to ask. I don't know if she'll talk to me. Adam says she's evading him, and it's possible she'll do the same with me. However, she doesn't know you so you may be able to convince her to talk to you. Will you go with me tomorrow to see her?"

"I need to spend time with *Daed* tomorrow. His physical therapist wants me to watch his session."

"Afterward?"

"If Celesta can stay to watch the *kinder*, I'll go with you. You may be right. Your sister might feel more comfortable talking to another woman, especially someone who isn't going to pressure her." She folded her arms in front of her and lifted her chin in her most determined pose. "I won't pressure her,

Samuel. I'll listen, and if she asks for my advice, I'll give it. Nothing more."

"That's all I ask. If you can persuade her to talk to me, I may be able to keep her from making a mess of her life as I made of mine." He touched her elbow, trying to ignore the sizzle that uncurled along his fingertips as they brushed her soft skin. All he could offer her was a living, walking, talking reminder of the worst years of her life. "*Danki*, Naomi. I owe you more than I can say."

"Let's not start adding up who owes whom what. You're helping me with *Daed*, and I'm helping you with your sister..."

"Kara. Her name is Kara Slabaugh."

"We'll do our best, and let's leave it at that." Opening the back door, she went inside. It closed, a firm reminder she had no place in her life for him.

Which was for the best, he told himself. Maybe if he repeated it a million times, he'd start to believe it.

Maybe.

Chapter Twelve

Downtown Strasburg was quite busy the next evening. *Englisch* schools were finishing their year, so families were swarming to Lancaster County for a vacation. The tourists, who had spent their day driving through the plain farmland or had finished their visit to the train museum at the eastern edge of town, wandered among the shops and restaurants. The earliest buildings had been standing when George Washington and his men wintered at Valley Forge, forty-five miles to the northeast. Beautiful brick townhouses had been built around the time the first routes of the Underground Railroad had been established through Lancaster County. From its center, the town spread in both directions along the railroad line and beside country roads.

The heart of the borough was its main intersection, where the stoplight kept traffic in check. Nobody but tourists paid any attention when a plain buggy was in line for the light to turn green. An antique store and a pizza shop shared one building and claimed a corner. A bank and a quilt shop were kitty-corner from each other on two other corners. The last corner held the Strasburg Creamery, where customers were still lined up though it was past seven o'clock.

From the passenger side of the buggy, Naomi saw people fanning themselves as the sun beat on them. The day had been as hot as midsummer, and not a breath of air had eased the rapidly escalating temperatures. Beads of sweat popped out on her brow when Samuel drew in the horse at the stoplight.

"At least when we're moving, there's a breeze," she said.

"I'm glad we didn't come tomorrow." He held the reins taut so the horse wouldn't get in his head to go around the cars in front of them and through the intersection. "I wouldn't want to be out in the thunderstorms that are going to break this heat."

She glanced at the sky. It was a perfect blue without a hint of clouds. "We may have to wait a day or two for that storm."

"It'll be here by tomorrow morning." He tapped his right knee. "This is never wrong. Since the accident, I'm more accurate with the forecast than any weather service. It started aching two days ago, a sure sign of rain within the next forty-eight hours."

"I thought such things were old wives' tales."

"So did I until I realized what was happening." His hand tightened on the reins as a big truck rushed past, startling the horse and the pedestrians waiting for the walk signal. "It seems any of us can be wrong in our assumptions. Of course, now that we've talked about it, you'll never make that mistake again, ain't so?"

She gasped. Just when she thought it might actually be possible he was the changed man he claimed to be, he reacted to a simple comment so cruelly.

Wishing she was brave enough—or *dumm* enough—to jump out of the buggy as it began moving again, she pondered for a moment whether it would be worse to risk herself or remain in the buggy with someone who taunted her as he used to do. She closed her eyes and prayed, asking for the strength to let Samuel's insults slide away like a fried egg out of a greased pan. She shouldn't judge him when he was on edge.

He must have realized how his words had sounded because he said, "I'm sorry, Naomi. Seems that no matter how difficult it is for me to move my feet, I still can put my foot in my mouth as easily as I ever did. I didn't mean that the way it sounded. I know it can't be easy never to be able to forget anything."

"It isn't, but I don't need your sympathy, Samuel King." She wasn't ready to let him off the hook yet. So weary that all she wanted to do was go home, hug her *kinder* and fall into bed, she had no patience with him. "I'm fine exactly the way God made me."

"You are. Again, all I can say is I'm sorry. What I said came out wrong. Everything seems wrong today."

Her shoulders drooped, and she nodded. With so much on their minds, it felt as if there wasn't enough space to weigh words before they rushed past their lips.

"I'm sorry, too," she said. "We're stuck in a tough place right now. In the middle. Neither moving forward nor backward, just in a neutral space while waiting for the world to start turning again. *Daed* isn't home and well, and your sister needs help to decide what to do with her life."

"She needs to go home."

"We know that, but until she does, nobody is going to be able to convince her."

"I don't want her to learn her lessons the hard way as I did."

"I agree." She sighed and stared at the light in front of them. "No wonder we're on edge. Let's call a truce."

"I didn't realize we were at war."

"You know what I mean."

"I do." He slapped the reins to urge the horse forward as the light changed, driving straight through the intersection and past one side of the building where the ice cream shop was located. He put on the turn indicator for a left-hand turn. As soon as the traffic had cleared, he pulled into a parking lot behind the building and drove to where another buggy stood by a hitching pole. Many *Englisch* businesses provided buggy and car parking for their clientele.

Pushing the brake so the buggy didn't hit the horse as it stopped, Samuel went on as if there hadn't been any interruption in their conversation, "I do know what you mean, and I agree. We need to forget our pasts. At least for now. We've got to focus on helping members of our family grasp on to their futures."

"*Ja.*" She blinked several times, amazed at how succinct he'd made her beleaguered thoughts. "It won't be easy to let go of the past." She frowned as he opened his mouth.

He laughed. "You thought I was about to say something snarky, ain't so?"

"Snarky?"

"A word used by *Englischers*. It means something sarcastic and annoying at the same time."

"A *gut* word...for you." She smiled.

"Odd, I was thinking *snarky* fit you quite well." He chuckled again. "That's a prime example of using the word *snarky*."

"We've gotten off the subject."

When his smile fell, Naomi was sorry she'd reminded him why they'd made the twenty-minute drive into Strasburg. She startled herself as much as she did him when she reached out and took his hand that was resting on his leg.

"It's going to be all right. Remember my *daed*'s favorite Bible verse? 'And we know that all things work together for good to them that love God, to them who are the called according to His purpose.'"

"Romans 8:28." He arched his brows, the left one pulling to an odd angle because of his scar.

She gave him a wry smile. "I can see how me doing that is annoying."

"But not snarky." He squeezed her hand gently. "*Danki* for reminding me God is in charge here. What happens—whether Kara will listen to you or talk to me—is in His hands."

Her gaze was caught by his, and she couldn't look away. No, she didn't *want* to look away. His eyes, the color of a stormy sky, appeared more serene than she'd ever seen them. How could that be?

As if she'd asked that question aloud, he murmured, "I'm going to try to keep my emotions in check when we go in the shop. I don't want to spook Kara, and I know I'm not likely to have a second chance."

Knowing the best thing to say was nothing, she got out of the buggy. She smoothed her black apron over her pale yellow dress with shaking fingers. Samuel was depending on her as she was relying on him to be there for *Daed*. They had their plan to approach his sister, and she prayed it wouldn't go awry.

Naomi walked with Samuel toward the white porch on the back of the building. A few tables had been set in the parking lot to take advantage of the sunshine, but it was too hot to sit out there. She opened the door.

It took a moment for her eyes to adjust to the dimness after the bright sunshine. To her right, she heard customers ordering their ice cream, but directly in front of her and to her left shelves offered knickknacks and handicrafts for sale. Booklets vied for space with jars of candy. She saw tiny plain buggies among miniature steam engines.

"This way," Samuel said behind her as he pointed to the right. "She's scooping ice cream." He gestured to a girl who looked younger than the others. "That's Kara."

She steadied herself. "I'm assuming we're going to get ice cream. I've driven past this place more times than I can count, but I've never been inside."

"So you've never had their ice cream?"

"No, and I've got to admit I'm curious what keeps such a steady parade of *Englischers* coming through the shop's doors."

"The ice cream is delicious. It's got so high a cream content that it melts slowly, even on the hottest days." A smile flicked across his lips, then vanished. "Today is a *gut* day to test that." Reaching into his pocket, he pulled out his wallet. He handed her a twenty. "Get me a hot-fudge sundae and whatever you want."

"You want me to order? I thought you wanted to talk to your sister—"

"If she sees me, she may scurry away as she did with Adam."

She didn't say anything, knowing how uncertain he must be. Would his sister speak with him? If she did, would she listen to his advice? Naomi took the money he held out. Was his hand shaking or hers...or both? She hadn't guessed he intended her to approach Kara by herself.

Naomi went to the end of the line of customers waiting to place their orders. From the corner of her eye, she noticed Samuel slipping into the booth farthest from the front door. A display carousel of brochures on the area half hid him from the long counter, and anyone behind it would have to peer into the shadows to discover who sat there. The teens were so busy preparing orders that she doubted most of them looked past the counter often.

The line moved too quickly and too slowly. She had more time than she wanted to think about what she'd say to Kara, but the moment she reached the counter, she had to find the right words. Watching the staff, she realized each teen worked with one customer at a time, no matter how many items were ordered. She counted the people ahead of her and the number of teens to figure out how she could get to the counter so Kara would take her order. She paid no attention to the odd looks she got when she motioned two parties ahead of her. When one of the teens disappeared into the back, throwing off her count, she waited until her position again matched Kara's.

Kara Slabaugh looked fragile, but it was an illusion. Naomi watched her dig into the containers of hard ice cream, working as hard as any of the others. She moved concisely, not a motion wasted. Her expression said she was focused on her tasks, but she smiled when she handed a dish or cone to a customer.

Naomi clasped her hands behind her back so nobody could see how they shook when Kara stepped in front of her on the other side of the counter.

"What would you like today?" the girl asked.

"Do you have any strawberry ice cream, Kara?"

The girl's eyes, the same odd shade of gray as her brother's, widened. Puzzled, she asked, "Do I know you?"

"No, but I know you." She kept her voice even. "Or more precisely, I know your brother."

"You can tell Lewis that—"

"Not Lewis. Samuel."

The girl's face paled to the shade of the vanilla ice cream. "Is he here?"

"*Ja*. Right there." She gestured toward where Samuel was pretending to be interested in brochures about escorted tours through Amish farms.

"*That's* Samuel?"

Naomi flinched at the girl's shocked tone. From where they stood, the scar on the left side of his face was barely visible, and no other signs of his injuries could be discerned. So what was bothering his sister?

Again it was as if she'd asked the question out loud. Kara said, "I remember him being much taller."

"When did you see him last?"

"Almost ten years ago."

Smiling in spite of herself, Naomi said, "You probably weren't more than four or five then."

"Six!" She raised her chin.

"I'm sorry. People used to think I was much younger, too. It comes with being short."

Kara's tremulous smile returned. "It happens all the time. I almost didn't get this job because the boss thought I was too young to apply."

"*Mamm* told me someday I'd be glad I looked younger, but I didn't care then." Naomi smiled. "I wanted people to stop treating me like a *kind*."

"Exactly." She laughed. "You understand."

"Not really because I don't understand why you're behind the counter when your brother is waiting to talk with you."

"Maybe I don't want to talk to him."

"If you didn't, you could have gone into the back the moment you realized he was here. Won't you *komm* and talk with him?"

"I don't know him."

"You know one important thing. He jumped the fence.

Have you considered that the reasons you've left and why he left might not be that different?"

She stared at Naomi for a long minute, before turning to one of her coworkers. "Buck, I'm taking my break now."

"Now?" A gangly teen rushed over. "Kara, did you see the line?"

"Five minutes. Okay?"

He looked from Kara to Naomi, and comprehension flashed through his eyes. "Five minutes. No longer."

Wondering what Kara had told her coworkers, Naomi waited until the girl came around the counter. Together they walked to the booth. She wasn't surprised when Samuel didn't get up. She guessed he wanted to talk to his sister before revealing the extent of the damage done by the car accident. Odd how Samuel never mentioned what had happened other than there had been a crash and he'd ended up in the hospital.

Kara sat next to Naomi in the booth. The girl was stick thin, and Naomi had to wonder if she'd been eating well since leaving home. She kept her questions to herself, not wanting to waste a second of the time Kara had been given.

"She's got five minutes," she said, hoping Samuel could say all he needed to in such a short time.

"All right." He folded his arms on the table. "So let's get right to it. What are you doing here, Kara?"

His sister puffed up like a cobra getting ready to strike, but Naomi could see tears in her eyes. "Why are you of all people asking me that? *You* jumped the fence when you were not much older than I am."

"I did, but it was a mistake."

She sniffed. "You say that now, but you didn't back then."

"I don't want you to make the same mistakes I did."

"Trust me. Any mistakes I have made or will make in the future will be mine and mine alone."

"You may think that, but everything you do has an impact on someone else." His eyes shifted toward Naomi, then quickly away. "Sometimes you know that. Sometimes you don't, but it doesn't matter. The outcome can be the same."

"Are you saying," Naomi asked in a voice only a breath above a whisper, "that unintended consequences are the same as intended ones? That it doesn't matter whether we meant what we were doing or it was by mistake?"

Naomi's question hung in the air. Samuel knew she and his sister were waiting for him to answer it, but like too many aspects of his life, it was doomed to failure. He didn't have an answer.

"What I mean," he said, choosing his words with incredible care, "is that we shouldn't be judged the same for mistakes we made as *kinder* as we are as adults. Isn't that what growing up means? Learning to see the results of one's actions and words before acting?"

"I'm grown-up," Kara insisted. "More grown-up than any of you seem to think. Because I'm the *boppli* of the family doesn't mean I'm a *boppli* any longer." Her voice caught. "I'm tired of being treated like I don't know anything."

"No one means to do that," he said. "I'm available if you need to talk."

Kara put her hands over her ears. "I don't need to talk. That's all anyone's been doing. The deacon, both ministers, *Mamm* and *Daed*. They've *komm* here and asked to talk to me. I didn't talk to them because I know what they're going to say. I need to come home and be a *gut* daughter and live the life they've chosen for me. I don't want to talk to them."

"You agreed to talk to me."

"I did, didn't I?" She looked as surprised as he'd felt when Naomi had come to the booth with Kara. "Maybe because I was curious what you'd have to say. After all, you left."

"I came back."

"I'd heard that." She glanced toward the line of customers snaking through the front door. "I should get back to work."

"It hasn't been five minutes yet."

"Almost." She pushed out of the booth. "Like I said, I don't want to talk."

"What *do* you want?" asked Naomi, putting her hand on his sister's arm. Not to hold her in place, but to create a connection between them. How he wished he could do that as easily as she did!

Kara didn't hesitate. "I want time to think about what I want my life to be."

"If you need a place to think things over, our *dawdi haus* is going to be empty." She didn't look at Samuel as she went on, "Now that your brother is going to be living in the main house to help my *daed*, who recently had a stroke, it's just sitting there. You might as well use it."

Had Naomi lost her mind? His *mamm* and step*daed* had closed their door to him. If he took in Kara when she was rebelling, they'd disown him.

How would that be any different? the logical side of his brain demanded. *What if you're able to convince her to go home before she makes a big mistake as you did? If you help her go back, it's possible they'll forgive Kara and you.*

"*Danki*, Naomi," Kara said. "You're so kind."

Naomi's smile was unsteady, and he fought the abrupt urge to take her hand and comfort her. That would have been the worst thing he could do. Anything he said or did might be the wrong thing, and any chance of them helping his sister could be gone.

He held his breath as he waited for Naomi to answer. When she did, he was amazed how she'd found exactly the right answer.

"It's not kindness, Kara. It's desperation. With three small *kinder* and my *daed* to take care of—"

"I thought Samuel was taking care of your *daed*."

"He is, but he also needs to work in the buggy shop and complete orders on time. I don't want the business ruined because people can't get work done on their buggies as promised." At last, she looked at him. "I can help in the shop, Kara, if you're willing to watch the *kinder* at least part of the day."

Naomi wanted to work in the shop? His head reeled at the thought of spending hour after hour in the cramped shop with her. What could she do other than get in the way? He wisely didn't ask as he listened to her find out what time Kara would finish her shift.

Smiling as his sister said she'd be done in an hour, Naomi stood and went to the counter with Kara. He strained his ears but couldn't pick out their words over the general buzz in the large space. His eyes widened when, a few minutes later, Naomi came back with a hot-fudge sundae, which she put in front of him. She set a strawberry shake on the other side of the table and slid in.

"I told her we'd wait," she said without preamble.

"She's willing to come to the farm with us?"

"*Ja*, though she insists it's temporary. Apparently, she's been sleeping on the couch at a coworker's apartment, and it's not comfortable." She took a sip of her shake, then said, "She wasn't—in spite of how she acted—surprised to see you, Samuel. She seems to have already known you were working with

Daed, and I think she'd rather spend time with the twins and May than serve ice cream."

"*Danki*, Naomi." He closed his fingers around hers on the table and gazed into her eyes when they rose to meet his. "You said all the right things while I stumbled not to say all the wrong ones. I'm grateful. More grateful than I can say."

"I'm glad I can help. Just as you'll help *Daed*."

Shaking his head, he said, "No, don't say that. You were right when you said we shouldn't be keeping score of favors done for each other." Should he ask her to stop counting how many bad things he'd done in the past, too? No, he couldn't risk this moment when they were working together as…

Working together!

He drew his hand back and reached for his spoon as if it were an ordinary motion. Without looking at her, he dipped his spoon into the fudge that had hardened over the ice cream. He took a bite before asking, "Did I hear you right? Did you tell Kara you're planning to work in the shop?"

"To get you through the backlog of work. *Daed* scheduled work based on two people. He's not going to be able to help for a while."

"True, but—"

She put her hand on his arm as she'd done to his sister. Had Naomi felt the explosion of sensation rushing like a spring flood along her skin as he did when they touched? No, there wasn't anything simple about Naomi touching him. It revived feelings he'd tried to bury since the night he'd drawn her into his arms and tasted her lips for the first and only time. She'd fit so perfectly there, and though he'd held other women while living among the *Englisch*, none of them had seemed to belong in his arms as Naomi had.

"Samuel." Her soft voice undulated like a caress. "I've been praying for a solution to the problem of needing to be two places at the same time. In the house and in the shop. Your sister is the answer to my prayer. At least for now."

"You're the answer to what Elvin's been praying for." He couldn't let his feelings get in the way of what he must do to help the man who'd given him the opportunity he'd waited seven years for. "Someone to keep the shop running."

"Can we work together?"

"Ja." He wondered if she had any idea how much willpower he was going to have to exert to keep his longing to hold her again from bursting forth while they worked side by side. "We'll do what we must for Elvin and the *kinder.*"

"And your sister."

"Now who's keeping count?" He glanced at his spoon where melting ice cream was dripping off. "The only thing I should be keeping count of right now is how many bites it takes me to clean this bowl."

When she laughed, he did, too. Maybe it would be possible to work together long enough for him to convince Kara to return home. After that, Naomi would have to stay in the house overseeing the *kinder,* and he could go on pretending that it was possible for him to be satisfied with what was at best a leery friendship and nothing more.

Chapter Thirteen

When Naomi said she should check on the *kinder* and send Celesta home before she came to the *dawdi haus* to make sure Kara was settled in, Samuel heard his sister draw in a deep breath. To protest? Or to ask a question? Kara might be having second thoughts about staying at the Gingerichs', and he didn't want her running away again. She might not be found a second time.

Whatever Kara might have said was silenced when Naomi smiled and said, "I'll be in to check on you in a few minutes."

"When can I see the *kinder*?"

"In the morning. They should all be asleep now. I try to have them in bed before the sun sets on these late evenings."

"Oh," Kara said with a nervous giggle, "I should have known that."

"You'll learn. I promise you these three *kinder* will keep all three of us grown-ups hopping."

In the dim interior of the buggy, Samuel could see how

pleased Kara was to be included as an adult. It shocked him each time he recalled she was only a couple of years younger than he'd been when he jumped the fence. Back then, he'd believed he knew everything there was to know. He couldn't have been more wrong then, and he couldn't be more wrong now if he treated his little sister as a *kind*. That might compel her to leave.

He unhitched the horse, then picked up two grocery bags of Kara's things from the back of the buggy, stuffing them into the crook of his right arm before reaching for his cane. Kara carried two more as they walked around the side of the house to go to the *dawdi haus*.

"The barn over there is the buggy shop," he said into the silence.

"How's he doing?" Kara hesitated. "She said he'd had a stroke and you were helping him."

"He should be home in a day or two. I'll be helping him with his physical therapy because, as you can see, I've had a bunch myself."

"What happened to you?"

He paused and faced her. "What do you mean?"

She gestured toward his cane. "Why do you use that? What happened?"

"You don't know?"

She shook her head.

"I was in a car accident. Didn't *Mamm* tell you about it?"

"No. *Mamm* refuses to let your name be spoken in our house."

He shouldn't have been surprised, but the revelation sent a piercing pain to the center of his heart, where his yearning for his *mamm* to acknowledge him lingered. "I see."

"I don't!" she said with every bit of a teenager's fervor.

"You're my brother. I should have known you'd been injured in a car accident. *Mamm* needs to think about someone other than herself once in a while."

Though he wanted to agree with her, he had to keep in mind that once she returned home, she might not be as willing to rebel against everything *Mamm* said and did. He remained silent as he led the way up the porch steps to the front door. Opening it, he motioned for Kara to go in ahead of him.

She hesitated, her face abruptly pale in the light of the setting sun. When she glanced toward the ruins of the chicken barn, he explained how it'd burned and was scheduled to be rebuilt. Instead of asking more questions as he'd expected, she nodded and stepped into the *dawdi haus*.

He lit the propane lamp by the rocker where he usually sat after supper. In the center of the braided rug, Kara turned to take in every inch of the space. A stove with only two burners was set beside a compact refrigerator. The sink was beneath a wide window that had its twin on the other side of the room behind the sofa. Two other doors opened off the room. One led to his bedroom with its iron bed and worn dresser. The other was for the bathroom, which had only a shower, a *gut* idea when elderly parents usually occupied the space.

"I'll get my stuff out of here in the morning," he said.

"You're still living here?"

"I was planning to until Elvin got home. I didn't want to intrude on Naomi and the *kinder*."

"Where's her husband?"

"He died."

"Oh." Understanding filled his sister's eyes. For him to move under the roof with Naomi, even with her *kinder* and May as unwitting chaperones, would tarnish her reputation.

There wouldn't be any question of impropriety once Elvin was home from the hospital. "That makes sense."

"Let me get a few things from the bedroom. You can use it tonight, and I'll sleep on the couch."

"I can sleep out here. That one looks more comfortable than the one where I've been sleeping."

"Don't be silly. This is your place. You might as well get used to it."

Before his sister could retort, the door from the house opened. Naomi came in with sheets and blankets. She dropped them on the sofa and smiled.

"Kara, why don't you strip the bed and remake it while I put sheets on the sofa for your brother?" Naomi gestured toward the house. "You'll have to get a pillow from the storage closet in the laundry room, Samuel. I couldn't carry one along with everything else."

In quick order, Naomi had them too busy to argue. He'd seen her do the same with the twins, and he grinned as she made one suggestion—that's what she called it, though he'd call it an order—after another for making the *dawdi haus* more welcoming for his sister. While Kara unpacked in the bedroom, Naomi sent him to get a pitcher of ice tea from the refrigerator in the main house.

"There are cookies in the jar," she said as he walked toward the connecting door. "Don't rattle the top. The boys can hear it even when they're asleep."

He did as she asked and returned to find the two women talking in the farthest corner of the bedroom. Naomi glanced over her shoulder before motioning to Kara to come out into the main room. His sister shut her mouth and followed. What had they been discussing that they didn't want him to know about?

The answer was simple: him.

His pulse of annoyance faded when, as she took the pitcher from him and poured three glasses of tea, Naomi said, "I was telling Kara about how you've been helping *Daed* with the shop and what a relief it'll be to have her here to watch Jared, Jesse and May."

"I like those names," his sister said as she selected a chocolate chip cookie from the plate. "So you named the *boppli* for the month you found her?"

"*Gut* thing it hadn't been March," he said, picking up a pair of cookies for himself before sitting on the rocker.

"For a lot of reasons." Naomi sat on the sofa beside his sister. "The poor darling didn't have a stitch of clothing on her."

"Not even a blanket?" Kara asked.

"*Ja*. There was a blanket, but it wouldn't have been enough to protect her in March." Naomi shuddered. "Poor little thing."

"It sounds as if she's doing well now." His sister's eyes sparkled with anticipation. "I can't wait to see her—and the boys—tomorrow."

"Don't stay up late tonight. They're early risers." She glanced at the clock on the wall. "I'd better say *gut nacht*. It's almost time for May's next feeding, and I don't want her crying to wake up the twins." Rising, she said, "If you need anything, let me know."

"We'll be fine," he replied. "*Danki. Danki* for everything."

She paused in the doorway, and he knew she'd understood what he hadn't said. He was grateful for her help in persuading Kara to come with them to the Gingerichs' farm. No matter what challenges tomorrow brought, and he had no idea what might happen, he was sure he couldn't have made this first tiny step without her help.

After telling them to sleep well, she gave him a slow smile that warmed the cold spot in his heart, which had been skewered out on the lawn at his sister's words about how *Mamm* never spoke of him. Shock raced through him. He'd been sure that perpetual pain would be his companion until he drew his last breath. He hadn't thought anything or anyone could ease it.

Ever.

Two days later, Naomi was smiling at the thought of *Daed* coming home that morning. Her smile lasted exactly as long as it took the medical transport people to open the back of the ambulance and wheel her *daed* up to the porch. Instantly it became clear that everything in her life had gotten far more complicated than she would have guessed. She'd assumed it wouldn't be easy to move her *daed* into the house and get him settled in the big bed in what had been the extra room, but it was more difficult than she could have imagined.

Two large sheets of plywood were leaned against the steps so the gurney could be wheeled onto the porch. Unlike when they'd left for the hospital last week, speed wasn't important. In addition, *Daed* wasn't unconscious. On each step toward the house, he grumbled and tried to direct the man at the foot of the gurney. When his words wouldn't come, he waved his right hand back and forth to make his point. His left one was strapped close to his side so it didn't fall off the gurney and bang into the door. That man didn't pay any more attention to him than did the taller one pushing the gurney into the house.

"Which way, ma'am?" the tall man asked.

She pointed at the open bedroom door where Samuel stood. He gestured for the men to bring *Daed* into the room. Stepping aside, he motioned with his head for her to go into the *dawdi haus.* She wanted to protest as she had over breakfast that she needed to be with *Daed* when he was brought into what she hoped would be his temporary bedroom.

"No," Samuel had said so firmly the twins had stared in astonishment.

"He's my *daed.*"

"A fact nobody is disputing. However, you've got to think about him, Naomi, not yourself."

"I'm not thinking of myself. I'm thinking only about him. I want to make sure he's comfortable and he knows—"

"I can handle that with the help of whoever brings him in." He'd waved aside any other comments and said with a note of finality, "Elvin isn't going to want you to see him looking weak and helpless."

Naomi hadn't been able to argue. It was the truth. Even so, she had to force her feet to walk into the kitchen as the gurney rolled through the living room.

"Here," said Kara, holding out some *kaffi.* "You didn't drink yours earlier."

"I know. I was too anxious to get *Daed* home and safe."

"He's home, as you can see. Drink up. It'll do you *gut.*"

"It's not like caffeine is going to soothe my nerves."

"True, but drinking it will keep you from bouncing around like a barefoot kid on a hot sidewalk." The teenager smiled as she lifted May out of her carrier seat. "In the meantime, I think this one needs to be changed. Again!"

"Danki." She was grateful to Kara and to God, who had sent the girl into her life at this perfect time.

When Kara went into the laundry room to change the *boppli,* the twins followed, leaving Naomi alone for a moment. She was like a stone in the middle of a tumbling stream. All around her things were going on. She could hear the men and

Samuel talking and the guttural sound of her *daed* trying to speak. In the other direction, the twins were asking questions, one after another, in the rapid-fire way that often drove her to distraction because she couldn't answer one before three or four more were posed.

The men with the gurney reappeared and pushed it across the living room. By the door, they paused, and the taller man picked up a clipboard. He walked to her with a sympathetic smile.

"Paperwork," he said.

"I guessed there'd be some."

"Always." He put the clipboard on the kitchen table, being careful to avoid where the twins had splattered *millich* from their cereal.

Naomi read each page before she signed it. The paperwork was straightforward. She acknowledged that her *daed* had been brought to the house by the medical transport company and she was satisfied with the service.

"Isn't there a charge?" she asked.

"The hospital will bill you," the tall man said. "We don't handle that."

"All right." She took the sheaf of papers he gave her, trying not to think about the charges that had accrued during her *daed*'s time in the hospital and what the costs would be of his recovery.

Thanking the men, she watched them leave before turning to check on her *daed*. She reached the bedroom door as Samuel emerged, closing it behind him.

"He's asleep," Samuel said before she could ask a question. "The trip home wore him out."

Naomi wanted to check on him, but she nodded. On her

visit to the hospital yesterday, *Daed* had seemed more exhausted than usual. She needed to let him rest while he could.

"*Danki*, Samuel, for helping with getting him settled."

"What's all that?"

She held up the pages. "Hospital forms I had to sign."

"Would you like me to give them to Adam so he can arrange for payment?"

"Would you do that?" Her heart soared for a second with happiness that she didn't have to speak to Adam Hershberger again so soon.

"Certainly." His brows lowered, pulling at his scar. "I know you didn't forget I said I'd help in any way I could. So do you believe my words had no intentions behind them?"

"No. I…" She closed her eyes and took a breath to bolster herself. "If you got that idea from my reaction, Samuel, I chose the wrong words. I didn't want to suggest anything like that. I'm deluged with the changes in my life. I'm more grateful than words can describe that you're willing to help."

"I said I would."

His terse answer warned he was still offended. It hadn't been what she'd meant.

Was it?

Had she been testing his resolve to see if he was truly willing to step up for her and her family?

Samuel sighed. "It's discouraging how little you trust me after I've shown you that I've changed."

"I'm trying."

"I agree." His smile returned as he chuckled. "You may be the most trying woman I've ever met."

For a moment, she was about to take offense at how he'd twisted her words; then she halted, realizing he was attempting to ease the tension between them. Slowly she returned his smile.

"You, Samuel King, are just as trying."

"Never said I wasn't." He motioned toward the kitchen. "How about some *kaffi* for me, too?"

"You know where it is," she retorted.

"True, but I thought you might want to sit and enjoy a sip or two with me while Elvin is sleeping."

Glancing at the bedroom door, she nodded. The idea of sitting and drinking *kaffi* in the middle of the morning seemed decadent, but she guessed Samuel knew—as she did—that such a quiet interlude might not happen again for a long time to come. She should take advantage of it while she could.

By day's end, Naomi was glad she'd enjoyed half a cup of *kaffi* before demands came at her from every direction. She hushed the twins more times than she could count so they wouldn't wake their *grossdawdi*. When *Daed* did wake about two hours after his return, she'd focused the rest of her time on him.

What would she have done if Samuel and Kara hadn't been there to help? Kara kept the *kinder* out from underfoot. When the boys got tired of coloring and wanted to do something louder and more active, Kara took them, as well as May, for a walk until all three youngsters were ready for a nap.

Samuel hadn't faltered in taking care of *Daed*. She was strong, but she doubted she could have picked up her *daed*'s deadweight and helped him shift in bed. Getting him fed she could have managed on her own, but she'd seen the strain on Samuel's face while he settled her *daed* against the pillows on his bed and made sure the covers were smooth around him.

No work had been done in the shop, and Naomi noticed another buggy parked in front of it when she stepped out onto the porch after dark. The lightning bugs etched their greenish glow into the sky over the fields, weaving abstract patterns that disappeared each time she blinked. Customers sometimes left their buggies, putting a note on the seat to explain the problem that needed to be fixed. She'd check it in the morning.

Sitting on the glider, she let herself sink into the cushions. The stench of humidity clung to them, but she leaned her head back and stared at the slender lath on the porch's ceiling. Paint was chipping, revealing the white beneath the light blue she and *Mamm* had painted shortly before *Mamm*'s death.

Two weeks, two days and four hours before she died, came the voice out of her memories. Marlin hadn't wanted Naomi to come to Bliss Valley for that visit. He hadn't—she realized now as she looked back—ever wanted her to leave the farm in Honey Brook. Why? It wasn't as if he'd loved her or the boys. If he'd loved them, wouldn't he have spent time with them instead of with other women?

She wasn't going to think about that tonight. Marlin Ropp was the past. She wanted to think of the future, especially one where her *daed* could walk again and talk clearly. Her home was once again in Bliss Valley. After the hot weather broke, she'd see if there was any leftover paint and redo the ceiling... as *Mamm* would have wanted it.

In her spare time...

She was torn between laughing at the idea of getting a moment to herself during the day and surrendering to the tears that had clung to the back of her eyes, refusing to dissolve. To see *Daed* so helpless, so hopeless, was almost too much to bear. She started to close her eyes to pray, but opened them when she felt moisture gathering in the corners.

She would not cry.

She wouldn't!

"It'd be easier to give in." Samuel climbed the steps with his uneven gait.

"Give in?"

"To your tears. I can't think of anyone who deserves a *gut* cry more than you do right now."

He was teasing her. Not as he had in school, but as a friend would. She knew that, but she'd never felt less like laughing.

"If I cry," she said, "*Daed* might see. That could make him discouraged, and then he'd lose his determination to get out of bed."

"Elvin Gingerich lose his determination?" He shook his head as he leaned against one of the poles supporting the porch roof. "I can't imagine that happening. He's going to get discouraged. He's going to want to quit because the physical therapy makes his muscles ache. He won't quit. He's so stubborn that if someone told him that he can't fly, he'd stand in the field and flap his arms until he lifted off the ground."

"He's not that stubborn."

"*Ja*, he is, but that's a *gut* thing. He's going to need that, and so will you. There are going to be times when you'll have to insist he complete the repetitions his physical therapist has given him."

"She's coming tomorrow. She left a message on the phone in the shop."

"His *doktors* won't want him to linger too long in bed." He held her gaze steadily. "Don't worry about the physical therapist, Naomi. He or she—"

"She. Her name is Lillian Rushmore."

"By now, she's already read Elvin's files and has formulated a program to help him regain as much use of his left side as possible. She'll evaluate him and make sure he's pushed to his limits, but not beyond. He's not going to want to listen to her and do everything she insists he does. That's where you're going to have to step in. You're your *daed*'s daughter. Just as stubborn."

Naomi looked across the field at the lightning bugs again. She *was* like her *daed*. Their mutual mulishness was a sure sign that they were *daed* and daughter. It had to be. She had to stop letting Skylar's assertions trickle into her thoughts.

Skylar was mistaken about Naomi being her half sister. Maybe that was why she hadn't called back as she'd said she would. She'd found the real missing *kind* she was seeking. She wrapped her arms around herself as she prayed Skylar wasn't busy because her *mamm* had taken a turn for the worse.

"Naomi?"

Raising her head, she looked up at Samuel. "What?"

"You looked as if you'd gone a thousand miles away."

"Not a thousand miles. I've got too much on my mind."

He smiled. "I can give you three fewer things to worry about."

She sat straighter, and the glider moved under her. "Which things?"

Sitting next to her, but leaving a cushion between them, he said, "Well, Elvin is resting comfortably. I'll be checking on him every couple of hours."

"I can do that. I'm up with May several times a night any-how."

"Kara said she'd take the overnights with May until we get adjusted to what Elvin needs. I moved the cradle into the *dawdi haus* a little while ago."

"Does Kara have any experience with such a tiny *boppli*?"

"If not, she'll learn the same way you did. Through trial and error."

"I'm May's foster *mamm*."

"The commonwealth isn't going to take her away because you've left her with a sitter for a few nights."

"You don't know that," she protested, though she hoped he was right.

"I'm not going to tell any social worker, and you won't, either. I can assure you Kara won't. She's as excited and happy as a *kind* with a new toy. Three new toys, because the twins adore her."

Naomi couldn't argue with that. Jared and Jesse had declared her "fun," the highest praise they could offer.

When she didn't answer, Samuel said, "Another thing is Adam stopped by earlier. I gave him the paperwork from the hospital."

"*Danki.*" Why was she bothered Samuel had chosen to sit as far from her as possible? She should be grateful. Yet dismay niggled at her like a mouse gnawing its way into a house. When he'd taken her hand at the ice cream shop, she'd been overwhelmed by a sweet delight she hadn't expected to feel again. Most certainly not with him. She'd tried to forget it, but during the chaos of the past twenty-four hours, she hadn't been able to.

Maybe she'd been the only one to experience it. Why would Samuel after all the times she'd made it clear that, even if she could have, she'd never forget each of the horrid things he and his friends had done to her and Laurene? He'd be a *dummkopf* to believe she could have any feelings toward him other than disgust. She hadn't been repulsed the night he pulled her to him and shared her first kiss...or her second or third. That night, until he'd laughed in her face and run off to brag to everyone how easy it'd been to convince her to kiss him, she'd savored that warmth surging through her with every thrilled beat of her heart.

As she had at the ice cream shop yesterday.

So many years, so many changes in their lives, but one thing remained the same. She melted when he touched her, and she yearned to share that sensation with him again.

"Don't you want to know the other thing?" Samuel asked.

"Other thing?" She recalled what they'd been talking about before she lost herself in thoughts of feelings she shouldn't be longing for. When she shifted so she could see his face in the thin light from the lamp in the living room, lightning flashed. She looked to the west, where the fireflies had vanished before the oncoming storm. As a thick rumble of thunder rolled across the fields, she added, "Oh, you said you'd taken care of several things."

"Actually to give credit where credit's due, Adam helped, too. He wanted me to let you know the lumberyard will start delivering supplies tomorrow. He figures everyone will be over to help rebuild the chicken barn toward the end of next week or the beginning of the following one."

"They don't need to do that, not when I've dropped all those medical bills on the *Leit,* as well."

"Naomi, I shouldn't have to tell you this because you've been a faithful member of the community and never considered jumping the fence, but you know how important it is for us to help one another."

"That's not true."

"What?" As another bolt broke across the dark sky, the light revealed the shock on his face. "Of course it's true that we wish to help—"

For once, she interrupted him. "I wasn't talking about helping one another. I was talking about how you believe I never considered jumping the fence."

"You?" The single word was almost lost in another roll of thunder.

"*Ja*. When Laurene vanished and everyone said she and her family had gone to live among the *Englisch*, I wished I could go, too. She was my dearest friend. As we'd said often, we were closer than sisters, and my life was empty without her. If I'd known where they'd gone, I think I would have gone, too. Not necessarily to stay, but just to be not alone."

"Against the three of us?"

"That wasn't the only reason, but, *ja*, I didn't know how I could endure your tricks and cruel jokes by myself."

He reached across the empty cushion and cupped her cheek with his calloused hand. "If there was any way to go back in time and change what happened, I would. Now all I can do is say as I've said before. I'm sorry for what went on when I was a heartless kid."

Closing her eyes again, she leaned into his strong fingers. Everything that had taken place in their teens disappeared as his skin warmed her face. As his fingers moved to tilt her chin toward him, she opened her eyes to discover his so enticingly near. She thought she heard him whisper her name, but her pulse throbbed so hard the sound was lost.

An explosion of thunder broke them apart. Naomi stared at him. He looked as if he were waking from a startling dream. She understood his disconcertion because she was shocked she'd let him draw her close and then closer still.

Hail suddenly bounced off the steps with a frightful clatter. She flinched, then heard a cry come from the house, followed quickly by frightened shrieks.

As she started to stand, Samuel motioned for her to stay where she was. "I can get the twins."

"I can't ask you to do that." Pushing herself to her feet, she said, "You need to check on *Daed*. I'll take care of the *kinder*."

As they stood, again face-to-face but with the memories of the past between them, she thought he was going to argue and accuse her once more of not trusting him with the twins. He edged aside, gesturing toward the door.

She slipped inside and up the front stairs to comfort her frightened boys. She should be grateful to the storm for protecting her from her own unrestrained thoughts. As she hugged the twins and soothed them, she couldn't keep from remembering how gentle Samuel's fingers had been on her face.

It was impossible for her to forget anything, but this once, she must do more than try. Otherwise, she could find herself being kissed again by the man who'd kissed and told, hurting her and her family.

Chapter Fourteen

The next morning, Naomi was amazed how everything seemed pretty much the same as it'd been the day before *Daed*'s stroke. Her whole world had shifted, but the furniture, the *kinder*'s toys and the *boppli*'s stacks of clothing that needed to be folded looked identical to what she'd seen the week before she'd called 911.

Yet nothing was the same.

Kara now lived in the *dawdi haus*, and Samuel had brought a mattress from the attic for his use in the living room. Naomi had urged him to get a bed frame, too, but he'd insisted that with the mattress, he could sleep close enough to *Daed*'s door to hear him at night.

"Also the mattress can be picked up, so there'll be room for Elvin to move around once he's on his feet again," Samuel had added.

Buoyed by his optimism that her *daed* would be able to get about on his own soon, Naomi had acquiesced. She was pleased how high *Daed*'s spirits had been when she took him his breakfast. While his left arm hung at his side and the only way he could move it was to pick it up with his right hand, his language skills were improving already. It took him a long time to get words to form, and he might say *"Ja"* when he intended to say the opposite, but he could string words together to make his meaning clear most of the time. When he'd groused about not having enough sugar on his oatmeal, she'd had to turn away to hide her smile. The complaint—which she'd heard every day at the hospital—seemed precious now.

Her happiest moment had been when she brought the twins to see their *grossdawdi*. Her fear they'd be frightened of his useless arm and his rough voice as he fought for each word vanished when she had to keep them from clambering onto the bed to spoon extra sugar onto the oatmeal. Hearing her *daed*'s laugh sounding almost like normal was such a blessing when last week, she'd been afraid he would die before he reached the emergency room.

Naomi was finishing the breakfast dishes when she heard a knock on the front door. Wiping her hands, she went to answer it. She guessed the caller would be the physical therapist sent by *Daed*'s *doktors*. Her neighbors would have come to the kitchen door, opened it, looked around and greeted whomever they saw before walking in.

"Back to the kitchen," she told the twins, who'd followed her like a set of shadows. She put her finger to her lips. "Let *Mamm* do the talking."

Disappointment dimmed their eyes, but they nodded. She wondered if they'd go into the *dawdi haus* with Kara. They already liked Samuel's sister, who kept the connecting door open in an invitation for the twins to visit whenever they wished, and she was watching May. The *boppli* fascinated the boys, but their glum expressions as they walked away revealed the infant wasn't as exciting as a visitor.

Opening the door, Naomi was startled she had to look down to meet the eyes of the woman on the porch. The woman was at least two inches shorter than Naomi's scant height. She was so thin that if she'd stood behind one of the uprights, she'd vanish. Streaks of gray in her dark brown hair and a few wrinkles announced she was older than Naomi by at least a decade. Her bare forearms and legs were strongly muscled. She wore a simple red T-shirt and black shorts. Her sneakers, also black, looked like the ones Naomi had upstairs in her closet. A box that seemed too big for such a slight person to carry sat on the porch beside her.

"I am Lillian Rushmore," the woman said with a warm smile. "I'm here to work with Elvin Gingerich on his post-stroke regimen. Are you his daughter?"

"*Ja*. I'm Naomi."

"Hi, Naomi. Can I come in?"

Opening it farther, she stepped aside. "Certainly. Please *komm* in."

After Lillian had lifted the box as if it weighed nothing and carried it into the house, she said, "I want to confirm one thing. You don't have electricity in the house, do you?"

"No. Will that be a problem?"

"We'll work around it." She glanced around, then flushed. "Sorry to stare. The only time I've been in an Amish house was at the museum on Route 30. I wasn't exactly sure what you'd have here." She laughed. "Looks like most farmhouses I've been in around Bliss Valley. Comfy furniture and a wood-stove. Nice space we'll put to use once Mr. Gingerich can get out of bed."

"You think he will?"

"I *know* he will if he'll put in the hard work ahead of him. He's already made good progress."

"I'm glad to help with whatever you need."

"Excellent." She bent, opened the box and pulled out a bag. Thrusting it into Naomi's arms who took a step back to balance the unexpected weight, Lillian said, "Show me where Mr. Gingerich is, and we'll get started." She smiled. "Oh, and please leave that bag out of his sight now. I don't want to freak him out by seeing the weights he'll be working his way up to in the coming weeks." Her eyes widened. "I'm sorry. Do you know what I mean when I say 'freak him out'?"

"We plain folks live separate from the rest of the world, but we can't help hearing things when we go grocery shopping and other places."

"Glad to hear that, and this is a good a time to let you know that if you've got any questions—any at all—about how I'm working with your father or why we're focusing on a certain aspect of his recovery, speak up. I tend to assume while I work that if nobody asks, they get what's going on."

Naomi nodded, but wondered how anyone managed to ask the voluble physical therapist questions. She seemed to have only one speed. Fast. There was no denying the compassion behind her smile when she walked into *Daed*'s room.

"Good morning!" Lillian boomed as if they were already the best of friends. "How are you doing this morning, Mr. Gingerich?"

"Elvin," her *daed* grumbled.

"Good. I'll call you Elvin, and you can call me Lillian. Or Lil, if you'd rather." She gave him a bold wink. "Don't call me 'Lil the Pill,' or I might give you twice as much work as they did at the hospital."

Naomi bit her bottom lip when she realized Lillian had

made it sound like a joke when she was letting *Daed* know it was all right not to try to say her whole name, which might be tough for him. She sent up a prayer of gratitude for this chatty, no-nonsense woman who was what he needed.

The twins peeked around the bed, their eyes round with curiosity. When Lillian put the box on the floor, both boys ran forward, eager to see what was in it.

"Ah, an audience!" Lillian laughed.

Naomi pointed to each boy and said his name before asking, "Is having them here going to be a problem?"

Lillian shook her head, her graying curls bouncing on her brow. "Quite to the contrary! I've found patients who have families involved in their PT do better and achieve more much faster."

"I need to let you know the twins won't understand you. They don't start learning English until they're in school."

"That's good to know, but don't worry. We'll find a way to communicate. After years of working with poststroke patients, many who aren't verbal any longer, I've learned there are plenty of ways to understand each other." She squatted to put herself on the twins' eye level. "Hello, boys. I'm going to need your help with your grandfather." She pointed to the boys, then to herself and to the bed. "Will you help me and your grandfather?"

The twins grinned and nodded, then ran to Samuel as he walked in. He must have seen Lillian's car in the yard from the shop.

Before Naomi could introduce him, Lillian appraised him. She must have taken note of his cane and lurching steps because she began bombarding him with questions about his own PT experiences. At the same time, she took a notebook and long elastic bands out of the box and began working with

Daed. Her steady patter kept them informed of what she was doing and why. On her first visit, she was confirming what the written reports from the hospital had shared.

Naomi stood to one side and watched, trying to remember the various terms Lillian used. Some were easy to understand, like *range of motion,* but others, especially the names of the various muscles, were unfamiliar. She promised herself that while the twins and May took their afternoon naps, she'd replay the whole session from memory and write down the words she didn't know. Next time Lillian came, Naomi would be prepared with questions.

Daed was drooping, his ability to talk sensibly flagging, by the time Lillian announced forty-five minutes later that they were done for the day. Naomi saw her relief reflected in her *daed*'s eyes and on Samuel's face.

When her *daed* made a strangled sound, she saw his mouth was twisted as he struggled to speak. She edged past the physical therapist and leaned on the edge of the bed to try to figure out what *Daed* was trying to say.

"He said, 'Out.'" She turned to the others. "It was a question. I think he wants to know when he can get out."

Lillian smiled. "We'll have you out of bed as soon as possible, Elvin."

Again Elvin made the ragged sound. Though his lips fought to form the word, his eyes pleaded for them to comprehend what he wanted to say. He tapped his chest, then made a circle with his finger before looking toward the door.

Not the door, she realized. He was looking in the direction of the shop. Instantly she wondered why she hadn't guessed what *Daed*'s first concern would be. He'd grown frustrated with each day of being stuck in the hospital with nothing to do but watch the television his roommate kept on from before Naomi arrived in the morning until after she left before supper.

"He wants to know when he can go to the shop," she said.

Elvin pointed at her emphatically and nodded.

"Right now, that's imposs—" Samuel began.

Lillian interrupted to say, "You can go to your shop as soon as you can get there under your own power. I'm not going to mince words, Elvin. It's going to take hard work. Lots of it, but you've got lots of people to cheer you on and make sure you don't skimp on your exercises." She closed her notebook and dropped it in the box. "Rest now, Elvin. You've done great."

"Weak," muttered *Daed*.

"Maybe now, but by the time I get done with you, you'll be amazed what you can do." Again she winked. "I'm not promising you'll be a superhero, but you're going to do more than you think you can, and you'll get back to your shop. Wait and see."

He arched a brow in a silent disagreement.

Lillian waved a hand. "Ah, ye of little faith, watch and see. God's got plans for you still. You wouldn't be enjoying my ministrations if He didn't."

Naomi laughed, surprising herself and everyone else. Then Samuel chuckled along with the twins, who had no idea what was funny but didn't want to be left out. When *Daed* made a rusty sound she hoped was a laugh, she wanted to throw her arms around him and Lillian. She contented herself with carrying Lillian's box to the front door while Samuel got *Daed* resettled in bed. Jared and Jesse were already firing questions at him before Naomi had stepped out of the room.

Lillian paused to pick up the bag of weights. "I knew I was optimistic bringing these today, but by next week, Elvin should be doing his exercises wearing the lightest ones." She answered the question Naomi hadn't had a chance to ask. "I was being honest with him about my expectations of what he can achieve, Naomi. Will he get any use of his left arm back? It's too soon to tell how much muscle motion we can recapture, but we'll be working on that. Will he be able to walk again? Yes, I'm sure he will, though I suspect he'll need a walker or a cane like the one your husband uses."

"Samuel isn't my husband. He works for *Daed*, and he's offered to help with his physical therapy because he knows much more about it than I do."

"I get it now." She smiled. "You should count yourself blessed to have someone who'll be able to empathize with Elvin and the long road ahead of him. Samuel's injuries have taught him plenty about PT and its challenges, as well as its benefits. You'll learn, too. In a month or so, you'll be using the lingo like an old pro." She opened the door. "I'll be back tomorrow and every day next week at the same time, if that's okay with you. Don't push Elvin to do any of the exercises we worked on today. We have to make progress slowly."

"All right. Tomorrow will be fine." She couldn't imagine anyone telling the miniature tornado of a woman no.

"Good. See you then."

Closing the door, Naomi leaned against it. She trembled with the emotion she'd kept hidden in *Daed*'s room. Seeing him feeble left her weak, too. She wished she could curl up into a ball and sob out all her fears.

She squared her shoulders. She had to be strong. For her *daed* and for her sons. When Marlin had cheated on her, she'd held back the tears and dismissed pain from her thoughts. The night she'd learned he'd been shot, she'd let her grief and anger and anguish pile up inside her and then had shoved it aside. She couldn't let herself wallow in fear and anguish, because once she released it, she'd have to relive it over and over and over again for the rest of her life.

On tiptoe, Naomi slipped along the upstairs hall and down the back stairs. She didn't want to wake the *kinder*. She didn't want to wake her *daed*.

Most of all, she didn't want to run into Samuel.

She was being silly. With someone extra in the house, there was a sense of everything not being as it usually was.

She couldn't blame that feeling on Samuel. No matter how much she'd hoped otherwise—and pretended to spare *Daed*'s feelings—coming home hadn't been what she'd expected. She wasn't the optimistic girl she'd been the day she'd left to begin married life. She no longer believed in happy-ever-afters or that dreams came true by wishing.

She'd come home, searching for a sanctuary. It wasn't here.

Those thoughts had bounced around in her head for the past two hours while she tried to sleep. Tossing and turning, she kept thinking of how difficult the next day would be if she didn't rest. That added to her anxiety, making it impossible to close her eyes for more than a few seconds before they popped open again.

She hoped getting up and walking around would tire her enough so she wasn't fighting herself any longer. She crossed the kitchen and shut the door to the living room. The door to the *dawdi haus* was already closed, though the back door was open to let in what little bits of cool breeze there were.

She lit the overhead propane light. The kitchen shone with her hard work, and the newspapers that once had been stacked on the table had been moved into the living room. Tomorrow, she should move the oldest issues into *Daed*'s bedroom. Reading *The Budget* would give him something to do.

When the door to the living room opened and Samuel walked in, Naomi didn't move from the center of the kitchen floor. His hair was tousled as if he'd been tossing and turning, too. The heat had plastered it to one side of his face, and he pushed it back as he blinked in the bright light. With his shirt half-buttoned and his suspenders hanging from his waist, she was aware that she was wearing only a thin nightgown and bathrobe.

He lifted his suspenders over his shoulders. She had to wonder if his thoughts matched hers.

Telling herself to stop feeling ill at ease in her own home, she asked, "Did I wake you?"

He shook his head as he edged past her and reached for the refrigerator door. Taking out the *millich* jug, he raised it in a silent offer to share.

"*Danki,*" she said. "Do you want me to warm it?"

"That sounds *gut.*" He held it out to her.

She took the jug and carried it to the stove. Carefully taking a pot out of the cupboard, so the clatter wouldn't awaken *Daed* and the *kinder,* she poured most of the *millich* into it. There would be fresh *millich* in the morning after *Daed* milked the cows, and—

She sighed. Her *daed* might not ever milk the cows again. She'd taken over the chore since his stroke, but now she wondered if she should sell the small herd and buy *millich* from a neighbor. That would be the smart thing to do. Yet she wouldn't. Not without discussing it with *Daed,* and she didn't want to add to his stress by suggesting he might not be able to do everything he used to.

"Are you all right?" asked Samuel from behind her. "That was a big sigh."

"I'm fine."

"It's everything else, ain't so?"

In spite of herself, she glanced over her shoulder. He stood by the refrigerator, his nearly useless arm cradled in his other hand. She wondered if his injuries still hurt. She quelled the question before it could reach her lips.

Looking at the stove, she twisted the dial. The flame roared out, and she jumped away before stretching to turn the fire down.

"Are you all right?" he asked again.

She nodded, but her voice shook. "That startled me."

"I'll check the burner tomorrow before I head out to the shop."

"Danki." A few minutes later, she asked as she poured the warmed *millich* into two cups, "How's *Daed* doing tonight?"

"I checked him a couple of times before I went to bed and then now. He's sleeping well, and he seems able to turn himself from side to side."

"That's important."

"Ja. Bedsores can become a real problem for stroke patients." He smiled sadly as his gaze turned inward. "For anyone who can't move around on his own."

"What do you think of Lillian?"

"She's just what the *doktor* ordered."

"You seemed to understand everything she said."

"I did. So far." He took the cup she handed him. Sipping, he asked, "Do you have any cinnamon?"

"I'll get it." She went to the tall cupboard next to the laundry room door. Opening one of the trio of stacked doors, she reached in and pulled out the container. "Here you go."

"You knew exactly where it was. I usually have to rummage around."

"I remembered where I put it the last time I used it."

He arched his brows. "I should have remembered you'd remember."

"Don't, Samuel." She walked past him and pulled out a chair at the table. Sitting, she curled her fingers around her cup. Though the air coming through the open windows was hot at almost midnight, she appreciated the heat coming off the ceramic. She'd endured a deep, gnawing cold since *Daed* had collapsed.

"Don't?" Honest curiosity filled his voice. "Don't what?"

"Don't pick on me now."

He pulled out the chair next to hers. She sensed the warmth emanating from his forearm beneath his rolled-up sleeve and wondered how long she'd continue to feel as if she were encased in ice. She leaned her elbows on the table and pressed the heels of her palms against her eyes. Maybe if she pushed hard enough she could force the weak tears back inside her.

"I'm sorry, Naomi. Bad habits are harder to break than I'd guessed." Now he sighed. "I didn't intend to tease you. I'm in awe of how you remember everything. Does your *daed* have the same ability?"

She raised her head, but kept her gaze focused on her cup. "I don't know. Why do you ask?"

"Because he can put his hand on any tool in the shop within seconds, even if it was tossed aside after the last time he used it. Just like you could find the cinnamon in the cupboard without searching for it."

"Maybe I inherited it from him." Hope spread through her, warm and comforting. If she'd been bequeathed her astounding memory by her *daed*, then she couldn't be Skylar's missing half sister.

"We'll have to ask him."

"Once he's well enough." She sighed and hung her head, her hope faltering again. "He's so weak now."

"He'll get better."

"How can you be sure?"

"Because he's survived the worst of it. The *doktors* believe most stroke victims who make it through the first twenty-four hours can live a somewhat normal life." He took a sip of the *millich*, then wiped the back of his hand across his lips as if no older than Jared and Jesse. "I appreciate you're willing to let me do what I can to help him, Naomi. He gave me a chance when no one else did."

"Because he thought you were someone else."

"*Ja*, there's that." A swift smile lit his face for only a moment. "When he learned the truth, he didn't send me packing. He's a *gut* man, and he deserves everything I can do to help him. Not to repay him, but because he'd do the same for anyone else. Was he ever put into the lot?"

She nodded. "Each time there was a vacancy, he was included, but he never selected the Bible with the slip of paper in it. *Mamm* was relieved, and he acted as if he were, too."

"For her sake?"

She wasn't accustomed to this version of Samuel King, this man who acted as if he cared for someone other than himself. Warning herself not to be drawn in as she'd foolishly been too many times before, she said with care, "*Ja*, because he gladly would have accepted the burden of serving the *Leit*."

"Like I said, he's a *gut* man. Watching him with you and the *kinder* has shown me what a family can be."

"Your family—"

"My family is different from yours."

Recalling the rumors she'd heard about the trouble Samuel had at home, she asked, "Why aren't you living with your family?"

"Because they don't want me." His quiet words shook her because there was more emotion in them than if he'd shouted.

"Even now?"

"To be honest, most especially now."

She was shocked into silence, wondering if she'd made a huge mistake by letting a man who wasn't wanted by his own family into her *daed*'s house, where three innocent *kinder* slept. If she had, how was she going to rectify it?

Watching emotions rippling across Naomi's face like shadows chasing the sun, Samuel clenched his hands on his lap. He didn't take pause to think about how startling it was that he'd closed his right hand. Strong emotions seemed to cure his body's weaknesses…temporarily.

He could read her thoughts as if she'd blurted them out. Maybe because he'd heard the same words from too many other people.

"I know," he said, forcing his voice to remain calm because what had happened—and continued to happen—wasn't her fault, "you think it's something I did that caused the schism between me and my family. You'd be right."

She drew in a sharp breath as her blue eyes widened. When her mouth tightened, he also guessed what she was about to say. She was going to tell him to leave. Maybe not the farm, because she needed his skills, nascent as they were, in the shop. She'd order him out of the house, maybe telling him he wasn't welcome to sleep in the *dawdi haus*.

Leaning toward her, he was glad she didn't pull back. She wasn't the skittish girl she'd been before he'd left Bliss Valley and she'd married Marlin Ropp.

"Naomi, what I did to cause my family to turn away from me was being born."

"I don't understand."

He laid out the whole story of how his *mamm* had rejected him when he was born before she married. He told Naomi how he'd returned to Bliss Valley after the accident. How *Mamm* had opened the door. How she'd told him to get out of her life. Hadn't he done enough already? How she'd slammed the door in his face. How he'd struggled in the years since until her *daed* hired him.

"I had no idea," she whispered when he was finished.

"I want you to know the truth of how grateful I am to Elvin for offering me a helping hand when nobody else would." He chuckled. "Not yanking it back when he found out the mistake he'd made in hiring one of the boys who'd picked on his daughter unmercifully."

"True."

When her lips fought a smile, he picked up his cup and drained the last of the *millich* from it. It was mostly cinnamon by that point, so it left him thirsty. Rising, he went to the faucet and rinsed out the cup before refilling it with water.

"So you can see," he said, facing her, "why I'd do anything to help Elvin."

"'He which soweth sparingly,'" she said softly, "'shall reap also sparingly; and he which soweth bountifully shall reap also bountifully. Every man according as he purposeth in his heart, so let him give; not grudgingly, or of necessity: for God loveth a cheerful giver. And God is able to make all grace abound toward you; that ye, always having all sufficiency in all things, may abound to every good work.'"

"I've heard Elvin reading that to himself several times recently."

Raising her pretty eyes to meet his gaze, she flushed. "Sorry. I know it bothers you when I quote from memory, but it's one of his favorite passages from 2 Corinthians."

"No, it doesn't bother me." He grinned wryly. "Okay, *ja*, it does. Most of the time. Not tonight. It describes Elvin perfectly. You, too."

She shook her head. "I don't want to believe what I've reaped is what I've sown."

Her voice was so discouraged he'd already taken a step toward her when he halted himself. Clamping his arms by his sides to keep from reaching out to offer her comfort, he wished he could erase the past they shared. Even if he could forget—and, *ach*, how he wished he could!—she never would be able to.

Those memories would always remain between them.

Chapter Fifteen

Naomi was surprised how Samuel managed to avoid his sister when they were living in the same house. Or maybe it wasn't that amazing.

Kara spent most of her time in the main house chasing the twins and helping with May. Once the *kinder* were in bed, Kara retreated to the *dawdi haus*. Samuel was seldom inside, other than to help *Daed* with physical therapy, during the day. Every other waking minute he spent in the shop.

She'd caught Samuel glancing with worry at her when he came in along with Lillian, but he didn't say anything. Just as he hadn't said anything three nights ago after she'd lamented about what her life had become. She wished she hadn't let those words slip out. Nobody in Bliss Valley must learn how Marlin had broken his vows and planned to divorce her. She didn't want his shameless actions to be his legacy to their sons.

But was Samuel worried about his sister? He'd never showed any sign on the few occasions they were together. Samuel's sister was equally to blame. If Kara saw Samuel coming, she found something to do in the *dawdi haus.* At meals, Kara focused on the *kinder* while Samuel acted as if he sat alone.

Naomi had let the days pass without saying anything. They'd been busy in the wake of the midnight conversation in the kitchen. Many buggies had been damaged in the hailstorm, so a new one seemed to show up every hour. She'd worked the past several mornings smoothing dents out of the tops and sides of buggies. She had to be cautious with the resins she prepared, making sure she worked where there was plenty of fresh air, but it was work she enjoyed.

Did Samuel or Kara enjoy anything? By the time another week was coming to an end, she'd put up with enough. Their antics had begun to upset the twins, as well as her *daed.* The only question was how to convince two siblings to bridge the chasm between them so they could reconcile and put the past behind them.

Like you've done?

She ignored the accusation in her internal voice. Nothing either Samuel or Kara had done could have been as bad as Marlin's cheating.

Even choosing an underhanded scheme to get your husband to come home and have a real marriage with you?

No, it hadn't been a scheme when she'd decided to try to carry a *boppli* to term to make Marlin happy. She'd wanted what other women had. A husband who loved only her and a family to share their lives. After so many losses, she'd been blessed by having the twins, but she knew that, though she'd wanted *kinder* with Marlin, she'd kept trying to carry to term because she believed that was the best—and maybe the sole— way to persuade her husband to value his marriage vows. How many times had she prayed for a *boppli* to bring her straying husband back to her? She'd believed, with all her heart, that was the answer.

It hadn't been.

She'd spent many hours walking the floor through the long nights with a colicky twin while she tried to puzzle out why Marlin had pleaded for her to marry him and then had left her to spend time with other women for days. Sometimes weeks. When she'd tried to discuss his philandering with him, he'd either walked out again or told her she should be grateful he'd given her his name.

He'd said a man deserved *kinder*, especially a son. He'd said that more than once after she'd miscarried. His words had eaten her like acid, searing and going more deeply into her until reaching her very soul. The wounds his words had engraved there refused to heal.

So she'd risked her health and her life, refusing to heed warnings from *doktors* and midwives. She'd done as he demanded.

Times two.

She'd given him two sons. Two beautiful sons.

He'd changed his hurtful words to complaints about how she never had time for him because she spent every minute with the *bopplin*. She'd never understood why he needed to make her feel inadequate and a failure.

"Hey, Naomi, where do you store the rest of the clean diapers?" called Kara from the other side of the kitchen. She held May in the crook of her arm.

Happy to push aside her dreary thoughts, Naomi said, "All the clean diapers are in the cupboard by the back stairs."

"Just these?"

She wanted to groan when she saw how few diapers were

there. Yesterday, it'd rained the whole day, so she'd taken the chance of skipping laundry.

"Let me start a load of diapers." She brushed a loose hair toward her *kapp*, knowing that today's sultry weather wouldn't be *gut* for drying clothes, either. "Three in diapers are two too many. I need to get the twins potty trained." She glanced around the kitchen, which was filled with the *kinder*'s toys. "One of these days, I should start."

"Don't worry. I can take care of that." Kara reached for a diaper, then closed the door. "I helped train my little cousins. It's fun to spend time with them."

"*Fun* is the boys' favorite word."

"I've noticed." She offered one of her rare smiles, and Naomi was surprised to see a dimple in her left cheek in the same spot as Samuel's.

Did the other Slabaugh siblings have the same dimple? She'd never spent any time with the other kids in the family because she'd been anxious that if she did, it'd draw Samuel's attention, along with his friends', to her again.

"If you'd start potty training them," Naomi said, "I'd be grateful."

"It's the least I can do when you've welcomed me to stay with you and your family." She made a silly face. "And this adorable little pumpkin seed. I think she's chubbier today than she was yesterday."

"The way she eats, that's no surprise."

"You don't think it's a problem, ain't so?" Kara's voice became agitated.

"*Bopplin* grow round and cuddly, and then they seem to grow an inch or two overnight and stretch out. My boys have done that since they were born. It's as if they need fuel to shoot up in a growth spurt."

"That's *gut* to know." She went to the refrigerator to get a bottle for May.

For only a second, Naomi considered asking why she was avoiding her brother, but bit back the words. She didn't want Kara to think that because she lived under the Gingerichs' roof, she didn't have any privacy. She and the girl barely knew each other. All their conversations revolved around the *kinder*.

After starting a load of diapers in the loud washer, which was run by a propane engine outside the house, Naomi went to check on her *daed*. His session with Lillian had left him frustrated because she was helping him try to make his left hand move at the same time as his right one. Each time his left arm had flopped like a dead fish against the bed tray she'd set across his knees. She'd halted when he refused for the first time to continue working. Lillian had reassured Naomi they'd try again during a later session.

The bedroom door was open to allow for cross ventilation on the hot afternoon, so she walked in. Making sure she was smiling, she realized it didn't matter. His eyes were closed, but she could tell he wasn't sleeping because his right hand was fisted on the dark-red-and-green diamond in the square quilt that her *grossmammi* had made as a wedding gift for *Daed* and *Mamm*.

"How are you doing, *Daed*?" She picked up his cup and popped the top as she would have the twins'. It was more than half-full of juice.

"*Gut*." He opened his eyes and glanced at her. "*Danki*, Na...omi."

As he said her name for the first time since his stroke, she drew in her bottom lip and held it before her shout of joy could explode out. It would embarrass her *daed*. She contented herself with saying, "You're welcome, *Daed*."

Had he heard her? His eyes were closed again, and the sound of soft snores rumbled through the room.

She left him to his nap. In the hall, she leaned her head against the wall and raised her eyes. "*Danki*, Lord, for my *daed* saying my name. I don't know when I've heard anything as beautiful. *Danki* for the precious sounds of my family."

Something abruptly crashed at the front of the house, and one twin howled. Jesse. Moments later, the higher-pitched cry that belonged to May rushed along the hall. Then Jared's voice rose in dismay.

As she ran to see what had happened, a laugh of joy burst from her. Who said that God didn't have a sense of humor?

Once it was nap time for everyone in the house, including *Daed* and Kara, Naomi debated between baking a cake and doing another load of laundry. Both would be hot chores when the stagnant air felt as if it'd come from a kiln.

Instead, she poured two glasses of ice tea. As hot as it was in the house, it'd be worse in the shop. She carried them outside and across the yard, knowing Samuel would appreciate the refreshing drink. He was an excellent assistant for her *daed*, in the shop and while doing physical therapy. The least she could do was bring him a drink, and maybe she'd find a way to discuss why he and his sister seemed to be living parallel lives.

"What's this?" she asked aloud when she stopped by what looked like tire tracks dug deeply into the grass along the side of the house. Seeing Samuel in the door to the shop, she called him over. "Did you see this?"

He took the glass she offered him and shook his head. "No. I came out the front door with Lillian this morning, so I didn't come across this part of the yard."

"Lillian! These tracks must be from her car."

"No." He shook his head, then pushed his straw hat back. "She was parked near the shop. These must have been made by the car I heard last night."

"A car here? In the middle of the night?"

Taking a deep drink of the tea, he swirled the cubes in the glass. "Someone must have been lost. They turned down the lane and kept going, hoping to find the main road. Looks like they gave up right about here and spun the car around."

"I hope that's all it was."

He frowned. "Why would you think it might be something else?"

She didn't want to admit how anything out of the ordinary sent chills down her back since the night she'd opened the door to the Yeatmans. "I didn't hear it."

"I'm glad. You've been looking peaked lately, like you could use a week's worth of sleep."

"Danki," she said, letting sarcasm slide in the voice as they stepped over the tracks and continued toward the shop.

"Being honest."

"Sometimes honesty isn't the best policy." She smiled to take the sting out of her words. "Especially when telling your boss's daughter she looks exhausted."

"I can get a hoe and pull the grass back together."

"Don't worry. When they bring in the supplies to rebuild the chicken barn, the big trucks will tear up the ground between here and the old foundation."

"Have you heard when that will be?"

"Not yet. They've got to finish the other projects they put in front of ours after *Daed's* stroke."

"I'll ask Adam the next time I see him."

She nodded, not wanting to talk about his erstwhile partner in crime. When they stepped into the shop, she glanced toward the phone answering machine, but it wasn't blinking. She'd thought she would have heard from Skylar by now.

"What's on your mind, Naomi?" he asked as he put his glass on the table holding the phone.

"I guessed you'd be thirsty." She was equivocating, and she could see he knew it as much as she did.

"So you decided to come and chat me up after hardly saying two words to me in the past few days."

"Me? You're the one who's given me the silent treatment." She waved aside his response before he could make it. "You're right about me wanting to talk to you. I'm worried about Kara and you."

"Both of us?"

She held the glass in two hands to make sure her quivering fingers didn't lose their grip. "*Ja*. Why are you shutting her out? She's your sister. She's going through a tough time. Don't you want to help her?"

"I'd like to, but she doesn't seem to want my help."

"How do you know?"

"Because I've asked her a bunch of times if she wants to talk about what happened to convince her to leave home, and she says no."

Naomi knew she must look as young as his sister when she rolled her eyes, but she couldn't help herself. "Samuel, you're a stranger to her. Why would she open up about what's in her heart because you asked?"

"She has to you."

"Not much. Mostly she likes to talk about the *kinder*, and a few times she's mentioned what her own childhood was like. As soon as she realizes what she's doing, she stops."

"If she won't talk to you, why do you think she's going to talk to me?"

"Because you're her brother."

He laughed curtly. "You think about siblings weirdly, Naomi."

"Probably because I've never had any."

"Is that why you've got an idealized version in your head?" He didn't give her a chance to retort. "I remember you loving stories in school about brothers and sisters playing together while they had exciting adventures that turned up a missing item or saved an abandoned puppy."

"You remember that?"

"You aren't the only one with a memory. I might not be able to pull up every little detail of every day, but I remember plenty of things from those years. I especially recall things that happened over and over, like you reading those books with such a wistful expression."

"Every kid wants siblings." She folded her arms. "I was pleased when my twins came along, because they each had an immediate brother."

"Having brothers and sisters isn't like in books where the kids never say a cross word to each other or disappoint each other or hurt each other because one's mad at the other. It's learning to live with someone who may share your blood, but not your interests or your values. It's learning to compromise when you don't want to and don't have any reason to, other than to keep peace under your roof."

"Compromise? You?"

"*Ja.* I compromised a lot."

"At home."

He nodded.

"Is that why you never compromised at school or any-where else?"

"I compromised a lot. You've got to remember how many times I did."

"No, the only time I remember you compromising was when you tried to compromise me by ruining my reputation."

He stared at her, his face as gray as the buggy beside him. She didn't wait for his answer before she turned on her heel and walked out of the shop. Talking about the past made it all seem too real again, and she couldn't bear to live through that torment again.

"Im-im…!" Elvin groaned the following afternoon as he tried to close his fingers around the soft ball Samuel held in front of him.

The older man grinned when Samuel stifled a yawn. How many nights could a man go without sleeping and still be able to function? He hadn't gotten a minute of sleep since Naomi had stormed out of the shop yesterday. She'd remained as cool to him as his sister was. Though he wasn't sure why Kara continued to distrust him after agreeing to move into the house where he lived, he was well aware why Naomi spoke to him only when necessary.

The past was still alive between them. He had no idea how to put it to rest. Apologizing hadn't helped. Also he was growing more convinced something had happened to Naomi during her marriage that kept her from forgiving him as she would have anyone else.

Almost anyone else, his brain corrected him. He knew that was true as sure as he knew his own name. Had her husband done something to her as atrocious as Samuel had before he'd jumped the fence? She'd spoken easily of Marlin Ropp's death, but he couldn't recall a single word she'd said about her life with him.

"Now, you know it's not impossible," Samuel said, trying to keep his eyelids from sagging. "You did it yesterday with Lillian. Twice."

"Better—"

"*Ja*, you're doing better, but you—"

"Looks better. Lil."

Samuel laughed. The older man usually managed to get his message across, though it took far longer now. His stroke had altered so much for his boss, but it hadn't changed Elvin's strong will.

Was being stubborn such a Gingerich trait that a near-death experience couldn't alter it? Naomi shared Elvin's ability to stand pat in the face of logic.

Most especially Samuel's logic.

"That's enough for today," he said.

Elvin, who hadn't let a second pass during the exercise session without grumbling about something, shook his head. "*Ja.*" His face puckered with frustration at saying the opposite of what he meant. It occurred less, except when he was tired. They were supposed to try the exercise with both hands at the same time, but it remained something Elvin couldn't master. Samuel wouldn't have been able to do it, either, so he skipped it most days.

"Go out?" Elvin asked. "Today?"

"I know your ears work as well as mine," Samuel replied, "and you heard what Lillian said. You can go to the shop when you can walk there."

Elvin snorted. "Walking now."

"*Ja.* From the bed to the bathroom and back, leaning on me or her. What's that? A half-dozen steps? The shop is all the way across the yard."

"Try. Want to try."

Samuel heard the yearning in the old man's voice. How well he understood it! Hazel, his physical therapist, had given him the goal of being able to walk the length of the hall before he could go outside. It'd taken almost two months before he was able to meet that goal, and then he'd been so weak and drenched in sweat he'd barely made it to his room to fall into a chair. He'd spent three more weeks building up the stamina he hadn't realized he'd lost before he attempted to walk on the sidewalks near the rehab center. It'd been another month before he had enough strength to lift his injured leg high enough to traverse the lawn.

"All right," he said.

The old man's eyes glistened with sudden excitement, and he sat straighter, using his right arm to help push himself up.

Hating to douse that hopeful light, Samuel nodded. "Let's talk to Lillian tomorrow about getting you practice." He glanced at the four-wheeled walker waiting in the corner. It had larger wheels, which were meant to help over uneven ground, something that would be necessary for Elvin to get from the house to the shop. Especially with that deep track gouged out by tires in the side yard. "You know what she's said about it."

"Need two hands." Elvin scowled at his left hand, and both sides of his face worked in tandem. Samuel didn't mention that, not wanting to let his boss know how closely he, Naomi and the physical therapist gauged each move he made.

"So let's work on that later this afternoon."

Again Elvin grunted, but Samuel noticed the fingers on his left hand twitched. It could have been only an involuntary motion. However, he guessed Naomi's *daed* was struggling to make them obey him. Progress was in small increments, but

Samuel took the motion as a reminder he needed to get back to work on the project he had devised for Elvin.

Making sure Elvin had water to drink and newspapers to read, Samuel returned to the shop. Naomi had been out there while he was tending to her *daed*, but she never was in the shop when he arrived. He couldn't stop from thinking of the *Englisch* fairy tale about the cobbler and the elves. Her work was excellent, far better than his own. If she'd been a son instead of a daughter, Elvin would have trained her to take over the shop.

Samuel was glad she wasn't a son...for many reasons. Not the least was that Elvin wouldn't have hired him if a son was ready to step in. A smile curled along Samuel's lips as he thought of other reasons why he was happy she hadn't been born a boy. The sparkle of her pretty eyes, her soft curves, the way her lyrical voice lilted in his ears... Those and other considerations were reasons to be thankful.

Chuckling to himself at his goofy thoughts, he got to work on a bent wheel. It had been caused, like so much of the work lately, by the recent storm. The owner had been caught out in it, and his horse had been spooked by the hail. The buggy wheels had skidded, and one had struck a rock on the side of the road. The damage had been worsened by driving the buggy to the shop.

An hour later, Samuel had appraised how the wheel fit on the buggy. He moved toward it again. Running his hand along the surface, he tried to discern any irregularities. He squatted, keeping one hand on the door opening so he could check the axle and the brake. When he'd learned Elvin preferred to replace old brakes with disc brakes rather than the drum brakes that were standard on buggies in the area, he'd been astonished the elderly man was so forward-thinking.

Elvin had explained it. "Young men want the newfangled gizmos on their buggies. Once one of them changed over to disc brakes and started spreading the word, every man under forty who brought his buggy in for brake work wanted them. I haven't stayed in business for almost fifty years by forgetting the most important thing: give the customer what he wants at a price he's willing to pay. Don't you ever forget that, boy."

Nodding, Samuel had kept his smile to himself. Elvin called anyone under fifty *boy*. Older than that, he called them *young man*. Samuel wasn't sure why, and he hadn't asked.

Samuel didn't feel like a boy. Sometimes, when his weak arm and leg refused to work as they should, he felt older than Elvin. He'd squandered his youth and had no idea how to get it back.

Naomi squinted as she looked across the yard from where she'd finished bringing in a load of diapers. The thickening gray of thunderstorm clouds made it almost as difficult to see as at dusk.

What was sitting in front of the shop? When she'd been there earlier in the day, there hadn't been anything outside.

After putting the basket of clean diapers in the laundry room, she strode across the grass. She jumped over the tracks in the grass, barely pausing because she was eager to make sure whatever had been left outside would be protected before the rain started.

It was, she realized as she got closer, the front seat from a buggy. Metal supports held the back to the main cushion. The structure beneath the seat had been replaced with wooden rails and legs. Though the dark blue upholstery was thin in spots, it appeared clean.

When Samuel stood from behind it, a screwdriver in hand,

she wished she hadn't come to check. Since their last conversation at the shop yesterday, she'd made sure someone else was around whenever he was nearby.

"It's going to rain," she said, feeling *dumm* for stating the obvious.

"Water won't hurt it. I put fabric protector spray on the cushions, so rain will roll right off it. When I pulled it out of the Stoltzfuses' buggy, I decided to rebuild it rather than throwing it away."

"And put it here for customers?" she asked.

He shook his head.

Her eyes widened, and her voice grew husky. "You built it for *Daed*?"

"*Ja*. Maybe you haven't noticed, but Elvin is getting antsy inside."

"Not noticed? I've been expecting I'll find him crawling on his belly across the kitchen floor to reach the door." She laughed, her heart leaping with happiness. Again, she had to ask herself which man Samuel was: the kind one who helped her *daed* or the nasty one who hadn't cared about anyone's feelings but his own? Could anyone change that much?

Marlin did.

The words stabbed at her so hard she almost gasped. Why was it easy to accept someone could take a turn for the worse but not for the better?

"He can sit here," Samuel said, revealing he had no idea of the course of her thoughts, "and supervise my work as he used to. It'll give him a sense of normalcy. It's important for him to believe he can control his own body again." He edged past the bench to go into the shop.

"And I won't be here getting in your way."

"You haven't ever gotten in my way, and you know what you're doing."

"*Daed* wanted to teach me everything he knew." She swallowed hard. "In case someday I needed to support myself."

"Fixing buggies is an unusual career for a plain woman."

"No more unusual than a widow taking care of her family's farm. We do what we must."

His eyes narrowed, startling her. His words were astonishing. "Be careful with that train of thought, Naomi. I said much the same to myself while I was on the other side of the fence. When we think we know more than God about the path our lives should take, we get into trouble. I thought I knew more than Him until He sent me a wake-up call in the form of that car accident." His hand clenched around the screwdriver. "Adam got God's message before we left. I got mine the night of the accident. I wonder if Joel ever figured it out."

"Have you heard from him since the accident?" She asked the question tentatively, unsure where the conversation could head.

"Not a word."

"I've heard he went to jail."

"I've heard that, too, but I don't know the truth."

"If the accident—"

"I was the one driving that night. If Joel ended up in jail, it wasn't for that."

"Or for running out on you."

He put the screwdriver on the table. "If you're hinting that it must have hurt that Joel never came to see me in the hospital, then come out and ask." He didn't give her a chance to reply as he hurried on. "*Ja*, it hurt. A lot, though I shouldn't have been surprised. We were so used to fighting against living plain that when we left for the *Englisch* world, it was impossible to stop fighting. Even when the only one we had to battle against was each other." He rubbed his right hand against his leg. "I never stopped thinking about him."

"I'm sorry he let you down."

"Maybe he did. Maybe he didn't."

"What do you mean?" she asked, stepping into the shop as a distant rumble of thunder announced the coming storm.

"While I was in the hospital, I was doped up with painkillers, so I had a lot of strange dreams. Some things happened I still find hard to believe weren't dreams. Other things felt as real as you and me talking now."

"What do you mean?"

He hesitated, then said, "One night I was hooked up to all kinds of machines and couldn't move because my leg was in traction. I'd been in the hospital for about three days, but I'd only been conscious for a day. In the hours after the accident, I can recall only bits and pieces about what happened. That's why it seems so strange this one night is so clear in my mind."

"What happened?" She flinched as lightning flashed twice.

"Joel came to visit me."

"You said he never came—"

"That's what everyone told me, but, Naomi, I remember him being there." He stared past her toward the roiling clouds. "He stood at the foot of my bed and watched me. He thought I was asleep, but I wasn't."

"What did he say?"

"Not a word. He stood there making a strange sound. I've wondered ever since if he was crying. Maybe he felt bad for me."

"If so, why didn't he come back when you were awake?"

He shrugged. "I don't know, Naomi. I don't know when he got there or when he left. I only know I can clearly recall him standing at the foot of my bed that night. When I asked the nurses, they said I hadn't had any visitors. I hated how they looked at me with pity."

"It must have been a dream. Your hopes manifesting themselves so starkly that it seemed real to you." She yearned to embrace him, comforting him as he revealed the pain that continued to haunt him.

"That's what everyone said, but…"

Comprehending what he couldn't find words for, she said, "You hope it was real. That Joel came to make sure you were okay."

"I *pray* it was real." He flung out his hands, the right one making only a portion of the motion of his left. "Then I wonder if I have the right to ask God to heed my prayers after I turned my back on Him. Every day when I look in the mirror while shaving, I see the truth in front of my eyes. It's not everyone who carries the signs of his sins right out in plain sight for the whole world to see."

Her heart ached for the guilt and pain he held deep within his. This time, she couldn't keep from reaching out to take his right hand and fold it between hers. "Is that what you think your injuries are? Signs of your sins?"

"What would you call them?" He looked at her fingers wrapped around his. As if he couldn't trust himself to meet her eyes.

"Signs of God's grace."

He stared at her. "God's grace? When I went as far from God and His grace as any mortal could?"

"If you think that's true, then you don't have any idea how far someone can go to turn his back on God." She released his hand and stepped back before tears ran along her cheeks like the cloudburst pelting the yard.

She ran toward the house, but couldn't escape the sight of the shock on his face at her words when he realized she was talking about her late husband. She'd finally found something she had in common with Samuel King.

Neither of them wanted to be pitied.

Chapter Sixteen

The following Tuesday was the date set for the barn raising. Activity began before Jonas's buggy turned onto the main road at the head of a parade of other horse-drawn vehicles at first light. On Friday and Saturday, large flatbeds had driven down the farm lane to deliver materials. Their large wheels obliterated the tire tracks that had been cut into the grass.

Naomi had taken the twins to watch the lumber being unloaded. They'd been thrilled with the big trucks, the stacks of wood and the collections of screws and nails. The latter she agreed to take inside so the frequent thunderstorms didn't ruin the cardboard boxes. Jared and Jesse had declared moving the boxes would be "Fun!" However, after they scattered nearly a whole container of nails in the grass, she'd convinced them to let her carry them while they opened and closed the kitchen door for her. She'd diverted their attention from the activity by convincing them to help her get *Daed* onto the porch with his walker.

She'd smiled as the twins explained to their *grossdawdi* what would happen when the volunteers arrived to rebuild the chicken barn. He'd listened as intently as if he hadn't participated in many barn raisings. He was *wunderbaar* with the twins, giving them the love they hadn't gotten from their *daed*.

The previous day, the job's appointed supervisor, Ephraim Weaver, had come to the farm with Adam. Ephraim was Adam's great-*grossdawdi*, and everyone called him *Grossdawdi* Ephraim, even men, like her *daed*, who were close to his age. She hadn't seen *Daed* have such a *gut* time since before her *mamm*'s death. Both men were patient with his faltering words and gaffes.

That morning the kitchen had filled with women bringing baskets of food and casseroles for the midday meal. Naomi's favorite hymn of praise played through her head when she welcomed them. She'd cleared out the refrigerator the night before and brought every table in the house into the kitchen to provide room to store the largesse. Cheerful voices lilted around her.

Kara walked in from the *dawdi haus* with May. She scanned the crowd, and her shoulders eased from their taut line. It must have been that nobody from the Slabaugh household was in the kitchen. Why hadn't Naomi thought about Slabaugh family members being part of the friendly onslaught of volunteers?

As fast as Naomi could make *kaffi*, the pot was emptied. She was glad when Laurene Nolt and her great-*aenti* arrived with a pair of big urns from the Acorn Farm Inn. It was more than an hour later before those were drained. By that time, dozens of eggs had been prepared and served along with toast and oatmeal and every flavor of muffin she could imagine.

Grateful Kara kept an eye on the twins because Naomi doubted she could do that and oversee the crowded kitchen at the same time, she smiled when the younger woman stopped her long enough to tout the twins's progress with potty training. Kara was doing a great job because the boys adored her so much for making everything into a game.

"Can I take them outside?" she asked as her eyes followed May, who was being handed from one admiring woman to the next. "They want to go."

"Only as far as the back porch. They'll have a *gut* view from there. Make sure they don't go off the porch. There are too many ways they can get hurt."

"Got it." Holding out her hands to Jared and Jesse, she said, *"Komm mol."*

Another hour passed before Naomi could take a break to go outside and see how the barn was progressing. After tying her black bonnet under her chin, she stepped onto the porch. She smiled when she saw her *daed* with Jesse sitting on his lap while Jared grasped the arm of the rocking chair. All three were watching the volunteers push up a side wall with long poles. Other men sat on the already constructed rafters and waited for the wall to come up to where they could nail it in place. Not all the builders were plain, she realized, when she saw *Englischers* working side by side with the Amish carpenters.

"Vol-vol…teer…firefight-firefighters," *Daed* said as if she'd spoken.

Kara, who was sitting on a step, looked over her shoulder. "From what *Grossdawdi* Ephraim told us, at least a few of the members of the Bliss Valley Fire Department have offered to help rebuild each of the buildings destroyed by those arsonists this past spring."

"I'm sure they did their best to save the originals."

"They did, but now…build up again." He bent to talk to

his *kins-kinder*. "Look! The truck! See white…lights? Means… back…"

Smiling at her *daed,* who was trying to teach the twins a lesson, she looked at the truck when she heard the hard sound of spinning tires. The driver had gotten caught in one of the big ruts left by the delivery trucks.

A half-dozen men moved forward to help. One was Samuel, because his odd gait was like no one else's. When he slipped on the raw earth near the truck, she gasped. His weak leg wouldn't hold him, and he tumbled. In one smooth motion, he rolled his left shoulder forward. Doing a somersault, which ended with dirty water and mud dripping off him, he scrambled to his feet and kept going.

Daed grinned as the twins crowed with excitement and clapped their hands at what they saw as part of the show.

Naomi was startled by her *daed*'s reaction. "If he's hurt—"

"Not." *Daed* pointed toward the yard. "Look."

He was right. Samuel was wiping mud off his trousers as if nothing unusual had happened. In short order, he was shouting to several other men. They brought horses from the field. He hooked them together with Waldo and connected the harness to the rear of the truck. Calling to the driver to put the truck in neutral, he gave the order to the horses to go. More cheers went up as the team drew the truck forward and out of the ruts.

Samuel unhitched the horses before going to the front of the truck. His voice carried to the house. "Sometimes less horsepower is better."

The driver chuckled. "I can't argue with that. Maybe I should get a team of my own for when I'm heading down one of these farm lanes after a big storm."

"There are plenty of horses around here. All you need to do is put out the call for help, and you'll find a nearby team."

"Thanks, buddy!"

Samuel stepped back and waved as the man backed out, carefully turning so he avoided people and the horses that were being led to the pasture.

Naomi listened to her *kinder* chattering about what they'd seen, but she didn't answer as she watched Samuel. He seemed comfortable with *Englischers*. As comfortable as he was around plain folk, especially Adam and her *daed*.

Like Marlin.

She shook her head in response to her own thought. *Ja*, Marlin had a lot of *Englisch* friends. Too many, it'd turned out, because one of them—and she'd never found out which—had taken him to Lancaster the night of his death. Having *gut* relationships with neighbors wasn't a bad thing.

Marlin had never been at ease around her *daed*. She hadn't understood why at first, because everyone liked Elvin Gingerich, even when he spoke his mind. Only later, when she'd discovered the truth about Marlin's cheating, did she think he might have been afraid *Daed* would discover his betrayals. Marlin had refused to come to Bliss Valley. She didn't understand why, if he was ashamed of being with other women, he hadn't stopped.

With the ease of too much practice, she pushed thoughts of her late husband from her mind. She spent the rest of the morning sitting with her family and watching the construction until it was time to help set up the midday meal. Leaving the twins under Kara's watchful eyes, she carried food and dishes to the tables that had been set up not far from the barn. The interior structure had already been completed. She guessed by nightfall, there would be clapboard on the sides and shingles on the roof.

The food disappeared almost as rapidly as the *kaffi* had. No matter how many dishes she and the other women carried to the tables, the food was gone and people were waiting when they returned with more. She also made sure *Daed* and the other older men got generous servings. A trio of women, led by Laurene, oversaw feeding the *kinder,* who were seated on sheets on the front lawn. Anything they spilled could be shaken or washed out.

When she saw Adam Hershberger on the porch with his great-*grossdawdi* and *Daed,* she knew she couldn't put off talking with him any longer. She collected a large manila envelope where she'd been keeping the bills from the hospital. Though she'd already paid more than a dozen of them, she'd need the *Leit*'s help with the rest.

"Adam?" She hated how her voice quavered when speaking his name.

He turned and smiled. "Naomi, the raising is going well, ain't so?"

"It is." She hesitated, then asked, "Could I speak with you a moment? As our deacon?"

"Of course." He followed as she stepped away from the porch and walked to the front of the house.

She paused by the steps. "It's about *Daed*'s bills."

"I assume they're in that envelope."

"*Ja.*" She held it out. "These are the bills we can't pay ourselves right now."

"Don't worry. We've already reviewed the current bills with the hospital. The *Leit* will cover what you can't."

"All of it? There's nearly fifty thousand dollars left to pay."

"Don't worry," he repeated. "The hospital offers discounts to patients without health insurance. The bills, after I speak with them next week, will be quite a bit lower. The billing office has gotten used to me coming in to negotiate."

"Danki." She released the breath she'd been holding almost from the moment she'd realized she couldn't put off talking to him.

"I'm glad to help." He rubbed the back of his neck and gave her a grin. "I thought God had lost His mind when I was selected to be deacon, but I've gotten so I like the job. This part. Helping people. Not the part about trying to convince members to live the life they vowed they would at baptism." His smile wavered as he asked, "How's Kara Slabaugh doing?"

"She seems happy. She loves spending time with May and the boys, and she's *gut* with them. She'll be a great *mamm* someday."

"I'm glad to hear that. I want you to know I never intended for you to take her in, especially with Elvin in recovery."

"It's okay, Adam. I'm glad I can help."

"Samuel appreciates this more than he's probably told you." He chuckled. "He's not one to talk a lot about how he feels, but he does feel a lot. Okay, that sounded silly."

"I know what you mean. He keeps things to himself."

"Ja, and not just how he feels about things. He's never forgiven himself for going with Joel, and he feels as if the accident was punishment for what he did."

She shook her head. "No, he doesn't." Knowing Samuel trusted his friend, she shared with Adam what he'd told her about the accident, leaving out the part where he thought he'd seen Joel Beachy by his hospital bed. She finished with, "He sees the accident as something that showed him the way home."

"That's the problem, ain't so? Samuel's never been able to come home because his family has closed their hearts to him. I know Jonas has spoken with them, but nothing has changed." He sighed. "Until he can truly come home, I don't think he'll ever be able to put the past behind him."

Telling her he'd let her know any updates on the bills, he walked away.

She stayed where she was, blinking back surprising tears. She hadn't cried when she'd learned Marlin was dead. She hadn't cried when she'd been evicted from what she'd believed was her home, but she battled against her tears at the thought of how unmoored Samuel was.

When the twins came running around the house, she captured them and hugged them close to her. She buried her face between theirs, thanking God she had them and *Daed*. Without them, she would have been as lost as Samuel.

She couldn't think of anything sadder.

May's first visit to the pediatrician couldn't have been deemed anything other than a great success. Though nobody had said a word, Samuel knew he wasn't the only one concerned that the *boppli* had suffered damage from being left on the porch in a grocery bag. Naomi hadn't stopped smiling since the *doktor* had examined the infant from head to foot and pronounced May was exactly average in her milestones for weight and height and reaction time.

Samuel admitted, only to himself, he'd been anxious as well about the skills of the *doktor*. Because May was a ward of the commonwealth, she couldn't go to the *doktorfraa* in Bliss Valley who usually saw plain *kinder*. Instead, they'd had to drive the little girl to an office building on the far side of busy Route 30, which cut through the heart of the county. The summer brought more traffic, and today hadn't been any exception.

They'd left the house almost an hour before the appointment, though the seven-mile trip usually didn't take more than forty minutes. He was glad that they'd departed early because they were more than five minutes late by the time they reached the low brick building and found the proper office among the maze of other specialists.

However, the *doktor* whose name was Dr. Elgar, had proved to be competent and compassionate. He'd worked with other foster families, though most had the *kind*'s parents' health history to share. Not knowing anything was something he'd taken in stride. He'd focused on the *boppli* in front of him and Naomi's report of how the little girl was sleeping and eating.

May had been cooperative except when she received her first shot. Her shriek must have been heard from one end of the building to the other.

"Don't worry," Dr. Elgar had said with a smile. "Our neighbors are used to hearing our patients express their opinions." He'd rubbed his hand on May's tummy to calm her. "I can't offer you a lollipop to make up for the indignity."

After answering their questions—and Naomi had many more than Samuel—the *doktor* had asked them to make an appointment for a month later.

"So you liked the *doktor*, ain't so?" Samuel pulled the buggy into the traffic along the road that led south to Strasburg.

"I did." Naomi smiled at the *boppli* lying on her knees. May had grabbed Naomi's thumbs, and they were playing a game of patty-cake. "How did you know?"

"You made an appointment for the twins for the same day as May's. You wouldn't have done that if you didn't like the *doktor*."

She wiggled the *boppli*'s hands gently. "We needed a new pediatrician, and May showed us the way. It's amazing how God works through the least of us."

"Don't let May hear you call her the least." He chuckled, but kept a wary eye on the long line of cars slowing to a stop at the light where the road crossed Route 30.

A policeman was walking along the parked cars. He paused by the buggy and said, "There's a pretty nasty accident about a half mile down the road. We're diverting traffic along the main road." He kept walking to deliver the same message to the car behind them.

"You know Waldo better than I do," Samuel said. "How will he do?"

She glanced at the number of cars speeding along the highway. "He'll be fine." She hesitated, then said, her voice wobbly, "Let me drive. I'm more used to him than you are."

"Are you sure? I can—"

"I'm sure. I drove him from Honey Brook, so getting through the detour shouldn't be harder than that."

Samuel climbed out while Naomi slid across the seat. When he got back in on the other side, she handed him the *boppli*. She handled the reins, he noticed, with easy competency.

"Why have you let me drive before now?" he asked when she guided the horse forward a few paces, pressing the buggy's brake as they stopped again. "You're a *gut* driver."

"After that long trip from Honey Brook, I was glad to hand over the reins for a while."

"You're okay now?"

She nodded and smiled as she moved them forward again, this time several car lengths. "I'm fine, Samuel. If you're worrying, I can take the *boppli* and let you handle the reins."

"No, you're doing great. I trust you to get us home in one piece."

"*Danki.* It's nice to be trusted."

"*Ja,* it is." He looked at May as she gurgled something to

herself, then stuck her fingers in her mouth. "I never thanked you for trusting me with Elvin's PT."

"It sounds as if you're keeping score again."

He shook his head. "Far from it. I wanted to let you know I appreciate your faith in me."

When she started to reply, they were motioned forward by the officer directing traffic. She focused on easing the horse around the corner and onto the shoulder, which was barely wide enough for the buggy.

Samuel said nothing, not even to the *boppli* as they drove west along the crowded road. Naomi must stay alert each time she came to an entrance to a shopping plaza or gas station. He frowned when a small red car zipped into a gas station less than a foot in front of the horse. Neither Naomi nor Waldo panicked as she slowed the buggy.

Cars and trucks sped by, too close for comfort. A memory flashed into his mind of Adam's parents being killed and Adam badly injured after being thrown from a buggy hit by a fast-moving vehicle. The echo of the car he'd been driving crashing into the telephone pole resonated through his head, along with the screech of metal and plastic crumpling into one another.

Why are You making me remember that *now, Lord*?

"Are you okay, Samuel? You're looking a bit green around the gills."

"I'll be okay once we're off this road. Seeing all this traffic makes me understand why folks are leaving Lancaster County to look for areas that aren't as overpopulated."

"Are you thinking of leaving?"

"Not now, but I did before Elvin offered me a job." He started to add more, but gritted his teeth as another car came by too close and too fast.

Naomi cringed away from the loud whoosh of its passing, but Waldo kept going as if the road were empty.

"You've got a *gut* horse," Samuel said. "Nothing upsets Waldo, ain't so?"

"He doesn't like mice. If a mouse gets anywhere near his hooves, he goes wild."

Samuel glanced across the road to a construction zone. It must be where the casino was being built. For now, it wasn't much other than raw earth. Blocks of concrete marked where another building had stood. Chain-link fencing edged the perimeter. Banners displaying the name of the contractors involved were hung along the fence.

"We've all got to be grateful that monstrosity wasn't built in Bliss Valley," he said.

"*Daed* told me there was talk about it, but nothing for certain." She frowned. "He said someone talked to him about purchasing his land to use for an access road. He told them not to come back again."

"Adam told me Laurene was working for the casino at one point."

She shook her head. "That can't be right."

"She was living an *Englisch* life then, don't forget."

"I can't forget that...or anything else." When she laughed, he was glad she'd taken his words as the unthinking comment they were. What a change from when she'd first arrived on her *daed*'s farm and bristled at anything he said.

Naomi turned on the left blinker to alert cars she wanted to move the buggy into traffic as they descended a hill flanked by hotels and restaurants and shops. She waited until a car held back enough to let her shift into the right lane, then into the left turn lane.

"It's time to get off the highway. There's too much traffic." As if to emphasize her words, a large minivan raced past so close Waldo tugged to the right.

Calming Waldo with gentle words and a steady grasp on the reins, Naomi kept him moving in a straight line. She waited for the backed-up traffic to clear, keeping Waldo from bolting as a pair of large tractor trailers whizzed past on either side of them. As soon as it was safe, she turned left onto Millstream Road in front of the Mennonite Information Center. Only a few cars were parked in the lot in front of the low brick building.

The rush of traffic faded as they went past the back entrance to the outlet shopping center and drove around a sharp corner at the rear of the Lancaster Mennonite School. Turning left at the next intersection, the buggy headed south along a road edged by plain farms with fields of rapidly growing corn.

They passed a narrow track leading out into one of the fields beyond a barn. Suddenly she grew rigid.

"What's wrong?" he asked, keeping his voice low so he didn't wake the *boppli,* who'd fallen asleep as soon as they left the heavy traffic behind.

"I haven't come this way since…"

He was about to ask, "Since when?" He halted himself when he realized where they were. The night he'd kissed her, he'd offered her a ride home. She'd refused, not wanting to be seen leaving the youth group with him. He'd waited until she left her friend at the third house along this road and continued on her own toward another friend's house. That friend had left with the young man with whom she was walking out.

Samuel had followed at a distance. Once he saw Naomi was alone, he'd come up alongside her and asked her again if she wanted a ride. As clouds were gathering along the darkening western horizon, she'd agreed.

Right by the road leading out behind the barn they were passing.

"If I say I'm sorry for what happened back then," he asked, "will you believe me?"

She stared in silence at the road. He waited. Anything he said, anything he did, could be the wrong thing now.

"I believe you're sorry now," she replied at last. "I don't believe you were sorry then."

"I guess there's nothing I can say to change your mind about that."

"No."

He sighed. "Then I can't expect you to forgive me."

This time when she didn't answer, he didn't press. Her lack of a response said it all. Nothing had changed, no matter how hard they worked together to help Elvin and to make a home for his sister and the *kinder*. The chasm he'd dug the night he betrayed was too wide.

He sighed silently. For years, he'd railed against the unfairness of how his *mamm* blamed him for his birth. He hadn't done anything except come into the world. He'd treated Naomi as badly, and he deserved every bit of her contempt.

"I'm confused," Kara said the following week as she pulled a diaper out of the basket in the laundry room and folded it.

Naomi dumped another load of clothes into the washing machine. From the front of the house, she could hear Lillian and Samuel working with *Daed*. May was asleep in her seat beside her while at the kitchen table the boys were finishing their midmorning snack of peanut butter and crackers.

When had this life become normal? She hadn't expected to return to live in her *daed*'s house with Jared and Jesse. She certainly never could have imagined Samuel would be on the farm, assisting *Daed* with his PT and moving the shop into the new barn. A *boppli*? That thought might have entered her mind, but only as the wisp of a dying dream after she learned Marlin had lied to her about wanting *kinder*.

Then there was Kara, another surprise. Naomi didn't want to become dependent on the girl's help, because at any point, Kara might decide she was ready to go home. She'd begun wearing plain clothing again, except for a *kapp*. Kara hadn't mentioned why she didn't put one on her hair she wore in long braids down her back, and Naomi hadn't asked. She'd figured that Kara would tell her when she was ready.

Was now the time? Was that why Kara felt confused?

Trying not to give away her thoughts, Naomi asked in what she hoped sounded like a casual tone, "What are you confused about?"

"My brother. At home, I heard how he ruined *Mamm*'s life, but he seems like a *gut* man."

"He does seem like a *gut* man," she agreed, startling herself at how uncomfortable the words felt on her lips. Not because she was lying. She didn't want to say he *seemed* like a *gut* man. She wanted to say he *was* a *gut* man.

That was a fact she'd been trying to ignore since before her *daed*'s stroke. Since she'd gotten home, to be truthful.

She reached for the laundry detergent and measured out enough for a load. She added a bit more because the twins got grass and food stains on everything they wore.

"Why did my parents say those things about him?" Kara asked. "They said he was no *gut*, that he never wanted to be part of the family, that all he did was hurt them."

"You need to ask him. I'm not part of your family." She reached to start the washer. "I do know sometimes people say things in an effort to protect themselves from further hurt."

"How could Samuel keep hurting them when he never came home?" Her eyes widened. "Maybe that was what hurt them."

"What?"

"Him not coming home."

"Kara, he tried to come home." She clamped her lips closed, wondering if she'd said too much.

"When?"

"Like I said, you should talk to your brother about this. It's about your family, not mine."

Kara grabbed her arm and jerked, twisting Naomi to face her. "I've got to know the truth. I thought I knew the truth, but now I'm wondering if everything I thought I knew are lies."

On the girl's face, Naomi saw her own desperation after so many nights alone, wanting to know the truth about where Marlin had gone and why. Those nights had been agonizing as she worried that something horrible had happened to him and he'd never come home. When she'd discovered the truth, she'd felt like the world's biggest *dummkopf*...and then one night he'd gone out and hadn't come home.

Her heart hadn't broken because it'd been turned to stone by his deceptions.

She didn't want Kara to suffer from the not-knowing, the struggling to comb through everything she thought she knew to find the truth, the pain of learning how wrong she'd been.

"Kara, right after he got out of the hospital after the accident, Samuel went to your house. He was turned away."

"Turned away? Did he and *Daed* argue?" Her hands shook as she continued to fold diapers. "They used to argue. All the time. In fact, it's the thing I remember most about Samuel from when I was a *kind*."

"No, it wasn't your *daed*. It was your *mamm* who told him to go away and not come back."

"Because he was born before she was married?"

Naomi didn't try to hide her surprise. "You know about that?"

"Everyone in the family knows about it." Kara rolled her eyes with the skill possessed only by a teenager. "*Mamm* likes to pretend it's a secret, but things like that don't stay a secret." Her mouth tightened. "Most especially when *Mamm* never keeps anyone else's secrets. As soon as something goes in her ears, it comes out of her mouth." She shook her head. "I learned that the hard way a couple of years ago."

"So arguing with your parents wasn't the reason you jumped the fence?"

"No." She glanced at May and then into the kitchen, where Jared was using peanut butter to decorate his brother's face.

Naomi took a step toward them when the boys started splashing water. She paused when Kara went on, riveted by what she heard.

"After Samuel left," the young woman said, "*Mamm* didn't have him to complain about. That's why she started in on Lewis and me."

"Who's Lewis?"

"He's the second youngest in our family, the youngest boy." She shook her head. "I don't know why *Mamm* picked on him. He's a *gut* kid, the one who did his chores without anyone nagging him. He did okay in school, though learning is tough for him. I'm not sure why he had problems learning his numbers, and *Mamm* refused to talk about it. She yelled at him for the slightest mistake. She called him stupid a lot."

"Where's Lewis now?"

"He's still at home. He left for a while, but he got taken

advantage of among the *Englisch*. He never said why he came back, but it was better for him after he did because by then, *Mamm* had decided I was the source of every bit of trouble in her life."

"Have you told Samuel about this?"

She shook her head. "I didn't think he'd want to know. I thought he was happy he'd escaped and didn't want anything to do with us." She began to cry.

Putting her arms around the girl, she held Kara and let her sob. She'd had no idea Kara felt unwanted by someone she cared about...as her brother did. As Naomi did herself. She prayed she could put aside her own residual anger long enough to help ease Kara's grief. She didn't want that sense of being abandoned to taint someone else's life.

Chapter Seventeen

Naomi stood in the doorway to the bedroom.

Though he didn't look in her direction, Samuel couldn't be unaware of her. He'd known she was coming to the room before her light footsteps reached his ears. He always knew when she was nearby.

He had to focus on Elvin. The older man was unsteady on his feet as he made the transfer from bed to his walker. He needed help again when he sat in a chair. He could lock the wheels with the right side handgrips, but his fingers didn't close far enough to do the same on the left.

Standing in front of Elvin, Samuel wrapped a belt around the older man's waist. He held it as Elvin slid forward on the bed to lower his feet to the floor. It was a ballet they'd perfected over the past two weeks. Once Elvin was on his feet and holding on to the walker, he could move about the house. He was impatient and wanted to go beyond the porch, but Samuel insisted Elvin wait for Lillian's okay.

Samuel sent up a silent prayer of gratitude for how much steadier Elvin was as he stood, swaying slightly. To speak that prayer aloud would embarrass the older man.

Glad he had his back to the door, so the sight of Naomi didn't distract him, he said, "Now, Elvin, I'm going to let you get to the chair on your own." He moved the belt so he could stand out of Elvin's way. "Grab the walker, and let's go. I'll be right here if you start to fall."

"I won't." His voice had become clearer and his words came more easily than a few days ago. It was as if he'd rediscovered his voice. "I've been sitting in a chair for more than sixty years, and I can do it another time without you hovering over me like a hen with a single chick."

A smothered laugh came from the doorway, and Elvin brightened, delighted to amuse his daughter. He continued to talk, but his words became disjointed as he concentrated on pushing the walker toward the door. Naomi smiled when her *daed* moved with slow, uneven steps toward the living room. When the twins burst out of the kitchen, she caught them and warned them to slow down.

"Let *Grossdawdi* sit before you start climbing on him," she warned.

"Fun!" called Jared.

"Fun. Lots of fun." Jesse hurried to the toy box and pulled out one of the books Elvin had read to them.

Jared followed and tripped over his own feet. He tucked into himself so he did a forward roll. Lying on the floor, he giggled. "Me fun. Like Samuel fun."

Hearing a gasp behind him, Samuel looked over his shoulder to see a vibrant flush climbing Naomi's cheeks. He'd never seen her blush before. Not even when he and his friends had teased her. So why was she turning red now?

He got his answer when she said, "Jared, it isn't nice to make fun of people."

"Fun!" crowed the little boy, bouncing to his feet. He pretended to stumble again and rolled forward to sit with a grin. "Fun. Right, Samuel?"

Dismay made Naomi's voice ragged. "Samuel, I'm sorry. I—"

"Don't worry." He chuckled. "Don't they say imitation is the highest form of flattery?"

"He's copying what you did when you fell."

"It took me a long time to learn to do that," Samuel said, moving closer to Elvin's side as they reached the old man's favorite chair. "Jared has already mastered it." He laughed when Jesse dropped into a roll and giggled. "Now you can help me teach your *grossdawdi* to do it, too."

"Not with these old bones," grumbled Elvin as he sat with Samuel's help. The fingers of his right hand dug so hard into the upholstery that the marks remained after he'd adjusted himself so he was comfortable. He waved both hands. "Go! I'm going to read to my *kins-kinder.*"

Samuel motioned for Naomi to precede him out of the room. When she glanced back a couple of times, he did, as well. Jared and Jesse were sitting cross-legged on the floor in front of Elvin. He awkwardly held the picture book but read the words on the page with surprising ease.

"He's making improvements in leaps and bounds," Samuel said as soon as they were out of earshot in the kitchen.

"That's what Lillian said would happen." She walked over to the counter where bread was rising beneath a dishcloth. Lifting it, she peeked under the cloth, then settled it into place. "She says he'll hit a plateau and could be stuck there a while. Then, all of the sudden, he'll make a big step forward."

"The next step will be going outside on his own." He

walked over to the window. Scowling, he asked, "Did you hear a car last night?"

"I thought I heard spinning tires, but I didn't see anything."

He pointed to the yard where a pair of deep ruts glistened in the morning light. "Those are new."

"Oh, no!" she said as she looked out the other window.

"What?"

"They must have hit the bench you made for *Daed*."

In disbelief, he saw the one-time buggy seat had broken off its wooden base and was bent and useless. Anger bubbled inside him.

Gentle fingers brushed his shoulder. Looking at Naomi, he saw her sadness. Not for her *daed,* who wouldn't be able to use the bench, but for him.

"I'm sorry," she said. "It was a *wunderbaar* idea."

"I'll make another one by the new barn." He was astonished how her kind touch and words had evaporated his frustration as if it'd never existed.

"He'll love it. He can sit and tell you what you should be doing."

He laughed, startling himself anew. "You've got that right."

She stepped away from the window to face him. "Samuel, I've got to speak to you about your sister. I don't like to interfere—"

The twins ran into the kitchen, chattering about the book Elvin had read them. It'd been their favorite about a fire truck, and they acted as excited as if they'd heard it for the first time. She glanced at him with an apology before she bent to talk with them. Whatever bothered her about Kara would have to wait.

When the boys asked for something to drink, he said, "I'm going out to clean up." He was careful not to say what because he didn't want to let Jared and Jesse know anything was amiss.

She gave him a quick nod, but turned her attention to her *kinder*. He wondered if Jared and Jesse knew how blessed they were that their *mamm* loved them so unconditionally. He yearned for that himself.

Not his *mamm*'s love.

Naomi's.

It was barely past dawn, and already Naomi was behind in her day's chores. The *boppli* had been fussy all night. Though Kara had urged Naomi to send May to her in the *dawdi haus* if the infant didn't sleep, Naomi hadn't wanted to waken the girl. Kara had been exhausted after watching all three *kinder* while Naomi canned tomatoes and made tomato sauce to store away for the winter months. The kitchen was as hot and uncomfortable as the steam bath used to sterilize the canning jars. Each time Kara had come in to get a bottle for May or a treat for the twins, she rushed right back out.

Today Naomi would be doing it all again. She wasn't sure why her *daed* had planted so many tomatoes, but she wasn't going to let a single one go to waste. They'd be glad they had fragrant sauce and delicious canned tomatoes when winter was at its worst.

Reaching for the pot to pour herself a cup of *kaffi* and maybe wrest her brain away from the sleepy cobwebs holding it prisoner, she halted as she heard giggles behind her. She looked over her shoulder. The twins had spilled juice and were slapping it. Juice splattered across the table. *Daed* was watching, either bemused or amused. She couldn't tell which.

She grabbed a roll of paper towels and the wet dish rag and rushed to the table. The twins brought their hands into the orange juice at the same time, and they laughed. *Daed* did, too, as he slapped his right hand against the table.

Rushing to the cupboard, she pulled out a pitcher. She filled it before taking two cookie sheets out of the cabinet beside the stove. Shoving them under one arm, she went to the table and wiped up the juice. The twins watched her, wide-eyed, obviously expecting for her to scold them for the mess.

"What's this?" Jesse asked when she put the cookie sheet on the table between the boys.

"You'll see," she replied.

"Fun?" Hope raised Jared's voice.

"*Ja.*"

She put the other tray in front of *Daed.* His puzzled look was identical to the twins'. A door opened behind her, and she heard Samuel emerge from the bathroom. As she went to get the pitcher of water, she glanced at him. Her fingers tingled at the thought of stroking his freshly shaved cheeks. Quickly lowering her eyes, she prayed her face hadn't displayed that longing.

She carried the pitcher to the table. Four pairs of eyes followed her motions as she poured enough water on each cookie sheet to cover the bottom.

"All right, boys," she said as she set the pitcher on the counter. "Splash!"

They looked at her as if she'd lost her mind.

"Go ahead. Splash!"

They didn't need a second invitation. With eager cheers, they slapped the cookie sheet. Water sprayed high in the air.

"Your turn, *Daed.*"

"Don't be silly, Naomi."

"I'm not being silly. Slap the water."

He flicked a single finger on his right hand against the water.

She looked at Jared and Jesse. "Show *Grossdawdi* how to

splash water. Hit it as hard as you can with both hands. Let's see how high you can make it go."

They exchanged a glance before donning expressions of disbelief that matched her *daed*'s. When Samuel came to stand on *Daed*'s other side, he didn't say a word, but she saw he guessed what she was trying to do.

"Okay?" Jesse was the first to ask.

"Okay hit hard?" Jared confirmed.

"*Ja*. Today." She lowered her voice to a conspiratorial whisper, hoping the twins understood what she was about to say. "*Grossdawdi* has forgotten how to splash. Can you teach him how?"

"Like he teach hammer?" Jared's eyes brightened with abrupt mischief.

Hoping that her son was talking about something *Daed* intended to do when they were older, not something they'd already done, she said, "*Ja*. Teach him. You're *gut* splashers."

"*Gut*," Jesse agreed.

"Fun," his twin said.

"That's right." She gave their wet fingers a gentle squeeze. "*Gut* fun."

With excited squeals, the two boys stood on their chairs and slapped the water. It sprayed along the long table and almost to the ceiling. Naomi wiped drops off her face and saw Samuel do the same before she turned to her *daed*.

"Okay, *Daed*. Your turn. Let's see if you can do better."

"Two of them," he grumbled.

"Your hands are more than twice as big as theirs," Samuel said, his lips twitching in a grin. "Sounds like a fair contest to me."

"Splash, *Grossdawdi*!" the twins shouted together.

"Both hands together," Naomi said as she moved next to him. "Try, *Daed*."

He looked at each of them in turn, and uncertainty dimmed his eyes. His jaw clenched. Samuel had called her and *Daed* stubborn. Maybe being stubborn was the way *Daed* could make his next breakthrough.

Using his right hand, he lifted his left arm to shoulder height. It wobbled when he released it, but fell as he brought his right hand down at the same time. Water erupted. The cookie sheet jumped into the air before clattering on the floor.

The twins cheered.

Naomi wanted to shout her joy, too, as she picked up the cookie sheet and put it in front of *Daed*. Samuel brought the pitcher to pour another thin layer on it. He glanced at her. When she nodded, he put more on the twins' cookie sheet.

"Now," she said once Samuel was done. "Do it together. All three of you at once. Both hands!"

Daed hesitated, "I'm not sure I can. I dropped my hand before. I didn't—"

"You can." She took his hands in hers and began singing in the rhythm of his palms and the boys' slapping the water, "Jesus loves me. This I know, for the Bible tells me so. Little ones to Him belong. They are weak, but He is strong."

As she got to the chorus of "Yes, Jesus loves me..." the twins joined in. They weren't sure of the words, but were enthusiastic and splashed hard.

Then she realized *Daed* was moving his left arm without her help. She released his hands as she continued with the next verse of the song. Backing up, she watched as *Daed*'s left hand moved up and down on its own. It didn't always hit the water at the same time his right one did. Sometimes it didn't strike the water at all, but he was making it move.

She kept singing, and Samuel joined in, his voice deep and strong beneath her soprano, until they'd sung the whole song twice. She stopped because *Daed*'s face was growing pale, a sign he was getting exhausted.

Applause sounded from behind her. Lillian stood in the kitchen doorway. Naomi had been so focused on what they'd been doing she hadn't heard the physical therapist come in.

Lillian arched her brows. "Did this start as a water balloon battle?"

"Bat-til?" asked Jared, his eyes glittering with excitement.

"I'll explain later." Naomi got a towel from a drawer and wiped her *daed*'s hands.

"Be careful," Lillian said as the boys ran to her, eager to share what they'd done. "I don't need to give them ideas like water balloons, do I?"

Samuel chuckled. "Trust me. They come up with plenty of ways to get into trouble on their own."

Walking to the table, Lillian looked at the cookie sheets. "So what were you up to?"

Naomi explained how she'd halted her boys from making a mess earlier and then realized how much fun it would be for everyone, including her *daed,* to do a bit of intentional splashing.

"Intentional splashing?" The therapist let the words roll off her tongue. "Both hands at the same time?"

"*Ja.*"

Lillian laughed as she put her hands on her hips. "Looks as if they've worked you hard, Elvin. I'm curious to see this in action. Would you show me?"

Naomi held her breath as her *daed* tried to hit the water as he had before. He missed.

"Sing," Samuel urged. "Sing to give him the tempo, Naomi."

Self-conscious of the *Englischer* listening, Naomi began "Jesus Loves Me" again. Her voice gained strength along with *Daed*'s motions. She smiled when his hands slapped the water together on some beats.

"Bravo!" Lillian clapped again when Naomi finished a single verse and the chorus. "Well done, Elvin! Keep strengthening that left hand, and you'll be able to steer your walker wherever you want to go."

Daed smiled, looking as young and eager as Jesse and Jared.

Naomi sent up a joyous prayer of thanks before asking, "Who would have guessed two little scamps' mess could lead to this?"

"You did." Samuel came around the table to assist *Daed* to his feet so they could go into the living room to continue his therapy. "That was brilliant, Naomi."

Heat climbed her face at the unexpected compliment. "I figured it'd be fun, if nothing else."

"Nonsense," Lillian said as she gauged *Daed*'s steps while he gripped his walker. "Physical therapy isn't a lot of fun. You've changed that for your father by allowing him to turn it into playtime with his grandsons. Well done. Promise me if you have any other ideas like this one, you'll let me know."

She nodded, too overwhelmed with the praise to speak.

"I hope you don't mind if I use your idea with other clients." Lillian grinned broadly. "I may ask to borrow your boys to help. " She held out her hands to the boys. "What do you say, Jared? Jesse?"

"Fun," they replied in *Deitsch*, though they couldn't have known exactly what she was saying.

"Fun!" she repeated back to them in the same language.

As everyone laughed and Naomi realized that her twins and Lillian were learning each other's language with an astonishing ease, the door to the *dawdi haus* opened. A bleary-eyed Kara walked in. "What did I miss?"

That set off a new round of laughter while everybody tried to fill her in at once. Samuel smiled. His gaze caught Naomi's, and elation danced its way along every nerve. She couldn't remember the last time she'd been so happy. She intended to savor every moment of it.

Chapter Eighteen

It was quiet.

Naomi couldn't remember the last time it'd been so quiet in the big farmhouse. She did hear voices from her *daed*'s bedroom, where in the middle of the afternoon, Samuel was working *Daed* on his exercises to follow up on Lillian's morning visit. *Daed* could get himself anywhere in the house without help, something he'd achieved a week ago, so Samuel spent less time inside. That had allowed him to move tools and supplies from the old shop to the new one in the barn, which he'd painted last Friday and Saturday.

The twins and May were napping, having gone down late because the boys had discovered charred timbers that hadn't been cleared away after the barn raising. They'd covered themselves with soot, requiring a bath before lunch.

Naomi couldn't remember the last time she'd had a free moment. Kara had been as *gut* as her word and had the twins almost potty trained, which meant they were spending longer each day without diapers. With less laundry, she'd gone from doing three loads most days to one or two.

Today, she hadn't had to do any. She'd harvested the squash and early beans before the dew had steamed away in the July sunshine. They waited in the cellar until she had enough to do another canning day. The kitchen floor was clean, though the twins begged to play "the splash game" again. She'd allowed it outside, but not indoors.

The bread was baked, and tonight's supper would be leftover ham and potato casserole with applesauce Naomi had brought from the cellar. Standing in the kitchen, wiping her hands on a towel, she realized she finally had the time to do the job she'd wanted to tackle for weeks. Cleaning the storage room would keep her busy for longer than a single afternoon. She'd have to check with *Daed* before she got rid of anything, but many items she'd peeked at belonged in a trash bin. Especially those close to the cracked window, where rain had gotten in.

Naomi tiptoed up the stairs, wanting to avoid waking the twins. Jared and Jesse would poke their noses into every box.

She didn't let the blocked door halt her. She put her shoulder against it and pushed until she got it open enough so she could slip in. She had to move two boxes and a bag of clothing into the hall before there was enough room for her.

When was the last time *Daed* had gone into this room? The way the boxes and furniture were stacked, she guessed they'd been shoved in, pushing the mess closer together and tangling up everything.

She reached for the next box and opened it to reveal the clothes she'd worn when she was a *boppli*. With a smile, she carried it into the hall. Her nose wrinkled when she noticed the damp smell. A *gut* washing and time hanging on the clothesline should take care of the odor. The clothing would be perfect for May.

Old toys. Old tools. Musty old books. Clothes that belonged to her when she first started school and clothing her *mamm* had worn. Everything was stuffed into boxes with no rhyme or reason. She found broken dishes and wondered if they'd been in one piece when put in a box or while being brought to the storage room.

Shifting boxes, she opened another one. It was filled with spiral notebooks. She smiled. She remembered *Mamm* writing in her journals, recording the weather and events around the farm. Simple things like how many eggs she'd collected that day or bigger events when someone visited or a birthday was celebrated.

"Why do you write in those?" Naomi remembered herself asking when she was a few years older than the twins. She halted her mind from telling her exactly how many years, months, weeks and days ago. She wanted to savor this memory as it played through her mind.

Her *mamm* had smiled. "Because otherwise I can't remember everything like you do."

"You can depend on me, *Mamm*, to remember. But you can make cookies."

With a laugh, *Mamm* had agreed, putting down her pen and pulling out her favorite mixing bowl.

Naomi brushed her fingers over the journal, savoring the memory she hadn't enjoyed for too long. After *Mamm* died, it'd become easier not to think of her instead of risking the pain each happy remembrance brought.

She hefted the box and edged her way out of the room. She checked to see May was sleeping. Peeking into the twins' room, she saw they were still asleep, Jared sprawled on top of his covers and Jesse beneath them, as tucked in as when she'd put them down. The boys were revealing more individual traits with each passing day.

Upending the box on the kitchen table, Naomi sorted the journals by the dates *Mamm* had written on the covers. The earliest journal had been begun the year she was born. Odd. She'd thought *Mamm* had kept a journal since she was married, almost a decade before Naomi was born. Maybe there were more journals in another box. She'd look later. For now, she wanted to read through these.

Picking up the earliest one, she opened it to discover a manila envelope taped inside the front cover. She couldn't help but be curious what her *mamm* had considered important enough to keep.

She tilted it and watched a flurry of yellowed pages tumble onto the table. She swept out her arms to corral them before they fluttered away. After gathering the rectangular papers, she laid them out in neat rows on the table. There were ten. In amazement, she realized they were canceled checks with her *mamm*'s name imprinted on them. Her *mamm* had had her own checking account?

Naomi hadn't known that. If she had, would she have insisted on having the same while married to Marlin? In retrospect, it might have been the wisest thing she could have done. He'd insisted they have a joint account, and he'd kept the canceled checks, not letting her see them. She'd come to understand why once she learned about his cheating. After that, he didn't care whether she saw the canceled checks, and she'd come to dread getting that envelope in the mail each month. It offered a trail of where Marlin had gone and what he'd done...without her.

Stop thinking about that, she told herself. She wanted to enjoy looking at *Mamm*'s journals, not spend a pretty afternoon lamenting about what couldn't be changed.

Why shouldn't *Mamm* have had her own checking account? It made sense. *Mamm* would have paid the household expenses, keeping them separate from the buggy shop's account. The checks didn't have *Daed*'s name on them. Had he known about the account?

"Of course he did!" she asserted aloud. Her parents had never kept secrets. How many times had they said that while chiding her for trying to hide the truth so she didn't get in trouble?

More than she wanted to remember, she thought as she shut down the count as memory after memory popped into her mind.

Mamm had emphasized one adage: Honesty Is the Best Policy.

Raising her eyes, Naomi stared at a sampler on the wall. She could count the number of times she'd pricked her fingers while sewing it when she was seven years old.

One hundred twelve times.

She knew how many drops of blood had threatened to stain the cloth, but *Mamm* had cleaned it before returning it to her to finish.

Three.

It was simple to recall how long it'd taken her to complete the Bible verse edged by lilies of the valley. Two months, one week, one day and eight hours.

The simple words from Colossians 3:9 had been sewn in cross-stitch.

"'Lie not one to another,'" she whispered.

Naomi looked at the table. There were ten checks, one for each of ten consecutive months. Every check was for one thousand dollars and made payable to Vikki Presley.

"Who is Vikki Presley?" She glanced toward the door leading to her *daed*'s bedroom, where he was deep asleep if his snores were any indication. "How did *Mamm* get ten thousand dollars to make these payments?"

Another question popped into her head. *Why* had *Mamm* been paying Vikki Presley so much money?

She stared at the subject line on the bottom of the check. On each was written a single word: "Naomi."

The money had been spent on something for her? Had she been ill as an infant? Her memory didn't go back that far, so she had no idea why *Mamm* would have paid someone ten thousand dollars and put Naomi's name on the checks.

One person must know. She rose from the chair and took a single step toward the bedroom before *gut* sense kicked in. *Daed* needed his sleep after his physical therapy sessions. She should try to find the answer without disturbing *Daed*. It was probably there in *Mamm*'s journal.

Picking up the envelope, she looked inside. A few papers had been stored with the checks. She drew them out, wincing as she heard one rip. The pages were fragile with age. She spread them out, opening each one with care.

She sorted the handwritten documents by the dates on each page. There were, she discovered, three letters. All were written to *Mamm* by Vikki Presley.

The facts were simple. Vikki Presley was a midwife who knew a young, unwed woman looking to find a home for her *boppli*. The pregnant woman had expressed a preference for her *kind* to be raised in a plain home. *Mamm* must have asked questions because Ms. Presley had stated certain matters were privileged information she could share only with the birth *mamm*'s permission. If *Mamm* wanted the *kind*, she should remit money to help cover medical expenses and give the birth *mamm* a chance to get back on her feet.

When she picked up the third letter, Naomi's hands were trembling so hard she could barely read the handwriting. It stated Ms. Presley would bring the newborn to Bliss Valley in exchange for a ten-thousand-dollar fee. She'd leave the *boppli* to be named Naomi with *Mamm*, and no further contact would be necessary as long as the rest of the checks were sent as promised. If not... Ms. Presley hadn't stated what she'd do, but the threat was inherent.

A *boppli* named Naomi.

Her mind reeled as she tried to make the facts come together in a logical pattern. Had there been a *kind* before her? Another daughter with the same name? She wanted to grasp that idea and hold it close to her, but her eyes were caught by the dates on the letters and the checks. They were close to when she'd been born.

No! She didn't want to believe what was right in front of her. She was the *boppli* discussed in the letters. The truth made her stomach curdle. How could *Mamm*—no, not her *mamm*, her adoptive *mamm*. No, not even that, she realized as she paged through the journal and the two after it, looking for further paperwork. It wasn't there. Naomi hadn't been legally adopted. Every document she had to identify herself must have been forged.

Then she realized something else. What Skylar Lopez had been telling her was true. When Naomi hadn't been much older than May had been the day they'd found her on the *dawdi haus* porch, she'd been given away by her *mamm*. Only instead of being abandoned, she'd been sold like a buggy or a dozen eggs.

She propped her elbows on the table, paying no attention

to the papers crackling under them. She pressed the heels of her palms to her eyes. She tried to pray for guidance, but couldn't. Her thoughts were too jumbled, her heart too full of anger. How could her parents have preached honesty when they'd lied about the most important fact in her life? That she wasn't their *kind*.

Sobs swelled in her chest, but she couldn't cry. She hadn't cried since the night she'd discovered Marlin's cheating. He'd belittled her for weeping, and she hadn't let a tear slip out of her eyes since then. Now, when she ached to release the pain tightening its grip around her heart, she couldn't. Had all the tears she prevented from falling dried up within her, blocking any new ones?

Please, Lord, let me cry away this anguish.

But the tears refused to fall.

Samuel was whistling as he walked toward the house. He'd gotten more moved today from the old shop to the new barn than he'd expected. Most of the smaller tools now hung on the pegboard he'd put in place a few days ago. It hadn't been easy climbing a ladder with his weak leg, but he'd managed it without falling. He'd need to get help to move the heavier tools. On Sunday, he'd ask Adam if he and his cousins could offer a hand next week.

His sister was standing near a window in the *dawdi haus*, staring out. She wore a strained expression, and her gaze was focused on the ruts in the yard. Was she worried the *kinder* might stumble into them? He'd reassure her at supper that he planned to smooth out the yard once the move to the barn was finished. When he waved to her, her face eased and she waved back. Kara seemed more accepting of him than she had when she first moved to the Gingerichs' house.

She refused to speak to him about *Mamm*, and he hadn't pushed. He didn't want to chance Kara running away again. As long as she was here, he could keep an eye on her.

Opening the kitchen door, he was about to call a greeting to Naomi. He halted himself when he saw she was leaning forward, her face in her hands. He didn't hesitate. He rushed forward and pulled out a chair so he could sit beside her. Reaching up, he took one of her hands hiding her face and lowered it.

"What is it?" he asked softly, seeing her devastation.

"She was right."

"She? Who? Right about what?"

"Skylar." Her hand trembled in his as she told him about finding her *mamm*'s journals and what she'd discovered in one. Not asking her permission, he gathered the pages. A quick scan told him she hadn't made a mistake.

"You're adopted?" he choked past his shock.

"No. There aren't any adoption papers here. I may have been sold as a *boppli* and never adopted."

"The paperwork must be somewhere else. Have you told Elvin?"

"I don't know how."

"You ask him about this before he hears someone else talking about it."

"Who else would talk about it?" Her voice broke. "Nobody else knows. I didn't know until a few minutes ago."

When she started to pull her hand out of his, he tightened his hold. "Naomi, other people know. This Vikki Presley knows, and so does your birth *mamm*. Skylar Lopez knows. She spoke to other people in Bliss Valley before she showed up here the first time."

Naomi deflated and looked at the papers and notebooks on

the table. "You're right. I would have realized that, too, if my brain wasn't at war with itself. One half says this is impossible. The other half says it must be true because, otherwise why would *Mamm* have kept these papers in her journal?"

"You've got to discuss this with Elvin."

"I know."

She added nothing more, so he put a finger on her cheek and turned her face so her gaze met his. He almost gasped at her agonized eyes. Wishing he had the words to ease her pain, he didn't.

"They lied to me," she whispered.

"Maybe it'll make sense once you talk to Elvin."

"How can it make sense that they lied to me while saying honesty was as important as faith?"

"Ask him." He squeezed her hand gently. "Don't convict him of a crime before you hear his side of the story."

"All right. I will." She stood and picked up the letters. "*Komm* with me?"

He nodded. He intended to stay silent unless either Naomi or Elvin needed him to step in. Wanting to put up his hands on either side of his head to make sure it wasn't spinning as it felt, he grabbed the canceled checks and followed her to the bedroom door.

Elvin was sitting in bed, reading an old edition of *The Budget*. He put it down, brightening when he saw Naomi. His smile faded as he looked from her grim face to Samuel's.

"What's wrong?" Elvin asked. "The twins—"

"They're fine. Napping," Naomi answered. "*Daed*, why didn't you tell me I'm adopted?"

"What? Is this a joke?" He put his hand to his chest. "You're not trying to give me a heart attack, ain't so?"

Her voice grew brittle. "*Daed*, this isn't a joke. Why didn't you tell me I'm adopted?"

"Because you aren't! What gave you that idea?"

Samuel listened while Naomi related what she'd found in her *mamm*'s journals. She held out the papers to Elvin, who took them with shaking hands. The old man paged through the letters, reading each one before going to the next.

Elvin spoke a word Samuel hadn't heard since he'd left the *Englisch* side of the fence. "You're my daughter. Your *mamm* gave birth to you right here in this house. Remember? I told you the story of how I came home to find you lying in that cradle and Flossie exhausted and happy you were healthy and beautiful."

"The letters—"

"Enough!" roared Elvin, shocking Samuel because he'd never heard his boss raise his voice. "I can tell you one thing—you are *my* daughter. I watched your *mamm* grow round with you, and I tended to her when the *doktor* insisted she must be on bed rest for the last three months of her pregnancy." He shoved the pages into Naomi's hands. "Know what I think? I think Flossie held on to those pages for someone else."

Naomi wanted to believe what her *daed* was saying. She adored Elvin, as he did her, and their connection was deep and strong.

Noise came from upstairs, the sounds of two little boys getting out of bed. She glanced at the ceiling, then at her *daed*.

"Take care of your *kinder*," Elvin said. "Forget this nonsense."

"*Ja, Daed.*"

In disbelief, Samuel watched her walk out. He started to leave, too, but paused when Elvin called to him.

"Get rid of this," his boss ordered, pointing to the papers.

"Naomi won't be happy if I do that."

"Keeping it will upset her more. Flossie shouldn't have agreed to hold on to those papers." He tapped his chest. "I *know* she's my daughter. I saw Flossie when she was pregnant. Naomi is the blessing we prayed for after so many years of not being able to have a *kind*."

Samuel glanced at the canceled checks he'd brought into the room. If he showed them to Elvin and forced the issue… He couldn't do that without discussing it with Naomi first. Gathering up the letters, he took them and left.

Hurrying up the stairs, he waited while Naomi redressed the twins after their sweaty nap in the hot room. May was wiggling on one of the beds, playing with her thumbs. Naomi turned, and he saw her relief he'd come upstairs to talk to her where Elvin wouldn't be able to overhear.

"Go to the *dawdi haus*," she urged the twins, "and ask Kara to give you each a cookie. One each!"

He stepped aside to let the boys scurry past him and waited until the sound of their feet on the stairs faded. Only then did he ask, "Why did you agree to forget about everything you've found out?"

"*Daed* believes I'm his birth daughter."

"You want to believe that, too."

"Of course I do."

"So you're going to pretend you never found this?" He tossed the checks on the bed beside May. "Just like that?"

"It's what I'm supposed to do. A daughter obeys her *daed*." She collected the checks and patted them into a smooth stack. "I want to believe that *Daed* is right, that *Mamm* held on to these papers for someone else."

"But…?"

"I've got to know the truth." Her mouth hardened into a

straight line. "I know what *Daed* said, but if there's any chance, I've got to find out." She lifted May, settled her into the crook of her left arm and faced him again. "I'm going to call Skylar Lopez and agree to have the DNA test. Proving I'm not that woman's daughter is the only way to be able to refute what I found today."

He didn't reply. She was overlooking one important fact. The test would only disprove she was Skylar's half sister. It wouldn't establish she was Elvin and Flossie Gingerich's daughter. Now wasn't the time to mention that. He'd made a mess of things with his own family. He couldn't risk doing the same with hers.

Chapter Nineteen

If Naomi had thought Skylar would be happy to hear from her, she was sadly mistaken. Skylar was her usual curt self on the phone and said she'd come to the farm later that afternoon.

"No," Naomi told her. "You can't come here."

"Then where?"

"How about the Acorn Farm Inn?" She was sure Laurene and her great-*aenti* would be okay with her meeting Skylar on their front lawn. Later, she'd apologize to Laurene for being presumptuous but she wasn't sure where else to go.

"All right. At four." The familiar sneer came into Skylar's voice. "Don't stand me up."

The phone clicked in Naomi's ear before she could think of a response. Her prayer that Skylar wasn't her sister was one she instantly regretted. She wasn't doing this because she was looking for a sibling, though as Samuel had guessed, she'd wanted one. She checked Kara could watch all three *kinder* and start supper before she went to hitch Waldo to the buggy.

Samuel stepped out of the shop. "Where are you getting the test done?"

"I don't know."

"If you're not going to get your DNA tested, then where are you going?"

"To the Acorn Farm Inn to meet Skylar." She glanced at the house and tried to ignore the guilt that thickened in her throat.

"*Gut.* You'll be glad to have Laurene there."

"*Ja.* She's been with me through so many other rough times in my life." She faltered. "I shouldn't have said that, Samuel."

"It's the truth."

"It *was* the truth. Now…" She went to the buggy's door and climbed in. "I'm not sure I can talk about that today."

"Go," he said. "Do what you've got to do."

Giving Waldo the command to go, Naomi resisted the yearning to turn the buggy around and run to Samuel. He'd been kind and understanding in the kitchen and generous to offer to stand beside her when she spoke to *Daed*. He hadn't teased her, taking advantage of her being at her lowest point.

She headed in the direction of the Bliss Valley Covered Bridge. She didn't want to have feelings for Samuel King, feelings that had grown stronger each day as she watched him with *Daed* and the twins. She'd been a *dummkopf* to get involved with Marlin, but she'd fallen in love with him without knowing him. She knew Samuel King. All too well. She'd been *dumm* to trust him before, and she would be as *dumm* to trust him again.

So why did she ache for his arms around her?

Nobody was working on the inn when Naomi pulled the buggy into the driveway, but signs of the rebuilding were everywhere from the skeleton of two-by-fours at the back of stone building to piles of sheathing and stacks of shingles not far from the pond where a single duck swam. She got out of the buggy and walked to the inn to knock on the door.

It opened before she reached it, and Laurene came onto the porch. Sawdust had gathered in her *kapp*. She brushed more off her black apron as she came down the steps, smiling.

"Naomi! How *wunderbaar* to see you! How's your *daed*?"

"He's getting better every day. I hope I'm not interrupting anything," she said, though it was obvious the day's work was done.

"Not at all. The workers have left, and I'm sweeping up inside." She plucked another bit of sawdust from her sleeve. "I'm trying to stay ahead of the mess so it'll be easier when *Aenti* Sylvia moves back in. Did you stop by for a reason or to see what's going on?"

A car came along the road, and Naomi turned to see if it was Skylar's. The vehicle didn't slow.

Looking at her friend, she said, "I stopped by to meet someone here."

Laurene's purple eyes narrowed. "Why are you meeting someone here?"

"Because I didn't want her coming to the house."

"What?"

"I didn't want *Daed* to see. If he gets upset, it could set back his recovery. I..." She halted herself, knowing she wasn't making any sense.

"Naomi, is everything all right?"

"*Ja*... No. Look, here's the short version. A woman came to our house right after I returned to Bliss Valley and said she was searching for her half sister. She seemed to think I could be that sister."

"You?" Laurene asked in a strained tone.

"*Ja*. I told her she was wrong, but she persisted." She wrapped her arms around herself. "Information has come to light that changes everything, so I thought it'd be a *gut* idea if we talked face-to-face."

Laurene's face had become an odd shade of gray. "Was the woman's name Skylar Lopez, by any chance?"

"How did you know?"

Her friend dropped to the steps. "*You* are the missing twin?"

"Twin? What are you talking about? The boys are fine."

"Not your twins." She stood slowly and clasped Naomi's hands. "My *mamm's* twins."

"You're not a twin."

"I am. Not in my adoptive family, but in my birth family. Wayne and Ida Nolt are my adoptive parents."

"Why didn't you ever tell me you're adopted?"

A sad smile played at the corners of Laurene's mouth. "Because I didn't know until this spring. My birth *mamm* is named Gina Marie Tinniswood."

"Skylar Lopez's *mamm*? You're her sister?"

"*Ja*, and if you are, too, then you're *my* twin sister."

"Yours?"

"*Ja*."

"Are you serious?"

Laurene smiled. "Serious as a stomachache."

Naomi stared. How many times had they joked that they were more than best friends, that they were as close as sisters? Twin sisters?

Another memory burst through her mind. Marlin's face had twisted with rage as he lashed out at her with language she hadn't ever heard. She'd known the words must be curses.

Marlin had often sworn when he was upset with her, hoping to anger her. That had worked early in their marriage; however, as the years went by, she hadn't taken the bait.

He'd been furious because she'd given birth to twins. He'd lambasted her for complicating his life with two *kinder*, though he'd used a word worse than *kinder*. Tired from hours of labor, she'd ignored him, which made him more furious. His raised voice had caught the nurses' attention. They'd had him escorted from the hospital. He hadn't come back, not to get her and the twins. When she'd gotten home, it'd been clear he'd been there, because dirty dishes and empty bottles were everywhere. She hadn't seen him, though, for more than a week, when he'd dragged himself home, drunk and hungover and furious again she wouldn't have time to take care of him because she was busy tending to their *bopplin*.

The image of Samuel's gentle smile flickered through her mind. He'd been there today when she needed someone to connect her to reality as her life whirled out of control. So many other moments burst into her mind like a cascade of popcorn. In each, he was taking care of *Daed* or his sister or the *kinder*…or her. How could she have thought the two men were anything alike?

"Naomi?" asked Laurene gently. "Are you okay?"

"I don't know."

A silver car slowed on the road, and Naomi recognized it as it drew to a stop by her buggy. Glancing at Laurene, she saw her own uneasiness on her friend's face. Her *sister's* face. Maybe.

How was it possible they were twins, but nobody in Bliss Valley had known? What other secrets had her parents kept from her?

Skylar got out of the car and walked toward them. Again

she was dressed in garish clothing with bold jewelry. Even her glasses had rhinestones on their pink frames. The streak in her hair was as orange as the sky at sunset, and she carried a bag large enough to be a diaper bag for all three *kinder*.

"What's she doing here?" Skylar's rude motion toward Laurene made it clear she didn't like Naomi's best friend.

Naomi's twin! Was it possible?

"She lives here," Naomi said. "Or she did before the fire."

"And," Laurene added in a tone Naomi had never heard her use, "if she's your sister, she's my twin. So I'm glad I'm here for this family reunion. Not that we had any idea we were family when we first became good friends in school."

"Look." Skylar fiddled with the shoulder strap on her purse. "I'll be blunt. I'm not interested in becoming one big, happy family. I'm interested in saving our mother. I don't want two Amish women dogging my steps and calling me out for the way I live my life. If you two want to form a family, go for it. My life and yours don't match up in any way."

"You're our sister," Naomi said.

"*Half* sister."

"Just words. You're still our sister, and we don't intend to judge you or intrude in your life."

"Like I've intruded in yours?" She gave a sharp laugh. "You'd have every right to kick me to the curb, and I almost wish you would. If not for Mom needing help, I wouldn't be here."

"So let's focus on helping her." Naomi glanced at Laurene, who gave her a bolstering smile. "Anything that happens or doesn't happen is God's will."

Skylar shook her head, making her dangling earrings dance. "That's what I mean. You bring God into everything you do or say."

"God is in everything." Laurene folded her hands in front of her. "Skylar, I've lived an *Englisch* life, as well as a plain one. I know the challenges of each of them, and I don't want to judge you or have you judge me. Can't we accept each other as we are?"

"Accepting each other," Skylar insisted, "isn't why I'm here." Looking at Naomi, she said, "You asked me to meet you. You may be the last chance our mother has to survive. Will you *finally* agree to be tested?"

"*Ja.*"

She reached into her bag and pulled out a piece of paper. "Here's a list of labs that do the testing. Go tomorrow. They'll swab your cheek. That's it."

"All right." She took the paper and glanced at it. The nearest lab wasn't far from the pediatrician's office. "Have either of you heard of Vikki Presley?"

Laurene's eyes cut toward Skylar, whose lips tightened into a straight line.

"Who is she?" asked Naomi. "I found canceled checks for ten thousand dollars. Checks my *mamm* wrote to her out of a checking account that apparently wasn't connected with my *daed*'s business's account."

"She's the one," Skylar said, "who created this whole mess. After Mom got pregnant, her no-good boyfriend skipped out on her when he learned she was going to have a baby. She was young and didn't have a job. So she decided to put the baby—babies, she found out later—up for adoption. Vikki Presley said she was a midwife, and she'd take care of everything so Mom could return to her life as if nothing had ever happened."

Laurene picked up the tale. "From what Gina Marie told me, Vikki took the twins and sold them to two families who wanted a *kind*. She told the families the money would be used to help Gina Marie. That's not unusual in private adoptions, but Vikki never shared a cent."

"Just dumped our mother back out on the street," Skylar said. "Where she fortunately met my father before she ended up starving or worse."

"Where's Vikki now?" Naomi asked.

"Dead, and good riddance." Skylar's eyes narrowed. "Wait a minute. Laurene, you said the two of you were good friends in school, but I thought you lived in Chester County, Naomi."

"I did. I lived there with my late husband on what I thought was our farm in Honey Brook. It turned out it wasn't."

"I don't understand."

Naomi wanted to say she didn't, either. "I was told that we'd gotten a mortgage on the farm, but apparently we were only renting."

"That's weird."

"It's more than weird," Laurene said. "It doesn't make sense. If you were renting the farm, why were you allowed to lease out your fields to others after Marlin died?" She smiled. "Or at least that's what Adam told me you'd done. He must have heard it from Samuel or your *daed*."

"Ever hear of subletting?" suggested Skylar before she turned toward her car. "Tomorrow, Naomi! Don't put it off any longer."

"How is Gina Marie doing?" Laurene called to her.

"Not good." Her voice softened in pain. "The chemo isn't working, and if she doesn't get that bone marrow, I don't know how much longer she's got. If you're not a match, Naomi, our only choice will be trying the bone marrow donor registry again. Though why a stranger would be a match when none of us are boggles the mind."

Naomi watched Skylar get into her car and drive away. Turning to Laurene, she said, "I'll go first thing in the morning."

"Do you want me to go with you?"

"No. You're busy helping your great-*aenti*." She swallowed hard. "I'll let you know what they say."

"It can take a week or two before you find out."

"Oh, I didn't know that, but I'll let you know."

"Danki." She embraced Naomi. "Even if we aren't sisters, you'll always be as dear to me as if you were."

"You, too." She went to the buggy and didn't say anything other than repeating she'd let Laurene know as soon as she heard the results. She drove away, more confused than she'd been on her way to the inn.

Every day when the mail carrier stopped at the box at the end of the lane before noon, Samuel held his breath until Naomi told him the DNA results hadn't come. It was exactly fourteen days later when she came to the new barn to let him know the letter had arrived.

"What does it say?" he asked, his words echoing weirdly in the space that was vast compared to the old shop.

"I'm Gina Marie Tinniswood's daughter."

He put down the wrench he was holding and pulled her into his arms. She clung to him, shaking but not crying. Against him, she felt fragile, and he held her as if she might shatter at any moment. There were so many things he wanted to ask her. Did that mean she could donate bone marrow to her birth *mamm*? What was she going to tell Elvin? How was she planning to explain the truth to her *kinder*? Would she leave the farm? He didn't want that. Not only would it devastate Elvin, but it would break his own heart.

She drew away more quickly than he'd hoped, but he let her go as he asked, "Are you a match for the bone marrow donation?"

"The cover letter said that report would come separately. It has to go to a different lab for testing, I think." She tried to smile and failed. "It does mean that Laurene is my sister." She stared at her bare feet. "I've got to tell *Daed*."

"I'll go with you."

"You're not going to ask if I want you to go with me? You're telling me you'll go with me?" Her words were clipped with abrupt anger, but he guessed it wasn't aimed at him. She was overwhelmed by the results from the test, because she must have hoped right up until she opened the envelope her DNA would prove she wasn't Gina Marie's daughter.

"If I'd asked, you might have said no because you aren't thinking straight, Naomi. This is going to be tough for you and Elvin. You're about to tell him the woman he loved his whole life lied to him."

"I know. I've been praying God will send me the perfect words."

"There aren't any perfect words. Tell him the truth and show him the letter. Nothing you say or do otherwise will make a difference."

"Okay, after we eat—"

"No, do it now. How are you going to sit through a meal knowing what you've got to tell him?"

She nodded. He put his arm around her shoulders as they walked out of the barn. He respected her silence while they went to the house. Neither of them spoke as they walked into the living room, where Elvin sat in his recliner. He looked over the top of a fishing magazine he was reading.

Samuel wondered idly if Elvin had finally caught up on all the back issues of *The Budget*, but kept his mouth closed.

"You two look grim," Elvin said. "Are you bringing me bad news?"

Naomi stepped forward. "It's not *gut* news or bad. It's simply news." She drew a sheet from the envelope and handed it to her *daed*.

"A DNA test?" asked Elvin. "Why would you do such a thing? I told you you're my daughter."

"No, *Daed*, I'm not."

"Don't be ridiculous!"

"Look here." She tapped the bottom of the page where a large box held an explanation of the results above it.

Samuel strained to read it upside down. He couldn't pick out the words, but saw the name Gina Marie Tinniswood as well as "confirmed" and a percentage above ninety-nine.

"Who is Gina Marie Tinniswood?" Elvin asked.

"The woman who gave birth to me."

He shook his head, tears filling his eyes. "This is wrong. It's got to be."

"Listen to her, Elvin," Samuel said as he put a calming hand on the older man's shoulder. "Has she ever lied to you?"

"If what she says is true, then my wife lied to me."

She knelt by his chair and folded his hand between hers. "I don't know why *Mamm* didn't tell you the truth. I suspect, knowing her, she wanted to give you what you'd been longing for. A *boppli*. So she made up an elaborate charade to pretend she was pregnant."

"She did a *gut* job," he said as tears oozed from his eyes. "Even convincing me the *doktor* had put her on bed rest, so she didn't lose another *boppli* before she got to term. I wish she'd been honest with me."

"*Daed*, this doesn't mean anything other than I may be able to help save a woman's life. You are—and always will be—my *daed*. *Mamm* will be my *mamm*. Gina Marie may have given me life, but you and *Mamm* gave me a place in your hearts. You and me and Jared and Jesse and May, for as long as she is here, are my family. Nothing in my DNA can change that."

Rising, she put her arms around her *daed*. The paper and envelope drifted on the floor as they held each other.

The twins came racing in, eager to see what had delayed their dinner. Samuel caught them before they could find their way into the private moment between their *mamm* and their *grossdawdi*. He steered them toward the kitchen with the promise of peanut butter sandwiches and a piece of pie for dessert. Envy bit him again. If his *mamm* could give him a portion of that love…

He shook away the thoughts that got him nowhere and focused on persuading the two-year-olds he didn't need their help spreading peanut butter on their bread and everything else in the kitchen. As he sat with them at the table and bowed his head to say silent grace, he added a prayer that Naomi and Elvin wouldn't lose the love they'd taken for granted.

"*Danki*," Naomi said as she walked back into the new barn later that afternoon. She loved the smell of the freshly cut lumber and how the rafters that hadn't yet been painted glistened in the sunshine. A row of windows along the back were open to let in air, so the space wasn't stifling.

When Samuel looked up from where he was sitting on a stool by the front wheel of a buggy, a paintbrush in his hand as he touched up the black paint that had been scratched, he set the brush on the small plastic container of paint. He pushed himself to his feet, grabbed his cane and came around the vehicle.

"I'd say 'you're welcome,' except I don't know what you're thanking me for." He grinned.

"You know what I'm thanking you for. For being there today when I had to tell *Daed* about the DNA test results."

"How's he doing?"

"He's distraught *Mamm* wasn't honest with him, but he has forgiven her. He admitted he'd talked a lot about wanting a *kind* of their own, even when *Mamm* was having trouble with miscarriages." She sat on the new bench Samuel had made for *Daed*. "He says he's regretted doing that and came to realize too much honesty can sometimes be almost as bad as too much dishonesty."

"I'm not sure I agree with that. Honesty still is best, but sometimes it's better to be silent than to say what's on your mind."

"I agree."

"How are you?" He sat beside her on the bench. "This has changed everything in your life."

"No, it hasn't. I'm the person I was before I found those journals. I have parents and *kinder* I love. Now I have more parents."

"Are you going to try to meet your birth *mamm*?"

"I definitely will if I'm a bone marrow match."

"What if you're not?"

"I don't want to think about that. I'm going to be grateful for the life I've had and the life ahead of me. To be grateful for family and my *gut* friends."

He slanted toward her. "Am I included among those *gut* friends?"

When his gaze captured hers, she didn't look away. Didn't

want to look away. "*Ja*, though I sometimes find that harder to believe than I'm adopted."

"I'm glad you consider me a friend, Naomi."

"Me, too." Her voice sounded breathless in her own ears. "Do you think of me that way?"

His hand curved along her cheek as he steered her face closer to him. "The only thing I've been thinking about is how much I want to kiss you."

"I know that." Her voice dropped to a whisper. "I've been thinking about you kissing me, too."

"I don't want you to think it's like it was back—"

"Sixteen years, six months—"

"Two weeks and three days ago." He smiled. "I don't need for you to give me the exact date, because I've never forgotten it. Each year when the date comes around, I remember it. With guilt and shame and sorrow that I made a mess of everything, and that I'd never get another chance to show you the truth."

"The truth?"

"That I didn't kiss you because of a dare." He gave her a cock-eyed grin as his breath brushed her lips with each word. "Or at least not *just* because of a dare. Though I don't know if I would ever have had nerve enough to kiss a beautiful girl like you if my friends hadn't dared me to."

"You never said."

"I was afraid to, Naomi. I was afraid you'd push me away like others had. If I kissed you and showed you how I felt and you'd rejected me, I didn't think I could have endured it. So I made sure I pushed you away first."

"I never thought of it like that."

"I did. I thought about it a lot beforehand and endlessly afterward. Now…" His other hand came up to frame her face, but he didn't bring her nearer.

She knew why. He wanted it to be her choice if they kissed. Unlike in the past, he was letting her choose.

She should think about the consequences of pressing her lips to his. She couldn't. Not when her mind was filled with questions about whether his kiss now would be as *wunder-baar* as his kiss had been then…before he made it into a joke.

"You can tell me if you don't want me to kiss you again." He sighed. "I won't, though I'll always want to."

She stared at him. If she said she didn't want him to kiss her, that would be a lie. She wanted his kiss, but she wanted them to kiss because they wanted to, not to fulfill some *dumm* dare.

When her fingers rose to his face, his eyes closed as if he could not bear for her to touch him and then watch her turn away. His cheek was rough beneath her fingers, but his lips were offering her what she once had dreamed could be hers. She drew his mouth to hers, and his arms enfolded her. This—this amazing connection—was what she'd wanted all her life. She leaned into him, thrilling in the quick skip of his heartbeat against hers. He murmured something on her lips she couldn't understand. She didn't try to guess. All she wanted was for him to kiss her again and again…and again.

"Samuel!"

At the shriek of his name from outside the barn, Naomi jumped to her feet and whirled to face the door.

Kara raced in so blindly she tripped over a toolbox on the floor. Jumping forward, Naomi caught her before she could fall.

The girl pulled away. "Samuel, are you here?"

"I am," Samuel said, standing. "Right here. What's wrong?"

She raced to him and gripped his sleeve. "May and Jesse are missing! You've got to save them." Dropping to her knees, she pressed her face to his leg. "Save my *boppli* and Jesse, please."

Chapter Twenty

Naomi rushed out of the barn, shouting the twins' names.

Samuel wanted to go with her, but his sister wouldn't release his leg. He pulled her up and tried to get her to tell him what had happened. She was too hysterical to make sense.

He finally steered her to the house, anxious to discover what Naomi had found. A hole opened in his heart, and fear, unlike any he'd ever known, not even the night of the car accident, strangled him. He sat Kara at the kitchen table and tried again to get her to talk so he could understand. It was useless. She kept crying out May's name and pleading for his help in returning the *boppli* to her.

Not "the *boppli*," but "my *boppli*."

A slip of the tongue?

Or the truth?

How could he have failed to see what was right in front of him? Everyone in Bliss Valley had known Elvin Gingerich had hired him, and plenty of people had thought it was a big mistake, so his job had been widely discussed. It was common knowledge he lived in the *dawdi haus*. May had been left on *his* porch a few weeks before his sister jumped the fence. Kara had refused to talk to anyone but him. When Naomi had offered her a place to stay, his sister had accepted eagerly.

So she could be back with her *boppli*? Kara had taken every opportunity to spend time with May, bringing her into the *dawdi haus* many nights. How often had Samuel chanced upon her playing with the *boppli*, cuddling her, whispering to her? Had she been reassuring the *boppli* that May was her own precious *kind*?

Naomi ran into the kitchen. She looked as shocked as he felt.

"I can't find them anywhere," she said.

Kara dropped her head to her arms on the table and sobbed more loudly.

"Jared?" he asked.

"He's safe," Naomi replied.

Steps, more uneven than his own, came into the kitchen. Elvin pushed his walker into the room with Jared holding to the side. The little boy had a bandage on one finger and streaks from tears down his face.

The *kind* ran to Naomi. She hugged him, but Samuel knew her arms must feel empty when Jesse wasn't also there.

"Do you know what happened?" Samuel asked.

Naomi urged, "Sit, *Daed*, first."

Elvin patted her cheek. The motion spoke volumes. Flossie's subterfuge couldn't drive *daed* and daughter apart. Their love was too solid, too strong. Moving past her, he took his seat at the head of the table.

"A…truck…pulled in," Elvin began, his voice unsteady, warning how distressed he was. "At… At the same time, Kara came in with Jared."

"For only a second," Kara said, raising her head and struggling to speak past her hiccuping sobs. She tried to add more, but couldn't.

"He'd scraped his finger on the swing. Pretty bad. She bandaged it, then went back out to watch the *kinder*," continued Elvin. "That's when I heard a scream. Kara's scream. The *kinder*...gone."

With a moan, Kara collapsed against the table and wept.

"Get that girl..." Elvin clenched his fist. "Water. Get her some water."

Hurrying to the sink, Naomi filled a glass and brought it to Kara. She sat and held Jared onto her lap. The frightened *kind* clung to her, his eyes huge.

"No fun," he whispered.

Samuel's heart broke at the pain in the *kind*'s voice. Though the little boy didn't have the words to explain, he must be feeling as if he'd lost half of himself.

"Take a drink, Kara," Samuel urged, holding the glass out to her. "You've got to tell us what you saw. Why you screamed."

She seized the glass and held it to her lips. Water dribbled down her chin. She ignored it as she gulped the water as if she'd just run a marathon.

Setting the glass on the table, she said, "I'm May's *mamm*."

He watched Naomi and Elvin exchange a shocked glance. "Who else knows?"

"Nobody! Do you know what *Daed* would have done to me? If *Mamm* learned I made the same mistake she did..." She burst into a renewed bout of sobs.

She'd disown me as she did you. He could hear the words Kara hadn't spoken. How *Mamm* had controlled them with her need for pity and forgiveness! Though he had offered both, it hadn't been enough. Nothing would have been.

Nothing could have been.

He froze at the thought. It liberated him from the burden of guilt he'd carried through his life. At the same time, he was filled with sorrow for what she'd thrown away.

When Naomi touched Kara's arm, his sister looked at her. "Kara, tell us what happened."

Kara's head swiveled from him to Naomi. "Get them back!"

"Who took them?" Samuel asked.

She began sobbing again.

Naomi stood. "Call the police, Samuel. I'll try to get her calmed down enough to talk."

He paused long enough to take her hand and give it a squeeze. She nodded, showing her faith and trust in him.

He wished he had the same in himself.

Naomi released an agitated breath as the door shut behind Samuel.

"Mamm." A small hand tugged on her skirt.

Scooping up Jared, she pressed her cheek to her son's. His tiny arms stretched around her neck as he clung to her.

"It'll be all right," she whispered, knowing God would forgive her for what might not be the truth.

No, she had to believe it was true. She couldn't bear the thought of losing someone so precious to her. God had given her *daed* a chance to live longer, and He would have His eye on Jesse and May, too.

"Daed, did you see anything?"

He shook his head. "I'm sorry, Naomi. I was tending to Jared's finger. If I'd had any idea…"

"If any of us did." She'd been savoring Samuel's kiss at the moment the *kinder* had disappeared. How could she not have known they were in danger? *For I the Lord thy God will hold thy right hand, saying unto thee, Fear not; I will help thee.* The words from Isaiah 41:13 flowed out of her memory as soothing as the first drops of rain on dry soil.

Samuel came into the kitchen, and her heart was comforted to know he would stand with her through whatever was ahead. For the first time, that didn't seem odd. He'd been a horrible *kind*, but he was a *gut* man. He'd shown her that over and over, waiting patiently until she was ready to admit he'd changed.

"I called 911," he said. "They said the police would be here as quickly as humanly possible."

"Maybe faster if they're given a bit of heavenly speed."

He brushed his fingers against her face, and she longed to lean into his caress. "From your lips to God's ears."

As if in answer, a siren shrilled through the afternoon. Less than a minute later, two police officers came to the door. A tall man and a woman who, after introductions were made, took a seat next to Kara, who stared at them in dismay. The woman's name tag read Monteith. The man's identified him as Hood.

Officer Monteith took the lead. "I assume you don't have a picture of the missing boy, Mrs. Ropp."

"He looks like his twin." She settled Jared in her lap. "Except he's got a chipped front tooth."

"Good. We'll get a description out right away." She gestured to Officer Hood. He stood and went to the opposite side of the kitchen to speak into the radio clipped to his shoulder.

Samuel's hand on her shoulder eased the frisson of fear as she heard the officer describe Jesse and add, "Also missing. A one-month-old. Female."

Her attention was pulled to Officer Monteith, who held Kara in her cool gaze. "You're the last one to see the children. Is that right?"

Kara nodded.

"Tell me what happened."

Haltingly at first and then more in control, Kara explained how Jared had cut his finger and she'd brought him inside to put ointment and a bandage on it.

The police officer listened, then said, "When you came back outside, the little boy and the baby were gone. Right?"

Kara nodded.

"Do you have any idea who might have taken them?"

"Ja," Kara replied in a fragile voice.

Naomi couldn't silence her gasp and saw her shock mirrored on Samuel's face. "Why didn't you say so before?"

"Please let us ask the questions," Officer Monteith said.

Naomi tried to keep her son occupied while the officers posed their questions to Kara. When he began to squirm, she stood, got him a cookie and set him on the floor with a coloring book.

"Who took the children, Kara?" asked Officer Monteith as the other cop moved to stand on the girl's other side.

"The *boppli's daed.* I mean…the baby's father."

Samuel stiffened, and Naomi took his hand as he had hers earlier. Beside her, *Daed* bowed his head.

"What's the baby's father's name?" Officer Monteith remained gentle, but Naomi could see she was annoyed with having to draw each word out of Kara.

"His name is Hayden Carpenter," the girl replied.

"Hayden?" Officer Hood frowned. "Which Carpenter family?"

"The one that lives on the farm behind my family's." She gave a description of the young man and his truck, though she didn't know the plate number.

When the police went to set up a search, Kara looked at Samuel.

He frowned as he said, "Hayden Carpenter has been here before, ain't so?"

"*Ja*. How did you know?"

"The gouges in the grass were made by wide tires like on a pickup. I learned a lot about trucks when I was on the other side of the fence. Also I saw you staring at the ruts with an odd expression on your face. Were you mooning for Hayden?"

"No! You don't have to tell me I was a *dummkopf* to get involved with someone from that family, Samuel. I know that."

"You mean you know it now?" he asked.

"No, I knew months ago when I found out I was pregnant, and Hayden, who'd told me he loved me and I was the only girl for him, was sneaking around and seeing someone else." Her lip twisted. "Several someone elses."

"How did you hide the truth?"

"About being pregnant?" She shrugged. "I kept my mouth closed and ate a lot when other people were around. That explained my weight gain…if anyone had paid any attention."

"*Mamm*—"

"You know better than anyone, Samuel, that *Mamm* is more interested in what everyone else thinks of her than her *kinder*."

Officer Monteith cleared her throat as she returned to the table, and Samuel nodded with a sheepish smile, but Naomi noticed how the fingers on his left hand had closed into a fist. He released them as if he hadn't realized what he was doing.

"What else can you tell me about your baby's father, Kara? That model of truck isn't uncommon. Why do you think it was his and he took the children?"

Anger slashed through the girl's voice. "He told me that his kid— That's what he called our *boppli*. His kid, as if I had nothing to do with the *boppli*. He said he wasn't going to let it be raised plain. He despised everything plain, including me." She turned to Samuel. "That's why I left the *boppli* with you. I didn't think he'd figure out you were my brother."

"Until you came here," Naomi whispered.

Her eyes filled with tears again, and she ran the back of her hand under her nose. "I couldn't resist when you asked me to help you with the *kinder*, Naomi. To have the chance to hold my little girl again and get to spend time with her... I know I shouldn't have *komm* here, but I couldn't say no." She took a steadying breath before adding, "Officer Monteith, you should know that Hayden drinks. A lot. Sometimes he starts with his first beer before noon."

"Do you think he was drinking when he came here?" she asked, frowning.

"*Ja.* If he'd been sober, he probably would have thought twice before snatching the *kinder*."

After asking Kara where Hayden might be if he wasn't at home and listening to a variety of places, including several friends' houses, Officer Monteith said, "We've got enough to get started. It's a black Chevy pickup, right?"

"*Ja.* With a cap on the back and extra lights along the sides and under it."

"Good. That'll help us narrow down what we're looking for." She motioned toward the back door with her head. "We'll keep you apprised of our efforts. If the children are returned here, let us know immediately."

"We can get together a search party," Samuel said.

"Let us do a sweep of the area before the word gets out. It's best if we can find them with as little possible fuss. Is the number you called from the best one to reach you?"

"It's in the barn," Naomi began, "and there's an answering—"

Kara pulled a cell phone from a pocket beneath her apron. "Call this one." She rattled off a number and confirmed it when the police officer read it back.

Silently, she handed the phone to Samuel as the officers strode toward the door. Pushing back her chair, she said, "I need to—" She didn't explain further as she ran into the *dawdi haus*.

In her wake, Naomi looked from *Daed* to Samuel. What did they do now?

As if she'd asked that aloud, Samuel said, "Now we wait."

"And pray," *Daed* added.

"And pray," she confirmed.

Chapter Twenty-One

The house was almost silent when Samuel stepped inside shortly after nine. They'd seen what might be a police car in the lane, so he'd gone to check.

"Was it them?" Naomi asked from the front staircase, then put her finger to her lips.

"Are they asleep?" he whispered.

"*Ja,* all three of them." Her fingers tightened on the banister before she stepped off the stairs. "Was that the police?"

"No, someone turning around."

"You were gone for a while."

"I stopped in the shop, in case there was a message on the answering machine. Nothing. I don't know what's taking so long."

She leaned her head against his shoulder, her *kapp* crinkling on his shirt. "Every minute is an eternity."

"We've waited long enough. I'm going to find Jesse and May."

Stepping back, she gasped. His face was as hard as the stones in the house's foundation. She recognized his expression. It was the one he wore when he tried to force his battered body to do something it once had done with ease.

Determination.

"All right. I'll go with you."

His brows arched. "You? You've never broken a rule in your whole life."

"It's about time, then, isn't it? Got Kara's phone?"

"*Ja.*"

"Then let's get our little ones back."

Lightning played across the tops of the trees on the horizon, but no thunder sounded through the night. The storm was far to the southwest, and Samuel hoped they'd have the *kinder* and be home before it broke over Bliss Valley.

When he turned the buggy onto a dirt road that twisted along a stream, she whispered, "Where are we going now?"

"The last name on the list of Hayden's friends. Guy's name is Riley Sabella Jr., and the man at the convenience store said he had a house out this way."

She recoiled when branches hit the buggy. The way was edged by trees and bushes that, left unchecked, would soon consume the road. They bounced from one pothole to the next, and he hoped the directions had been accurate. Peering into the darkness, he searched for any sign of light.

"There!" She pointed to the right. "Through those bushes. I saw a light."

"*Gut.*" He slowed the buggy so the wheels dropped in and out of the holes without rattling. The dirt road softened the sound of Waldo's horseshoes.

Abruptly the shrubs and trees lining the road opened to a small bridge.

"Is *this* the place?" she asked.

He heard her dismay and understood it as he saw the house, which looked as if it were about to fall down. Lights cut through the undergrowth and put the slanting porch in silhouette. The moon, as it was being swallowed by the clouds, showed the building's roof line sagged like a swaybacked horse. Shrubs grew wild, and he guessed in the spring, lilacs and azaleas blossomed everywhere.

"It's a jungle," she said.

"There must be a way in. Someone's inside there, and I doubt they used a machete." Squeezing her hand, he stepped out of the buggy. "Even if they did, the path must still be open. All we have to do is find the entrance."

"Like a maze," she replied as she slid across the buggy and climbed down beside him. She was about to add more when a thin sound came from the house. "That's May! I'd recognize her cry anywhere." She turned to him. Though he couldn't see her face, he could guess how intense her expression must be by her taut voice. "I'm going to get her out of there."

"You?" He caught her arm as she was about to bend her head to duck into the small opening in the bushes. "You can't go in alone." He pulled out the cell phone. "I'm going to call the police."

"It's going to take them time to get here. I can't wait. You heard May. She's in distress. Let me try something."

"Naomi—"

Her face was pale in the light from the cell phone. "Don't stop me, Samuel. I've had enough of men pushing me around."

"Like me?"

He was astonished when she said, "No, not like you. Not any longer."

"Then who?"

She hooked a thumb toward the house. "Like Hayden and his buddy Riley. Like Marlin. Men who don't care about anything or anyone but themselves and what they want, even when they don't want it." Her voice broke. "Especially when they don't want it."

She was talking about her late husband. Rancor welled in him as it did each time he thought of Marlin Ropp. But had Samuel been any better to Naomi? She was asking him to trust her.

"All right," he said. "Look in the front windows. I'll go around back. Once we find out where the *kinder* are, I'll call the cops. Don't let anyone see you."

"I won't." She gave him a quick kiss on the cheek. "Stay safe."

He pulled her to him and kissed her sweet lips. He didn't want to let her go, but couldn't forget Jesse and May needed them. Smoothing her hair back from her face, he whispered, "You stay safe, too. I don't want that to be our last kiss."

She touched his cheek, then disappeared into the bushes.

The interior of the house didn't look much better than the outside. Naomi moved from one window to the next, but froze when she heard May cry out again. Throwing aside caution, she reached for the front door. She twisted the knob. It turned, but the door stuck on a raised board as she struggled to push it open. With a shove, she swung it back, scraping the floor.

May's cries became louder. The *boppli* must be close by. Praying both *kinder* were together, she wondered why nobody had come to see who'd opened the door. She inched in, hoping Hayden and his friend weren't hiding, ready to ambush anyone who came through the doorway.

An arch to her left opened onto a living room. It was a

pigsty. Dirty plates were stacked on a low table by the couch, jumbled together with squashed pizza boxes and takeout containers. From where she stood, she could see crumbs mashed into the carpet and empty cans and bottles. A miasma of sweat and alcohol hovered like a dank fog. A television blared, but she didn't see anyone.

May's cries continued...from the far side of the room. She inched into it.

"Hey!"

She whirled to see a man rising to his elbow from where he'd been stretched out on the stained couch. How could she have missed seeing him?

"What are you doing here?" the muscular man drawled. The hems of his overalls were covered with what looked like tar. Did he work on a road crew? Or maybe he did roofing. His hair, so long it brushed his shoulders, was the same dark brown as the stains on the cushions. For a moment, she had the bizarre thought that maybe he dyed it and had dripped the color on the sofa.

Focus! Think of something to say. Now!

Naomi clasped her hands in front of her so he couldn't see them trembling. Taking the offensive, she asked, "Are you Riley Sabella?"

"Yep, the one and only, if you don't count my old man." He laughed as if it were an uproarious joke. Lightning brightened the room, but he ignored it. "I'm Riley T. Sabella Jr. My old man is—"

"Let me guess. Riley T. Sabella Sr."

He chortled. "Oh, honey, you're a hoot and a half. What's a pretty thing like you doing here? And Amish to boot!" His eyes narrowed. "Don't tell me Hayden got himself another plain gal."

"I'm here to babysit." As if on cue, May let out a screech that warned she was furious with the whole world and someone had better take note of it.

"Hayden send you?"

"What does it matter? It sounds as if you could use help with the kid."

"Kids," he grumbled.

Naomi's heart hammered at her chest with excitement. Both *kinder* were in the house! Now she needed to find them and get them out.

How, Lord?

She got her answer seconds later when the man yawned. Pasting on a smile, she said, "Sit here and close your eyes. I'll get that little one to stop crying."

"She hasn't shut up for the past hour. The kid is as bad. Been sniffling and bellyachin'. I told him to be quiet, or he'd have a real reason to cry."

She restrained her anger and somehow she kept her voice calm. "Don't worry about it, Riley. Relax while I take care of the kids."

"When you're done putting them to bed, c'mon back and I'll let you do the same for me."

Her stomach roiled, but she forced her smile not to waver. "Give me a few minutes."

"Okay. Hurry back."

"I will." She inched around the table with the dirty dishes. Another shiver raced along her when she saw a cockroach crawl out of a pizza box.

Once out of the living room, she found herself in a filthy kitchen. She averted her eyes as another bolt lit the space. She grimaced at the greasy stove and a sink that overflowed with dishes while a slow drip eased past the counter to fall into a puddle on the floor. Her sneakers stuck to the floor, and she grimaced.

Three doors opened from the kitchen. Which one should she try first?

She held her breath. No sounds came from any direction, but then she heard the faint sound of Jesse's favorite lullaby coming from her left. She inched toward the door, forcing her fingers to close around the gummy knob. Inside, the song continued, and she wondered if he was trying to help May get to sleep.

The door clicked open, the tiny noise like an explosion in the quiet. When Jesse opened his mouth, she jumped forward and put her finger to his lips. His eyes grew wide, and she glanced back, fearful Riley had followed her.

No one was there.

The terror in her son's eyes had been burned in there by what he'd experienced since he and May were abducted. Renewed rage pulsed through her, but she squashed it. Now wasn't the time for reacting. It was the time for acting.

She started to tiptoe around the bed to get May, then realized speed was more important than stealth. Riley already knew she was in the house. She needed to get out before Hayden arrived.

"Shh," she murmured as she bent to pick up the *boppli*.

May was wet and smelled as if she hadn't been changed since she was grabbed from the Gingerich farm. Again Naomi pushed down her ire. She'd have time enough for it once the *kinder* were safe.

She didn't say anything else as she held May close with one arm and drew Jesse to her with the other. He gave a soft mew when lightning was followed by the dull concussion of distant thunder.

Bending, she whispered, "Are you okay, *liebling*?"

He started to answer, and she put her finger to her lip, then to his. He nodded, his eyes as wide as saucers.

She guided him off the bed. He grasped her hand so tightly he squashed her fingers. He was determined not to let anyone separate them again, and she agreed.

A twinge cut through her as she looked at the *boppli* in her arm. Kara was May's *mamm*. Now everything would change. The Lancaster County Children and Youth Social Service Agency would help Kara take care of her *kind*. That was the way it should be, but if Kara moved out of the *dawdi haus*, Naomi wouldn't be able to see sweet May every day. The thought sent a dagger of pain into her heart, even as she was thanking God that Kara had been honest with her and Samuel.

Had Kara gone to work at the ice cream shop knowing someone would see her and contact Adam, who would then alert Samuel? So many questions needed to be answered, but now wasn't the time to think about them. She must get the *kinder* out of the house while she could.

"We must be as quiet as a mouse *boppli*," she whispered.

Jesse nodded, his eyes large and fearful. She wanted to smile when he rose to his tiptoes and tried to cross the room without making a sound. He tottered on every step. She put her hand on his shoulder to bring him down onto his heels before he tumbled to the floor.

Praying May remained quiet, Naomi led the way into the kitchen. Each creak of a board beneath her feet or Jesse's made her stiffen, but she didn't hear anything from the living room. She understood why when she reached the room.

Riley was sprawled on the sofa, one foot on the floor and his arm flung over the side. As she paused, he began to snore.

The sound battered the walls, and she knew he'd never hear their footsteps.

Bending, she whispered, "See the door, Jesse?" She pointed.

He nodded, biting his lower lip with his chipped tooth.

"Go there. Samuel's waiting on the other side of it."

His eyes lit with hope for the first time.

"Let's go!" she urged.

Too late she realized her foolishness. Jesse ran and stumbled over the uneven carpet. He hit the low table. A dish crashed to the floor.

She froze, then scooped Jesse against her hip. The little boy started to apologize, but she shook her head. He turned frightened eyes toward the sofa.

She held her breath while Riley muttered something in his sleep, then turned his face toward the back of the couch. Edging around the table, she set Jesse on his feet again. She motioned with her head toward the door.

As soon as they were on the porch, she urged, "Run, Jesse! As fast as you can to the buggy. See it? There!"

He obeyed, and she was on his heels. She hoped neither of them tripped on something in the long grass.

A shadow appeared in front of her. She screamed. Then she saw it was Samuel. She ran forward to him.

"Oh, thank the *gut* Lord!" Samuel swung Jesse up into his arms, cautioning the toddler to be quiet. "I was hoping that was you running across the yard. How did you get the *kinder*? I saw a guy in there."

"He's drunk. I'll explain later." She didn't have time for his consternation at what she'd done. Later he could be as mad at her as he wanted to be. For now, they needed to get out of there.

He led the way to the buggy. "Are they all right?"

"Hungry and dirty, but otherwise okay."

"How did you get them out?" he persisted.

She waved aside his question. "I'll tell you on the way home. I want to put as much space between us and that house as possible."

"*Gut* idea."

Less than a minute later, they were in the buggy. Jesse sat between them, his hands clutching Samuel's arm and hers. May began to whimper, but quieted when Naomi began to sing to her while Samuel turned the buggy toward the bridge.

"Watch it there, buddy," he said to Jesse. "I've got burdocks all over my trousers, and you don't want them pricking you. It was the biggest, nastiest bush in the world." His laugh was genuine, and it ran through her like heated maple syrup.

"At least you didn't run into a skunk," she said.

"No, but I smelled one."

"Me, too." She didn't add that the skunk she was talking about was human.

He gave Waldo the command to go. As the wheels clattered on the bridge, she couldn't keep from looking back to see if anyone was following.

The buggy stopped, and she rocked forward into a hard pole. No, not a pole. Samuel's arm. It kept her and Jesse from hitting the dash.

Before she could ask what was wrong, lights glared. A pair of lights, almost on eye level. More lights glittered beneath it and around the windshield. The rumble of a powerful engine exploded through the night, louder than thunder.

The truck slid to a stop less than two feet from the horse's nose.

"Go around him!" Naomi shouted.

"There isn't room." He backed the horse toward the bridge.

She gasped when the door to the truck opened.

A man jumped out, slapping a tire iron against one palm. He stepped in front of the truck.

"Wait here, Naomi." Samuel pulled out the cell phone and handed it to her. "Call the cops, but if you see a chance, get the *kinder* out of here."

"But you'll—"

"I'll be careful. I've had to deal with his kind before. If you see your chance to get out of here, don't hesitate."

She slid over to pick up the reins, shifting Jesse to her other side.

"*Mamm*, no fun," he said.

"You're right." She hit the button on the phone to activate the screen as she'd seen others do. As she tapped 9-1-1, she murmured, "No fun."

Chapter Twenty-Two

Samuel felt rain strike his hat as he walked toward the truck. Raindrops were backlit by the headlights. He patted Waldo as he walked past him, then edged in front of the buggy. He wanted to keep the sides of the road open in case Naomi had the chance to drive the buggy around the truck and toward the main road.

He stopped beyond the reach of the tire iron the driver held out like a sword. He assured Naomi he'd be careful. He hoped those wouldn't be his final words to her. He hated to think that the last thing he said to her was a lie. He'd be cautious only if he could still protect his niece and Naomi and her son.

The driver edged toward him unsteadily. Samuel didn't back away as he stared at the scrawny driver.

"Are you Hayden Carpenter?" Samuel called.

"What's it to you?"

"Original," he fired back. "You going to offer to make my day next?"

Hayden lurched toward him. The tire iron fell out of his hand, and he bent to pick it up and almost toppled on his face. Leaving the iron on the ground, he stumbled backward against his truck. "Who are you?"

"Samuel King, Kara Slabaugh's brother."

The teen spit on the ground. "It's my kid."

"If you're willing to admit that in court, then you can pay support for your *kind* until she's your age."

"Huh?"

Realizing the young man was too drunk to follow any sort of conversation, Samuel said, "You should go inside and sleep it off with your buddy Riley."

"How can I sleep when the kids are screeching?"

"They're not your problem anymore." He walked closer to the teen, who was having a tough time staying on his feet.

"I want my kid. Leave him here."

"Her."

"What have you heard?"

"No, not heard. Her. Your *kind* is a girl."

He shrugged, and his knees bent. Pulling himself upright, he said, "Doesn't matter. I didn't plan on taking your kid. I just want mine."

"So why didn't you leave him?"

"'Cause I didn't want him squealing." He scowled, weaving on his feet. "How did you find me?"

"That doesn't matter. Do you need help getting to the house?"

"I'm not going to the house." He slid along the truck. "I'm going to find Kara and tell—" He choked back a curse when Samuel stepped between him and the driver's door. Balling up his fist, he raised it.

"Don't do it." Samuel opened the door and switched off

the engine. Stuffing the keys in his pocket, he faced the teen. "You're not driving tonight."

"Look, dude. I don't know who you think you are."

"I told you. I'm Samuel King, Kara's older brother."

"You?" He squinted through the headlight's glare. "Aren't you dead? I thought you died."

"I almost did. In an accident like the one you could have if you get behind that wheel."

"I'm not drunk, man." He abruptly grinned. "Just a little buzzed."

"How many beers have you had? As many as your friend inside?"

He swayed and put his hand on the hood. He tried to wave Samuel aside, but banged his knuckles against the truck. "Get out of my way."

"Your friend is passed out in the house."

"So?"

"So what do think's going to happen if you get behind the wheel?"

"I'll get out of here." He swore again as he tried to open the door, but couldn't get his fingers to close around the handle.

Samuel stepped back as he saw another pair of lights behind the truck. Hayden didn't notice because he was intent on trying to open his door.

When doors slammed behind the truck, Hayden mumbled something, then whirled to run. Samuel backed away as a large form exploded from the darkness and seized the teen. In one smooth motion, the police officer had Hayden in cuffs. He marched him toward his cruiser as he read him his rights and announced it was time for a breathalyzer test.

Another police officer walked over to Samuel. He smiled

at Officer Monteith. He'd been pretty sure the other officer was Officer Hood. He handed her the truck's keys.

"I thought I told you two to let us handle this." She looked along the road. "I assume Naomi is in the buggy."

"Along with Jesse and May."

A smile edged along her stern face. "Good to hear. Get the little ones home. We'll deal with this kid. Thanks, Samuel."

"*Danki*, Officer Monteith."

"If you take the road on the other side of the bridge, it'll connect with Bliss Valley Road not far from the covered bridge."

"*Danki.*" He steered Waldo to where there was room to turn the buggy.

He climbed in. Naomi threw her arms around him and gave him a kiss that sent a tingle from his lips to his toes. He kept his arm around her as he left the glare of lights from the vehicles behind. Overhead, the lighting continued to embroider the clouds together with quick stitches as thunder grew louder.

"That was brilliant," she whispered because the *kinder* had fallen asleep. "You distracted him until the police got here."

"I didn't tell him about the dangers of drunk driving as a distraction. I told him because I didn't want him to make the same mistakes I did."

"You drove drunk?" Shock heightened her voice.

"You must have heard the stories about the accident."

"A few, mostly about how badly you were hurt."

"We'd been drinking and should have known better." He gazed at the stars being extinguished by the clouds. "God offered me His grace, and I survived. Facing the mistakes I made that night forced me to think about the others I'd made in an effort to get my *mamm* to notice me." He shook his head.

"No, I can't blame it on her, though I've tried to. She didn't open the bottles of beer. She didn't make me drink them. She didn't force me behind the wheel of that car. Those decisions were mine and mine alone."

"Maybe you're right about trying to catch someone's attention. Maybe God wanted you to notice Him."

"There would have been simpler ways for Him to let me know." He shook his head. "Probably He tried, and I didn't listen."

"*Daed* told me it's not easy to listen to God when I'm doing all the talking."

"You?"

She smiled at his teasing. Her response was serious, however. "If you hadn't experienced what you did, you might not have been determined to stop Hayden."

"If you're saying God was trying to teach me a lesson..."

She shook her head. "Our God is a loving Father. When you were hurt, so was He. Because His heart is so much bigger than ours, it's impossible for us to comprehend the depth of His pain when one of us turns away." She grasped his hands in hers. "Or His joy when one of us comes back."

"I'm no prodigal son." He grinned. "Most of the time I was away, I didn't have two cents to my name."

"*Prodigal* doesn't have to describe someone wasting money."

"No? Isn't that the meaning of *prodigal*?"

"*Ja*, but there was a book I read in eighth grade that spoke about how we can be prodigals by wasting God's gifts, things more precious than money."

His brows lowered, tugging at his scar. "I don't remember reading that book. I would have because I'm sure Adam, Joel and I would have made fun of it."

"I didn't say I read it at school." Faint color was visible on her cheeks in the lights on the buggy. "It was in a book I borrowed from the library in Strasburg."

"You?" He widened his eyes in mock horror. "Miss Always-Follow-the-Rules went to the public library?" He put his hand over his heart and pretended to wobble. "I'm staggered. I can't believe *you* broke a rule."

She laughed. "See? I told you I wasn't perfect."

"I've got to disagree. In my eyes, you're about as perfect as any imperfect human can be."

She leaned her head onto his shoulder, and they drove through the night toward the farm. There was still a lot that needed to be said between them, but for right now, he wanted to enjoy this special moment.

"Naomi Ropp, would you please call the office of Charles Satterfield, attorney-at-law, at your earliest convenience?" The message was followed by a phone number.

Naomi stared at the answering machine in the old shop. She'd seen the light blinking on it when she came out to get a manual *Daed* wanted before Lillian arrived for his therapy, which was now three times a week. It was the first quiet morning they'd had in the last week.

In the wake of the kidnapping and the arrest of Hayden Carpenter, the house had been chaotic with comings and goings. The police officers had arrived the morning after Naomi and Samuel had found the *kinder* and brought them home. They interviewed each adult member of the house individually and spoke with the twins while Naomi watched. The boys were delighted with the officers and showed off their toys and books. However, Officer Monteith called it quits when all she could get from them was the whole set of circumstances had been "No fun!" She and her partner, Officer Hood, had left soon after with bags of Naomi's snickerdoodles and pictures colored by Jared and Jesse.

Mr. Tedesco, the social worker from the Lancaster County Children and Youth Social Service Agency, also had come. He'd spent time with Naomi and with Kara separately, then together. Returning later in the week, he'd focused on Kara, talking with her out of earshot of the house and the barns.

Now a message was on the answering machine from an attorney. Why was a lawyer calling her?

Her fingers trembled as she started to dial the number from the message. Hearing uneven footsteps, she faced Samuel, who stood in the doorway. Jared and Jesse ran to her. With the tools moved to the new barn, there wasn't much risk for them in the shop.

"Elvin sent me for the same book he asked you to get," he said with a smile. "He figures you couldn't find it because you've taken more than two seconds to bring it back to him."

She relished seeing his genuinely happy expression. In the week since one of the worst nights of her life, he'd grinned often. She loved how his lips twitched before he smiled as if he were so delighted with what amused him, he wanted to relish it a moment before sharing it. As he'd had so little to be elated about in the past, she guessed he was basking in every morsel of mirth.

"You know," he continued as he walked in, his cane tapping against the floor, "the old shop seems sad now that we've moved into the new barn. Elvin likes the extra space so he can guide his walker around the buggies when he visits, but I miss the cramped clutter of this building." His smile faded. "You're letting me babble, Naomi. That's not like you. What's wrong?"

She pointed to the answering machine. "A lawyer wants me to call."

"About what?"

"I don't know. Do you think it's about Hayden's arrest?"

He shook his head. "No self-respecting defense attorney would contact a witness like that. He'd get disbarred."

"Then why is a lawyer calling me?"

"The only way to find out," he said as he closed the distance between them and took her hand, "is to call him back."

"Will you stay here?" she asked.

He nodded, then reached past her. "Before you call, I'm putting it on speaker. That way, both of us can listen and talk."

"You can do that?"

He grinned. "Even this ancient one has speaker capability."

After he'd pushed a couple of buttons, Naomi found the boys some pipe cleaners *Daed* kept to clean out small spots in buggies. She showed them how to twist them into the shape of animals and flowers. While they tried to make their own, she placed the call.

The phone was answered on the second ring, and a female voice said, "Offices of Charles Satterfield, attorney-at-law. How may I direct your call?"

"This is Naomi Ropp. I received a call from Mr. Satterfield."

"Ropp, did you say? Oh!" Naomi could almost see the woman sit straighter. "One moment. I'll get Mr. Satterfield on the line."

"Danki."

"One moment."

It was actually closer to two minutes later when a man's voice came from the other end of the line. "Hello? This is Charles Satterfield. Mrs. Ropp?"

"Ja," she said. "I'm Naomi Ropp. Samuel King is also here, and we're listening to you on speakerphone."

"I'd like your permission to speak plainly in Samuel's hearing. If you're willing to grant your permission, please say so."

"*Ja*, it's okay. Can I ask why you called me?"

"I called for two reasons. The first is that I represent Gina Marie Tinniswood." His deep sigh came through the phone. "I've received the report on your bone marrow test, Mrs. Ropp, and you are not a match for Gina Marie."

"I'm not?" She pressed her fingers to her lips. "Skylar was sure I would be."

"We all *hoped* you would be, Mrs. Ropp."

"Please call me Naomi."

His smile came across the line. "I should have remembered that from speaking with your twin sister."

"How is Gina Marie doing?" she asked.

"Disappointed, as you can imagine."

"Skylar mentioned something about a bone marrow registry."

"It's for people to donate sample swabs to put on file in case someone needing a transplant can't find a match within his or her family. The registry was built by holding donation events, sort of like a blood drive." Without a pause, he said, "Speaking of Skylar Lopez, she's the other reason I'm calling you."

Naomi exchanged a baffled look with Samuel. She couldn't imagine why her half sister would have spoken to their *mamm*'s lawyer about her.

Mr. Satterfield went on when she didn't speak, "Skylar shared concerns with Gina Marie about a dispute over property in Honey Brook. Gina Marie asked me to look into the matter."

"The matter?" Naomi stood straighter. Had Skylar spoken to Gina Marie about the farm?

"The farm you thought you and your late husband had purchased. The whole situation sounded peculiar to me, so I contacted the office of the recorder of deeds in Chester County. That's where any records of any property transfer are kept." His voice lightened as he went on, "Naomi, you were lied to. The paperwork for the transfer of the property from Mr. and Mrs. Cole Yeatman to you was there, signed by you and your late husband."

"Cole?"

"Cole Yeatman Sr. and his wife, Amber."

Naomi leaned her hands against the table, her knees abruptly weak. "Cole Sr. and Amber really did sell the farm to Marlin and me?"

"Yes. I can have copies of the paperwork sent to you."

"I'll need them to prove ownership, because everything I had disappeared." She looked at Samuel, who was giving her the widest grin she'd ever seen. She could feel a matching one on her face. "Thank you, Mr. Satterfield."

"Thank your sister and Gina Marie for bringing it to my attention."

"I will." *God*, danki *for their generous hearts. Help me not to judge others when I can't see the truth within them.*

"So," Samuel asked, "the farm has been Naomi's all along?"

"Yes."

Naomi frowned. "But the Yeatmans told me they owned the house."

"The Yeatmans? They sold it to you."

"Not Cole Sr. and his wife. Cole Jr. and his sister."

"There's no record of them ever owning the property." There was a pause, and she heard something rustling. The lawyer must be looking through his notes. "Ah, here it is. Let me read you what I received from the Honey Brook Borough Police Department."

Samuel took a step toward the phone, and she guessed he didn't want to miss a single word.

However, Naomi said, "One moment please. The *kinder* are here, and I don't think they should hear a police report."

"That's true," Mr. Satterfield said. "Shall I wait for you to call back?"

"No. Give me a minute."

As she took the boys outside and told them to go to the house, she watched to make sure they obeyed her. *Daed* opened the kitchen door as he had for her so often when she was young. He waved to them, then to her. Joy glowed on his face as he guided the twins inside.

Naomi turned to go back in but paused when she heard the lawyer say, "How's she doing, Samuel? This is a lot to take in all at once."

"She's disappointed, of course, that she can't help her birth *mamm*. Otherwise, I'd say she's shocked."

"She hasn't heard the most shocking part of this yet. I'm glad you're there. She shouldn't be by herself when she hears what the police shared."

"What's that?" asked Naomi as she walked back into the shop.

There was silence on the other end of the line, then Mr. Satterfield said, "This may not be easy for you to hear, Naomi. According to what Leslie Yeatman told the police, your husband took the proof of your ownership of the farm and destroyed it. Leslie Yeatman was—"

"I know what she was," she replied.

"She says the whole idea was Marlin's, and she didn't know anything about it until after he'd slipped the papers out of your house."

"Why would he do that?" Samuel asked.

"Because," she said, "Marlin didn't want to give me any-thing when he divorced me."

"Marlin was planning to divorce you?"

"*Ja*, because I objected to his affairs with other women. He was killed before he could file." She spoke emotionlessly. She'd lived with the shocking truth for so long she'd become inured to it.

"Ms. Yeatman claims," Mr. Satterfield said, "Marlin cooked up the scheme on his own, planning to hoodwink you. After his death, the Yeatmans decided to continue with the plan and get their hands on the property they felt their parents should have left to them instead of selling."

"Do the Yeatmans have any claim on it now?" she asked.

"None. The property is yours, Naomi."

"*Danki*—I mean, thank you, Mr. Satterfield."

"My pleasure. It's nice to see things go the right way." He paused, then asked, "Do you have any other questions for me?"

"I do," Samuel said, startling her. "You've been involved in the search for Gina Marie's *kinder* who were surrendered for adoption. Does that mean you handle adoptions, too?"

"We have."

"That's *gut* to know. We may be calling you soon." Thank-ing the lawyer, he ended the call.

"What was that about?" Naomi asked.

He curved his arm around her waist and brought her to him. "Kara told me this morning she isn't ready to go home."

"She knows she can stay here as long as she wants."

"She does, but she's not ready to live plain now. After watching Lillian and me work with your *daed*, she's inter-ested in becoming a physical therapist. She intends to enroll in high school—maybe public, maybe Lancaster Mennonite

School—and then go on to take physical therapy classes if she still wants to do that. She plans to talk to Lillian about it."

She put her fingers over his heart and felt it skip at her touch. "If that's what she wants—"

"Then she can't take care of May."

"Why not? She could still live here. Lancaster Mennonite School isn't that far from here by buggy."

"She tells me she'd be able to get a bus to and from school." He gave her a sad smile. "Though she didn't say so, Naomi, I think she wants a chance to be a teenager. She's loved taking care of the *kinder* as if she's babysitting during summer vacation, but she wants to have—as the twins would say—fun while she figures out what she wants to do with her life. She asked if we would adopt May and raise her with the twins. That way, Kara could see her and be part of her life."

Her head spun. "We? *We* adopt her?"

"Would you consider it, Naomi?" He awkwardly dropped to one knee. "Will you marry me and let me be part of your family?"

All she had to do was say *ja*, and her dreams would come true. He would sweep her into his arms and kiss her. It would be a kiss from a man who loved her, who would always love her, who wouldn't betray her with other women.

Go away, Marlin! She didn't want him in her mind, especially when Samuel posed the question she'd never thought she would hear from him. Why had it been easier to banish Marlin from her heart than her thoughts? The answer was simple. Because she'd come to believe every man she dared to trust would betray her.

But *Daed* hadn't.

Samuel hadn't since she'd come home.

Even so, she turned away, unable to look at his face as she said, "No."

"No?"

"You need to have a *gut* wife, Samuel."

"You'd make me the best wife." He stood and stepped around her so they were face-to-face again. "I love you, and you love me. Isn't that enough?"

"I thought it was, but it isn't."

Rage like she'd never seen washed over his face, but his anger wasn't aimed at her. "This is about Marlin, ain't so? He cheated on you. Yet you're the one who acts ashamed. What do you have to be ashamed about?"

"I should have known what he was doing. If I'd been as *gut* a wife as he—"

"Stop that right now!" He grasped her shoulders and held her still. "When did his cheating become your shame?"

"I should have—"

Again he interrupted her. "Should have what? Done more for him? Risked your life again and again while you tried to give him the *kind* he claimed was all that was missing to make your marriage perfect?"

"You know about that? Who told you? Not *Daed*!"

"I don't think Elvin knows. You've said enough that I've pieced together what I thought was the truth. I'm right, ain't so?"

"*Ja.*"

"I know you, Naomi. I've seen you give one hundred and twenty percent of yourself to everyone in this odd family we've created under Elvin's roof. You didn't hesitate to offer May as much love and care as you've given your boys. Your greatest distress once Elvin survived his stroke has been that you can't do more for him. After you learned Gina Marie might be your *mamm*, you've been ready to give the marrow in your blood to save her."

"At the beginning, I hesitated—"

"Because Skylar came on like a loaded semi with her demands and her questions that shredded everything you believed about your life. Anyone would have pulled back." His hands softened on her arms. "I'll respect your opinions, Naomi, but you being a *gut* person isn't an opinion. It's a fact. You're the best person I've ever met. The kindest, the most giving, the most honest person in my life. You've got to believe that instead of the abuse your husband piled on you."

"Abuse?" she whispered. "Marlin never raised his hand to me."

"There are other kinds of abuse. Your husband beat you with his words as surely as he would have if he'd hit you."

"Like your *mamm* did to you?"

Her question stunned him. His mouth opened and then closed without him making a sound. Clearing his throat, he said, "I never thought of her being abusive. She treated the other kids all right."

"Until you left."

"What?"

She related what Kara had told her how after Samuel jumped the fence, his *mamm* had turned on her other *kinder*. His face lengthened with sorrow, and she realized he was blaming himself.

Grabbing his shoulders as he had hers before, she gave him the best shake she could. It was like trying to move a mountain. "It…is…*not*…your…fault. What your *mamm* said to you and to Lewis and to Kara, none of it is *your* fault. Her words were abusive like Marlin's were. Because we loved them, we couldn't see they were twisting our hearts. They were afraid of their mistakes, so they blamed us." She shook her head. "Do you know what the worst part is?"

"No."

"We've continued to punish ourselves after they can't any longer. But they were wrong."

"Like you telling me no when I proposed is wrong." His eyes searched her face, beseeching. "If you don't love me, tell me so. If you don't want to marry me, I'll accept that, but I won't stop asking you because I love you with all my heart. I have since the moment my lips first touched yours that night when I gave you a ride in my buggy."

"Twelve years, two months…"

He silenced her by capturing her mouth beneath his. As she melted against him, she knew she'd let her stubborn pride keep them apart. She'd been so intent on showing him how he'd wronged her, she hadn't stopped to see how many things he'd done right for her and her family.

"Say *ja*, Naomi," he murmured against her lips. "Tell me you'll be my wife and May's *mamm*."

"*Ja.*"

He bent to kiss her, then halted. "You're crying, Naomi."

"I am!" She raised one hand to touch her cheek. "I thought I'd forgotten how to cry." Looking into his loving eyes, she whispered, "Even tears of joy."

"You forget?" he asked in the teasing tone she'd grown to love. "I didn't think that was possible."

She slapped his arm playfully as healing tears ran down her face. "You know what I mean."

"What I mean is that *I* will never forget this moment when you agreed to be my wife." His lips seared that promise into hers.

Epilogue

"Found them."

Naomi looked up to see Samuel walking into the kitchen with the twins. The two-year-olds were dripping water and mud on the floor, and neither Jared nor Jesse could stop grinning, clearly pleased with what they'd been doing.

Until she looked at them and said, "I told you that you could play outside *after* we get home from the adoption ceremony."

"Be fireman," Jared said.

"Like Samuel." Jesse grinned at him.

Samuel smiled back. He'd offered to help with fund-raising for the volunteer fire department. It'd allowed him to connect with friends, old and new.

"*After* the adoption ceremony," she repeated.

"Told ya," Jared said, ready to pin any misdeed on his younger brother.

"No, told *you*." Jesse had begun standing up for himself

more in the past month since Naomi and Samuel had exchanged wedding vows in front of the *Leit*.

One month, one week, six days and twenty-three hours ago, came the exacting voice in her head. How fast the time had gone since she and the twins had welcomed Samuel and May into their family.

Maybe Jesse was standing up for himself because he'd seen Samuel do the same. Samuel had returned home. Though his *mamm* still refused to acknowledge him, his half siblings had welcomed him and Kara for the visit. Even his step*daed* had greeted him warmly. It wasn't all Samuel had hoped for, but it was a beginning. He was, she knew, grateful for that.

Interrupting before the inevitable back and forth of blame could get started, Samuel asked, "Where do you want me to put their muddy clothes? In the bathroom or the washing machine?"

"Washing machine. I'll do a load as soon as we get back."

"'Doption day!" cheered Jesse.

"Fun!" Jared said, not to be outdone. "'Doption day fun!"

"*Ja*, it is." Naomi couldn't keep from smiling as she looked at May, who was eyeing the puddle left behind by the boys. Picking up the little girl, she said, "We don't want you getting dirty, too, *liebling*, on our special day."

"All right. I'll get them changed and…" Samuel's voice faded at the sound of a car driving into the yard. "Who's that? I don't have any appointments today. I told Dale to take the day off."

She hurried to the front door. Dale Hershberger was Adam's cousin who was interested in anything with wheels. He worked with Samuel on buggies and had another job at a local car repair shop near the Bliss Valley Covered Bridge.

When she came out on the porch, *Daed* tossed the latest

issue of *The Budget* onto the glider and reached for his walker. He looked at her, and she started to say she didn't know who'd be calling today.

Her eyes widened when she recognized the silver car. Skylar! She hadn't seen her half sister since their meeting with Laurene at the Acorn Farm Inn. Doors opened on the car. Skylar's hair was streaked with purple and pink, but Naomi's eyes were riveted on the older woman emerging from the passenger side.

She was thin, almost gaunt. Lines were dug deeply into her face, half-hidden behind glasses as large as Skylar's. Her short, curling hair was fine and graying. She leaned heavily on Skylar as they walked toward the house.

With her usual lack of tact, her half sister said, "Meet your mother, Naomi."

Time stopped as Naomi drank in the sight of the woman in front of her. The woman who'd given birth to her and been tricked by a heartless woman who'd sold the *bopplin* to line her own pockets. She had so much to say, so many questions to ask, but all she could do was stare.

"Won't you come up and sit?" asked Samuel from behind her.

Loving him more because he was there—yet again—when she'd needed him, Naomi said, "Please."

As soon as they were seated on the porch and the boys were happily playing in the mud again, Gina Marie asked, "Are those boys your children?"

"*Ja.* My twin sons. Jared and Jesse. Your *kins-kinder.*"

"*Kins-kinder?* What a lovely word for grandchildren! How old are they?"

"Two."

"Ah, the terrible twos. You must have quite a time with two two-year-olds."

"*Quite a time* doesn't begin to describe it."

"And you've got a baby." Gina Marie looked from Naomi to Samuel. "Skylar didn't mention you were married."

"Just recently," Naomi said at the same time Samuel explained, "May is our foster daughter. We hope to adopt her soon."

"Oh, you sweet thing," the older woman said. "She'll be a real blessing."

"As Naomi has been a blessing for me and my wife," *Daed* said.

"I want to thank you," Naomi said, "for talking to your lawyer about the farm in Honey Brook."

Gina Marie's smile added light to her face. "He told me about it. I'm so glad he could help you."

Her *daed* cleared his throat. "*Danki* from me, too, Mrs. Tinniswood. By signing those papers, you're making it possible for me to adopt Naomi today."

"'Doption day!" Jared and Jesse chortled as they spoke at the same time.

"I'm delighted," Gina Marie said. "You raised her. I'm sorry it took so long. I thought I'd signed the papers then." She looked at Naomi. "The painkillers I was on after your birth addled my brain, making everything fuzzy. Just as the chemo has. However, I clearly remember the day you were born. It was December 20."

"No," Naomi said, "my birthday is December 22."

Gina Marie shook her head. "You were born on December 20, as Laurene was."

"We weren't sure which birthday was our real one."

"December 20. The day, a Thursday, was unseasonably warm, seventy degrees by noon. At exactly three minutes after one, as I was bringing in laundry, my contractions started. That was twenty-nine years, eight months, one week—"

"Five days," whispered Naomi, "and twenty-two hours ago."

"You can do that, too?" Gina Marie asked. "Remember dates and times?"

"From around the time I was the boys' age. I don't remember being born, but I calculated the date years ago, and I haven't forgotten it."

"I've got a memory like that." Her eyes lowered. "Or I did until chemo clogged my brain. The doctors tell me it should pass if I can beat this cancer."

"I'm so sorry that I wasn't a match for—"

"No," the older woman said. "Don't be sorry for anything. I should be apologizing to you. Let's enjoy this time we've got together."

And they did. *Daed* regaled everyone with stories about when Naomi was little. Though he had a few gaps in his memory and mixed up events, she didn't correct him. She loved his stories, and she could see Gina Marie did, too.

So did Samuel. He was listening intently, and his sparkling eyes warned he'd be teasing her later about how she'd unwisely thought she could lasso a sheep and ride it like a cowboy.

When Gina Marie left a half hour later, she gave Naomi a warm embrace and asked her to come to Lancaster for a visit soon.

"I will. I promise."

"I know you won't forget." With a laugh, Gina Marie got into the car.

As it drove away, *Daed* called the boys so he could help them get cleaned. "Hurry," he urged. "We've got to be there in an hour."

Samuel smiled as the boys raced to catch up with their *grossdawdi,* who was excited Naomi would soon be his adopted daughter. Soon, May would be a true part of the family, too. Holding the door for Naomi and May, he said, "God has given you a *wunderbaar* gift on this special day."

"I'm glad I got to meet Gina Marie. I thought I was the only weird one."

"You aren't. You're like your birth *mamm*."

She smiled as she looked across the living room to where *Daed* was tossing the twins' muddy clothes on the floor and herding the boys toward the bathroom, where he could wash their faces and hands before they put on fresh shirts and trousers. "I'm like my *daed* and my *mamm*."

"I wish I could have met Flossie."

"No, you don't." She laughed. "She would have taken one look at you and chased you off the farm with a broom."

"Rightfully so. Naomi, the sale on the farm in Honey Brook closes tomorrow. Are you sure you don't want to go back there?"

"No."

"Not to see it one last time?"

She tapped her finger against her temple. "I have memories of each and every room in the house right here. Home is here. In Bliss Valley." She hooked her arm through his and rested her head against his shoulder. "With you and the rest of our family, making fun memories neither of us will ever forget."

★ ★ ★ ★ ★

If you enjoyed this story, look for the next book in the Secrets of Bliss Valley series,
A Search for Redemption *by Jo Ann Brown, available June 2022 from Love Inspired.*

*Joel Beachy's return to Bliss Valley—and the Plain People—
is his last chance to redeem a life filled with missteps.
Can Amish* maed *Grace Coffman help him find a new
beginning—if he can face his past?*

Read on for a sneak preview of
A Search for Redemption
by Jo Ann Brown.

"Joel," he said when he realized that while he knew her given name, she didn't have any idea what his was.

She took a step back, then another. "I'm sorry, but I need to finish closing the shop so I can get home."

"I'm the one who should apologize for not realizing I'm keeping you from your husband and family."

"Just family," Grace said, then flushed.

Again he wanted to apologize. He hadn't been fishing to try to find out if she was married. Or had he? Why else would he have probed to discover her marital status? If she knew the truth about how he'd spent the past ten years, she'd know he didn't have any right to think about her as anything other than a shopkeeper.

He stuck the watch cover in his pocket. Groping for the doorknob, he fumbled to open the door.

As he opened it, she said, "Have a nice evening."

"Danki."

Her eyes widened, and he wanted to take back the single word that had betrayed too much. He'd been so focused on escaping without another mistake that he'd put his foot in his mouth with the next thing he said.

"You're Amish?" she choked out.

Joel nodded. "I was raised that way."

"In Lancaster County?"

Again he nodded.

"But you left." She didn't make it a question.

"I did." He held his breath, waiting for her kindness to turn to cool disdain or a fervent determination to point out the error of his ways. He knew the mistakes he'd made. He didn't need anyone else pointing them out.

"Then welcome back, and enjoy your visit to Bliss Valley." She'd switched to *Deitsch*, the language of the Plain folk.

An odd sensation bubbled deep within him, something he couldn't name. He nodded as he rushed out of the shop. Hearing her lock the door behind him, he almost laughed. Not in humor, but something that was the utter opposite.

"Enjoy your visit to Bliss Valley"?

Not likely.

Don't miss
A Search for Redemption *by Jo Ann Brown,*
coming soon from Love Inspired.

LoveInspired.com

LIEXP53003TR

LOVE INSPIRED

Stories to uplift and inspire

Fall in love with Love Inspired—
inspirational and uplifting stories of faith
and hope. Find strength and comfort in
the bonds of friendship and community.
Revel in the warmth of possibility and the
promise of new beginnings.

Sign up for the Love Inspired newsletter
at **LoveInspired.com** to be the first
to find out about upcoming titles,
special promotions and exclusive content.

CONNECT WITH US AT:

f Facebook.com/LoveInspiredBooks

🐦 Twitter.com/LoveInspiredBks

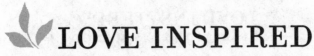
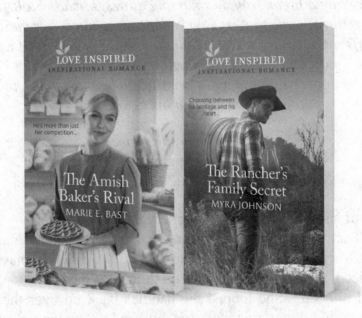

"Your sister's still your willing servant."

"That wasn't the idea," Matt said stiffly, his temper flaring that Miriam could read him so easily. "In case you haven't noticed, it makes her happy to do things for me."

"I noticed." She looped the handles back up over the bar and pulled down a pair of stretchy bands. "As long as she's helping you to get stronger, I don't object."

"Stronger." He almost spat out the word. "Stronger for what? None of this is going to do any good. It's useless. I can't be the person I was."

She seemed unaffected by his anger. "We'll never know that if you don't try, will we?"

He glared at her for a long moment as a thought formed in his mind. He turned it over, looking at it from all angles. Would it work?

"I'll tell you what," he said. "I'll make a deal with you."

"What kind of a deal?" Miriam's expression was cautious.

"I promise to do everything you say…to try my hardest…for a month. If I'm not much better by then, you agree to quit."

Miriam stood very still, considering before she spoke. "I can't speak for Tim. Just for myself."

"Yah. Just for yourself."

"Who's going to decide whether or not you're much better?" she said. "You?"

His jaw hardened. She wasn't going to make this easy.

"No," he said abruptly. "How about…Betsy?"

Her lips twitched. "Don't you think Betsy has her own reasons for wanting to be rid of me?"

He raised one eyebrow, a gesture that used to attract the girls. "If you're really making progress, you'll have won her over by then. What's wrong? Don't you have any confidence in your work?"

She seemed to wince at that. After a long moment, she nodded. "All right. It's a deal."

Don't miss
Nursing Her Amish Neighbor *by Marta Perry,*
available January 2022 wherever
Love Inspired books and ebooks are sold.

LoveInspired.com

LIEXP75897TR

With her family's legacy on the line, a woman with everything to lose must rely on a man hiding from his past...

Don't miss this thrilling and uplifting page-turner from *New York Times* bestselling author

LINDA GOODNIGHT

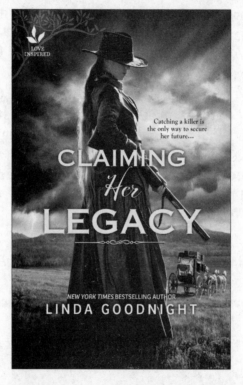

"Linda Goodnight has a true knack for writing historical Western fiction, with characters who come off the pages with life."
—**Jodi Thomas**, *New York Times* and *USA TODAY* bestselling author

Coming soon from Love Inspired!

LOVE INSPIRED
LoveInspired.com

LI41876BPATR